After Such Kindness

Also by Gaynor Arnold

Girl in a Blue Dress
Lying Together

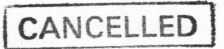

After Such Kindness

Gaynor Arnold

**Tindal
Street
Press**

First published in 2012
by Tindal Street Press Ltd
217 The Custard Factory, Gibb Street, Birmingham, B9 4AA
www.tindalstreet.co.uk

A CIP catalogue reference for this book is available
from the British Library

ISBN: 978 1 906994 37 2
Export ISBN: 978 1 906994 94 5

Typeset by Tetragon

Printed and bound by
CPI Group (UK), Croydon, CR0 4YY

For Nicholas

Oxford, 1862

S HE'S COMING TO LIFE UNDER MY HANDS. THE DARK, untidy mass of her hair, the bright eyes, the frill of her white dress, her sash, her parasol. She's floating in the liquid, becoming more and more real. I jiggle the tray and peer closer. She is ready now; finished; perfect. I lift her out, shake the paper, peg it up and let it drip. I sit down on the stool in the dark room and gaze at her.

I catch my breath when I think how easily I might have missed her. And even so, I have to remind myself that she will soon be gone from me, because in spite of her slight and childish form, she is already eleven years old. I see the number like a shadow of doom upon her, signalling the end of the golden years, the moment when she will start to spin away from me like a top: slowly at first; and then so fast – so horribly fast – that I won't be able to recognize her. And when she stops spinning, she'll be a woman.

That is why I must make the most of what may be our only summer together, the only time I may be able to enjoy her pure perfection. I cannot dawdle and bide my time, bringing her to eat from my hand little by little like a tame robin, winning her trust by stillness and kind words. I must act robustly, as if my life depended on it – as in the quiet watches of the night I almost believe it does. I must put aside any shyness, and channel all my forces into the resolution of this one desire. I must strive to know my child, to earn her love. My dearest hope is that one day I will be able to take her warm little hand in mine as we walk along the meadow, and feel her little bones press trustfully against my breast as I lift her carefully over a stile. And best of all, if I have deserved it through my attentiveness and good actions, I will be able to sit her in my lap under the shade of a sycamore tree and tell her a story that no one in the world has heard before. And she will reach up and kiss me gently on the cheek. And I will feel her lips as soft and moist as the ripest of fruit. And I will kiss her in return, just as if I were her father or her brother. And she will lie cradled in my arms, daydreaming – sleeping even – in perfect trust and friendship. The thought is so sweet I feel I might almost faint. But I must not anticipate the moment. Though I wish for it so fervently, I do not know if it will ever come about. I do not know if I will deserve her, my Daisy, my Day's Eye, my meadow flower. All I can do is hope and pray.

1

I CAN SCARCELY BELIEVE THAT I SPENT SO MANY MONTHS in the company of Daniel Baxter without being aware of the existence of his delightful daughter. But ours was originally a friendship not given to matters such as daughters, however delightful. In fact, our acquaintance had begun on an indifferent – dare I say, hostile – note.

I had heard of Baxter, of course; all Oxford knew him as the successful and popular vicar of St Cyprian's – but he was the kind of clergyman I disliked; a man given to whipping up his congregation simply by the power of his voice and the fervent light in his eyes. I had by no means gone out of my way to avoid him, but I spent a large part of my time – then as now – quietly studying and teaching within my college walls, while Baxter was an energetic saver of souls with missions in the poorest parts of the town. It had seemed unlikely that we would meet, let alone find common ground. I certainly did not imagine that we were to become friends.

It was the Dean, strangely enough, who brought us together. I say 'strangely' because I have never sought the company of my fellow dons. I dislike having my privacy intruded upon, which has given me the reputation of being aloof, but that reputation protects and suits me. However, on coming out of my rooms one particular evening I saw the Dean scuttling across the college quadrangle, heading, I feared, in my direction. He then took the liberty of falling into step with me, taking my arm in his. It is a peculiar habit of his, this linking of arms, and as I am six foot and he is not more than five foot two, it is a particularly annoying one. I had to bend low to accommodate him as we progressed across the quadrangle, his sharp elbow digging into my side.

'I am delighted to have caught you,' he said; as if he were addressing a plump salmon just pulled from the river. 'You are just the man for my purpose. I need someone of a High Church view – for my colloquia I mean; there are too many men of the Rugby persuasion at the moment – too much doubt; too much Broad Church laxity. It won't do at all.'

I knew there had been talk in the common room of a series of debates that were to take place between High and Low Church interests, but I had taken little notice, being in no way interested in the minutiae of Church politics, although I was classed as a clergyman by the requirements of the college rules. Faced with the alarming possibility of being asked to speak on such a matter, I pleaded my ignorance and general incapacity as a speaker.

But the Dean would not be deterred. 'No, no,' he insisted. 'If you, with your logic and cleverness, cannot add to the debate, I don't know who can.'

'But if I have any c-cleverness, it is only mathematical,' I replied. 'I fear I have a very superficial knowledge of anything else. Indeed, the more firmly held an opinion is, the more I am inclined to make fun of it.'

'And very amusing you are too, sir. I have read some of your satires in the London magazines. But I cannot imagine that you are likely to make similar jokes at the expense of Dr Pusey's learned writings. You are a man in Holy Orders after all – even if they are minor ones – and, if I may say so, you have seriously neglected your spiritual duties at the college. I don't believe you have read the Lesson in chapel more than twice this whole year.

No, no, Mr Jameson, mathematician you may be, but you will oblige me by coming along. We start tomorrow immediately after Hall dinner. Half past eight o'clock in the Old Buttery.'

I was utterly dismayed. My opinion is that the Church of England is an utterly illogical institution and it no more deserves the thousands of words expended on its behalf than, say, a lobster. In fact, a lobster may deserve more words, and is certainly a good deal tastier. There have been times in the past when I have almost dreaded entering the senior common room for fear of what I would encounter: dirty teacups set down everywhere and no place to sit that did not put one within spitting distance of a theological argument. I often found myself squashed up between a mad vicar from Fairyland and an equally certifiable archdeacon from Nurseryland, who both seemed set fair to put my head into the teapot if I did not agree with them. I had thought that by now all the sound and fury generated by the Tractarians had largely dissipated. But it seems that as soon as any controversy threatens to die down, there is a man like the Dean who will breathe fire into its embers and start it up again.

He smiled. 'By the way,' he said. 'You will be interested to know that Daniel Baxter will be in attendance. He was my pupil, you know, once upon a time. He will bring a certain liveliness to the debate, you can be sure.' And, with that, he flitted off into the cloisters like an absent-minded bat.

Of course, at the time, I was unaware of the magnitude of the favour he had done me. Rather, I was irritated to have been ambushed in this fashion; and the notion of Daniel Baxter's presence at the proposed meetings in no way allayed my annoyance at having to leave my comfortable chair and be bored on a bench for two hours a week. So, the following evening, when I took myself to the Old Buttery and saw the person I presumed to be Baxter – a handsome and athletic man surrounded by a coterie of admirers – I declined to acknowledge him, and sat in a corner, well away from him. Baxter was clearly used to being the centre of attention, and I had no wish to increase his self-importance. And, during the course of the debate, whenever he got up to speak – and he spoke often, loudly and enthusiastically – I yawned and made amusing sketches of him in my notebook – depicting him as a preaching toad, or even a monkey in a mitre.

Yet, I could see he was by no means as confident a man as he pretended. He would often lose the thread of his argument and his eye would fall upon mine in an anxious way, as if seeking encouragement or approval – although why my approval was of any importance to him was beyond my understanding; I am a poor speaker at best, and in that feverish atmosphere I tried not to speak at all, rising only to correct any matter of fact or an aberration of the rules of grammar. Perhaps Baxter was made nervous by my stony manner and the scribbling of my pencil every time he rose to his feet. Perhaps he saw me simply as another opponent to be won over by his charms.

But whatever it was, as the weekly meetings continued, I found myself beginning to like him. He possessed an earnest sincerity that was hard to resist, and made a point of detaining me after the meetings to ask my opinion on this or that. On one or two occasions he had even accompanied me as far as my rooms, engaging me in serious conversation for up to half an hour, deferring to me in a way I found most flattering. I have to admit I had not enjoyed such a demonstration of friendship since my schooldays, and I looked forward each week to the time when we would meet. The debates themselves were no better than I had expected and my notebooks quickly filled up with drawings of ancient theologians and bits of comical verse. But I was surprised to discover that Baxter – in spite of his enthusiastic speeches – was also unimpressed by the polemical nature of the proceedings. One evening, he took me by the arm. 'Well, we have all spoken loud and long, but I find myself no nearer to the answers I crave. What about you, Jameson? Are you satisfied?'

I shrugged. I had not anticipated satisfaction, so its absence was a matter of indifference to me, yet Baxter's face lit up. 'I see you are like me, Jameson. You long in your soul for something more intimate. Maybe we could find a private time to examine our consciences honestly without the need to take up a position? A kind of mutual confessional – if I may use so Roman a word?'

Although such intimate exchanges were generally anathema to me, I did not wish to lose Baxter's friendship so soon and I nodded my agreement. He was delighted, and clasped me to his bosom, a gesture which disconcerted me considerably. (I had noticed his frequent habit of touching people on the arm and hand, and clapping them on the back. Even pens, books and the corners of tables were subject to his caress.) 'Splendid,' he said. 'I cannot tell you how much this means to me.'

It was readily decided that I should be the host, as I was lucky enough to have a comfortable set of rooms overlooking the college garden, whereas he was a busy paterfamilias in a house where callers were a continual cause of interruption. So, once a week after Evensong, we would drink a modicum of sherry and eat two or three fairly dry biscuits while we examined our position with regard to the spiritual authority of the Anglican Church – ending always with a solemn prayer by Baxter for guidance in the week ahead. The discussions were generally interesting, in spite of Baxter's tendency to generalities. 'What are candles?' he would say. 'What is incense? What is the wafer at the altar and the draining of the cup, if we do not carry the Love of God in our hearts?' He would then go on to question High Church practices in general and the Popish notion of celibacy in particular, in an attempt to persuade me that the life of a bachelor don was neither good nor healthy.

'Christian life is family life,' he would say, heartily. 'Without my family, I am nothing. They are the better part of me. I rejoice in the Lord's goodness to have given me such a loving wife and four healthy children.'

When he was in this vein, I let him expound – although his words held such an implicit reproach to my bachelor status that it was hard not to take offence. But I did no more than gently intimate that family life was not meant for everyone. 'I am rather crabby and crotchety, as you know. No sensible woman would have me.'

'You never know, John,' he would always conclude. 'You never know.'

But I do know, of course. I know my nature very well.

But it was part of Baxter's generous nature to share all his thoughts with me and during these times of heart-searching I learned a great deal about him – in particular that his afore-mentioned loving family comprised a wife, three girls and a boy – the boy, Benjamin, being the youngest by some ten years. And one day when he was being particularly intimate, having imbibed more than his usual amount of sherry, he confessed that he had once feared he would never see the day when he would hold that son in his arms.

'After Daisy,' he said, 'Mrs Baxter was very unwell and it seemed unlikely she could survive the rigours of another con-finement. We had to practise – discretion. For years I was forced to hold back from my desires, to fight every night the demons of the flesh. But I have to confess to you, John, that one night I gave in to temptation. God forgive me, but I did. It is hard, you know, to go without love – without the physical expression of love, I mean – and that night I fell short of my duty.'

He looked searchingly at me then, as if wondering if I myself had ever known the love of a woman or the nightly temptation of the flesh; that I might confess some similar failing on my part that might mitigate or excuse his own lack of chastity. I said nothing. There was, of course, nothing to say. I am a single man, a college tutor and a deacon of the Church of England. No woman sets a foot in my chambers. I lead perforce a chaste and blameless life.

Clasping his hands as if in prayer, and taking no heed of my considerable discomfort with the topic, he added, 'And when it became clear that our night of bliss had borne its fruit, I feared my punishment would be to lose that wife I so much cherished. I prayed, then, John – how I prayed! We both did, Mrs Baxter and I, every night side by side in our night attire, down on our knees, asking most earnestly that her life should be spared not only for the expected infant's sake, but for all three of our girls, that they might continue to know the guiding hand of their mother as they grew to womanhood. A father, you know, however loving, is no real substitute for a mother as the daily mentor and companion of young girls.'

I felt quite put out to hear him say that. I am of the opinion that a father, if well-intentioned and conscientious, can do all that a mother might, and more. But I have no children, and I know Society takes parental advice very ill from an unmarried man, so I bit my lip. 'Well, that is fortunately a theoretical matter now,' I said. 'You have your son, and your wife is happily still with us.'

He nodded, his eyes filling with tears. 'Yes, oh, yes! God is full of grace and listened to our prayers. Mrs Baxter survived her ordeal – although it was a long and painful one – and Benjy was delivered safely, nine months to the day. He is my special treasure. A gift from the Lord; a sign of forgiveness.'

'Amen,' I said, touched at his emotion. 'I am glad that you have a son and heir, Daniel, and that you take such delight in him. Many men seem to favour their sons, I have noticed. A child to carry on the family name, to follow in their father's footsteps – play cricket and go to university and so forth. But, in general, I find little girls far gentler and more appealing.'

He looked surprised, as if he could not conceive of such a preference. Then he laughed. 'But of course you know nothing of the reality of the fair sex. You spend all your time hidden away in your college room, teaching young men who are equally confined. Little girls are no doubt as strange and fabulous to you as unicorns.'

'On the contrary, I am very used to the company of girls,' I said with some asperity. 'I had seven younger sisters at home and entertained them for many years – with considerable success I might add.'

'John, you astonish me! Who'd have thought it?' He gave me a close look, as if to see in my face something previously hidden – maybe the impression of my sisters' features, or a ringlet or hair ribbon he had somehow overlooked in our months of companionship. 'Well, in that case, I absolutely require that you come up to the vicarage and entertain *us*. We have more than enough to spare of female company there. Daisy is only ten, but Christiana and Sarah are of an age for conversation, and it might do them good. And Mrs Baxter will, I'm sure, be delighted. She cannot see what takes me away from her so long every Wednesday evening and has tired of delaying supper for me.'

'Thank you,' I said, somewhat agitated at the prospect of a family gathering, even with the inducement of three young girls to be entertained. 'Although you must warn your wife that I am an inept figure in the drawing room. My stammer, you know. It's worse when I am in company, as you'll have noticed. But I am at ease with children – especially the younger ones.'

Even then, the very name 'Daisy' conjured up in me a vision of innocence that made my heart quicken.

I was thus full of mixed emotions when, in response to a written invitation from Mrs Baxter, I climbed the hill to Westwood Gardens one day in late March. It was some time since I had visited the family home of anyone except my married sisters, as I took all my meals in Hall whether in or out of term (except for a seaside holiday once a year). I feared that perhaps my bachelor ways had become set, and my manners out-of-date. Not that I care about 'manners' as such. Indeed, I often find the goings-on of family life comedic in the extreme. However, Baxter had tried to put me at my ease by saying the family was 'as you find us – harum-scarum to a degree'.

As soon as I saw the house, I doubted that. The vicarage was rather grand – a spacious and comfortable new house, entirely Gothic in style, with patterned brickwork and double-arched windows, each with mottled granite columns and individual carved capitols. The handsome front door had stained-glass panels each side of the big brass knocker (itself in the shape of a lion's head), and there were stone pots of budding hydrangeas on each side of the porch. Through the tinted glass I could spy large vases filled with flowers, gilt-framed pictures, Italian statuettes, pots of ferns, silver candlesticks, rich brocade cloths and tasselled curtains. The whole house reflected Baxter's status as a successful member of society as well as a successful clergyman.

He'd made no secret of his path to success. I knew how, after leaving the university the very year I myself had come up, he had worked hard and long hours as a curate in the poor parishes of London, doing much good there it would seem. But he had married early and, although still anxious in his heart to do God's work, judged that his wife and young daughters were too delicate for a life in the slums. He had therefore been rewarded with a well-endowed Living in his own alma mater and had been established back in Oxford for over ten years. The parish he now administered was tremendously genteel, but Baxter contrived to steer his genial Broad Church way through the doctrinal extremes that had wrecked many of his predecessors, and not a few of his contemporaries. He was practical, too. He had instituted parish committees for the care of the poor, ignorant and sick, even beyond his parish boundaries. He was a man with a finger in a good many pies.

A housemaid with neat white cap and well-ironed streamers opened the door to me. 'Reverend John Jameson,' I enunciated with difficulty, as I gave her my hat. 'C-Compliments to Mrs B-Baxter. I am expected.'

To my relief, Daniel appeared at a door near the back of the hall. He looked different – more lightly clad and comfortable. In fact, I noticed, he was wearing carpet slippers and something approaching a smoking jacket, although I had never seen him smoke and hoped sincerely that he did not do so. 'My dear Jameson,' he cried. 'Delighted to see you! Welcome to my humble abode!'

'Not so humble,' I couldn't help saying, as I eyed the particularly fine silver-gilt looking-glass that dominated the hallway.

He looked disconcerted, as if the opulence of his surroundings had never occurred to him. 'It's not mine, remember,' he said apologetically. 'The house goes with the Living, as you know. And most of the furniture belongs to my wife.' Then he gave a grin. 'But it is rather impressive, isn't it? Built by subscription, in the Ruskin style. The parishioners insisted that only the best would do to glorify the Lord as He deserves, and I'm the first fortunate recipient of their generosity. But come in, come in!' And, dismissing the servant, he ushered me into his study.

I always feel at home when I am among books, particularly in the special quietness that a book-lined room bestows. Daniel, I could see, had many books, but not so many as I did, and as far as I could see, not so varied: a little entomology and botany, the usual Classics and theology, but no mathematics. He made up the lack with many sporting trophies – silver cups on his mantelpiece and a wooden oar suspended above it with dates and names, indicating, no doubt, some achievement of note. There were some daguerreotypes too – a group of oarsmen in sporting gear and caps, and another group of men in clerical garb. One picture was slightly blurred, as if the camera had been carelessly moved, and the other was overdeveloped and dark. This annoyed me and I remember wishing people would take proper care with photographic work. It is an art on a par with drawing or sculpture and needs just the same amount of concentration and finesse.

'Head of the River 1845,' he said, seeing me look, and pointing first at the picture, then at the oar. 'I was Stroke, and I set the best pace that season.'

'Congratulations,' I said, conscious of a dryness in my tone. 'You are undoubtedly a fine, athletic fellow and all should bow their heads to you.'

He laughed. 'You are hard on me, as always. But you must allow a man a little justifiable pride from time to time.' He smoothed his impressive set of whiskers in a smug manner.

'Must I?' I said, with as straight a face as I could manage. 'When we both know pride is the worst of sins?'

He looked at me as if to ascertain if I were serious, and I continued with my solemn look. Although I did not care a jot if he was (or was not) proud of his rowing achievements, it seemed to me that if he accepted the seven sins as deadly, it was logical to have a healthy respect for them.

'You are right of course,' he said after a while, his face almost comically full of self-reproach. 'I am a proud man – a vain man, in fact. It is a terrible failing and one I fight against every day. Forgive me, John.'

'Oh, it's not for me to forgive,' I said, airily. 'You'll need to ask for mercy in a very different quarter.'

'Yes, yes, of course. And I will again add it to my nightly prayers.' He seemed flustered, and I thought again how easily he was put off his stride. 'It wasn't meant as a boast, you know,' he said with a wry smile. 'Just a passing remark. But, as usual, some *pernickety* person takes it up and makes much of it.' He ran his hand through his hair and in the good light I noticed for the first time how brown it was, how deeply wavy. 'You see what you have done, John. I am now filled with guilt.'

'Are you? Oh, dear,' I said. 'And a guilty man is no better than a stoker.'

'And why is that?'

'Well, they both heap up coals of fire all day.'

He laughed. 'You say the most absurd things, John. But you always make me *think* – that's what I like. You always bring me back to the point.'

'Glad to be of service,' I said, wishing *he* would come to the point and take me to meet his children.

As if he had read my mind, he suddenly brightened and said, 'Come, I must introduce you to my wife. She is most anxious to meet you.' To my relief, he took off his quilted jacket and donned his clerical coat, straightening his stock and smoothing his hair back, running a hand along his whiskers.

'And am I to meet your daughters too?'

'I have asked them to join us for tea. I will show you my son, first. It's de rigueur, even though you are not a devotee of boy-children.'

He ushered me across the hall and into the splendid drawing room, furnished in the same plush way, the glitter of mirrors and the green of potted plants being much in evidence. I was nervous, as always, when entering a lady's domain and hardly dared raise my eyes to take in more detail.

'Evelina, my dear, this is the Reverend John Jameson, the clerical friend I have spoken so much about, the one who keeps me from your side every Wednesday evening, and keeps me on the straight and narrow every day. John, may I present my wife?'

I could see the pattern in the brocade of the chaise, and the small boots peeping out of the frilled hem of Mrs Baxter's deep green gown as she reclined along it. I raised my eyes and there was a delicate and beautiful lady, with pearly skin, thick dark hair, and remarkably bright eyes. She was much more youthful than I expected, and, seeing her look so fondly at her husband, with his manly bearing and glossy head of hair, and seeing him hold her glance in return, I could sense that their marriage was not simply one of true minds, but was still alive with the breath of conjugal passion. Of course, I could not put from my mind what Baxter had told me of his nightly struggles and, as she turned her eyes to mine, I immediately had an image of her sitting up in bed in her white nightgown. It was most awkward and I felt quite unpleasantly hot, but I made an effort of will and, to my relief, the impertinent image disappeared.

Mrs Baxter held out an ivory hand. 'How do you do, Mr Jameson? I have tried hard to forgive you for taking my husband from me for so many hours, but I regret to say that I have not yet succeeded. You will need to work very hard to gain my favour.' And she gave me what I felt was almost a flirtatious smile. At which point my tongue became a tortured ball of string, which filled my mouth and would not unravel. I took her hand and nodded, making a dreadful half-choking sound which I hoped would be taken for a heartfelt assent.

She must have taken it as such, because she laughed and said, 'Excellent.'

Such was my discomfort, I was unsure I could maintain the required level of civilized conversation through the whole of teatime. But I was saved by the arrival of young Benjamin Baxter, brought down from the upper regions by his nursemaid to spend half an hour with his progenitors. The nurse was a sensible body of about thirty, and she seemed both modest and conscientious. She also spoke of her other charge, and my ears pricked up. 'Miss Daisy has learned a poem she would like to recite to you,' she said. 'But she wasn't expecting visitors to be here.'

'It will be good practice for her,' said the vicar. 'She must learn to accommodate a larger audience than her parents if she is to learn the art of public speaking. Mr Jameson is a connoisseur of verse, so he will be well-placed to offer his comments on her performance.'

'Well, p-perhaps not yet,' I added, afraid I would predispose the little girl to dislike me by first encountering me in the role of critic. 'It might make her shy. I will listen, but I won't interfere.'

'I'll tell her, then, shall I, that there'll be an extra gentleman but not to take no notice of him.' The nurse gave me a droll look.

'Exactly. I like it b-best when I am not noticed,' I said, and I got up and moved myself to a place behind Mrs Baxter's chair where I was partly in the shadow of the curtain.

I could hardly contain my excitement at the prospect of seeing the little girl. Of course, I said to myself, she might be ugly, or lame or sickly, or, even worse, spoiled. But I had a strong premonition that she would be as delightful as I had imagined. With a handsome father like Baxter, and a beauty for a mother, I felt she must surely have the best of attributes. I was not mistaken. When the door opened and the nurse ushered her in, I beheld the most graceful and charming of children – small-boned, delicate, with pale skin and wonderful dark, rather wild-looking hair. She looked like a fairy creature, a fawn. She seemed made for the meadows and woods of the Garden of Eden, where, like our first forefathers, she could walk naked and innocent. But of course she was heavily clothed, as is our regrettable fashion. A blue cotton dress and a substantial embroidered pinafore obscured the childish curves of her arms and neck, and her well-shaped little legs were covered in dark woollen stockings. She was very self-possessed, however, and without a glance at me, approached her mother and handed her a book before taking up her position in the middle of the room.

'Off you go,' said Baxter, with a smile.

'"How Doth the Little Bee", by Isaac Watts,' she announced, folding her hands in front of her in the approved classroom manner. I groaned inwardly. I dislike that poem with its mincing platitudes, but I was still keen to see how Daisy would perform it. She fixed her eyes on some spot out of the window and began. Both Mr and Mrs Baxter nodded with approval, and I buried the urge to laugh as Daisy metrically informed us of her need to keep permanently busy in case Satan found mischief for idle hands to do.

I looked at Daisy's sweet face, her little hands, and thought how unlikely it would be for such a child to be doing any serious mischief in the world, and how wrong it was that she should be preoccupied with imaginary sins in this way, spouting sickening cant about work and duty, and devoting herself to stultifying dullness. How natural and enjoyable it would be for her to cast off the chains of duty and propriety that Society was forcing on her, and to do exactly as she wished in the short golden time of childhood, before she was obliged to conform to the absurd rules and regulations of adult life. Even then I determined to devote my powers to this end: Daisy would know what it was to have days of enchantment; to know amusement and freedom and laughter; to explore the wild ways of the imagination. Of course, in order to do so, I would need to have her to myself – and that would not be easy to bring about.

With the fourth verse, Daisy's recitation came to an end, and she executed a deep curtsey, her face flushed with relief, her cheeks dimpling with pleasure. The nurse, I saw from the corner of my eye, clapped her hands discreetly together, and Mrs Baxter handed back the book saying, 'Well done! Word perfect.'

'Nettie helped me,' said the child, giving the nurse a grateful glance.

'Then well done, Nettie, too,' said Mrs Baxter, somewhat languidly.

'But we won't let ourselves become too proud, will we?' said Baxter, rising and placing his hand on his daughter's shoulder. 'It is only a recitation and there is much more of worth to be striven for in this life.'

I thought this speech somewhat rich after our conversation in the study, and for the first time thought it might be possible that Daniel Baxter was a hypocrite. I also noted that the child's pleasure in her achievement was on the instant undermined, and that her face fell. To be frank, I could have wrung her father's neck. But I was immediately put into a mixture of confusion and ecstasy as he steered her towards me. 'Daisy, this is Mr John Jameson, a good friend of mine, and a very clever man. I hope we will be seeing much more of him at the vicarage.'

'How do you do, sir?' she said politely, holding out her hand.

'I do very well as it happens. How do *you* do?'

'Very well, too.' But she looked somewhat disconcerted, and quickly pulled back the hand I was holding so reverently in mine. I was afraid that she did not like me. Many people don't at first acquaintance. I could see that I would need to develop a repertoire of suitable distractions if I was to overcome this antipathy: I would need to practise words and actions that would appeal to a child's mind. Puzzles, perhaps, or jokes – or some of my little inventions. I opened my mouth to say more to her, but she was gone, whisked away by the nursemaid. I gathered she would not be joining us for tea.

The rest of the afternoon was very much an anti-climax. The older girls were duly brought in and presented to me, but I could see they were the sort that would have no time for a plain and awkward fellow such as myself, and, frankly, I returned the compliment. They were handsome, certainly, but they were rather haughty and somewhat pleased with their new-found womanly charms, and in their presence I blushed and found that my stammer redoubled. They clearly thought this circumstance amusing, and exchanged several smiles and even sniggers when their parents were not attending. 'Some j-jam, Mr J-Jameson?' one even whispered as she brought me a plate of bread-and-butter. I am usually unprepared to sanction rudeness in young people, and have a selection of withering replies for any undergraduate who steps even slightly out of line, but I did not feel that insulting his older daughters would be the best way to insert myself into Baxter's intimate household. So I nodded and looked meek. I felt the Baxter ladies all regarded me with a kind of condescending pity, and from that day onward I did nothing to counter that judgement.

2

   MARGARET CONSTANTINE

I'VE BEEN MARRIED NOW FOR EXACTLY SEVEN WEEKS
and two days. But life is not at all how I imagined it would be.

I've been busy, of course, doing all the things a new wife
should do. I've inspected every room in the rectory, including
the broom cupboard and the wash-house; I've counted every
jar of preserve and pickle in the larder and made a note of
the quantity in the household book Robert has given me; I've
checked every silver knife, spoon and fork in the pantry, and
made a note of them too; I've counted the sheets and pillow-slips
a dozen times, and then the tablecloths, tray-cloths, napkins and
towels, noting as I go; I've made little lavender bags to hang in
the closets to keep away moths, and I've embroidered initials
on all my husband's handkerchiefs; I've spoken to Cook in the
mornings and arranged the day's menus in minute detail; and
every day, whether it's fine or not, I've walked in the garden,
inspecting the fruit and the vegetables.

In addition, I've spent two whole days unpacking the wedding
presents. I've set out the new ornaments on the mantelpiece
and the piano, and moved them around until I am satisfied.
And then, not being satisfied at all, I've moved them again.
I've carefully mounted the photographs we had taken for our
wedding in the album Robert has bought for the purpose,
and I've shown them to him after supper when we've sat in
the drawing room together. I've written long letters of thanks
to all who kindly sent us presents, and I've answered all the

congratulatory notes that have welcomed me to my new home. I've noted who has left visiting cards and, on selected afternoons, I've chosen fashionable new outfits from my trousseau and taken the carriage to leave my own card in return. I've written every other day to my mother and sisters, and once a week to my brother Benjamin, who is still at school. I've written as often as is reasonable to my dear friends, Annie, Enid and Emma. And when I've completely exhausted every possibility of duty and entertainment, and my husband is still busy in his study with his sermons, I've sat at the window-seat in the upstairs drawing room, looking over the yew trees in the churchyard, reading the latest novel about love.

In spite of all this housewifely activity, I can't help feeling that the house belongs more to my husband than to me. In my more rational moments I know this is not Robert's fault. After all, he has been established here at St Aidan's for almost a year, and he has his ways and patterns already in place. He's all ease and familiarity as he walks around, and has a purpose in all he does; whereas I feel awkward and unsure, and have no one with whom to confide my uncertainties. I can't confide in Robert; I feel too foolish. Besides, there are other, more difficult, matters that occupy the ground between us. But I'm embarrassed to find that the servants seem to know my husband's preferences better than I do: when he likes to be convivial and when he likes to be quiet; his dislike of fuss, and his desire, on the whole, to be left alone during the day, a period that has seemed longer and longer when I have only myself for company. Robert has been generous: he has given me carte blanche to make whatever changes I wish. Anything, he says, that will make me happy. He wants me to be happy – he wants both of us to be happy. He holds my hands and kisses me to show how much he wants it. And of course I want it too.

*

But this afternoon I've had an exciting diversion. I've come the six miles right into Oxford, to the house where I was brought up – and more particularly, to the attic nursery where I spent a large part of my childhood. It's bare now, the furniture gone. But in the middle of the room is a large toy-chest. It was left behind when my family moved out a month ago, and now, by a kind of default, it has come to me. An inheritance, almost – although Mama doesn't appear to have attached much value to it. Indeed, it was only last week that she even remembered to tell me of its existence – and then in a hasty postscript to a letter full of other matters to do with her settling back in Herefordshire.

I am very sorry, but the box was overlooked in the general frenzy and only discovered at the eleventh hour, covered in old carpets. I glanced inside, naturally, but it was so packed with childish rubbish that I found it impossible to do more than sift through what was on the top; and with the removal men gone and the carriage to take us to the station practically at the door, I decided not to have it sent on. Your brother is not interested in toys any more – and Christiana and Charles hardly wish to be reminded of the fact that they have no children. I had half a mind to let Mr Arbuthnot have it – after all, he has five offspring, and it would save the expense of moving it. But then I saw you had written your name on it – although it was almost too faint to see without my spectacles and your writing was never very clear – so I suppose it is yours. And as I hope you and Robert will enjoy the good fortune of having an infant of your own in the near future, it makes sense for you to see if there is anything to salvage. In my opinion, it is mostly jumble – things that should have been got rid of long ago. But then, if I remember rightly, you were a child who never threw anything away.

Mama manages as usual to sound disapproving towards me, as if the mere existence of the toy-box is my fault, and its late appearance in the removal schedule were deliberately engineered by me. But I thought it would prove a pleasant way to spend the afternoon, so here I am, up in the nursery at Westwood Gardens, with a meagre fire in the grate and two hours to sift through what remains of my childhood memories. My initial delight at the prospect of a diversion from my house-wifely routine has faded a little. Even entering the house again has made me feel apprehensive. I stare at the box. It's years since I've opened it and I don't remember at all what's inside.

Other memories are clear, though. This room, for example: I'm familiar with every inch of the sloping ceiling and the high view from the dormer window, right down to the garden below. And Nettie's gentle face is clear, too. I see her in my mind's eye, bending over me, putting on my petticoat and frock and patiently brushing my hair. Nettie is part of this room, part of the best time of my childhood. She loved me in a way that no one else did. And I know that I was happier in this room than I have ever been – even now, as a newly married wife, which everyone has told me is the pinnacle of a woman's joy and aspiration.

I pull my shawl around my shoulders. The house feels damp. It's been closed up for some weeks, of course. There was some difficulty about the appointment of my father's successor, the circumstances of his life being somewhat unusual, but now it's all settled. My brother-in-law has been relieved of his position and Mr Arbuthnot has sent his housemaid in advance to clean and air the property. Yesterday, passing the house en route for the draper's shop on an errand for some new cushion material, I saw the upstairs sash windows had been opened wide and that a steady stream of smoke was coming from the kitchen chimney. So I sent a note and today the servant has let me in, saying she 'supposed it was all right', before grudgingly lighting the fire with three sticks and four small pieces of coal. I forbore to say that it was my mother's coal she was being so frugal with. There seemed to be little point in making her even crosser.

I stand for a while, looking at the box. There's my childhood name on the lid: *Daisy Baxter*, written in chalk. And then: *Private*. I can't remember writing it. And the word 'private' brings an uncomfortable warmth to the back of my neck. What secrets could I have had in those days that I so much needed to protect? And is it right to uncover them now? But, all the same, I kneel down and unclasp the lid, letting it drop backwards on its hinges. The chest is full to the brim, just as Mama said. In fact, things start to fall out immediately. There are pieces of paper galore: old drawings, attempts at French and mathematics, exercises in syntax, dreadful poems by the dozen. I sit back and smile at my creations, examining them one by one before piling them up on the floor beside me. Under the schoolwork I find jigsaw puzzles and games and, below them, a large store of reading matter: children's books, nursery rhymes and fairy stories, all very well-thumbed – some so much so that their binding is coming adrift. Everything is very tightly packed and it's awkward to dislodge even a single object, but I persevere – tugging out each new thing, turning it over, and placing it on the rug beside me until I'm sitting in a sea of childhood reminiscence.

After a while, I notice that my hands feel dry and dirty, as if I've been digging in the ground, and my back is aching with the effort of bending forward. But I'm almost at the bottom and there has been little of consequence; certainly nothing to deserve the warning sign on the lid. I'm both relieved and disappointed. My mother was right; apart from my books, most of the contents can be left behind for the Arbuthnots. I peer in at the last few items: an album of pressed flowers (incomplete), an India-rubber ball that Nettie once gave me (which I will certainly keep) and something coyly nestling in the corner, something flat and rectangular, wrapped in an old linen bolster-case.

Seeing it makes me feel faintly sick, and my first instinct is to pretend it's not there. Because I know exactly what's inside. I'm aware that I am holding my breath and that my heart is thumping. Daisy buried it deep; she never wanted it discovered. 'Private', she said. And there is part of me that knows I should go no further; that I should let it alone; put it out of sight, let my mind dwell on happier things. But another part of me is horribly curious; it tells me to ignore that clutch at my stomach, that dry feeling in my throat. After all (it assures me in its most rational voice), what could there possibly be in an eleven-year-old's diary for a woman of twenty to fear? It will be interesting, surely, to see what young Daisy has to say for herself. But my heart goes on pounding all the same and it's some time before I have the courage to reach down and touch the thing – and, even more, lift it out. It feels unexpectedly heavy, just as it did all those years ago when I used to drag it on to my knees and write so carefully between the pale blue lines.

I unfold the linen wrapping still holding my breath – and there it is – with its red cover, just as I remember, and with bits of loose paper poking out from between the gilt-edged leaves. I look at it – I look a long time – but I don't open it. My fingers tremble as they even touch it. A warning voice sounds in my head. *Best left alone,* it insists. *Best left alone.* I don't know what to do. I sit with it in my lap for a long while, unable either to open it, or put it back, drawn by curiosity and held back by fear. Then some sound comes up from the landing below – the servant's voice perhaps, or her broom knocking against the skirting board – and I wake from my daze. I must follow my instinct. There is something dangerous about this thing. It must go back where it belongs, where I won't have to think about it ever again. I thrust it back into the chest, covering it in a kind of frenzy with whatever comes to hand: the backgammon board, the nursery rhymes, the box of chess pieces, the exercise books, the French grammar, the drawings of kittens and flowers. Finally, I slam down the lid.

But even as I do so, I know that this is not the answer. Far from being out of harm's way, it's simply biding its time, festering until it's uncovered again. And it *will* be uncovered if I leave it here. Some Arbuthnot child will come across it, in an innocent quest for toys and games, and set free its secrets. Because I know there are secrets even though I can't remember what they are. They are part of that hidden time, those dark years that I cannot account for. And while I remember writing in the book, I don't remember hiding it, or indeed why I did so – except there is a horror attached to it all. Daisy did well, burying it here. My sisters were far too grown-up to go rooting around for toys, while my brother would have disdained to engage himself with such girlish items as books and board games. Time and neglect (and a covering of carpet) have done the rest. But now it has come into my hands again.

But what to do? The word 'private' won't protect it now. It must be destroyed. And not just torn up, but burned to unknowable cinders. I delve back through the contents of the chest, pitching out everything that I have just replaced until I come to it again. I seize it and make for the grate. But the fire is paltry, a mere cage of powdery grey coals. I take the poker and try to ginger up a blaze, but I can only manage a small flame or two. And this book is too robust. The pages will only smoulder, leaving blackened words to be deciphered by the servant when she rakes the cinders or (worse) to be spotted by my husband when he comes to fetch me home. No, I need to take it to the scullery, shove it deep into the kitchen furnace, turn it to harmless ash in seconds. I should go now, immediately, down the back stairs, pell-mell, before I have time to think. My mind is ahead of me, already going down the staircase, sensing the familiar curve of the wall as it descends to the next floor. But my feet don't move and the book seems to grow heavy in my hands, as if it, too, is resisting leaving the room. A new voice cajoles me. *Read me*, it seems to say. *Read me now*. I feel an absurd degree of panic at the thought. And yet, to cast such precious childhood writings unread into the fire seems suddenly too drastic, too irretrievable. Again that voice tempts me. *Don't destroy me*, it says. Read a little at least. *You never know. I may have the answer.*

I finger the cover. The scarlet leather is still soft, the gold-leaf decoration still bright. It seems hardly to have aged, like a saint found whole and incorrupt after years in the grave. But in the end, it's only leather and paper bound together. And as for what's inside – well, Daisy always had such an imagination – it ran away with her at times. There'll be no great secrets here. In fact, I'll probably smile when I see what foolish things she's written.

I sink onto the threadbare rug, careless of my fine new honeymoon frock, and open it. There on the flyleaf, reassuringly bland, is the greeting from my parents: *To our dear Daisy on her eleventh birthday*. It's in my father's handwriting, precise and firm, and the roots of my hair ripple a little with remembrance. And underneath, in my own unformed copperplate, I've recorded my full name and address with exceptional neatness. I can still remember how I measured each line to make sure that the words fitted in exactly.

I turn the page. And there it is: my very first entry, the same clear, pencilled writing.

Saturday 7th June 1862. My birthday.
All sorts of things have happened today. I had some extremely nice presents and my friends came for a picnic, and Mr Jameson and Papa punted us up the river further than we have ever been. It was all extremely exilarating. But then just when I thought nothing could be more perfect, it was all spoiled.

(Oh, dear God, of course – the fateful birthday party. And the even more fateful trip up the river. It was the day that my friendship with John Jameson started in earnest, the day when I noticed him properly for the first time.)

Mama says we must all be grateful that it wasn't worse. And I am, of course, although I wish it hadn't happened on my birthday all the same. Nettie said I was Tempting Fate with my parasol, which made me think the accident was a little bit my fault, although Mr Jameson said it was no such thing, which I hope is true. (I can't write more as Nettie is looking at me with a pretend glare and saying I must go straight to bed this minute, so I have to leave off until tomorrow.)
Signed, Daisy Elizabeth Baxter (aged eleven).

PS This journal was a present from Mama and Papa but I had a much superior present from Mr Jameson. I will write more anon.

How it all comes back: my eleventh birthday and the picnic treat I'd been promised for so long. It had taken weeks to plan. Mama had asked me what I wished to include in the luncheon hamper, and I'd thought about it every day for weeks, consulting poor Nettie at tedious length before deciding on poached salmon, potted shrimps, roast chicken, egg-and-cress sandwiches, cucumber sandwiches, sugar buns and cream jellies. My mother had smiled when she read the list and said she wouldn't promise that there would be *absolutely* everything I'd asked for, but that she was sure Cook would do her best to oblige. I'd also been allowed to invite three of my friends – but only three, as my two older sisters and baby brother were to be of the party; and with my parents, Nettie and Mr Jameson, we would more than fill the two hired punts. By chance – or so it seemed – my very best friends happened to number exactly three, and I'd been very excited to hand them stiff white invitation cards with all the details inscribed, and a request for an RSVP to Miss Daisy Baxter at St Cyprian's Vicarage, Westwood Gardens, Oxford. All three had sent back equally grown-up cards saying they would be delighted to accept, and we'd spent every minute between our lessons with Miss Prentiss talking about the outing – what we would be wearing, and what we would do to entertain ourselves. My father had said he had a secret up his sleeve 'for our delectation', and I was dying to know what it was. I was looking forward to the whole thing so much I was practically sick with nerves. I was particularly worried about the weather. If it rained, Papa said, we could not go on the river, as getting drenched was 'dismal stuff', and an alternative picnic would be held at home instead, maybe in the summerhouse, with games later in the drawing room with the carpet rolled back. I could hardly bear to contemplate so tame an option, and prayed every night that the weather would be fine.

In fact, the day dawned so bright it seemed as if the air were made of solid sunlight. When I opened my eyes, I could see the slopes of the nursery ceiling almost shimmering in the heat, and the air was already warm. I pushed back the bedclothes and rushed to the window, slipping my head under the muslin and standing on tiptoes to gaze out. Ahead of me was the bright blue sky – not a single cloud – and directly below me, the garden. It seemed a long way down, with the flower borders, and the line of the hedge, and the summerhouse and the croquet lawn all as small and neat as items in a toy village. Matthews was already watering the beds, and the boy was on his knees pulling up weeds and putting them in a barrow next to him on the lawn. 'Oh, Nettie,' I cried out excitedly. 'We'll be able to go on the river. The weather has stayed fine after all!'

'That's because you've been a good girl all year, Miss Daisy. The Lord has rewarded you,' said Nettie, coming up behind me and putting her hands on my shoulders. I could feel her warm, comfy chest against my back as she pulled me towards her, swaying a little. 'Now, make sure you thank Him properly when you say your prayers tonight.'

'Oh, I will!' I replied. I'd prayed so often for it to be fine, it would have been churlish to forget my thanks now that my request had been granted. I was sure I would have no trouble at all in remembering, but I whispered a quick intermediate prayer against the windowpane just in case God was under the impression I did not appreciate His goodness.

After I'd washed my hands, Nettie said I might have breakfast in my petticoat as there was no point in putting on my day dress just to take it off again later, and even more foolish to put on my best dress with the chance of getting it dirty, which she wouldn't thank me for. So I sat at the nursery table feeling strangely free and cool with my bare arms and neck, and helped myself to bread-and-butter and jam. Nettie was busy making up a porridgy mess for my brother, and whenever her attention was elsewhere, I quickly dipped the jammy slices into my glass of milk before putting them in my mouth. I suspected she saw me, but she pretended not to, partly because it was my birthday and also because I was in my petticoat with nothing pretty to spoil. When the porridge was ready, she took Benjy from his cot, sat him on her lap, and began to spoon it into his mouth. He wasn't at all interested and kept turning his head to look at me, holding out his hand and gurgling, so that the spoon traced a porridgy line across his cheeks from mouth to ear, in a shape rather like Papa's whiskers.

'Do you know what day it is?' I asked him after a while, unable to contain my joy. He didn't reply, of course, but he smiled at me and gave a little shouty noise, and I put my head close to his and gave him a kiss. 'It's my birthday!' I whispered. 'And we are going to have the best treat ever! A picnic *miles* up the river with all my favourite things to eat. Only you must be very good and not cry, as that makes Papa cross and then everyone is miserable.'

It was a mistake to go so close to him. He grabbed my curl-papers with his sticky hands and pulled so hard that my eyes watered. The curl-paper came right off and a lock of porridgy hair flopped down into my eye.

'Serves you right for interfering with the child,' said Nettie. 'Don't blame me now if your front curls won't sit straight.' But she put Benjy in his high chair and took a wet comb and wound the curl-paper up again really tight. 'That'll soon dry in the heat,' she said. 'Not that I knows why we has to dress up in order to go and sit on the grass for hours on end when a body has work to get on with.'

I knew Nettie was not altogether keen on this picnic party. Or at least she thought that she and Benjy would be better to stay at home. 'The child doesn't like the heat, Mrs Baxter,' she'd said to my mother a couple of days before. 'And he'll be fussing all day.'

But it was no good. 'The vicar wishes the entire family to be there,' said my mother. 'There can be no argument, Nurse. Take plenty of cooling drinks and a sun bonnet. I'm sure you can manage perfectly well. You always do.' And Nettie said no more.

After I had washed my face and hands, Nettie had laid out my best frock on the bed together with my new white stockings, and Hannah came up from the boot room with my newly polished shoes. 'All the servants wishes you the best, Miss Daisy,' she said, dropping a quick curtsey. 'You've got a lovely day for it.'

After she left, I kept an eye on the door, hoping my parents or sisters would come up to the nursery to offer their good wishes as well. I was even hoping to have a present or two, although my mother always told me not to be greedy and never to expect anything, so I was trying to be grateful for what I already had, which was so much more than the poor children had, especially if they were in Africa or India. And of course the picnic was a great thing in itself. 'I wonder if Mama and Papa will come up,' I said idly to Nettie. Then, with a sudden feeling of horror, I added, 'You don't think they've forgotten, do you?'

'Course not, miss. It's just that your ma and pa are very busy with all the arrangements just at the minute. It's like a madhouse in the kitchen, I can tell you.' But she must have seen the disappointment in my eyes, as she hesitated and added, 'But I've got a little something for you to be going on with. It's from me and Master Benjy.' She went to the big chest of drawers and took out a lumpy parcel wrapped in red and white paper, with a red ribbon around it and a large label tied on with string: *Best Wishes on Your Birthday from Your Brother Benjy and Loving Nursemaid Nettie.* It was quite light, and the wrapping was awkwardly put on, with blobs of sealing wax holding the edges together. I broke the wax and pulled the paper away. Inside was the most perfect India-rubber ball, all the colours mixing together like the patterns in the marble columns at church. It was much nicer than the plain red one belonging to my sisters, which they wouldn't let me play with even when they were sitting down doing nothing. 'We might want to play at any moment,' they'd say. 'And you'd be sure to lose it.'

'Oh, thank you so much,' I said, putting my arms around Nettie. 'I shall treasure it for ever and ever.'

'Well, I don't know about that. Just don't go losing it,' she said, looking cross and pleased at the same time.

At a quarter past nine, Nettie, Benjy and I went downstairs. I had on my best white dress with blue piping and a blue silk sash, and was already feeling very hot. Nettie had put more ribbons than usual in my hair so as to fix the ringlets in position, but I knew the curls would be out before the end of the day, especially once I'd put on my straw hat. It was the absolute sinful desire of my life to have natural curls like my sisters. Each strand of their hair was always very well-behaved and fell in exactly the same way at the end of the day as at the beginning. I watched them now, sitting demurely side by side on the piano stool, wearing grown-up dresses with extremely puffed sleeves and with silver bangles around their wrists. They always seemed so much older than me, although Christiana was only fifteen and a half and Sarah a year younger. They were both tall, like Papa, whereas I was small for my age and, to my continued mortification, always being mistaken for someone much younger. Mama looked ravishing as usual. I remember Papa said: 'My dear, you look ravishing,' when she came into the room with her dainty print frock and straw hat, and carrying a furled parasol. She smiled and said he looked handsome too. He'd taken off his clerical collar and was wearing a light-coloured coat – suitable, he said, for the exertions of the river.

Mr Jameson, by contrast, was wearing his usual dark suit and a shirt with a very high collar. He looked ill at ease and I couldn't help wondering if he was really capable of steering the punt all those extra miles upriver that Papa had promised. My father was strong, and I knew from previous excursions that he was able to negotiate a punt under every kind of bridge and overhanging tree. But Mr Jameson was rather a weedy fellow, and I felt he might make a hash of it. I didn't really like him; he rarely spoke when I was in the room, although he always seemed to be looking at me, taking notice of everything I said and did, as if he were committing it to memory. I was always afraid he was going to ask me a difficult question about geography or arithmetic, but so far he hadn't. He came to our house two or three times a week to talk about important things with Papa, and was, as Mama said, 'quite a fixture' in the drawing room. When the expedition was first being planned, he'd offered his services immediately, and no one had liked to ask him if he were capable of managing a boatful of people for a whole afternoon. As a result we were rather stuck with him.

My father was standing in the centre of the drawing room and when we were all assembled, he addressed us as if he were in his pulpit, although smiling a good deal more. 'Our dear little Daisy is eleven years old today, and we are celebrating her birthday in a way in which I hope she – and all of us – will remember for many years to come. And now, a small gift to commemorate the occasion.' And he took a rectangular parcel down from the top of the piano and presented it to me. 'From your loving parents. We hope you will make good use of it.'

'Thank you, Papa. And Mama.' I kissed them both, then pulled the pretty wrapping open very carefully. I knew it was a book, a very heavy one, and was excited to think which of my favourite stories it would be – or indeed if it would be a new one I'd never read. It was a handsome red and gold volume, but it had no title and, when I opened the cover, I discovered all the pages were blank, except for the faint, ruled lines clearly waiting to be filled. I wanted to weep with disappointment, but held my chin firm.

'It's a journal, Daisy,' said my father, in explanation. 'And, as its name suggests, it is for daily use. It is never too early to learn habits of reflection and contemplation and, as such, it is an invaluable aid for recording the successes and failures of one's battle towards self-improvement in this life.'

My sisters smiled brightly at me, as if echoing these senti-ments. I couldn't recall whether they themselves had been given journals for their eleventh birthdays and, if so, whether they had taken the trouble to write in them daily. Since they had moved out of the nursery years before I knew little of what went on in their lives. They had their meals downstairs, and no longer shared the services of Nettie; Hannah now seeing to their clothes and hair. However, Mama could see I was dismayed, and touched my hand, adding, 'You're so very good at reading, Daisy, and although your spelling can be a little uncertain, Miss Prentiss says all your essays show great imagination and have such excellent punctuation! We thought it would be nice for you to have somewhere to write down whatever you pleased. You could record all about the picnic, for example.'

'Yes, Mama,' I said, rather more dully than I intended, disappointment stinging in my throat. When I looked up, I caught Mr Jameson's eye, and I thought he gave me a sympathetic glance, but he looked away so quickly I couldn't tell.

Christiana and Sarah then presented me with a set of six fine cotton handkerchiefs, on each of which they had embroidered the letter *D* intertwined with a daisy flower. 'So you won't lose them and have to borrow ours,' they said, laughing. I couldn't help wondering why everyone was under the impression I would lose things. I considered I was very careful with all my belongings. I had once – *once* – lost my hair ribbon when playing blindman's buff, but Hannah had found it under the piano the next day so it wasn't really lost.

Then, just as Papa began to look at the clock and fret, saying he hoped that my little friends would not be late, Mr Jameson darted out with a long, thin object in his hand and said in his stammering way that he hoped he would be permitted to offer his own small gift. He thrust the parcel into my hands awkwardly, and retired to his habitual spot behind Mama's chair. I was very surprised, and my parents looked quickly at each other, as if it were an unexpected turn of events for them, too. I stood there with the object in my hands, not quite sure what to say.

'Say thank you, Daisy,' said Mama quickly. 'Really, Mr Jameson, there was no need to have gone to such trouble.'

'Thank you,' I said automatically, and I heard him murmur that it had been no trouble at all.

The gift was wrapped in a good deal of brown paper which, once unfixed, came off in a long spiral, and I could see that it was printed with the name of the umbrella shop in the High. Had Mr Jameson given me an umbrella? As the paper fell away, I saw it was in fact a parasol. A most beautiful parasol in fine stripes of white and cream, with a frill all round the edge and a bow at the top. A most grown-up parasol, quite as nice as Mama's, only smaller. I remember feeling pink with delight, the memory of the wretched journal quite erased. Mama, Papa, Nettie and my sisters all stared as I went to put it up.

'Not in the house, miss,' said Nettie in alarm. 'That's bad luck. Wait until you're outside.'

But, headstrong as I was, I couldn't wait. 'That's just a super-stition, Nettie,' I said as I pushed up the lever, and Nettie said nothing more. The parasol opened as smooth as oiled silk. I held it over my head and then rested it on my shoulder and twirled it around as I'd seen young ladies do as they walked with their beaux in the park. 'Oh, thank you, Mr Jameson,' I said, this time with true feeling, and half wanting to embrace him as he stood, cramped and awkward, in the corner. He just nodded his head and smiled quietly to himself.

'How extraordinarily generous,' said my mother with a strange note in her voice. 'You must be careful not to turn her head, Mr Jameson. She is only eleven, after all.'

I thought for a moment she might take the precious thing from me and insist on keeping it until I was older, but at exactly that moment my friends turned through the front gate with Annie's nurse Deedee in charge, and Papa sprang to his feet, saying it was time to be off. They were carrying presents, however, and were anxious that I should open them, which I did as quickly as I could. Emma had brought a jigsaw puzzle of the Crystal

Palace in two hundred pieces, Annie a game of Ludo decorated with birds and flowers, and Enid a copy of *Robinson Crusoe* with coloured illustrations. Normally, I would have been delighted at such gifts, but my mind was full of the parasol.

On the walk to the landing stage, Papa took the lead with Mama, and the rest of us followed, crocodile-style, Nettie bringing up the rear with Benjy in her arms and carrying a large cloth bag of nursery supplies. She had taken off her apron in honour of the occasion, although I could see she would have felt more comfortable with it on. She'd put Benjy in a cotton bonnet as a precaution against the sun, and he was squirming about all the time, trying to remove it. Mr Jameson walked ahead of my sisters, wheeling a small cart in which there was a heavy object covered in canvas, which he said he had to be very careful with. Matthews and the garden boy carried the wicker luncheon hamper between them. Hannah carried the summerhouse cushions and a folded rug. I walked along proudly with my parasol, and my friends took it in turns to come under its shade, linking arms with me and squeezing close. From time to time I threw a glance at Mr Jameson. His generosity had suddenly cast him in a much more interesting light and I thought I should try a little harder to be nice to him.

My father, as had been arranged, was to be in charge of one punt and Mr Jameson the other. Papa insisted that Benjy and Nettie should be of the party with himself, Mama and my sisters, and that Mr Jameson would take us four younger girls, as we were light, and Mr Jameson's mysterious canvas object and the luncheon hamper were both heavy. Mama feared Mr Jameson would be too busy managing the pole to pay us children attention, but Father said that we were sensible girls and he trusted us to behave ourselves and not stand up or walk about. 'And we shall be in sight of each other all the way,' he said. 'Nothing can go wrong.'

And so we got in and prepared to set off. Mr Jameson had taken off his dark jacket and rolled up his sleeves and, in spite of his thin build, he had us out into the middle of the river in no time, setting a straight course upstream. Papa was quite left behind, having become entangled with a punt full of undergraduates who were going in the opposite direction, heading for the Thames. He called out, 'Jameson, you wretch, wait for us!' and Mr Jameson pulled up his pole and let the punt drift while Father pushed out from the bank and set off after us with energetic strokes.

Enid and I lay back on the cushions with the parasol above our heads and with Mr Jameson directly in our line of sight. He kept the punt moving at a steady pace apparently without effort, whereas I could see Papa behind him making much heavier weather, with a lot of water splashing up as he lifted the pole. Mama must have been surprised too, as when their punt came up alongside, she called across saying, 'You are an excellent punter, Mr Jameson. And a dark horse, too; I had never taken you for an athlete.'

'I'm not, Mrs B-Baxter. It's not so much strength you need, as p-precision. I'm no oarsman, unlike the vicar.' He was somewhat breathless, and he stammered as usual, but I thought his voice by no means as squeaky as it had previously seemed. I felt he might be quite nice, deep down, and that was why my father liked him so much. As the journey progressed, he certainly ensured that we four girls were well-entertained. Sometimes he pointed out wild flowers growing on the river edge, or a water vole running along the bank, or a shoal of little fish in the water – and after a while he encouraged us to sing songs or recite poetry.

'Daisy has a poem she can recite,' he said at one time, making me blush. 'How does it go now? *How doth the little crocodile?*' and we all chorused, '*Busy Bee*! It's the *Busy Bee*!' He laughed at that and said he didn't know how he'd made that mistake and were we *absolutely* sure we didn't know the one about the crocodile? And we said we were sure. 'Or the lobster?' he said. 'I am *sure* you know the one about the lobster.' And we said we were sure about that, too. And then he said, 'Dear, dear! Education is not what it was. I shall have to have a word with Miss Prentiss. In the meantime I shall teach it to you.' And he began to recite:

Said the Stork to the Lobster, 'I'm quite a fair man.
I'll give you a penny; you give me a ham.'
Said the Lobster, in dudgeon, 'It's worth so much more,
I'd rather quite frankly it went to the Poor.'
'Then I'll give you a shilling,' replied the Old Stork.
'As long as you throw in a knife and a fork.'

We all laughed and he made us recite it with him until we had learned it too. Then he recited some Wordsworth, but again that was all wrong and I hoped Mama could not hear as she was very fond of Wordsworth. What I particularly remember, though, was how delightful he seemed to find the four of us as we chatted and laughed and contradicted him.

It took us two hours before we arrived at our destination. The first stretch of river was shallow and overhung with willows, but once we had passed the bathing pond, the river was deeper and more open. Here, strength was more advantageous than style, and my father shot ahead. I could see that he hadn't been pleased that Mr Jameson had demonstrated such prowess at the start, and was anxious to show off his skills. I remember wondering, as I watched his smiling face, whether Papa ever recorded the sin of pride in a journal of his own.

The chosen picnic spot was on a sloping bank and we could see the roof and upper windows of a big house just beyond the trees. We were far upstream, well beyond the range of undergraduate punters and oarsmen, and the river was quiet.

It was ten minutes past midday, so there was hardly any shade to be had, but Papa said the sun would soon come round, and in the meantime we ladies were all to keep on our straw bonnets and make use of our parasols – 'Those that have them,' he said laughingly. He and Mr Jameson drew the punts into the bank and secured them with the poles, skewering them deep into the Cherwell mud and gravel. Then Papa helped us all disembark, and Mr Jameson brought the cushions and rugs for us to sit on, laying them out at the top of the slope so we could view the river and the countryside beyond. It was the best prospect along the whole river, said Papa. Then he and Mr Jameson struggled to lift the hamper from the punt. Papa took the strain, and with a great effort they brought the hamper onto the bank. 'Rowing muscles, you see, Jameson,' Papa said with a laugh, and I thought of all the caps and trophies in his study, and the great brown oar that hung over the mantelpiece.

Mama sat Benjy next to her and held him under her parasol while Nettie unpacked the hamper, starting with the cloth, then the plates, cups and cutlery as well as glasses for our lemonade. Cook had packed the bottles in ice and the lemonade was very cold, so we asked if we could drink it immediately, and Papa agreed. Cook, at Mama's request, had packed several bottles of ale for Papa and Mr Jameson, but Mr Jameson said he would prefer the lemonade, and drank a great deal of it all in one draught, which made me worry that we would not have enough left. He assisted Nettie in taking the items from the basket and setting them out on the tablecloth: poached salmon on a plate, little jars of shrimps and potted meats all sealed with oiled paper, dainty white sandwiches of egg and cress, and others of cucumber, soft bread rolls with curls of butter in a cold dish with the water still glistening on them, two cold fowls divided into portions, a bacon and egg pie, asparagus tops, and a half of very best game pie for the gentlemen.

Benjy was most taken with the game pie, and my mother had difficulty preventing him from helping himself. 'Do take him now, and give him something suitable to eat, Nurse, or he'll be crawling all over the tablecloth. Cook's minced him some lamb and potato, and there's a rice pudding for afterwards.' So poor Nettie had to sit and feed Benjy while the rest of us tucked into the delicacies before us, and I began to wonder why Papa had insisted that they come on the outing. Benjy would have been none the wiser as to what he had missed.

We had jellies afterwards, and then some cake. We all felt rather dozy after all the food, and Benjy fell fast asleep in Nettie's lap while Mama lay back under a tree. My sisters went off with Papa in search of insects for his collection, but my friends and I lay in a heap under the parasol. Annie's sister was shortly to be married, and Annie was to be a bridesmaid, so we had to hear all about the preparations and the immense dullness (so she said) of the fiancé. Then we turned our attention to Miss Prentiss and her shortcomings. 'Everything she teaches us is dull,' said Emma, plucking a stem of grass and chewing it. 'All she says is, *Look up, speak nicely, and don't twiddle your fingers all the time!*'

After a while I noticed that Mr Jameson had taken out a sketch pad and was drawing us. He was watching us very intently and had a smile on his face. 'You young ladies find everything remarkably dull,' he said. 'You are like the four sisters in the story.'

'What four sisters?' asked Annie, who was always bold and didn't seem to mind addressing Mr Jameson in spite of not knowing him at all. 'I haven't heard that story.'

'Why, the four sisters who lived in a well,' he said.

'In a well? Why would they live in a well? That's silly!' she said, pouting.

'On the contrary, it's very *sensible*,' he said. 'They lived in a well so they could learn to draw.'

'But how can you learn to draw in a well?' said Enid, in her tiny, breathy voice. 'It would be dark and wet and you wouldn't be able to see. And what would there be to draw?'

'Water, of course, Miss Enid. These four sisters became very good at it and drew water all day long. Of course, water is a very *dull* thing to draw and they complained and complained, saying how they wished they could be drawing breath or money from the bank instead.'

I laughed, thinking again that Mr Jameson was really a lot funnier than he looked. And I noticed that while he was talking to us his stammer had almost disappeared. But Annie interrupted. 'Are you drawing *us*?' she said eagerly.

'Indeed not. The four young ladies in *this* picture are busy killing time and I'm sure that none of you well-brought-up children would dream of such an act of homicide.'

'But "killing time" is a metaphor,' I told him, pleased to be able to show off my knowledge. 'Or maybe it's just an expression. At any rate, you can't *really* do it.'

He raised his eyebrows. 'Can't you?' he said. 'Maybe you've never tried hard enough. Supposing Time was stopped in his tracks right this minute? Just think – you'd never have to go to Miss Prentiss's lessons ever again or learn about simile or syntax, précis or parsing, superlatives or subjunctives, let alone the capital of Hindustan and the theorem of Pythagoras.'

'Well,' I said. 'I suppose it would be nice.' Although, secretly, I liked school and learning all about history and geography.

'But on the other hand,' he said, 'it would always be your birthday, which might not be so nice.'

'I think that would be *very* nice,' Annie said, butting in as usual. 'I like birthdays.'

'You wouldn't like them so much if you had one every day,' he said. 'Just think – you'd have to eat that immense picnic luncheon over and over again, starting with the sandwiches and chicken; and working through the salmon and shrimps. And then, as soon as you finish with the jellies and cake, you have to start again with the sandwiches, and so ad infinitum.'

'We'd be sick,' said Emma, making a face. 'My brother Ralph was horribly sick after eating too much at his birthday party.'

'But he's a little boy,' said Mr Jameson with a shudder. 'And boys are full of snips and snails as you very well know.'

'What are little girls full of, then?' Enid asked shyly.

'Well, don't you know the song? *Sugar and spice and all things nice?*' he said, smiling at her. 'I wouldn't wish you to get swell-headed, little Enid, because it would hurt too much – but girls, in my opinion, are the most delightful creatures in the world.'

'Not always, Jameson.' My father came up behind us. 'Girls always have a lot to say for themselves.'

'Well, it would be strange if they had a lot to say for *other people*.' Mr Jameson laughed.

'Yes,' said Annie. 'Because you'd have to get inside other people's brains first. You'd have to coil up really small, and be squashed against the sides of their heads.'

'Ugh, that's horrid,' said Emma.

'Quite horrid. But there's no need for such bodily contortions,' said Mr Jameson. 'Try using your imagination, little ladies. That's the best way to get into someone else's head. There's space for everything there – whole countries and universes if you have a mind to it.'

I couldn't help thinking about this, and how you can carry so many pictures in your mind even though your actual head is so small in size, and I thought Mr Jameson was very clever and not at all like the rest of the grown-up people I knew.

I am astonished at how much I remember, now my mind has jumped back to that time. But did Daisy remember that day as I do now? And did she remember John Jameson the same way?

I lift the journal from my lap and turn the page. The next entry is very long, and I'm obscurely cheered at her diligence. If she writes as much for every other day, I'll be here for hours. But I must take every word and paragraph in the strictest of order.

Sunday 8th June

I am writing my journal very early, while it is still a bit dark. I think I am what Nettie calls Overtired which means I can't sleep and the same things keep going round and round in my head, so I thought I would write them down before I forget. I've taken the old bit of candle from Nettie's bedside. I don't think she'll wake up yet. She's snoring a little bit which she always does when she's worn out, which she is of course, after all that happened.

The first part of the picnic party was a Great Success. We went a long way up the river and had our picnic at a very nice place. The sandwiches and cakes were very nice too and Mama said I had chosen well. That made me very pleased although I know Papa would say that is the Sin of Pride, but as it was my birthday I hope God will forgive me. Papa says He is a Loving God so that must mean He will *forgive me – although He punishes people too and I don't quite know how He decides which of the two to do. For example, I don't know why He should want to punish my brother as he is an Innocent Infant who has done no wrong, but when I asked Papa about it, he just said that the ways of God are a Mystery. It's hard to understand these Mysteries as they are most contradictery but the miracle is that Benjy was saved and I must try not to mind about my party ending so quickly without all the games, although if I am truthful, it was very disappointing.*

Before it happened Mr Jameson amused us with funny drawings and told us jokes that weren't jokes really, but still funny. I still don't know whether I like him or not. Of course he was very kind to give me such a lovely parasol, and I am very, very grateful to him for rescuing Benjy but there is something peculiar about him all the same. However, the most exciting thing is that he took real live photographs of us all in the open air! Papa said this was his Great Surprise although I thought it was Mr Jameson's surprise really. That was why Papa wanted Benjy to come with us, so the Whole Family could be recorded for posterety (I am not sure of the spelling of this). We all had to sit on the ground close to each other except Emma, Annie and Enid (who are not our family) and Mr Jameson took his photograph apperatus out of the canvas bag and set up the camera on three wooden legs which unfolded outwards in a very neat way. Then he made a kind of tent with the canvas bag and laid out all sorts of bottles and dishes inside it and took out the glass plates which he said would be used to make the pictures. They are called 'wet-plates'. Then he told us to keep very still while he put his head under a large back cloth and looked at us through the camera while we all waited for what seemed like ages! And then he lifted out the plates and crawled back into his tent and clinked about with the bottles and trays of liquid before coming back and saying everything was fine and now he would take a photograph of Mama.

When he'd finished that (which took a long time as it is very compli-cated), he took a photograph of my sisters and then he said he'd like a photograph of the Little Fairies too – by which he meant just me and my friends (as Christiana and Sarah are too grown up to be fairies). And he asked us to lift our dresses up at the sides and pretend we were dancing in a circle except we couldn't move but had to be like statues. My arms started to ache after a while and Annie was going to laugh which she had been told expressly that she must not, but luckily Mr Jameson said he had finished and we were able to move again. We all wanted to put our heads into the tent to see the pictures, but Mr Jameson said he had to print them first and he would do that in his room later which was disappointing, and we all asked him to do it as quickly as he could as we were all impatient to see them!

Papa then said we needed to take some healthy exercise and Mr Jameson said we must have a corkus race (I don't know how to spell this either and I am not really sure what it is). He said that he had brought prizes for us all whether we won or not which Christiana said was unfair but

Mr Jameson said was the fairest of all as no one was left out. So we all climbed up the bank until we came to where it was flat, except for Mr Jameson who was still putting his camera and tent things away, and Nettie was clearing away the picnic things with Benjy beside her.

We were just lining up when we heard Nettie screaming at the top of her voice and we looked back down to the river – and there was Mr Jameson up to his knees in water, and Benjy in his arms all brown and dripping as if he was made of mud. We all rushed down as fast as we could but Mama got there before anyone else. And she held him very tight even though he was dripping mud all down her nice dress. 'Thank God he's breathing,' she said. And 'Thank God for you, Mr Jameson.' And then Papa slapped Benjy on the back to make him cough. And all the time Nettie was standing with her hand at her mouth, and Papa glared at her, saying why wasn't she watching the child when that was what she was paid to do and didn't she understand that Benjy might have drowned? And Nettie just burst into tears and said that the last time she'd seen him he'd been sitting quiet beside the picnic box and she didn't know how he could have crawled that far without her seeing. And Mama said, 'He did though, didn't he?'

Of course we couldn't go on with the games after that as Mama said she needed Dr Lawrence to look at Benjy straight away to make sure he hadn't got a chill or something worse from the river water. Papa said he would see if anyone at the house near by had a horse and cart or anything that would take Mama and Benjy back to Oxford quickly. And a footman in a long silk coat answered the door and said there was a convayance which he was sure the lady of the house would let us borrow, and she did very kindly, and Mama and Christiana went together with Benjy in an old barouche with the footman driving.

The rest of us packed up everything and got back into the punts as quickly as we could, although I felt sorry that everything was ending so quickly and Papa was cross with me saying I was dawdling and holding everyone up. Mr Jameson was wet up to his knees and elbows but said not to worry as he would soon be dry if he recited Cicero to *himself which was by far the driest thing he knew. Papa gave a little smile, then. But he wouldn't smile at anyone else and wouldn't speak to Nettie at all, and made her sit in Mr Jameson's punt with me and Enid, and he put Annie and Emma into Nettie's old place. Nettie sat next to me and she was very quiet all the way back, and then just before we got to the landing stage, she started to cry and said that she wasn't surprised that things had gone wrong because of People opening Parasols inside the house which everyone knows is bad luck. I was struck to the heart to think everything might be my fault for Tempting Fate (what Miss Prentiss calls Nemesis and it means a punishment that comes back to you later), but Mr Jameson said that was all supersticious nonsense and he'd have no more of it, and Nettie looked more downcast than ever. I squeezed her arm and told her she mustn't worry and that everything would come out in the wash. This is her favourite saying if I am cross or upset about anything, but she didn't seem to take it to heart herself.*

When we got home Dr Lawrence was already here but Benjy wouldn't stop crying. The doctor said he was quite well and no bones broken, but had had a shock and we needed to keep an eye on him over the night-time. Papa didn't want Benjy to be left with Nettie any more, but Dr Lawrence could see that Nettie was the only one who could settle him. So Benjy slept with us in the nursery as usual, but there was a lot of bustle with Mama and Papa both coming to say goodnight to him and Christiana and Sarah hanging over him and singing lullabies, which they have never done before although they have singing lessons and very pretty voices. Benjy knew that something strange was going on and he was ever so fretful. Nettie just sat in a corner until they were all gone, and then she picked him up and rocked him and he went quiet. Then I undressed and had some bread-and-butter and milk and wrote the first bit in my diary but Nettie said I must stop and say my prayers and go to bed, as we were both dog tired (although I am not sure why a dog is particularly tired). I didn't feel I could truthfully thank God for the picnic because Benjy had nearly drowned, but I thanked Him instead that Mr Jameson had been there and had saved Benjy's life. And I asked God to forgive Nettie as she had so many things to do and generally she loved Benjy like a mother. And I asked Him to forgive me for being vain and opening the parasol when I shouldn't have. And Nettie patted me on the shoulder and said I was a good girl and she was sorry she mentioned the parasol but she was overought and it was not my fault in any way. The she kissed me and put out the candle. I could hear her rustling about getting undressed and she seemed to take a long time about it. Then I thought I heard her go and stand over Benjy's cot for even longer, though he was fast asleep. DEB.

I put down the journal, an awful sadness in my heart. Of course, I'd had no idea, as I scribbled away, what was in store for poor Nettie. I knew that my parents were angry, but the full impact of her transgression hadn't come home to me. I thought she'd be given some kind of scolding and that would be that. And Nettie, as she calmly went about her usual tasks, gave me no clue as to what was about to happen.

I was a little surprised, therefore, when Hannah came to take Benjy down to see Mama in the drawing room before church. This was unusual; and I recall now how Nettie was loath to let him go, fussing far more than usual about his clothes and his hair and giving him extra kisses. 'Bye-bye, my darling,' she said as Hannah bore him away and, although I sensed something different in her voice, I was preoccupied with finding a safe place to keep my journal, and I took no notice. Then Nettie tidied her hair and settled her apron and cap and said she had to go down to speak with Papa as she was 'on the carpet'. She gave me an odd little smile. 'I shan't be long,' she said.

I spent the intervening time idly admiring my parasol, although I didn't dare open it again in case it brought even worse luck. After about ten minutes, I heard Nettie coming back up the stairs, and I put the parasol down quickly. I thought I heard her crying, but the sound stopped once she got to the door.

When she came in she was wiping her eyes with her pocket-handkerchief and trying to look businesslike.

'What's the matter, Nettie?' Suddenly I knew something serious had occurred.

'I'm to go, Miss Daisy,' she said flatly.

'Go?' I stared at her blankly. 'Go where?'

'Your ma and pa don't feel I am fit to look after Benjy and I can't say as I blame them.' Then she started to cry. 'It don't bear thinking about – what would have happened if Mr Jameson had not been there. Oh, Daisy, he might have drowned as easy as winking – and I might be up on a murder charge! I thank the Good Lord it's no worse. Your mother is giving me a good reference as I've been reliable for twelve years, but she says under the circumstances it would always be between us and she could never trust me again.'

'But you've *always* looked after him,' I said incredulously. 'I shall tell Papa and Mama that you have to stay.' I got up, ready to do battle, enraged on Nettie's behalf and more than a little fearful on my own. I couldn't imagine life without Nettie.

She caught my arm. 'Now, Miss Daisy, you are a dear girl, the best ever, but things is better left as they are. I'm sorry to leave you so sudden but you're getting a bit old for a nursemaid now and I expect you'll manage fine without me. You'll be a proper little lady like your sisters before you know it. And I'm sure Benjy will get to like his new nurse as quick as anything.' She turned away, and I knew she was crying some more and didn't want me to see. 'Now get your clothes on for church,' she said in a muffled voice, 'or I will be in trouble for that, too.'

'Aren't you going to help me dress?'

'Sorry, Miss Daisy, I'm to pack straight away.'

'Aren't you even coming to church?' Papa was strict about everyone attending even if they had a cold or headache and I could not imagine he would excuse Nettie now.

'I have to pack, Daisy. I told you, I have to go.'

'What, today?' I couldn't believe that Nettie, whom I had known all my life, was to depart with such awful suddenness. *'But who will look after me?'*

'Like I said, you're old enough to manage on your own. Hannah will help you with your hair I expect, and you can pretty much do everything else for yourself; and what you can't do you must learn.' Nettie pulled her old portmanteau from under her bed and started to open the drawers of the wardrobe and remove neat piles of white linen which she put inside the bag with a good deal of steady attention, as if she was doing arithmetic in her head.

'But you'll still come back and see me, won't you?' I felt a terrible numbness descend. It was like the world coming to an end.

'Better not,' she said, at the wardrobe again, with her back to me. 'Your ma says a clean break is the best. And I expect I'll have my time cut out with the new children I'll be looking after, especially if I have to go to London for a position. I couldn't keep popping back to ask after you every five minutes.'

The idea of Nettie with some other children cut me to the quick; especially the notion that she might enjoy herself with them so much that she couldn't be bothered to see me. 'Don't you love me any more, Nettie?' I cried, my voice thick with grief.

She turned to me, and the face that I'd thought was so familiar to me seemed that of a stranger. The way her face was puffy and the tears were rolling uncontrollably down her cheeks made her look so different from the Nettie I knew.

'Oh, Miss Daisy,' she cried, putting down a pile of linen. 'I love you more than anything. Don't you know that? And Benjy's like my very own child. I always knew I'd have to go one day and leave you all behind – but never like this. Never like this.

It's too cruel!' She gave out a kind of howl and opened her arms and I howled too and ran to her and breathed in her warm, biscuity smell and felt the scratch of her starched apron against my cheek.

'I won't let you go!' I said, hugging her as hard as I could. 'I'll hold on to you so tight they won't be able to separate us, and you'll have to take me with you wherever you go.'

She laughed through her tears. 'My, that would be a bit of an inconvenience – me carrying you round my waist like an extra apron and you clinging on for dear life! We'd never get as far as the bottom of the street like that.' She took her work-worn thumb and wiped my tears outwards, one side after the other, so that I felt them roll wetly by my ears and down my neck. 'You have to be brave. We both have to be brave. Things is painful sometimes. We can't do or have what we want all the time. It's part of growing up.'

'Then I don't want to grow up,' I retorted, hugging her tighter than ever.

'We all have to,' she said. 'It's the way of life. You can't be a child for ever. Now get your Sunday clothes on and show me how well you can dress yourself.'

'If I make a mess of it, will they let you stay?'

'I don't think so, Miss Daisy.'

'Why not?' I cried out.

'Because I've been paid a month in lieu of notice and I've agreed to go. Them's the rules,' she said, trying to disentangle my arms from around her back.

'Whose rules?' I said.

She seemed a bit flummoxed by this. 'The rules of England, I suppose – what everybody agrees to in order to make the world go round smoothly.'

'But it's not going round smoothly for you!' I cried angrily. 'Or for me! I think they're silly rules!'

'Look, Daisy,' she said. 'Life is a good deal more complicated than it seems when you're eleven. But you know I love you and I know you love me, and we'll always know that, won't we? Won't we?' She made me look her in the face, and I began sobbing anew. 'And if you don't get ready for church, you'll only make it worse for yourself – and me. You know how your papa can't bear anyone to be late and he's cross enough already.'

'Will you dress me one last time?'

'Yes, of course.' She seemed relieved to have something to do for me, and I was dressed in no time, Nettie's practised hands doing up buttons and tying tapes as she had done hundreds of times before. Outwardly I was calm, turning obediently and holding out my arms for my sleeves and standing patiently as Nettie combed my hair. But I was seething inwardly at the injustice of it all.

'There, you look really pretty. That's how I shall think of you in the future.'

'*Will* you think of me, Nettie?' I asked, a horrible pang of grief filling my throat.

'Course I will. You and Benjy both, and all the happy times we've had together.'

A dreadful thought occurred. 'Will you still be here when we come back from church?'

She hesitated. 'I don't know, Miss Daisy. It depends.' But she avoided my eye. And when I returned from church two hours later, she was, as I expected, gone. Her wardrobe was empty, her bed stripped and bare.

I have to confess that at that point I threw all my birthday presents around the room in a wild fury, including the parasol and journal and especially the India-rubber ball that Nettie had given me, which no longer seemed so pretty. I hated her then; I hated her for going and leaving me. And I hated the world for making the rules that meant she had to.

Monday 9th June

Yesterday was the unhappiest day of my life! *My dear Nettie was sent away and I'll never see her again! Mama says I mustn't mope, but I don't see why not. Everything is different – and horrid! Mama has made Hannah sleep in the nursery for the time being but she doesn't like looking after Benjy and keeps asking me what she should do to stop him crying. I told her I didn't care and everything was Benjy's fault anyway. I was sorry afterwards and said I didn't mean it and Hannah said the sooner we had a new nursemaid the better it would be for all concerned as she couldn't be in two places at once and she was supposed to be a parlourmaid after all and had three ladies to look after as it was. I shall be glad when she's gone. She's* very *ill-tempered and doesn't do my hair at all nicely.*

Everyone at Miss Prentiss's knew about Benjy nearly drowning and Mr Jameson saving his life and everyone crowded around me and asked lots of questions, even girls I didn't know and who had never spoken to me before, which made me feel quite important. I told them Mama and Papa had been very cross and Nettie had cried all night and then she had packed her bags and gone off to London with a month's wages, saying she would never forget me. DEB

Oh how I remember the excitement of having a near-drowning in the family! I felt rather notorious and played up to the drama of the situation, quite putting aside all my sympathy for Nettie, and enjoying the feelings of importance that her misfortunes aroused. 'Serve her right,' said one older girl. 'Some servants are so lazy; they need to be kept in check.' That brought me up short; I knew Nettie was never lazy and she certainly didn't deserve her punishment. None of us had thought Benjy could have crawled so fast, and we'd all merrily left Nettie to get on with the packing while we went off to enjoy ourselves. And then I began to wonder why Mama hadn't watched over Benjy herself. After all, she was his mother and was always saying what a jewel he was. Yet she did surprisingly little for him. She rarely fed him or played with him or put him to bed. In fact, she rarely put me to bed either. Indeed she only spoke to me when I went down to the drawing room in the afternoons, or when we were out visiting or going to church. Nettie had done everything else, yet she had been dismissed on the instant.

The more I tried to make sense of it all, the more nonsensical it seemed. The rules of life seemed arbitrary and cruel. It seemed that Mama and Papa had to be obeyed and honoured whatever they said or did, just as God had to be obeyed and honoured even when He allowed bad things to happen. I could not help feeling that it was a topsy-turvy arrangement, and that if I had charge of the world, I would make sure children would be listened to, and people like Nettie treated as they deserved. But of course I did not have charge of the world. I hardly had charge of myself.

3

⁖ JOHN JAMESON ⁖

I FEEL THAT EVENTS ARE CONSPIRING DISTINCTLY TO MY advantage. I am *persona* very definitely *grata* in the Baxter household since my adventure in the watery mud of the Cherwell. In fact, I can do no wrong. Even the supercilious Mrs Baxter cannot thank me enough. Not only did she send a note (rather over-scented with lavender) in her own hand to express her lifelong gratitude, but she also sent a gold propelling pencil engraved with my initials, and a brace of wood pigeon, which was deposited at the lodge with the porter and conveyed thence to the college kitchens to be prepared for a small supper in my rooms. It would have been bliss to share the repast with Daisy, and to see her delicate little face and grey eyes looking at me from across the table; but that is a bridge too far. Instead I sent an invitation to Smith-Jephcott (who occupies the rooms below me), and we passed a pleasant enough evening picking at the bones. After dinner, I showed him my new photographs and he was very complimentary. He said he particularly liked the one of Mrs Baxter reclining on the ground, and remarked that she seemed to be something of a sweet little pigeon herself – a comment which sickened me. I hardly felt inclined to show him the study of Daisy and her friends after that, but I was so proud of it I could not resist. He glanced at it rather carelessly, then passed over it without a word, giving his attention to the family group instead, and showing especial interest in Daisy's sisters. 'This may be your chance, Jameson,' he said. 'In a few years the eldest will be seriously marriageable.' The man is an idiot, and a crass one. If it had been in my power, I would have turned him upside-down and shaken every scrap of pigeon out of him before kicking him downstairs.

But even Smith-Jephcott's coarseness cannot damp my good humour. I know it is not right to exult at the near-drowning of a little child, but I cannot help feeling it is Fate that I was on the spot when the nursemaid's vigilance failed, and that my quick actions have endeared myself to the family in a way I could not otherwise have brought about. In addition, I find my dear child much more at liberty than formerly. The nursemaid has been sent away and no other has as yet replaced her, so the Baxters are only too grateful to me for entertaining her when I visit, which I now do every day. Daisy is still reserved with me, which is to be expected, but I know that I can win her round, and that it will not be too long before I see again that immediate and natural delight which flashed across her face when she unwrapped the parasol. That was an exquisite moment for me; a proof that I understood the things that made her happy. Which is more than her parents seem to do. I cannot help wondering what on earth possessed the Baxters to give their daughter such a dull and worthy present for her birthday. Daisy is far too young to be cultivating the heavy art of introspection by committing her daily doings to paper. She has only just ceased to be ten; she has no need of the discipline of self-examination. She needs to be free, to play and wander at will, and to read and listen to amusing stories – ones that will take her into the realms of the magical and absurd. And if I have my way, she will do so. She will travel with me along the golden pathways of the imagination.

And yesterday I took a small step towards this goal. When I made my way to the vicarage as usual in the mid-afternoon, I was carrying under my arm a fine leather album in which I had carefully mounted all the photographs I had taken at the picnic. I had spent three days finding an album that satisfied me; and the assistants in five separate stationery shops in the Cornmarket and the High had given voice to their impatience as I rejected one after another of their showy volumes. (I really cannot see why they were so incapable of supplying what I needed: I described exactly what I required in terms of size and shape: linen-jointed, four photographs per page, fifty pages altogether – but they seemed to have no idea of proportion, or indeed, of taste.) I did eventually find a decent enough one, with deep brown pages eight inches by five, of a nice stiff quality with a double golden line running three eighths of an inch in; and, I have to say, the photographs looked very well on them.

Mrs Baxter summoned everyone to the drawing room to look, and all were delighted at what they saw. Mrs Baxter ran her elegant fingers over the pages as if they were velvet, and the once-disdainful Christiana and Sarah exclaimed over their likenesses with evident approval. Thus emboldened, I asked the Baxters if it would be possible to make some additional studies. I said I was particularly pleased with how the composition with the younger children had turned out and would like to take my amateur practice a stage further by setting up the photographs in more steady surroundings.

'The bright sunshine of the riverbank is all very well,' I said. 'But when I am indoors I can arrange the light for the pictures to suit myself. I have a special place in college where my equipment is kept and I have some fancy costumes that the little girls would no doubt like to dress in. Do you think their mamas would agree to such an arrangement? Chaperoned, of course,' I added.

Mrs Baxter said she thought this an excellent idea and would ask the parents of Daisy's friends if they would agree. 'I will advocate most strongly for you, Mr Jameson. It is the least I can do in terms of the debt of gratitude we all owe. Once we have their answers I will set a time, and send Hannah along with them. She'll like an outing, no doubt, and I'll release her from her duties here. Tell me, how long will you need?'

I said an hour or two would suffice on the first occasion (I was careful to plant the idea that more occasions would follow), but that I would be happy to give the little girls some tea and bread-and-butter once the picture-taking was over. I said that I would not wish to keep Hannah too long from her duties, and that I would be happy to entertain the children afterwards and walk them back to their respective homes. 'That is, if you think they will agree to such a rogue and v-vagabond as I being in charge of their precious offspring.'

Mrs Baxter laughed. 'I cannot think of a more respectable and reliable person than yourself, Mr Jameson. If one cannot trust a clergyman, whom can one trust? And they are only children, after all.'

I bowed. 'Indeed. But the world is full of Mrs Grundys. I would wish everything to be kept utterly respectable – most of all for the little girls concerned. They are the most precious and innocent of beings.'

'I will deal with it, Mr Jameson. Rest assured, there will be no difficulty of any sort.'

And I am sure there will not be. I can see that Mrs Baxter has her own sort of vanity, which prides itself on its ability to assess character. And she is equally convinced of her capacity to charm away any kind of opposition.

Daniel then having to go out on parish business, and the older girls to attend an archery lesson, I was treated to a whole hour alone in Daisy's company. It was another lovely day, and Mrs Baxter sat in the shade of an acacia tree with a novel in her hand and the baby asleep on her lap, while Daisy and I walked around the vicarage's extensive and well-kept garden. Daisy showed me the marigolds she had been trying to grow in a plot near the kitchen wall. 'I'm afraid the caterpillars got to them,' she said, bending down in that delightfully pliant way that children have, and stroking the few ragged leaves that remained.

'What a shame,' said I, squatting beside her, feeling how small she was and how large I was in comparison, and enjoying the protective feeling it gave rise to. 'Although, without caterpillars, we would never have butterflies to delight us with their beauty, would we? We would think that a shame too.'

She looked up at me then. It was the first time she had looked at me so directly, and she was so close to me that my insides nearly melted. 'But why do the marigolds have to suffer?' she asked. 'Can't things have their place in the world without eating others or being eaten themselves?'

She is such a kind child, it was hard to disabuse her. 'Nature is quite indifferent you know,' I said gently. 'Everything has to fight for its place.'

She looked perplexed and rather upset. 'Nature?' she said. 'But I thought God made everything the way it is.'

In her innocent way, she had brought down the axe. 'It's a conundrum,' I said.

'What's a conundrum?'

'An enigma. A mystery. Something we don't know the answer to.'

'Don't *you* know the answer, Mr Jameson?'

'I less than any man. Maybe your father does. He's a deep thinker.'

She did not seem very satisfied with that answer. 'Papa says you are the cleverest man he knows, so if *you* don't know, he won't either. He said you were a "Double First".' She looked up at me. 'What does that mean?'

'It means I have spent too much time with my nose in a book.'

'So why are there still things you don't know the answer to?'

'I don't know the answer to that. In fact, there are things to which I don't even know that I don't know the answer.'

She laughed at that, and I felt again how wonderful it was to be the cause of laughter in a child. Bubbles of happiness welled up in me and I wanted the moment to go on for ever. But she straightened and brushed down her pinafore and started to walk further along the path, further away from her mama. I fell into step beside her as we skirted the shrubbery. 'May I ask you a question?' she said.

'You certainly *may*. After all, a cat may look at a king. But I think it's not the *question* that is at issue; it's the answer. And, as you see, I cannot guarantee that I will have one.'

She pondered that for a bit, then she murmured in a low voice, 'Things aren't always fair in this world, are they?'

'Depends what you mean by "fair",' I said. 'What's fair to one person isn't fair to another. Is it fair that I am good at arithmetic, for example, but that your father is good at rowing?'

She considered this gravely. 'You and Papa are just different,' she said at last. 'I don't think that matters. But why are some people poor and others rich? And why are some people allowed to tell others what to do and they have to do it whether they like it or not?'

'A very good question. And one I have often asked myself – without, I have to say, getting much sense in return. But, on the second point, I suppose you could say that in general parents know more than children do, for example, and therefore they have the right and the duty to guide them in their actions. And this might entail forbidding them certain things, or telling them they must accomplish certain things. And, again, the rich have certain duties towards the poor; and those with knowledge have obligations to those who are ignorant. I am sure you have heard your father preach such things.'

She shook her head. 'No, I mean why was Nettie told to go away and not be able to stand up for herself because she is a servant and has no money? Just because there is some sort of rule that says she mustn't. And I mustn't say anything about it, either, in case it makes things worse.'

Suddenly I understood her sad demeanour. Daisy was pining for her nursemaid – her poor, wretched nursemaid who had given many years of loyal service night and day, but who had fallen prey to a moment's inattention and had been summarily dismissed. 'You must miss Nettie, naturally,' I said, recalling how the servant had been so proud of Daisy's recitation the day we first met, and how Daisy had smiled at her so warmly in return.

It was as if I had uncorked a bottle of seltzer. Daisy began sobbing in the noisiest and most abandoned way. 'Oh, yes, Mr Jameson,' she sobbed. 'I miss her all the time. I love her more than anything and now I'll never see her again!'

I was somewhat alarmed at this outburst, thinking Mrs Baxter might imagine I had said (or done) something untoward. But she was a long way off, and seemed to be asleep, and there were no other people in the garden to hear or see. 'Please don't cry,' I said, wanting to put my arm around her, but afraid to do so.

Daisy shook her head. 'I know I shouldn't say so,' she declared through her tears. 'And you mustn't tell anyone, Mr Jameson. But I love Nettie better than Mama or Papa. I love her more than anyone else in the whole world. Benjy loves her, too, and he doesn't understand why she isn't here any more. He keeps looking round for her and crying because she's not there.'

'Well, he's not crying now,' I ventured, casting my glance once more at Mrs Baxter in her shady spot. I couldn't help thinking how enormous the baby seemed as he lay across her delicate lap. He had always struck me as a fat child, and was certainly a lead weight when I pulled him out of the water. But now he looked pink-faced as well – more like a young pig than a boy.

'He's asleep,' said Daisy. 'That's the only time he's quiet. It's driving Hannah to distraction and she says she'll give in her notice if things go on like this.'

'I expect you will have a new nursemaid soon enough,' I said. 'And I daresay you will get used to her before you know it.'

Her colour rose. 'No, I wouldn't! How could I? No one is as nice as Nettie. And, anyway, Mama says I am too old to be in the nursery now. I'm to move downstairs next to my sisters and start to be a grown-up girl. So Benjy will be on his own with the new nurse and I won't even be there to comfort him. It's all so horrid.' She turned to me. 'Oh, Mr Jameson, you are so kind. Couldn't you speak to them? Ask them if we can have Nettie back so everything will be as it was before?'

It was wonderful to be appealed to in this way and I was in half a mind to do what she asked. After all, such an intervention would inevitably bring us closer. But I knew that even in my current state of grace I would not be able to prevail against the Baxters on such a matter. And I knew Mrs Baxter would not take kindly to interference in her domestic sphere. 'It's not possible,' I said eventually.

'Why not?' she said, giving me the most imploring look. 'All they have to do is write to her and say she can come back.'

'It's possible in theory,' I said. 'But it's impossible in fact.'

'How can it be possible and impossible all at once? That's nonsense.' Her voice was rising now, and I was afraid Mrs Baxter would hear this time and put an end to our conversation.

'Life is frequently nonsensical,' I said. Then, aware that this remark was unlikely to quell her tears, I adopted as calm a voice as I could, and fell back on the well-known phrases that always come to hand in situations of grief. 'But you have to believe, Daisy dear, that everything is for the good in the end. We have to believe that. Life will become clear eventually, at the time of reckoning, when all doubts will be set at rest and all suffering assuaged.'

'When we die, you mean?'

'Indeed. Exactly so.' Faced by the child's straightforward questions, I was feeling less and less fit for my task as sermonizer, and could think of no more to say. After a few minutes, during which she continued to weep, I took out my pocket-handkerchief and handed it to her. 'You will cry a whole puddle-full of tears at this rate,' I ventured. 'If you carry on, you may even cry a lake-full, and you and I will be up to our necks and will have to start swimming for the shore.'

She smiled wanly. 'I can't swim – at least not very well.'

'All the more reason for stopping now. You may keep the handkerchief and return it when it is laundered. I always carry a spare, and I have three hundred and sixty-five of them in college so they last me a whole year. I find a good pocket-handkerchief an essential item which can be put to no end of uses. In fact, I am infinitely surprised you do not have one yourself.'

'Nettie always made sure I had a fresh one every day. But I couldn't find any at all this morning and Hannah said I'd have to do without as she was too busy to go looking. I couldn't even find the ones my sisters gave me for my birthday and I've never even *used* them. They've always said I lose everything I'm given, and I thought they were wrong, but maybe they're right after all.' She looked at the point of tears again.

'Not at all,' I said gaily. 'Handkerchiefs have a habit of going for walks. I often see mine walking hand in hand around my chest of drawers or taking a promenade along the mantelpiece as airily as if they were at the seaside. Of course, when they see me coming, they fold themselves up and get into the smallest possible space under the coal scuttle or in the butter dish. And, if they can, they delight in getting themselves lost in the laundry. In fact, every washerwoman in the world must have several bedrooms-full of pocket-handkerchiefs that refuse to go back to their owners, and I rather think the poor women have had to put their children to sleep at the next-door neighbour's on account of the lack of space in their own establishments.'

Daisy laughed. 'You *are* funny, Mr Jameson,' she said.

'Well,' I said, 'I don't want to boast, but my sister Mary used to say that if she had a cough or a cold, all she needed was for me to come along and she'd quite forget her wretchedness. And if you could be persuaded to spend time with me in your spare afternoons, I could be very funny indeed. I'd make you forget all your woes. Would you like that, Daisy?' I queried.

She looked up at me again, the tear stains on her face as charming as the face itself, and her wild, untidy hair the most fetching it had ever been. She considered me for a long time. 'Yes,' she said. 'I think I would like that very much.'

I had never been happier than at that moment. It was as much as I could do not to shout with joy. But instead I put out my hand and said, 'Is it a bargain, then? I will tell you stories and cheer you up, and you will give me your pretty smiles in return. And maybe a kiss or two if you wish. Only if you wish,' I added, afraid I may have gone too far.

She held out her little hand and I took it in mine. It was warm and slightly damp from the hot weather and her own tears. I almost shivered with delight. 'In fact,' I said, trying hard to keep my voice light, 'we could be meeting sooner than you think. I am to take some more photographs of the little fairies and I hope you and your friends will come along and have tea with me afterwards. Your mama is to arrange it very soon.'

She considered. 'Papa says you live in one of the colleges. Are children allowed to have tea there?'

'Yes, indeed. You are more than allowed; you are actively encouraged. People in colleges spend a great deal of their time having tea. Sometimes I think life in college is one great tea party that goes on for ever. But you and your friends will be my guests in my own private rooms. I have a very nice set on the first floor and a very nice servant who looks after me. He is called a "scout" and he will see to the tea. He is quite old, so I hope that all you little girls will eat up what he brings you and not send him up and down stairs for extra jam or milk.'

'Oh, no. We'll be very good.'

'I am sure you will all light up my old bachelor rooms with your happy faces.'

She hesitated. '"Bachelor" means that you aren't married, doesn't it?'

'Indeed. As I said, there is only myself and the college servant. And Benson is responsible for the whole staircase, so I have only one-sixth of his services. And he has to wait at Hall table too, so I have even less of his time. He makes but a poor wife, I fear.'

'Would you like to be married? To a lady, I mean?' She looked at me with such earnest sweetness I could hardly forbear to kiss her on the spot, but I inwardly recited pi to the twentieth decimal place and managed to retain my sangfroid.

'I prefer to have friends instead. The general rule – unless you are the Caliph of Baghdad – is that you may marry only one person at a time – but you can have as many friends as you like. I think that is a far better arrangement.'

'You may marry and have friends too,' she persisted. 'After all, Papa is married, and you are his friend.'

'True,' I said. 'But I especially like to have child-friends, and I cannot marry a child-wife. So, all in all, it is better the way it is. I can give you and your friends all my attention when you come a-visiting. I find many adult people don't pay much attention to children, except to scold them or tell them what to do, whereas I prefer their company to that of anyone else, and hardly ever tell them what to do. Now don't you look forward to being my friend on such advantageous terms?'

She nodded, her grey eyes almost lively now. Then, at that precise moment, Benjy woke up and started to howl. Daisy's attention was immediately upon him and she flew down the path, her hair spreading behind her. By the time I had come back to the garden chair where Mrs Baxter was ensconced, she was already playing with him and diverting his attention with a rattle she had picked up from the ground. The child was so glad to see her that I felt almost sorry for him, to be deprived of his substitute mother and his best playfellow in one fell swoop. The Baxters had been cruelly obtuse in the matter, I thought. Sometimes it is as if adults have no idea of the feelings of children; as if they forget their own childhood once they pass into the years of so-called discretion. I sincerely hope that will never be my fate.

The servant Hannah, alerted by the infant's cries, came hastening down the lawn and bore him off for nursery tea, Daisy following in their wake. 'I shall see you very soon, then, Mr Jameson,' she said, giving me a very nice curtsey as she passed.

'I hope she has not incommoded you,' said Mrs Baxter. 'She is rather an intense child and latches on excessively to adult company. We feel her reliance on Nettie was somewhat un-healthy and we're hoping she will develop a closer relationship with her sisters soon. Once the new nursemaid has arrived, she will be moving down to her own room next to them.'

I could have said something then, but I didn't. If there were to be an adult that Daisy would latch onto, I wanted it to be me.

4

❧ MARGARET CONSTANTINE ❧

I TUCK MY SKIRTS AROUND ME TO WARD OFF THE CHILL. Now I have started Daisy's journal, I cannot leave off reading it. I have time, I think. Robert won't come for at least another hour.

Monday 16th June

Everything is so upside-down *at the moment that it's hard to find time to write and I don't want Hannah to see me doing it as I am sure she would read what I had written and it must be Secret. But I have found a good place to hide this journal which is in a little cupboard under the eves. You have to stoop really low to get at it, and it is painted the same colour as the walls so that it is hard to see. It has a little keyhole but there is no key and Nettie told me there hadn't been one all the time she'd lived in the nursery, and what would anyone want to put there anyway as it was so small and dark and full of cobwebs? To make quite sure Hannah doesn't see it I have pulled the washstand in front, which was quite easy as it is on casters. I think Hannah noticed something was different in the way the furniture was arranged but she couldn't remember what, and decided not to bother about it.*

I thought the best time to write would be when Hannah is taking Benjy out in his perambulater but she usually takes him in the mornings when I am at Miss Prentiss's. Then in the afternoon Mama often has Benjy in the drawing room with her and she wants me there too so I can fetch and carry while Hannah has other things to do, so I don't have much time to myself. It's strange to be in the drawing room at that time of day and even stranger that Mr Jameson is there when Papa is out. He sits on the very edge of the sofa and Mama says over and over again how grateful she is for him saving Benjy's life and he says he is glad to do anything for such a delightful family as ourselves. Then he asks, Is Benjy quite recovered? and Mama says Dr Lawrence is still coming every day but can see no ill effects. It's all very dull and Mama must think so too as usually she goes to play on the piano after a while and we both have to sit quietly and listen. Once when she was playing Mr Jameson asked if he could make a drawing of her and took out his sketchbook and made a very nice portrait of her with her head back and her eyes closed. He then asked if he could draw me as well and did a picture of a daisy flower with my face in the middle where the yellow bit should go and wrote The Prettiest Flower in the Garden underneath. And Mama said, Don't turn her head, Mr Jameson, and he said he certainly wouldn't as it was the right way on as it was. He says the funniest things but all with a straight face. I don't want to laugh as I am sad about Nettie but sometimes it is hard not to. DEB

I'd forgotten those awkward afternoons. Indeed, I've only a partial recollection of the days immediately following Nettie's abrupt departure. I know that I was very angry with the world and – although I was surrounded by a whole houseful of people – I felt as isolated and lonely as if I were an orphan. Nettie didn't write; or, if she did, I never saw her letters. Hannah was a most unsatisfactory replacement – not very much older than Christiana, and far too busy and brisk – and without Nettie to help me, I felt strangely uncomfortable in my clothes; seeming either to have one too many petticoats, or a tickly collar, or an apron that wouldn't sit straight. And the darns on my stockings, so painstakingly executed by Nettie, seemed always to be showing at my heels. Hannah, who did my sisters' hair so beautifully, had little patience with mine, saying she had never known hair like it. It was forever in my eyes which annoyed me considerably, and I carried my comb around in my pocket and tried to scrape it back into place whenever I had a moment to myself. But it had a will of its own and refused to stay in ribbons, so I usually ended up throwing the comb down in a fury. Truth to tell, I felt neglected and sorry for myself. I even had fantasies of running away from home and being found dead in a ditch; my parents only then realizing the enormity of the pain they had inflicted on me. I pictured them in deep mourning bending over my coffin, while Christiana and Sarah wept in the background. For some reason, I also imagined Mr Jameson giving the funeral sermon and saying what a lovely little flower I was, and how badly looked-after I had been in my short life.

Tuesday 17th June

Today Mr Jameson brought us the photographs he had taken at the picnic. He had put them into a lovely Album and everybody thought they were very lifelike and Papa said that he would like the one of Mama to put in a frame on the mantelpiece.

Christiana and Sarah thought their portraits were very good too and they were quite nice to Mr Jameson for once, saying how clever he was. It made me sad to see Nettie in the family picture, sitting to the side with Benjy on her lap and none of us knowing what was going to happen just a few minutes later.

Although I am mainly sad, I am also a little bit excited because Mr Jameson is going to take some more photographs of me with Enid and Emma and Annie pretending to be fairies like before but this time with costumes. He has asked us to go to tea with him at his college with his old servant Benson who is like a wife to him. Mr Jameson is not married, which he told me today but which I knew must be the case as he has never brought his wife to call on Mama. Papa says lots of University Men can't get married while they live in college which seems very strange and unfair. But I think almost everything about life is unfair

*at the moment. Even Mr Jameson agrees that is the case, although when
I begged him to talk to my parents about Nettie coming back he said
it was impossible so I suppose I have to stop thinking about it. I still
remember her in my prayers, though, and hope she is happy with her
new family in London. DEB*

How easily one switches allegiances as a child! Although I felt
so passionately about my loss of Nettie (weeping quietly into my
pillow every night), yet I couldn't help responding with pleasure
to Mr Jameson's growing interest in me. It was the first time any
adult had noticed me in that particular kind of way – listening
to my questions and giving me proper answers. I didn't count
Nettie, of course, because she was with me every day and was
required to take an interest, but it seemed that Mr Jameson had
specially chosen me, and I was flattered, especially as Christiana
or Sarah would have been a more obvious choice of companion.
They were so much more elegant and grown up – and much
more accomplished. They had art lessons and music lessons and
archery lessons and sometimes spoke spontaneously in French or
German, which impressed me mightily. And my parents – my
father in particular – were always singing their praises. Indeed,
I had the impression Papa had hoped Mr Jameson might show
a romantic interest in Christiana. He hadn't heard my sisters
mimicking him behind his back, parodying his stammer and
his awkward manner.

Naturally, the gift of the parasol was the first inkling that
Mr Jameson might value my company. And then, on the picnic,
he gave me such kind looks, and I noticed that whenever he
made one of his funny remarks he always looked at me to see if
I was smiling. Although Annie was more forward and delighted
him with her bold answers, I somehow knew in my heart that
it wasn't Annie he liked best. Of course, the catastrophe with
Benjy overshadowed all our jollity that day, and on the silent

journey home Mr Jameson had said very little. But he'd stood up for me when Nettie had suggested that my opening the parasol might be to blame for the whole affair. I'd given him a quick smile of thanks then, and he'd smiled back at me very warmly indeed.

And so I became attracted to him, not because of his looks (which were plain), but because he was kind and took trouble with me, and noticed things about me that no one else had noticed. In saying I was 'attracted', I use a phrase common in romantic love, but I am, of course, talking about friendship. At the age of eleven, having lost the one person I could truly rely on, I was open to tenderness, understanding and good humour.

So, I began to look forward to the times when he visited us, and then to the times when I visited him. The first time I called on him in his college was quite an adventure for me and I drove Hannah half mad with my demands that she should curl my hair extremely tightly and starch my dress extremely crisply. The prospect of a grown-up tea in the private rooms of a grown-up gentleman – combined with a chance to dress up and have my photograph taken yet again, seemed the most wonderful opportunity: a debut into a different, more adult world. I spurned my childish playthings, especially poor Nettie's rubber ball, which now seemed far too infantile for me in my new, exalted role. I was indeed in danger of having my head turned.

Thursday 19th June
Today Annie, Emma, Enid and I all went to tea with Mr Jameson. Hannah walked us through the centre of Oxford and said she had never been inside any of the colleges before. None of the rest of us had either, and we were excited when we came to the one where Mr Jameson lived, which was apparently one of the oldest. Hannah took us into a kind of lodge by the entrance gate and said we were looking for a Mr Jameson.

The porter said Reverend John Jameson you mean? And when Hannah said yes, he asked a younger porter to show us where to go. He said we needed Staircase Five Three (which is different from fifty-three) and then we crossed a big quadrangle where there were undergraduits walking about in their gowns reading and laughing and then the porter's boy showed us up some stone stairs under a pointed archway which was marked V (that is five in Roman numbers). We went up one flight of stairs and the boy knocked on a door marked III (which is three in Roman numbers). It was a big heavy door, with old, cracked wood and large metal hinges. I heard Mr Jameson call out 'Come in' and the boy opened the latch. It was a very nice room with windows that overlooked some gardens at the back, and there was a big fireplace with a looking-glass over the mantelpiece and a nice carpet and two comfortable chairs. Mr Jameson was sitting in one and a white cat was sitting in the other. When the cat saw us all come in, she leaped down and fled and Mr Jameson said, 'Oh you have frightened Dinah away – but she will come back when she knows there is milk to be had.' And then he got up and shook each of us by the hand and nodded respectfully to Hannah, who curtseyed. Then he asked us to take off our hats and gloves and he hung them on some hooks behind the door, putting the gloves very neatly inside the hats.

Then we looked around at all the books in the bookcases, and the beetles and butterflies in the glass cases and he let us peep under the white cloths that were covering the sandwiches. Then he said he would show us where he kept his Photographic Equipment as we had to earn our tea before we could eat so much as a crust. But first he said that we should go with Hannah and put on the fairy costumes which were laid out ready on his bed. His bedroom was next to the drawing room, through a door in the corner, which was very odd but colleges are not the same as ordinary houses. As well as having lots of staircases, they are more like monastries with carved stone and cloisters, and each one has its own chapel. I don't know why, but Hannah didn't like the idea of going into Mr Jameson's bedroom, although she goes into my parents' room every day to do Mama's hair. 'I hope you are not coming too,' she said rather rudely, and he looked upset and said 'Oh no' except he wanted to point out where the costumes were. Hannah said she thought she could manage to dress us without his help and I felt quite sorry for him as his stammer started to get very bad and he said it was all right and he'd leave it to her – except that we had to take our shoes and stockings off as fairies were always barefoot.

His bedroom was very plain and rather dark and his bed was a narrow one like mine. He had laid out four sets of fairy dresses in a row on top of the counterpane. They were made of white muslin and had muslin wings attached to the backs which looped over our fingers at the other end. The skirts had silk petals around the waist pointing downwards. And there were four head-dresses made of silk flowers. The dresses didn't fit very well, but luckily Hannah had her needle and thread with her so she tacked them to fit. When Mr Jameson saw us come out he was very excited and said we were just how he imagined. Hannah said she hoped he'd be quick as although it was summer we weren't used to going without stockings and shoes and she didn't want the blame if we all caught our deaths. So we went straight in to Mr Jameson's studio which was on the same bit of staircase, but more like a large dark pantry with no windows. Then he showed us all how we should stand, pretending we were moving our wings but not really moving at all. He put my arms higher and Annie's lower, and told Emma she should look at the ground and Enid should look at the ceiling. When he was satisfied he put in the plates and took the photographs. Then he explained how everything worked and showed us how he developed the pictures from the plates. It was like magic watching the shapes gradually appear – all four of us looking like real fairies, almost transparent against the dark background. Then we dressed again and Mr Benson brought up the tea and Hannah drank a cup standing up before going home to attend to Benjy. Then the rest of us sat down around the table and Mr Jameson asked Annie if she would like more tea and she said she couldn't have more as she hadn't had any yet. And he said what she really meant was she couldn't have less. And we all laughed because it was true, although Annie looked annoyed.

We had a very nice tea with cucumber sandwiches and Mr Benson did not have to go for more milk or jam, but he put a saucer of milk in the grate for Dinah, and she came back from wherever she was hiding and lapped it up. We all wanted to stroke her but Mr Jameson said she was an old cat and set in her ways and those ways were of an old Oxford don and not the ways of sprightly young ladies and so she was best left alone. Annie asked Mr Jameson why, if his ways were those of an old don, he had invited us to his rooms in the first place, and he said he was the opposite of Dinah as he loved sprightly young ladies more than anything. And after tea he said would we like to know how to turn a cat into a dog and we all said yes, thinking he was going to do magic with Dinah. And then he gave each of us a small notepad with our names written on very neatly and a very sharp pencil, and showed us how to change one letter at a time of the word cat *so it changed to* cot, *then* lot, *then* log *and lastly* dog. *He said we could change* pig *into* sty *the same way and suggested we wrote down as many others as we could think of. Enid thought up fourteen and I did twelve and Annie and Emma both did ten. The he asked us to make up the first line of a poem and he would carry on with it. And he made up the funniest Limericks and put us all in them, including Benson and Miss Prentiss and Dinah, and we all laughed until we were red in the face. Then Benson cleared away the dishes and Mr Jameson said he would take us all home, and he handed us down our hats and gloves and put on his top hat. He held my hand on one side and Annie's on the other, and Emma and Enid held on to us in turn. When we walked out through the quadrangle some of the undergraduits seemed to be laughing behind their hands and making comments which we couldn't hear but which seemed to be rather condersending but he took no notice and nor did we. We walked back along the High past the colleges, and he pointed out all sorts of interesting things and where famous poets and other important people had once been students. He said the poet Shelley had been sent away for aitheyism and serve him right – but when I asked what aitheyism was he said never mind, my fault for mentioning it. When I got home I asked Hannah and she said it was not believing in God, which I don't understand as everybody knows there is a God, except the Heathen, of course. I don't understand how a great poet can be a Heathen when he has grown up in this country and has read the Bible. I shall have to ask Mr Jameson. He has arranged for Hannah to take me to tea again next week, but this time with only one friend as four young ladies are far too trying for Dinah's nerves. But no doubt I shall see him here tomorrow in the drawing room as usual. I shall be disappointed if he does not come. DEB*

He was in many ways a strange companion for a child of eleven. I suppose he was about thirty-five years of age at the time – a little younger than our father, although he didn't look it. Father was handsome and well-built, and had elegant clothes, even though they were mostly clerical black; and when he came into a room, you always noticed him. But Mr Jameson was thin, awkward and weak-looking, and his clothes, although immaculately tidy, looked droopy and slightly odd; and when *he* came into a room, no one at all noticed. Of course, he had that terrible stammer that came and went, but seemed to be at its worst in company, so I understood in a way why he preferred intimate chats with one person at a time to the generality of polite conversation. And in fact he was not particularly polite, now that I recall. He was quiet, and that can be taken for politeness; but when there was something that interested him, he talked very fast, and was not above contradicting every-body in the room. He had very decided ideas, and expected his friends – young and old – to conform to them. For some reason, I was always happy to conform. I made no effort; he and I simply seemed to share some common understanding, an appreciation of each other that the world at large did not share. I didn't realize how strange it was; it seemed perfectly natural to me and I am sure it was equally natural for him. All the afternoons we spent together seemed to exist in a kind of sunny haze. Poor Nettie's image faded swiftly into the past as Mr Jameson absorbed my waking hours. When I was with him, it was as if I were living in a different world, a world I wanted to be in more than anything else.

My sense of dislocation from my family was heightened by the arrival of the new nursemaid, Mrs McQueen, and my subsequent move from the familiar attic to a small square room on the first floor. Instead of overlooking the garden, this room had a window facing the road, and the clatter of early carts and late carriages, the drudging step of the postman and the comings and goings of the milk cart, baker's cart and grocer's boy, all seemed to mirror the change from a protected and enclosed life, to the more worldly one I was about to embark upon. I spent hours alone for the first time ever, and it felt strange. There was no Benjy to distract me in the daytime, and no Nettie or Hannah sleeping across the room to make me feel safe at night. Mama, I recollect, thought I would be pleased to have a room of my own, as even Christiana and Sarah were obliged to share, and she said she hoped I would make the most of it, although in what way she did not say. She supervised the removal of my bed and chest of drawers down one flight of stairs, and got Matthews to bring up a new washstand with Delft tiles and a blue and white washing set, as well as a bookcase Papa said he could spare for my increasing collection of books. Hannah brought down my clothes from the nursery wardrobe and put them away for me with quite a good grace. (Ever since Mrs McQueen had arrived, Hannah had been in good spirits, and she even put a posy of flowers into the vase on the mantelpiece as a gesture of welcome.)

All the time the removals were going on, however, we could hear Benjy howling upstairs and Mrs McQueen trying to placate him. 'She'll have her work cut out,' Hannah said to Matthews on the stairs, nodding her head to the source of the cacophony.

I remember Matthews glancing up too, saying, 'Poor little sod. He doesn't know whether he's coming or going –' then stopping because Mama came out of the bedroom and said, 'That's enough, Matthews. Thank you for your help.'

I never knew whether she had heard or not, but it made me feel guiltier still that I was abandoning Benjy in his hour of need. He had only just got used to Hannah, and Mrs McQueen was a complete stranger. I asked Mama if I could go up and play with him for a while, but she said I would only upset him and it was better to let him settle with Mrs McQueen, as he had to learn.

Wednesday 25th June
I am now in my own room on the first floor so I can write in this journal whenever I like. This is a great relief. But now I must find somewhere new to hide it as Hannah still comes in to do my hair and Christiana and Sarah are in the next room and I know they are very curious and would certainly laugh at what I have written if they found it. They came in to see me as soon as I moved in and went around picking everything up, reading the titles from my books and smiling to each other in a condersending way. As it is summer and there is no chance that we will have a fire, I am putting this journal under the grate inside the screen. There are no coals or ashes so it's quite clean, but when the worse weather comes, it will be no good, as I expect I will have a fire from time to time though not every day like in the nursery, and Mama always has the chimneys swept in the autumn.

I am to eat my evening meals with Papa and Mama now, and lunch with my sisters in the morning room when I am not at school. If Christiana and Sarah are out, I am to eat by myself in the breakfast room, served by Cook. It seems as though everything is changing very quickly and I hardly know who I am any more. DEB

5

⏤ JOHN JAMESON ⏤

D AISY REALLY IS THE MOST DELIGHTFUL CHILD. SHE
tries so very hard to be good, but she is also very natural,
as all children are, and says what she thinks at the moment she
thinks it. We adults rarely say what we think – indeed, I do not
know how long it has been since I have said exactly what I think
to another adult human being. But when I am with Daisy I feel
at liberty to say whatever comes into my head – and it makes
her laugh. I can scarcely believe my good fortune. I feel I am
walking on air. My head is full of ideas and thoughts and wild
imaginings, and she is sharing them with me.

But I anticipate myself. This state of bliss has not come about
without effort, and I congratulate myself on the effectiveness of
my strategy, beginning with the pleasant tea party I was able to
arrange for the four little friends. The photographic experiment
produced some interesting effects and the tea itself went well,
although I was surprised at the amounts of bread-and-butter
and cake such small children could consume. I don't recall my
sisters ever falling upon the tea table with such enthusiasm, but
my father was strict (stricter than I am, at any rate) and we all
had to wait our turn in order to begin, which was only ever after
grace had been said and the eldest among us had partaken first.

After tea and games (of which the limericks proved a decided
hit), I took all four children home and begged that on the next
occasion I should limit myself to *two* young visitors on account of
Dinah's nervousness with company. This was agreed and Daisy

elected to bring Annie with her. Annie is a very forward child with a wide face and a bold expression. She is as ignorant as an eleven-year-old should be, but she is always ready with her opinions, which can be amusing. However, she does not in any way compare with Daisy, around whose natural charm there is now an air of sadness that I am making it my daily work to dispel.

I managed to arrange it so that it was not long before their second visit, and Hannah brought them as before, marching them across the quad in their neat cotton dresses, white stockings and jaunty straw hats, where they rightly drew the admiring attention of all who had eyes in their heads. But this time the servant did not stay. I explained that I planned to take the two girls for a walk in the meadow before tea and there would have been nothing for her to do except walk along behind us. She was not anxious to remain in any case, saying she had some errands to do at the haberdasher's in the High, but hoping I would not let the girls walk too far in the afternoon warmth. I promised I would take the greatest care of them and she took herself off. Hardly had she gone when Annie piped up asking if we were going to play games later on, as she found walks extremely uninteresting.

'And do *you* find walks uninteresting too, Daisy?' I enquired.

'It depends,' she said, wrinkling her forehead in a delightful way. 'On whom I'm walking with, and where we're walking. Sometimes it can be dull. I mean it's very dull when Miss Prentiss makes us walk in line for half an hour without speaking to one another.'

'And then makes us stand and look at some old bones in a glass case,' added Annie. 'In fact, I think museums are the most uninteresting places in the world.'

'Well, I promise there will be no museums today. And no old bones. Although I can't promise about young bones. There are inevitably a goodly number of them disporting themselves in the meadow, bowling hoops and playing at cricket. Unfortunately, they are mainly of a male variety.'

'But what will we *do* in the meadow?' moaned Annie. 'We can't play cricket because that's a boys' game. Could we play at shuttlecock? We play that at home on the lawn – but you'll need the battledores. Do you have battledores, Mr Jameson?'

'Sadly, no. Most of the games I know are in the mind. I think you can have even more fun with those, if you've *a mind* to play them. But there'll be a lot to do and talk about on the way, I assure you.'

Annie looked unconvinced, but I picked up my hat and said, 'Now, let's begin by walking in the opposite direction and see where we get to.'

'Opposite from where?' Annie said, pouting.

'Well, from here, of course.'

'But in which direction?'

'You ask a lot of questions for one who is only four and a half foot high,' I said. 'I've half a mind to make you sit down and answer an examination paper on all the questions you don't know the answer to, while Daisy and I go a-walking on our own.'

'But I won't *know* the answers!' She looked alarmed.

'Ah,' I said. 'Maybe there are no answers. I find there are far more questions in the world than answers, don't you think? Otherwise school wouldn't be the bother it is.'

They both laughed, and Annie being thus satisfied, we set off in good spirits as the clock in the tower chimed three.

'Do you teach *all* the young gentlemen in the college?' asked Daisy, eyeing a group of undergraduates who were reading on the grass and looked up as we trod by in our threesome.

'By no means. It is hard enough to teach the ones I do. They are so very deaf.'

'Oh, poor things!' cried Daisy, instantly sympathetic. 'But how can they learn when they are deaf?'

'With difficulty,' I said. 'When I ask a question, I often have to ask it twice. But that may be on account of the distance.'

She looked up. 'The distance?'

'Well, they will insist on taking their lessons on the kitchen staircase, and I have to call out my questions aloud from my room and Benson has to scurry down and pass them on, and due to his imperfect knowledge of mathematics and their imperfect hearing, equation becomes "evasion", and theorem becomes "peer at 'em" and we have to start all over again.'

'Is that really true?' asked Daisy with a sideways look.

'Well, not altogether,' I answered. 'I made up the bit about Benson. And the students are not actually deaf.'

She laughed. And my heart shivered into many delicious pieces.

We left the college buildings and set off across the Meadow. As we walked along the path I was able to point out various butterflies and day-flying moths, and give them their proper Latin names, which the little girls attempted to learn by heart. Once by the river there was quite a congestion of rowing boats and punts and even the odd hopeful fisherman. 'We might see people catching crabs later,' I said.

'Oh, you don't get crabs in the Cherwell,' said Annie confidently. 'You only get them at the seaside.'

'That's what you think,' I said. 'I wouldn't be surprised if there weren't half a dozen people catching crabs at this very moment, down by Folly Bridge.'

'It means when you miss your stroke, doesn't it?' said Daisy. 'And wave your oar around in the air? That's what Papa says.'

'And your papa knows everything about rowing that there is to know,' I said. 'So you are right, Daisy.' At which she blushed and looked pleased.

And I was pleased too, to be walking along with two such pretty children, as if I were their father or, even better, their uncle. We chattered away about this and that, and picked up the balls that rowdy schoolboys let run towards us, and answered innumerable requests for the 'right time' from all manner of people who only have to see that you have a watch about your person to think that you are obliged to keep them informed about the progress of the planet. However, the little girls were only too delighted to take out my pocket watch and read the hour and minute hands on my behalf, and supply the questioners with their answers. There were a number of people I knew by sight to whom I tipped my hat, and who acknowledged me similarly before passing on. However, one person hove into view whom I did not wish to encounter. It was Smith-Jephcott, strolling about in that purposeless way of his. I attempted to usher the girls off the path in an effort to evade him, but when he saw us, he came over. 'Ah,' he said, doffing his hat. 'Two of your little fairies, I believe? Won't you introduce me?'

And I was obliged to do so, even though I was very loath. When I said Daisy's full name, he raised his eyebrows and said, 'Any relation to Daniel Baxter, the renowned Christian Athlete of St Cyprian's?'

'Her father,' I said shortly.

'Indeed? And so the charming lady in the picture was her mother?'

'Mr Jameson photographed us all,' added Daisy, with a sweet eagerness to impart information that I could have dispensed with on that occasion.

He bent towards her. 'And I was privileged to have, as it were, an advance view of the pictures. They were very good. Very good. What a lovely family you all are.' Then he raised himself and addressed me sotto voce: 'I had no idea when you showed me the pictures that it was *Baxter*'s family you were so intimate with.'

'I assume you don't know him, then?'

'Only by reputation. But that's enough.' He laughed unpleasantly. 'But look here, Jameson, why don't we all have tea together? I was just about to turn back, and could do with a little livening up.'

'No,' I said. 'I have other plans.'

'You? What plans?' He laughed again. 'Are you going to introduce them to Dinah and play slapjack around the table for half an hour?'

'What's that to you?' I replied, incensed.

'Nothing at all. I just thought these two young ladies might rather see the musical box I have just purchased. It has a singing bird.'

'Oh, may we, please?' said Annie, her wide face made even wider with pleasure.

Daisy looked at me, and I think she could see the consternation on my face. But at the same time she was eager to see the toy. 'May we?' she asked quietly. 'Just for five minutes?'

'There you are!' said Smith-Jephcott. 'And while you are looking at it, I'll get Benson to give us tea.'

'But I have tea arranged in my own room. I have already p-purchased walnut cake,' I faltered, my tongue tight in my mouth.

'Then bring it down! I have some Bourbon biscuits, and Benson can see to the teapot and the bread-and-butter. The girls can know what it's like to have proper college hospitality!'

I looked at their shining eyes: Annie's bright and bold, Daisy's softer but no less eager. I could not deny them. 'Very well,' I said. But I was terribly put out by this alteration to my plan.

Daisy must have sensed my disappointment because she reached out her little hand and touched me on the arm. It was as if her touch had melted right through the black worsted, and I could feel her fingers on my very flesh. 'Do you mind very much, Mr Jameson?' she said.

At that moment I loved her so much for her kindness and sympathy that I almost felt gratitude to Smith-Jephcott for being the cause of it. 'Not if it makes you happy,' I replied, daring to squeeze her gloved fingers.

And so we repaired back to college and Benson was obliged to bring down to Smith-Jephcott's rooms the walnut cake and the bread-and-butter that he had already laid out upstairs. Smith-Jephcott, in spite of his boast, made no attempt to provide proper hospitality, or even a table, and put the plates down willy-nilly all over his desk and sideboard, mingling the cake with his bottles of port wine and muddling the bread-and-butter with his books.

The girls, meanwhile, were enchanted by the musical box, and in between forays to the cake and tea, they wound the handle over and over again while the bird moved back and forth and opened and shut its beak in time to the fluting music. Smith-Jephcott told them he had bought it for one of his nieces, who was ten years old in a week's time. Annie said how lucky that little girl was and expressed the wish that she could have one like it. 'Did you buy it in the High?' she asked.

'I got it in the Burlington Arcade. Do you know it?'

They both shook their heads.

'Ah, maybe you are not acquainted with London?'

They shook their heads again. 'My sisters were born in London,' volunteered Daisy. 'But they can't remember very much about it and Mama says Poplar was not very nice.'

'Poplar?' Smith-Jephcott raised his eyebrows. 'What were they doing in *Poplar* of all places?'

'What do you think?' I replied, somewhat testily. 'Baxter had a parish there. Before he came to Oxford.' Smith-Jephcott really is a fool.

'Ah. That explains it. An excellent opportunity for Good Works.'

'Papa says it was very *hard* work,' added Daisy solemnly. 'He often had to preach to a half-empty church. But I'd like to visit the interesting landmarks like Buckingham Palace and the Tower. Is the – Bullingdon Arcade interesting too?'

Smith-Jephcott laughed, and murmured, 'Not unless you are interested in a certain sort of fine art. In fact, there is a photograph shop there that might interest you, Jameson. Also specializing in interesting images.'

I felt myself go quite red with embarrassment and anger. 'I order all my necessaries by post,' I said. 'There is no need for me to linger in such places.'

'Such places? I'm sure I don't know what you mean.' But he smiled in a lascivious way I found quite nauseating. I was beside myself to think that I had brought the little girls into such a situation, with such a man, and was only thankful that their innocence protected them from his foul insinuations. I never cease to be surprised that such a man can be a member of a respectable college and I determined then that I would ensure that Daisy – and Annie too, of course – would not be exposed to any further grossness. I indicated – slightly deceitfully – that Hannah would soon be coming for the children and that they would need to eat and drink quickly before returning to my rooms. They were rather reluctant to leave the mechanical bird and his songs, and I thought I might have to drag Annie away with main force, but Daisy, remembering she had originally pleaded to spend five minutes only with the toy, persuaded her friend to finish the cup of tea she had carelessly left in the grate and come upstairs with me.

It was such a relief to be back in the comfort and familiarity of my own rooms. But it was brought home to me again that, to keep the attention of the young, one needs toys or amusing artefacts to occupy them, and I promised myself that hence-forth I would always have about me some small item for the purpose. But Dinah, bless her, provided an alternative on this occasion, as she was in a sleepy mood and prepared to let the children stroke her fur. They looked so lovely, both of them, kneeling beside Dinah's chair, their glossy hair spreading over their shoulders, the line of their sweet profiles more beautiful than any duchess's.

Annie was the first to break the spell. I think she saw me looking at them in an attentive way and asked, 'Are you not taking any photographs of us today, Mr Jameson? It would be nice to have one of us with Dinah.'

But just then, Dinah, as is the way with cats, chose to rise and stretch herself, jumping deftly away from the stroking hands and leaping up to sit on the windowsill, which is her second-favourite perch. Annie rose and made as if to fetch her back, but I put out my arm. 'If you annoy her she is likely to scratch you. And I wouldn't want to send you home covered in blood. Blood, in my view, should remain inside the skin where it belongs. But, to answer yet another of your questions, Miss Annie, I fear there is no time for photographs today, largely owing to my honoured neighbour's unexpected intervention. I won't rush things, you see, and Hannah is due at any moment.'

'I'm sorry. Are you very disappointed?' asked Daisy, as always concerned about others.

'A little, I own it. But we had a good walk, did we not? We counted six different butterflies and five kinds of beetle in less than a mile. The photographs can wait for another day.'

'But I am going away to Ilfracombe next week!' Annie wailed. 'I won't be able to come.'

'Dear, dear. That is a shame. One little fairy less.'

'I could ask one of the others,' said Daisy – rather reluctantly, I thought.

'Well, Enid can't come. She's going to her grandmother's in Wales now that school is finished,' said Annie.

'And Emma's got a chill,' added Daisy. 'Her mother thinks it was caused by putting on thin clothes and says she won't be allowed to come again.'

'So it looks as though it will only be you and me, Daisy,' I said, hardly able to restrain my delight at the prospect. I thought Daisy, too, looked pleased at the idea of meeting *à deux*.

At that moment, Hannah arrived, looking a little flushed. I put it down to the exertion of climbing the stairs to my rooms. They are quite steep and, if one is in a hurry, one can become out of breath. Benson is forever complaining of them. 'Did you get what you were looking for?' I asked her. She looked as if she was unsure of my meaning. 'At the haberdasher's,' I added.

'Oh, yes. Three yards of petersham ribbon and several bobbins of thread.' She held up a small paper packet, as if to confirm the transaction. It crossed my mind that she had been away for a long time if these were her only purchases, but I assumed she had had to go from one shop to another to get exactly what she wanted as I had had to do for the album, so I said nothing.

She was brisk, as usual. 'Come now, Miss Daisy, Miss Annie. Get your hats and gloves on – we've got to hurry if I'm to have you both back in time.'

'More walking!' complained Annie, pulling her features into a terrible pout. I could see immediately that she would grow up to be the languid sort of beauty who is more at home in the drawing room than on a country path. She will also, I fear, be the kind of young woman who will tease her suitors to within an inch of their passion and patience. I am glad I will never be among them.

'Oh, beg pardon, but I forgot to give you this, sir,' said Hannah, pulling a folded envelope from her pocket. 'It's from

Mr Baxter. I'm sorry not to have given it you when we arrived but it went out of my mind.'

It was an invitation to dinner the next day. Although I had frequently taken tea with the Baxters, I had never before dined with them. And I understood from Daisy that she was now a frequent attender at the family table. I hastened to my desk to write a reply and handed the sealed envelope back to Hannah, who stared at it in surprise.

'What neat handwriting!' she exclaimed, staring at the superscription.

'I hardly expect a compliment on account of that,' I said, a little tartly. 'If it were *foot*-writing now, I would understand your surprise.'

The girls chuckled at this and Hannah herself smiled, which I thought improved her somewhat sharp demeanour.

'Be sure to give it to Mr Baxter immediately,' I said. 'It would embarrass me considerably to turn up when I was not expected.'

'I will, sir. Don't you worry.'

I turned to Annie. 'So it seems, young lady, that I am to be deprived of your company from now on because of your selfish desire to take the sea air. However, you can make it up to me by sending me a picture postcard of the seaside when you arrive. I am very fond of the seaside and especially of watching all the young people disporting themselves on the sand. And if you write to tell me that you have been taking off your shoes and stockings and paddling in the waves in your bare legs, I shall be able to imagine you and wish I were there too. Now, will you give me a farewell kiss?'

She came forward boldly and lifted her face. And I bent down towards her and she planted a smacking kiss on my lips. 'I don't mind kissing *you*,' she said as she drew back. 'Because you have no whiskers.'

'I promise never to grow them on that account,' I said.

Then I looked at Daisy, who seemed uncertain whether to come forward or not. Hannah pushed her towards me. 'Give the gentleman a kiss, too,' she said, as if expiating for her forgetfulness earlier. 'He's been very kind to you both, having you all afternoon and that.'

Daisy raised her face. She was such a beautiful picture that I lost my courage and merely grazed her cheek with my lips. 'Goodbye, Daisy,' I said, my heart hammering away under my shirt and my tongue feeling enormous in my mouth. 'I will see you again very soon.'

'Yes, Mr Jameson.' And suddenly they were all gone. And, not for the first time in my life, my rooms seemed empty and lonely.

6

⤳ Margaret Constantine ⤲

'Margaret! What on earth are you doing up there?'

It's my husband's voice. I hear his footsteps on the uncarpeted stairs as he gallops up two or three at a time. I close the book quickly and hide it under my skirt. He appears in the doorway, a little breathless. 'I couldn't find you anywhere.'

I smile. 'You can't have searched very hard, Robert. I haven't moved for at least an hour.'

'Yes, I see.' He comes into the room, looking past me to the open toy-chest, with its contents spilling around in disarray. 'But what have you been doing, exactly?'

'Looking at things. Remembering.'

'Well, have you decided what to take?' He surveys the scattered objects with his hands on his hips. 'Not all these things, surely? I thought you were going to decide on just a few.'

'I can't decide. Maybe I won't take anything. Leave it all to the Arbuthnots.'

'Surely not. Look at this ball – and these books . . .' He picks up a pile of them. '*Holiday House, Robinson Crusoe, the Wide, Wide World, Uncle Tom's Cabin, The Water Babies, Oliver Twist, Hans Andersen's Fairy Tales* . . . My, you were quite a reader, weren't you? And good heavens, what's this parasol doing here?' He lifts up a limp and yellowed object that had been jammed into the lid of the box. It looks so different, I can hardly believe it was the one Mr Jameson gave me.

'It was a birthday present,' I tell him. 'When I was eleven.'

'Well, it hasn't benefited from lying in a toy-box for eight years.' He tentatively starts to unfurl it.

'Don't open it in the house!' I cry, stopping him with my hand. 'It's bad luck.'

'Bad luck? You don't believe that, do you?' He's smiling, trying his best not to be critical.

'Of course not, Robert.' I smile back. 'It's simply that the last time I opened it, my brother nearly drowned in the Cherwell. So it makes me apprehensive.'

'Well,' he says in his best jovial manner, as he lowers the parasol. 'I'll indulge you, in that case.' He bends and attempts to kiss me.

I turn away deftly so that his lips just skim my cheek. And he in his turn, not wishing to look foolish, pretends he has bent low simply to inspect the toys. 'Look,' he says. 'Why don't we put everything back and get Matthews and young Frank to put the whole thing into the carriage? You can sort it out at home then. We don't have much more time. Shall I help you?'

'No,' I say, rather too quickly. 'Just call them, if you would. I'll put everything back myself.'

He hesitates, but I smile sweetly up at him, and he turns and thuds back down the stairs shouting for Matthews. I quickly slide the journal under the threadbare carpet. Then I start to put back the contents of the toy-box. I pile them all in haphazardly, not in the careful way they were stacked before, and the lid won't close properly. I pick up the parasol, wondering what to do with it. I'm still holding it when Robert comes back.

'All done? You're not keeping that parasol, are you? It's rather past its best.'

'Yes. I mean, no, you're right, I'm not keeping it. It's no use to anyone now.'

'That's the spirit.' He takes it from me, looks round to see what he can do with it, then, at a loss, stands it in the corner. 'The maid can clear it away.'

'Yes.'

Then Matthews and Frank come up, and Matthews nods to me. 'Miss Daisy,' he says, forgetting I am married now. They pick up the toy-chest, and carry it off between them, bumping it against the walls as they round the narrow bend in the back stairs.

'Are you ready, then?' Robert is making every effort to be cheerful.

'You go down first. I want to say goodbye to this room.'

He smiles, indulgent. 'Five minutes, Margaret. Then we have to go.'

'Yes, Robert, I know.'

He leaves the room and I hear his footsteps echoing through the empty house. I stoop quickly and remove the journal from under the carpet. I know I'll have to secrete it on my person; there's no other way. With some difficulty I thrust it up next to my corset. It looks lumpy and square and it makes my bodice so tight it seems to constrict my heart. But I have no option if I am to keep it safe. I pull my shawl around me, hoping Robert will not try to embrace me in the carriage.

I stand in the middle of the room and look round me. All that remains are two broken wooden chairs, the worn carpet and the dusty muslin curtains at the window. All my life was spent in this house, and much of it in this very room. And now the house will belong to new people, and I'll never have the right to come here again. I walk to the door and turn round for one last look. I see Nettie in her cap and apron with Benjy on her lap. I see the two narrow, neatly made beds; the iron cot; the big oak wardrobe; the washstand; the meal table always with its white cloth; the hob with the kettle always on the boil. 'Goodbye,' I whisper.

'Margaret!' Robert's voice, from downstairs, a little sharper now.

'Yes, I'm coming.' As I turn to go, I hold out my hand and touch the ragged, yellowish parasol as it leans into the corner. I can't decide whether it makes me feel happy or sad. But I pat it gently before closing the door.

On the carriage ride, Robert talks about ordinary things: the weather, the state of the roads, the cost of keeping a horse in livery. He is wary of me, I know. He is afraid of putting the wrong foot forward. He is a dutiful husband and wants to be kind. But he also believes a man should be strong and not let weakness in his wife flourish and become a burden, or perhaps a sin. So I know it is only a matter of time.

We pass the University Parks. Little children are playing hide-and-seek. They look as if they have no cares in the world. I hold the journal tight against my stomach. When we arrive home, I let him take my free hand to help me down. 'I'd like to rest before supper, Robert, if I may.'

'Are you unwell?' He'd like to think ill-health would explain matters.

'No, just tired. I'd like to read for a bit.'

'Very well.' He looks businesslike. 'I've a good deal of work to do. I'll come up at six and see how you are.'

'Thank you, Robert.' I try to kiss him on his cheek. But he wants my lips. The dark bristles of his whiskers are rough against my skin as he presses against me. I tighten every muscle in my body and endure him as best I can. Then I pull away. 'Not now; everybody will see.'

'And what does it matter if they do? You are my wife, after all; it's not such a great scandal. And I hope you will truly be my wife before long. Otherwise I shall think you don't love me.' He gives a little laugh, and I laugh too. Reassuringly.

Once in the bedroom, I unhook my bodice with relief and release the journal. I don't bother to refasten my dress, but sit by the window and open the pages straight away. I'm greedy for the words now. The whole of my forgotten life seems to be opening out again.

Friday 27th June
Mr Jameson came to dinner tonight which was most exciting. We had Mock Turtle Soup, Fried Whiting and Jam Roly-poly. Papa and Mama had some pale-coloured wine they called Hock and so did Mr Jameson, although he would only have half a glass and kept filling it up with water. Hannah brought in the soup as usual, but when it was time for the fish, Cook came in herself with a big oblong dish and banged it down in front of Papa and seemed very cross about something although she didn't say a word, just wiped her hands on her apron and stalked out! Hannah had her lips folded very tight when she brought the plates and vegetables, and later we could hear a lot of clashing coming from the kitchen which we all pretended not to hear.

Mr Jameson was quiet during the meal even though Papa was trying to make him talk to Christiana, saying things like, Have you ever tried archery, John? Which he hadn't, although he said he didn't mind a game of croquet now and again in spite of being in general against Blood Sports. Mama said croquet wasn't a Blood Sport but Mr Jameson said it had been whenever he'd seen it played. Everyone laughed at that including my sisters who are very good at croquet and are not above hitting you on the ankles with the mallets.

Then everyone started to talk about poetry. Mama is very fond of poetry. Papa told us Mr Jameson wrote poetry himself but Mr Jameson said no it wasn't poetry, not like Wordsworth or Tennyson, it was just verse and he'd never put himself in the same catagory as those Great Men. Mama said she'd like to read his verse all the same or perhaps he could recite some for us after dinner? Mr Jameson said he didn't ever recite in public because of his speech impedament but he would send her some if she really wished but it was just light stuff, nonsense really. And Mama said she'd like that but surely he wasn't too shy to speak among friends and she hoped that he regarded us as friends and how did he manage to give his lectures if he didn't speak in public? He said he had to steel himself to it because he had to earn his crust, but he hoped that at such an agreeable dinner party he would not be expected to put himself through such agonies. I noticed that while all this was going on that his stammer had got worse and worse and it was difficult to listen to him because of the long pauses when I wanted so much to put in the word for him but thought it not quite polite. Christiana didn't look very sympathetic though, and she and Sarah did *try to finish his words from time to time, muttering them under their breath as he asked for things on the table: j-jam roly-poly and c-c-c-custard. I felt very sorry for him as he is such a kind man and sometimes my sisters can be horrid.*

I'd forgotten how Mr Jameson was willing and even eager to suffer the humiliation of a family meal when he could have eaten in college among men who ignored his shortcomings. But I do remember how much I'd looked forward to the event. It was the first time we'd had a guest to dinner since I'd been allowed to dine with my parents, and I was anxious to show off my grown-up etiquette. I had no proper idea then of quite how much pleasure Mr Jameson took in my company, but I was sufficiently aware of myself to want to look my best, and I'd combed my hair again and again, almost weeping that Nettie was not there to help me. Mr Jameson, I knew, liked little girls to look pretty. But even as I'd struggled in front of the looking-glass it didn't occur to me that his fondness for me was anything out of the ordinary, or that there was any impropriety in returning that fondness. My mother and father seemed glad to promote his attention towards me; and the previous day, when I had hung back, hesitant to embrace him, Hannah had positively pushed me into his arms. I'd been surprised by the pleasant nature of his kiss. I usually disliked kissing grown-up men; they were invariably covered in whiskers, and smelled strongly of tobacco, especially Mama's Uncle Bertie who always took hold of me very tight and had a very wet mouth. He would breathe very heavily, as if he was intent on passing all the breath from his mouth into mine, and stale old rum-smelling breath it was too. I always had to go into a corner and cough it out afterwards. Even kissing my father was not altogether pleasant, and thinking about it now makes me give an odd kind of shudder. But Mr Jameson had skin like a woman and smelled only of soap. He'd also kissed me very delicately and respectfully, so I didn't at all mind the prospect of doing it again.

After dinner, Mr Jameson stayed behind in the dining room with Papa and 'we ladies', as Mama now called us, returned to the drawing room. Christiana stood on tiptoes in front of the mantelpiece mirror and adjusted her hair saying Mr Jameson was such a dull man and why couldn't we have someone more interesting to dinner? Mama asked her whom she thought was more interesting and she said someone like Mr Gardiner, the archery teacher, and Mama said, Nonsense, we couldn't ask someone like that to dinner, and Christiana said why not? and Mama said she knew perfectly well why not, and if she didn't by now, she'd better learn quickly. Christiana went very red *and said was it because we paid him money? And Mama said that would do as an answer for the time being although it was a lot more complicated.*

I keep thinking that grown-up life is extremely complicated and it doesn't seem fair that you can't invite someone you like to dinner because you give them money. But it seems that paying people is part of these silly Rules of England that meant Nettie couldn't stay with us although she wanted to. Christiana went to the window then, and stared out at the garden in an annoyed way, and I wondered what sort of person Mr Gardiner was and why she liked him. And I wondered if he liked her in return in spite of her being so very contradictery.

Papa and Mr Jameson came in to join us quite quickly after that as Papa said John had no head for port and neither of them enjoyed a pipe. And Mama said what has happened to your thealogical arguments? And Papa said he was writing his sermon tomorrow and sufficient unto the day. Then Mama played the piano for us, and then Christiana played a duet with Sarah. Mr Jameson asked if I could play and I played Rondo which is the only thing I can do properly with both hands, and Mr Jameson clapped a great deal at the end although I did make some mistakes with my left hand. He then said 'Why don't we play Consequences?' and Mama said 'Why not?' and Sarah got some pencils and paper and we started to play. Most of the Consequences were about famous people like Lord Palmerston and Queen Victoria, but when it came to my turn, I unfolded my paper and found I had The Rev. John Jameson meeting Mrs E. Baxter on a London omnibus. He said: Will you marry me, delight of my life? And she said: We need some more coal on the fire. And the consequence of this was: They both took a dozen lessons in Elementary Logic. (Mr Jameson did this last bit as I recognized his writing.) We all laughed, especially my sisters, and neither Mama nor Mr Jameson looked the slightest bit put out as of course it is only a game! I wanted to do another round but Mama said it was time for me to go to bed and so I had to say goodnight and leave them all. I kissed Mama and Papa and then Christiana and Sarah, and then Mr Jameson was looking so left out that I went up and kissed him on the cheek too. He said he'd take my kiss and put it in a box and take it home with him as it was the sweetest thing he'd ever had. Christiana sniggered and Mama said, Oh, Mr Jameson, I thought I was the one you wanted to marry! And everybody laughed. Then Papa said 'Goodnight, Daisy dear' in a way I knew meant I had to go.

When I crossed the hall to go upstairs I could hear Cook and Hannah and Matthews all arguing down in the kitchen. I would have dearly liked to know what it was all about but didn't dare try to listen. I hope Cook is not going to give in her notice as I could not bear more changes.

When I got to the landing I could hear Benjy crying and Mrs McQueen stamping back and forth across the nursery floor. I have maybe forgotten to mention that Mrs McQueen is a very strict *person and I am glad that I don't have to sleep in the nursery any more as nothing seems to please her and she is even worse than Hannah ever was. If I speak to her she always contradicts me and tells me to mind my manners although I think it is* she *who is rude, always making personal remarks and telling me my hair is untidy and that my apron needs a good wash! She is even a bit stern with Mama who always agrees with her suggestions and says she must do as she thinks fit and please not to bother her about every small thing. I think Mama is afraid she will leave us and Benjy will be without a nursemaid again. She also says she wants someone who will be sure never to let Benjy out of her sight like Nettie did and Mrs McQueen is very experianced and reliable. She certainly sticks to him like glue, rocking him so hard I think he must get a headache but Mama says that gives her peace of mind.*

Oh, yes, the dreadful Mrs McQueen. What a bane and blight she was. Poor Benjy was kept to such a strict routine, and pressed so hard against her stiff, black frontage that he was eventually cowed into submission. In just a few days he'd become a wretched, grizzling creature, and he seemed frightened of everyone – even of me. Mrs McQueen would never let me hold him or even feed him, and said what was important in raising children was getting the Upper Hand. 'Children know when they meet a soft-willed person,' she said. 'They cry deliberately, just to annoy and tease. They must be put in their place.' And she'd poke me with her finger to bring her point home. She poked very hard, and I often had a bruise on my shoulder or in the middle of my back.

I knew I wouldn't be able to sleep knowing he was so upset. So I knocked on the nursery door because Mrs McQueen said I must, although I never did it when I slept there, but she says it's not my room now and I can't go marching in as if I own it. She didn't open the door but her voice came out in a kind of hiss asking who it was. When I said it was 'me', she asked what 'me' wanted at this hour, and when I said I had only come to say goodnight to my brother, she said it was a pity I'd decided to do it so late as she was just calming him down and didn't want me exciting him all over again. But he was already excited, or at least he was still making a noise, so she let me in. But Benjy didn't seem to want to know me, just bent his back in a big arch so that I thought he was going to fall out of Mrs McQueen's arms and when I tried to whisper soothing things to him he hit me in the face (without meaning to, I'm sure) and gave me a scratch on my nose which stung very hard. I told her Benjy had never been so grizzly before but Mrs McQueen said he'd been spoiled before and now she was making sure she got the Upper Hand and that of course Benjy didn't like it. I could see he was simply overtired as Nettie always said but when I said this, Mrs McQueen said Don't contradict me, child! So I had to leave him.

He's still crying, now. I really don't know what to do about it. I fear Mama won't listen and I daren't speak to Papa unless he speaks to me first, which of course he won't as he doesn't know about it. I wonder whether Mr Jameson would know what to do. He is not a married man but he likes children very much and I am sure he would not want any child to suffer. He is also very clever. DEB

I recall now, how I lay in bed that night and many others, wondering why people chose to look after children when they didn't seem to like them very much, and why ladies like Mama didn't look after their babies themselves, but paid someone else to do it on their behalf. I knew, of course, that Mama was not strong. I knew that giving birth to me had weakened her dreadfully, and having Benjy had nearly killed her; so she always needed to be careful not to overstrain herself. I was used to her spending a good deal of time lying on the sofa, reading a book or sleeping. Sometimes she used to say to Papa that she regretted not helping him more with his parishioners, and all these committees and associations and groups that he was involved in at St Cyprian's.

'I have fallen away from all the good habits I had in Poplar,' she would say from time to time. 'I should really go out and visit the poor. I will do so tomorrow, Daniel. I have decided.' But Father used to laugh and say there was not a single unvisited pauper in his entire parish and, if one were to be found, Mrs Carmichael would be there before her, making cabbage soup or washing babies at a great rate of knots. And if Mrs Carmichael didn't do it, there were at least half a dozen other ladies eager to enter the fray as a change from arranging the altar flowers and supervising Sunday School. 'Yes, I am sure there are many ladies eager to please you, Daniel dear,' she'd say. 'But I feel as if I am not doing God's work as I should.'

Papa would press her hand to his heart and say, 'We are all called in our different ways. Remember: *They also serve who only stand and wait.*'

That was a favourite saying of my father's and at the time I wasn't sure how anyone could serve God simply by standing (or sitting) around doing nothing, especially when I was being constantly told that Satan found mischief for idle hands. When Sarah had once taken my father at his word and declined to help with the Christmas blanket-sewing on the grounds that she had decided to serve God by prayer instead, she was given short shrift by my father, who made her stand on a footstool in the middle of the parlour for an entire afternoon, saying she was setting a bad example of Christian life. Sarah wept for hours afterwards. 'It's so unfair,' she said. Indeed, it seemed as if there were different rules for us and for Mama. She was curiously detached from our lives, and our time in the drawing room was always strictly limited in case it tired her. But the more remote she was, the more I longed to be close to her, and the more I was a prey to any perceived preferences she gave my siblings. Envy, I knew, was a mortal sin, and one I prayed to be delivered from every night, but I still resented Christiana and Sarah for being older and more beautiful than me, and enjoying a greater measure of Mama's attention. I would have given anything for her to spend even a few minutes combing my hair or reading the English compositions that Miss Prentiss had sent home with an 'Excellent' at the bottom, but she simply gave them a glance and smiled: 'Well done.' Occasionally she took it into her head to walk along the river at Binsey and all three of us would traipse behind as she strolled languidly along, gathering wild flowers, telling us their Latin names. We'd press them afterwards between sheets of blotting paper, and we'd copy out the names with pride when we put the specimens into the book.

The best times of all were when she read us stories – *The Little Mermaid* or *Uncle Tom's Cabin* – when we would sit around her armchair like ordinary children. I cherished these precious times of intimacy, and afterwards I'd return to Nettie in a state of high excitement, saying 'Mama this' and 'Mama that', and wondering why Nettie had such a sad expression in her eyes. But these glorious times were few. Mama always seemed less interested in us and more interested in things that were not-us – my father mainly and, to a certain extent, the Christian life; but also music and poetry. She often used to recite poetry as she lay on the sofa or walked about the drawing room, smiling at us as if she were on one of Wordsworth's mountaintops amid the wild grandeur and sublimity of nature, and we were dull toilers down in the valley, of only peripheral interest.

However, since Nettie had gone, I'd had more opportunity to observe my mother. I couldn't help noticing how very solicitous my father was for her welfare, especially if he was going out on parish business late at night (which he did a great deal), or when he had a summons in the middle of a meal to attend the sick or dying. Hannah would come in with a note and Papa would read it and say, 'I must go, my dear. Old Mrs So-and-So is at her last breath. Will you be all right?' And I'd wonder why she shouldn't be all right, as she was at home, surrounded by servants and family and quite as comfortable as she had been a minute before. And he'd kiss her and pat her hair and fuss over her to an excessive extent before putting on his coat and picking up the Bible and prayer book he always kept ready in a bag on the hall table – a bag that had been embroidered by Mrs Carmichael for his special use.

I knew she had been brought up to a life of ease. I also knew that she and my father had fallen in love when she was very young – fifteen when they had first met, as they enjoyed telling us – and how he'd had to wait for almost two years before declaring his intentions, and another two before Grandpapa would agree to the marriage. Then there had been some strife after the wedding because my father had his curacy in the East End, which Grandfather did not consider a suitable environment for a lady of my mother's sensibilities, but she had defied him and gone to be with Papa, supervising the Sunday School and teaching sewing and cooking to the women of Poplar. 'I don't think they could believe such an angel had come amongst them,' my father was fond of saying. I always imagined her in white clothes, standing out like a vision among the poor people in their dirty rags. But, according to my father, Mama had turned up her sleeves, donned an apron, and set to with a will, scrubbing and polishing and setting the best example of Christian work. It was hard for me to believe that; she was so ethereal and fragile by then. Even Christiana, who was born there, hardly remembered the time in that poor London parish. And by the time I was born, everything had changed. We were in Oxford, and there was a wide circle of helpers – especially female helpers – and my father could attend to his parish duties without my mother's help. But he hated being apart from her, even for an afternoon. Nettie said you could tell they were still in love and I thought perhaps this was the reason they had less time for us children. I certainly often felt excluded from their mutual bliss.

But even if Mama didn't choose to spend time with *me*, I couldn't understand her callousness over Benjy – Benjy who had been her pride and joy, the longed-for son, the unexpected gift from God. I remembered her desperation when she thought he might have drowned, how she had held him so tight and cried over him so loudly. How, then, could she leave him to the devices of such a person as Mrs McQueen? It seemed another instance of the ways of the adult world, which no one except Mr Jameson seemed to find at all odd.

Saturday 28th June
It is so exciting! I have received a proper grown-up letter from Mr Jameson! It was in an envelope with my name on but no stamp. He hadn't put it in the post but left it with Mama last night. She gave it to me at breakfast after I had finished my milk and toast. When she put it in front of me, I recognized Mr Jameson's handwriting straight away. I asked her what it was about, and she said I'd have to open it as that was the usual way to find out what was in letters. It was very neatly written and had some little drawings around the edge – Mr Jameson as a Tired Old Bird and me as a Daisy Flower.

The letter is attached, pinned to the journal. I recognize Mr Jameson's neat hand and his very strange little drawings.

My dear Child,

This is a short letter, but 'short is sweet'. At least I hope you will think so. I am very fond of going to the theatre, and there is a play at the Theatre Royal, Drury Lane, in London, which I think you will like. It is called Sylvie's Wish *and is a kind of fairy story and has no horrid moral to it, but is all fun and lightness. If you are willing to come with me, we will take the half past twelve train from Oxford next Thursday and see a matinée (which is the French word for morning, as I am sure you know, but in this instance it has perversely decided to mean the afternoon), then I will take you for tea in a nearby hotel. After that we will return in the train and you will be tucked up in bed by nine o'clock. Does that sound nice? I hope you think so. I am already getting my opera hat ready and hope you will wear your prettiest dress so that everybody will be ridiculously jealous of us.*

Your good friend,

John Jameson.

P.S. I have already spoken to your papa and mama and they have no objection provided you are back before midnight and don't turn into a pumpkin.

I was so excited I had to read the letter over and over to make sure I was not mistaken. I could not believe that Mr Jameson wanted to take me to the theatre, in London *and (although it is horrid to say so) I was pleased when Christiana and Sarah both looked at me as if they simply could not believe it either! Mama asked if I would like to go, and I said it would be the most exciting thing ever as I have never even* been *to London, let alone to a theatre there. Christiana caught hold of the letter as if she still did not believe what I'd said and then when she saw it was true, looked at Mama saying how was it that I should be the first to go to a London theatre considering I was only eleven, and shouldn't Mr Jameson have asked* them *first? Mama said it was because I had spent time with Mr Jameson and he was fond of*

me, and the play was a children's play anyway. Then Sarah said if
it was a children's play, then why was Mr Jameson going? And Papa
said that Mr Jameson knew one of the actresses in it, and anyway
it was his business what he did and where he went. Then he folded
his newspaper and looked at Christiana and Sarah very crossly and
said they had both had an opportunity to be nice to Mr Jameson and
had chosen to be proud and unkind instead, and God does not let these
things pass unpunished. 'Go and eat the bread of mortification,' he
said, 'and see how you like the taste.' Then he got up and went to his
study to write his sermon and my sisters became very quiet. *Mama*
said I should write back immediately and I could use her notepaper
if I liked. So I went with her into the morning room and she got out
a sheet of lavender-scented paper and the inkstand and asked if Miss
Prentiss had taught me how to write a formal reply. I felt Mr Jameson
was not the sort of person who wanted a formal reply but as Mama
was being so nice I didn't like to say so.

I wrote: 'Miss Daisy Baxter thanks Mr John Jameson for his kind
invitation to the theatre next week, and has great pleasure in accepting.'
Then I put the date and sealed it with sealing wax and Mama gave
me a penny stamp to affix to the outside, above the address. 'You
may take it to the postbox yourself, if you like,' she said. 'I know
how exciting it is to begin one's first grown-up correspondence.' And
she smiled at me as if she really understood how I felt and I was
so happy!!!

It remains with me now – the excitement of putting on my coat
and hat, walking the fifty yards to the postbox at the corner,
and letting the lavender-scented letter slide slowly inside. I held
onto it until the last possible moment, then let it fall: down into
the dark. I stood back, imagining the postman collecting it and
Mr Jameson in due course receiving it in his college rooms with
Benson presiding over the tea table and Dinah sitting on his
lap with that funny half-smile she always seemed to have. And

Mr Jameson opening it and saying to Benson: 'She *can* come!' And his pale, quiet face lighting up with pleasure. And part of *my* pleasure, I recall, was to be so favoured by Mama. She not only helped me with the letter, but also planned what I should wear; and on the day of the outing, she came to my bedroom and dressed me herself, saying I had to do her justice when I appeared in public at Drury Lane. She was not as good as Nettie in tying tapes and putting on petticoats, but to feel her slender fingers pat and stroke my body and to smell the delicate scent of lavender-water arising from her neck as she stooped and tied my sash, was complete bliss. I felt that almost everything that was happening to me then was new and exciting, and it was Mr Jameson who was making it all possible. I was beginning to see him as a kind of hero and, in my childish way, to fall a little in love with him.

7

❧ DANIEL BAXTER ❧

I LOOK AT MY FACE IN THE SHAVING-MIRROR – THE HAND-some nose, the fine whiskers, the sleek brown hair – and realize that I hate myself. I've hated myself for a long time, but it's easy to keep unwanted thoughts at bay if you keep hand, brain and eye busy. And I've kept very busy. I'm a veritable whirlwind of surplice and cassock. I throw myself with abandon into the matters of the moment, the daily concerns of the physical world that is, and always will be, too much with us. I'm a wonderful man when it comes to action: the committees, the vestry duties, the morning services, the evening services, the Sunday sermons, the visiting of the sick, the celebration of funerals, weddings, baptisms – the whole panoply of rituals that can be so satisfying when you do them well and are duly praised for it. People look at me and think I'm a fine man, a God-fearing man. They grasp my hand with fervour, or murmur a blessing under their breath, and I lap up their good opinion. Truly, the sin of pride rides high with me. But underneath it all, I'm a Doubter.

Looking at myself now – pallid, hollow-eyed – I can deny it no longer. Piece by piece, my faith has fallen away. I'm a hypocrite; standing in the pulpit every Sunday and urging my congregation to live their lives well in the hope of eternal bliss, and yet having no belief myself that such bliss will be forthcoming. I claw pathetically at the idea of Heaven, of which I was once so certain; that I saw reflected in human love and in the wonders of nature. But is there such a place? And was that Jesus of Nazareth, to whom I have dedicated my life, in truth divinely inspired? And is there beyond Him a divine watchmaker who has articulated all the parts of the universe according to a most wonderful plan? Or is everything a product of pure chance, of a rolling evolution that takes care of itself and owes nothing to a Supreme Maker? Is it all chaos, meaninglessness, absurdity? And am I, Daniel Baxter, absurd to believe in it? Or am I destined to burn for my disbelief, to add forever to the burden of mankind's sins that Christ died for in agony? I do not know. *I do not know.* I fear I will go mad in my confusion. And I cannot openly speak of it to anyone.

I have tried several times to confide in John Jameson. I'd once hoped for some comfort from a man who is both honest and clever; but I sense increasingly that he shies away from such discussions. He's happy enough to talk about points of principle, but I don't feel that he has ever had to endure desperate feelings such as mine. I suspect he is a cold fish under all the cleverness and whimsy. Indeed, he looks uncomfortable when I express doubt about the smallest point of faith, and becomes quite petulant if I persist in more rigorous questioning, saying I am enthusiastic enough in my torments to be a Methodist. At other times he has come close to suggesting that, like Newman, I'm tempted to go over to Rome. Perhaps that reflects the confusion of my own thoughts. Once I took a pride in the sensible pragmatism of the Anglican Church, but now it seems a nothingness, a compromised middle way that has nothing in it of true belief. Perhaps I would do better to strike out and nail my true colours to the mast – but which colours? And what mast?

And John is strangely elusive these days. We no longer meet every week in the old, intimate pattern that was such a comfort to me. He's become so much a friend of the family now that our private discussions have become more superficial and ad hoc. In fact, I sometimes think he spends more time with Daisy than with me. Even Evelina has been forced to entertain him on the many afternoons when I am out on parish business. But when opportunity arises, I still bring my questions to him in the hope that I might find illumination, if not comfort. Only yesterday, as I was struggling with my sermon and John was picking about in my bookcase for a particular illustration of a tropical bird, I found a great heat rise in my breast as I attempted, without success, to find a justification for the concept of Eternal Punishment. I suppose I am unduly sensitive to the concept of damnation, being perhaps so much in danger of it myself. But how could God condemn me to perpetual pain for an honest struggle with my conscience? How could He, who is perfectly good and merciful, deal out a punishment which I myself regard as abhorrent, and would not confer on the worst of my enemies? The more I thought about it, the more wretched I became. 'How can there be such a thing as Eternal Damnation?' I cried. 'Suffering with no hope of reprieve? That is an act of savagery, not of a wise and loving Father. I cannot believe in it. I simply cannot.'

John looked up from his book. 'In that case, Daniel, you will be denying the sacred truth of the Bible.'

'Then either the Bible is wrong, or God is wrong, or there is something badly wrong with my conscience,' I snapped, heedless of the enormity of what I was saying.

John closed his book, put it back on the shelf and considered. 'I admit it is a problem,' he said at last. 'But all religions rely on interpretation, and where a variety of languages are involved, interpretation is at its most unreliable. Perhaps "eternal" is not quite what we think it is. Perhaps in the original Hebrew the word does not mean "for ever" at all.'

If true, I thought, what a solution that would be for so many of the problems that have exercised all our minds for years! 'But how do we *know* if the word has been misinterpreted?' I said.

He shrugged. 'All other answers are contradictions and our religion cannot be a contradiction, can it?'

A great sense of disappointment came over me. I had hoped that he would bring me genuine enlightenment, stop up the hole in the sand into which the grains of doubt were pouring so fast. 'But everything we believe depends on *words*, John – and if we can juggle with them at will, how can we know the true meaning of anything? We could each gloss our own version of the Bible entirely to suit ourselves! Words must mean what they *say* they mean – they must be immutable and fixed – otherwise we are lost.'

'Are we?' He smiled. 'A reader may have a partial – or incorrect – understanding of the words, but that is not the Bible's fault. It is certainly not God's.'

I was exasperated. 'You might as well contend that the Bible means what it says because it – well – says what it means.'

'For some people it is the same.' He looked quietly pleased with himself, but I felt cheated. I've always hated that kind of hair-splitting theology. It is passionless and dry; and I want nothing to do with it. I need explanations that are strong and simple – that move the soul. They are what brought me to God in the first place, and they are the only things that will bring me back to Him.

And so every day I long to feel again that first careless rapture when Heaven and Love and Passion and Desire were all overwhelmingly present in my heart; when I woke each day with such a sense of freshness and purpose, my limbs firm, my eyes bright, and my whole body ready to be active in the work of the Lord – and when my love for Christ was entwined and reflected so gloriously in my love for Evelina. Not just because of her beauty, but because she seemed to offer – in her piety, her sweet smile, and the soft movement of her limbs – a way to a better future; a future in which I could be as God intended, and carry out His work.

I'd been a lost soul before I'd met her. I'd gone up to Oxford intending to follow in my father's footsteps and become a country parson; but it was not my vocation, and certainly far from my choice. Even at school, I had been uncertain of my suitability for a life of probity and restraint, but once at the university, I fell in with dubious companions and proceeded, in my own quiet way, to go to the dogs. I drank too much and I gambled at cards. I did as little work as I could and very often I woke with my head in such a hazy state that I would attempt to clear it by smiting my forehead on the bedpost until the blood ran. The mark would remain with me all day, a fearful reminder of my excess; but if, when night fell, there was nothing to distract me, I would drink again, seeking out the most disreputable places in which to hide myself. And when I was drunk, my passions had full reign. I would fall out of the public houses and into the muddy streets, and thence into the clutches of the nice girls who fleeced me of my money and gave me little satisfaction in return, although I yearned after the sight of their pale, naked breasts and the secret dusky places beneath their petticoats. I always repented most sincerely when I woke, and chastised myself once more with the wretched bedpost, but it would not be many days before I got more soddenly drunk, fell deeper into debt, and made myself more shameful in the very houses of shame themselves.

Of all my diversions, only nature was capable of holding me steady. I'd leave my studies behind and walk along the river, or across the fields, sometimes twelve or twenty miles at a stretch, the wind in my face and the firm earth at my feet. Only then would I feel myself cleansed and close to God. Yet, once back in the world of paper and pen, I would immediately suffer from pains in my head and sickness in my stomach. I'd creep wearily between the dreariness of my college room, the dreariness of the lecture hall, and the dreariness of chapel, utterly despising myself and my whole life.

It was in that state that Evelina took pity on me. It's still a source of astonishment and delight to me that she did so. I have no idea what I would have made of my life otherwise; to what depths I would have fallen if she had not been there to encourage and inspire me. And yet – such is the mysteriousness of God's ways – it was one of my disreputable companions who proved the means of bringing us together. Wilfrid Chauncey was by no means the worst of my cronies, more of a sportsman than a drinker, running hares along the Oxfordshire hedges and keeping hounds in his college rooms. One night, after extolling the virtues of his uncle's estate which had 'acres of shooting and no one to take advantage of it', he invited me to spend the week before Christmas at the house. His uncle spent most of his time in the library, he said, and was happy for his guests to drink and play cards as much as they wished. It was a very Liberty Hall – provided one did not encounter Wilfrid's cousin Evelina, who was something of a prig.

I'd accepted with alacrity, having little else to do at the end of term and not relishing a sermon from my father about my dissipated ways. I'd hoped not to encounter the priggish cousin. Well-brought-up ladies didn't interest me; I thought them vapid to say the least. But I'd scarcely arrived – and was still in my travelling clothes, grimy and dishevelled – when I opened the door to the drawing room, and there she was – standing at the window, gazing out at the distant mountains, her dark hair coiling down her back and a volume of poetry in her hand. She looked like any other modest and pious young lady, and I began to introduce myself with the kind of nonchalant swagger that had become habitual with me. But when she turned to look at me, the careless words died on my lips. Her eyes in that moment seemed not to be the eyes of a young girl at all, but of an angel. An angel who could see through me and read my mind.

Wilfrid strolled in behind me. 'Hello, Evelina. You're back from Caerwen, then? Let me introduce Daniel Baxter, the best fellow in Oxford – and the best shot too.'

'I'm sorry to hear that,' said the angel. 'Such proficiency usually means a man has spent more time with his gun than with his books.'

Wilfrid gave me a sly grin. 'You see, sporting prowess doesn't impress Evelina. She only cares for reading. And don't think of making love to her, Dan, because it's a hopeless cause. She's destined to join the Misses Venables and be lost to the world for ever.'

His words pierced me like a sword. This beautiful young creature lost to the world? But Evelina smiled patiently. 'You do exaggerate, Wilfrid. It's not as though I'll be locked up all day like a nun.'

'You might as well be,' he grumbled.

She shook her head in mock despair and turned to me. 'I need to explain, Mr Baxter. Caerwen is nothing terrible or medieval – just the Misses Venables and their friends trying to lead a good life. I plan to join them as soon as I am old enough. But in the meantime I'd be obliged if you would talk to me as if I'm an ordinary human being. Young men are often so put out when they know my intentions that I'm obliged to take my walks on my own.'

'You will not walk alone while I am in this house,' I replied, amazed at the boldness of my words as they came tumbling out with no apparent composition on my part. Suddenly – for the first time in my life – I realized that I was in love, and that it was Heaven. I felt I'd been raised a good six inches above the ground and harmonious music was playing in my ears. All at once, the thought of spending a whole day shooting and a whole night playing cards was anathema to me. I wanted to spend all my time with this divine creature amidst billowing clouds and everlasting sunshine. 'I'm a great walker,' I added breathlessly. 'And to walk with you, Miss Chauncey, would be an honour.'

'I will keep you to that, Mr Baxter,' she said with a smile of such pure limpidity that I nearly fell down dead. 'Tomorrow I shall walk up to Baycastle Crag immediately after breakfast. If you accompany me, I fear you will have to forgo the morning's shooting. We will know then where your loyalties lie.'

'I'll be there,' I said, not caring about Wilfrid's chagrin or the loss of sport as long as Evelina's grey eyes were fixed on mine.

The next day, as we mounted the steep path to the Crag, our talk was all of religion, a topic I had long found tedious, but she infused it with such emotion and longing that I wanted to break away from my wretched, sinful body, to cleave to her side, to draw breath with her, to see with her pure eyes, to taste with her tender mouth. I wanted so much to be at one with her that I could not bear the idea of keeping even the smallest thing back. I felt instead obliged to confess all my sins in a headlong jumble of self-abnegation.

She was not shocked. In fact, she seemed animated, and full of an eager kind of passion. 'Do you really intend to mend your ways?' she said, clasping my hands and sending a thrill through my veins. 'Will you turn back to God this very day?'

'Oh, yes, Miss Chauncey!' I squeezed her hands in return. 'But I need you to help me. I cannot do it alone.'

'I'm only a girl,' she said. 'And not yet sixteen. There must be better people than me to guide you.'

'God has sent you to me. I am sure of that. He will guide us both.'

'Yes,' she said, her bright eyes fixed on mine. 'That will be my mission; I understand it now. I cannot be a minister myself, but I can, through my prayers, draw you back to the ministry.'

I knew then that I would do everything to save her from a life of chastity. She would be my wife; I was determined on it. 'Yes,' I declared. 'Yes, Miss Chauncey! Do with me as you will.' As the wind whipped round us, and the fields and rivers were laid out below in a myriad of colours like a shimmering marriage bed, I kissed her hand fervently. And we walked on up the hill with our eyes shining.

All that week we were inseparable. I was so willing to be reformed that I would have sat at her feet every day for a month. As it was, I hardly spent any time with my gun, and left poor Wilfrid to the dubious companionship of the local farmers. I touched not a drop of wine and enjoyed a clear head for the first time in years. When the time came to part, I thought I might go mad to be, even for a moment, without her. But I was saved by her promise to write every day.

Once home, I presented myself to my father with a sincere wish to follow my vocation, and, once back at Oxford, my life changed in every way: I was punctual, hard-working, sober and chaste; and yet life was not dull. Evelina sent me her spiritual thoughts and quotations from her favourite poets; I sent her back details of my philosophical reading. I took up rowing, and was down on the river every morning at dawn, feeling the rush of pleasure as my oar sliced through the water and my muscles strained against the pull of the blade, knowing that every stroke made me stronger and more worthy of her.

Even now I cannot think of our courtship without feeling again those heady raptures of heart and lung and, looking at John Jameson, with his meaningless words and pernickety interpretations, I cannot imagine that he would ever understand what it is to be wrapped in the sublime embrace of the holiest and most intense sensations that it is given human beings to know.

Of course, I was wary at first of expressing my love in case I set Evelina's delicate sensibilities to flight – and even more wary lest my letters should fall into the hands of her father. But I could not keep my joy to myself. As I wrote to her, my blood roared in my ears, my limbs tingled, my whole body burned. *Meeting you, knowing you, and loving you has put me under a heavy debt to God. And how can I pay this better than by devoting myself to the religion I once scorned, making of the debauchee a preacher of purity and holiness, and of the destroyer of systems a weak, though determined, upholder of the Only True System.*

Evelina wrote back that she had never been so happy as to think she had been the humble means of bringing a sinner to repentance. *I think of you every day*, she wrote, *and I pray for you every night. Your face is with me as I lie on my pillow, and I only wish my heart was pressed against yours and you could feel its joyful beating.*

Once I had read this, I knew that if marriages were made in Heaven, then surely mine with Evelina could not be too far postponed. I asked her to be mine, and she consented. I knew there would be difficulties: she was due to inherit a considerable fortune, whereas I had little money and no particular prospects. But the day after I went down from Oxford, I immediately rode to Herefordshire and asked for her hand. 'She is all the world to me, and I will never cease to strive to be worthy of her,' I said to her father, studying the carpet in his library and filling my lungs with the dusty powder of thousands of ancient books.

My request was politely declined. 'The young are changeable,' Mr Chauncey said, not unkindly. 'One moment Evelina is committed to a celibate life, the next to matrimony with a man she hardly knows. I would have her wait at least two years before she is in a position to make such an important choice.'

It was a blow, but I wrested from him an agreement to our continued correspondence. That was my life blood and I could not do without it. 'I am to be ordained this month,' I told him. 'I am determined to find a parish where there is good Christian work to be done. I will work as hard as any man can to bring the Gospel to the poor and ignorant, and to make myself worthy of offering my hand again. She is willing to wait for me, and I will wait for her. Permit us to correspond in the meantime. Evelina is extremely well-read, as you know,' I said. 'And she takes great pleasure in the study of so many things – poetry, nature, theology. Indeed, those are the things that have drawn us together. I can share with her all that I am learning in my new situation. She in her turn can guide me with her simplicity and faith. There will, I promise you, be no more talk of marriage for the next two years.'

And so I entered into a most blissful phase of my life, in which anticipation was more glorious than consummation, in which Evelina and I shared our thoughts and feelings so completely it seemed that we were already One. Every day I would go about my business as curate at St Barnabas-in-the-East, sitting at the bedsides of the sick, baptizing newborn infants in their brief sojourn between birth and death, giving comfort to the living, and burying the dead – and every night I would retire, exhausted, to my small bare room and write to my love. I was almost in a delirium, then. I seemed to be able to envisage her completely naked, to see her lovely white body before me – although, in truth, I had seen nothing more than the whiteness of her neck and wrists. But my imagination went ahead of me and, when I wrote, I could no more refrain from talking of the ways of love than I could willingly condemn myself to death.

With each letter I became bolder, using every lovely biblical phrase I knew. *When you go to bed tonight,* I urged her, *forget that you ever wore a garment, and open your lips for my kisses and spread out each limb that I might lie between your breasts all night.* And she replied: *O, My Dove that art in the cleft of the rock, in the secret places of the stairs, let me see thy countenance, let me hear thy voice.* Sometimes I would have to take hold of the water jug and pour its contents over my yearning body. Sometimes I would sleep on the floor and rise at three o'clock to pray. Once I walked into the woods and lay naked upon thorns all night and came back with my body torn. Such bliss, such reckless bliss!

But night-time bliss was balanced by the gruelling demands of the day, and it was becoming daily clearer to me that my efforts at spreading the Word of God would falter unless society itself was changed. Many of us working in poor parishes throughout London had joined together to demand clean drinking water for all, fair wages for the working man, and schools for their children. Our motto was *Hard Work and Clean Water* – demands so self-evident that no Christian person could deny them. But we were laughed at by those who should have known better, and basely accused of neglecting the spiritual (which was apparently our business) for the physical (which apparently was not). Such accusations enraged me; I have never been able to see why the two things were set in opposition. In my anger I wrote a pamphlet denouncing the government's inaction, which was reproduced all over London, to general acclaim. I sent a copy of it to Evelina and she wrote back to say how much she admired it – but that her father had remarked that I sounded 'too radical'.

Soon after that (and maybe consequent upon it), Evelina was sent to Germany and then to France to complete her education and to let her 'see the world'. But at ten o'clock each night, she and I, according to our arrangement, would turn our thoughts to the other and imagine that we were together in body as much as in mind. We would both undress, then kneel and pray, knowing our thoughts were ascending together to Heaven like twinned spirals of smoke.

What will give us more perfect delight, I wrote, *than when we lie naked in one another's arms, clasped together, toying with each other's limbs, buried in each other's bodies, struggling, panting, dying for a moment? Shall we not feel, even then, that there is more in store for us; that those thrilling writhings are but a dim shadow of a union that shall be perfect?* Even then I was sure that the union of the marriage bed was a foretaste of the delights of Heaven, that chastity is at best an insipid virtue and at worst a cause of unnatural vice.

At last her father permitted our engagement. Evelina had told him that if she could not have me as a husband, she would have no one else, and would retire to Caerwen House as she had first intended. So Mr Chauncey gave in. I was the lesser of two evils; and at least I gave him hope of a grandson. From then on, Evelina and I spent as many hours together as we could. I had little opportunity to travel, and no money to do so. But Evelina's father allowed her to visit me and, to my astonishment, we often found ourselves alone and private. What delights then, as we explored that which we had only imagined before! Whenever she left me, be it day or night, I knew my hands were perfumed with her delicious limbs and I could not (and did not wish to) wash off the scent. And as I lay apart from her, the thought of those mysterious recesses of beauty, where my hands had so recently been wandering, caused my soul almost to faint.

So why cannot I confess to her now? To the woman who is the darling of my heart? Why cannot I lay before her, as I once did on that high hill, what is now so heavy upon my conscience? She is no less lovely and good than she was, but much has passed between us since – times of great trial – and I fear that we have in some ways grown apart; that the ardent couplings which were once so vital to us have ended, and left us less than we were. And, if I am honest (as I now try to be), I am afraid that she will not pardon me quite so readily this time. The doubts of a dissolute young man of twenty are one thing; the doubts of a practising clergyman of mature years with the care of hundreds of souls are another. Evelina has always believed in me. Her belief is at the heart of our marriage. In fact, I feel sometimes that she came to love me precisely because she had saved me. And now to tell her that her act of salvation was incomplete, and that all her efforts were for nought would be like smiting her in the face. I cannot disappoint her. I cannot destroy the only sure and certain love I have left on this earth. I will have to go on as I am, tormented and wretched and, at times, I think, half mad.

8

﹌ MARGARET CONSTANTINE ﹌

THE TRIP TO THE THEATRE IS NOW SO VIVID IN MY mind. It was one of the most memorable days I ever had. And I see Daisy has recorded it in detail.

Friday 4th July

I have had the most wonderful *day ever. I have been to London with Mr Jameson and we have seen a proper play! It was all about a gypsy prince who fell in love, and there was a chorus of girls in gypsy dresses and they looked so pretty that I really wanted to be one of them. There were forests that moved and real caravans, and coloured lights and music and ever such pretty costumes. And Prince Florizel was so handsome I wished I could marry him but Mr Jameson told me that it was his niece Miss Garfield and not a gentleman after all – which was very disappointing!! We went behind the scenes afterwards and I saw all the people pulling ropes and moving big pieces of scenery about, getting ready for the Second House when the play is done all over again (which must be* very *exhausting!). The big opening you look into from the audience is only part of the whole stage and there are bigger spaces at each side called the Wings and even bigger spaces up above called the Flies where all the curtains and canvases are kept hanging up like giant blinds. Mr Jameson said: 'Now, Daisy, tell me – why is a theatre like a bird?' And I couldn't think of the answer and he said: 'Because it has wings, and flies!' which of course I should have guessed.*

As we went up the little winding stairs to the dressing-rooms he said he hoped that it didn't spoil the magic for me, seeing how it all worked.

And I said no it was very exciting as all the girls looked so pretty still in their costumes with their faces powdered and roudged, and the boys with brownish stuff on their faces and felt hats and high boots. When we met Miss Garfield she had taken off her boots and leather jerkin and had on a very nice patterned frock and a very pretty straw hat with pink roses and a little veil. It was a bit disappointing in a way, as I thought she was so handsome as Florizel. But she was very nice and we went to have tea in a hotel near by, and everybody turned to look at her and she called all the waiters and waitresses by their first names, including a very important-looking gentleman in a tailcoat whom she called Henry, but they all called her Miss Garfield which I thought very respectful. She looked at me quite a long time while I was eating my scones and said I had exactly the right face for an anjenou. (I think this word is French but I don't think the spelling is at all right!) But she said that if I was ever to go on the stage I'd need to cut my hair shorter at the front so the audience could see my eyes properly.

How I cherished that remark of Miss Garfield's, and the steady and approving way the famous actress looked at me as if I were more than just a small and not very interesting child, but someone who was capable of doing something out of the ordinary if I chose. That was when I first realized that cutting my hair was possible and I couldn't imagine why I'd never thought of it before. With a few decisive snips across my forehead, I could be rid of the daily struggles to keep the wretched mane under control. It was a kind of liberation to my spirit – and from that time I began to think about how I could bring it about. Hannah, I knew, wouldn't attempt it without my mother's permission, and my mother didn't care for short hair. She had very abundant hair herself, and I suspect she was secretly vain about it, even though it was put up in pins and kept very plain as appropriate for a vicar's wife in a parish where there were many ladies ready to criticize. But I was determined that I would do the deed somehow. I regretted only that Miss Garfield hadn't had any scissors about her to accomplish the task on the spot.

After tea, Miss Garfield had to go to get ready for the Second House and so Mr Jameson paid the bill with two half-crowns and we got a handsome cab to Paddington. In the train I fell asleep and had a very strange dream full of animals. Then Father came to meet us at Oxford station and took me home in another cab. I was very sleepy by then as it was nearly nine o'clock and so Mama came upstairs with me to listen to my prayers and put me to bed. She asked me if I had been good, and I said yes and she asked if Mr Jameson had looked after me well. And I said he did and that he was very funny and had bought a bag of chocolate limes which were my favourites. I told her how we had gone to the backstage afterwards and that he had introduced me to Miss Garfield who played Prince Florizel and we'd all had tea together in an adjoining hotel and I'd had fruit cake and scones as well as bread-and-butter and Miss Garfield had lifted up the teapot and said, Shall I be mother? And Mr Jameson said, I hope not for a good while, my dear. Mama said Hmm, and asked if she had been a ladylike person as actresses were not always ladies and I told her that Miss Garfield was not always a lady — because she was sometimes a gentleman! I thought that was a very good joke and will try to remember to tell it to Mr Jameson. I told Mama that Miss Garfield had said that I would look nice with shorter hair, and Mama said, Really, I hardly think it is up to her to decide, so I know Mama will probably not let me cut it. DEB.

I can recall how wonderful it seemed to me then that Mama was on the doorstep ready to welcome me back. And even more wonderful that she put me to bed with her own hands and engaged in such an intimate conversation with me. Even then, though, I sensed something wary in my mother's demeanour, which I couldn't fully comprehend, some slight sense of unease about the kind of world I had been exposed to. Was she perhaps concerned that she had let me go so far afield and to have such novel experiences without being there in person to watch over me? It was my first intimation that theatre people, even those as great and well-known as Miss Garfield, might not be thoroughly respectable. All the same, I assumed it couldn't be a matter of great concern, otherwise Mama would not have allowed Mr Jameson to take me in the first place . . .

'Margaret?' Robert has come in so quietly that I haven't heard. I colour, close the journal quickly.

'What's that you're reading with such rapt attention?' He comes towards me, smiling, conciliatory.

'Nothing of importance, Robert.' I slide it down by my side, against the inner arm of the chair, and give him my most confident smile.

'On the contrary, you were quite engrossed. More engrossed than I've seen you for a long time. I think I have the right to know what it is.' He is holding out his hand, certain that I will surrender it to him. 'Is it a romance?' he teases. 'Now, don't be ashamed to admit it.'

'Maybe,' I say, equally playfully. 'Or maybe not.'

He's encouraged by the playfulness. He comes towards me, rests his hands on the back of my armchair and bends to kiss my neck. I feel the tiniest edge of his tongue as he does so, lapping at me, awakening – what? A thin tremor of desire? I'm not sure; I hardly dare think about it. He whispers in my ear: 'Come, now, let me see what you're hiding.'

'No, Robert, it's a secret.'

'Is it indeed? Have you forgotten so soon – there should be no secrets between a husband and wife. We are one person – one flesh, in fact. Or will be soon, I hope.'

The word 'flesh' seems to excite him, and I can sense that he wants to kiss me, and hopes that this time I will kiss him in return. But I can hardly breathe. It takes me an effort to control my voice, to turn the conversation back to the mundane. I pull back from him, laughing gently: 'It's not really a *secret*, Robert. Just a book from the toy-box; hardly your sort of reading matter.'

'Oh? And are you sure you know what my "sort of reading matter" is? I believe I have quite catholic tastes: adventure, comedy, ghost stories – even romance.' He smiles knowingly. He explores down the inside of the chair, his fingers contriving to caress the contours of my hip before they tighten over the book. 'Here it is! Now I'll find out what your secret is!'

I trap his hand with a deft sideways movement. 'Please, Robert,' I say. 'I'd rather you didn't. As a favour to me. Please.'

'Ah, my wife asks a favour, and I'm happy to grant it.' He retracts his empty hand. 'But what will she give me in return?' I can see his long, dark face reflected in the looking-glass, hovering expectantly next to mine. His eyes drop to my breast, and now he can see my unfastened bodice, my loosened stays. I feel his breath quicken. 'What's this, Margaret? *En déshabille* at six o'clock?'

I'm horrified that he will misinterpret this. 'I was a little uncomfortable, that's all. A little breathless after all that effort this afternoon.'

'But you are recovered, now, it would seem,' he says. '*Very much* recovered, if I am any judge. I don't know what is in that book, but I would say it had made you quite *pink* and *rosy*.' His voice has taken on a caressing quality, which makes me feel uneasy. I don't like that silken tone of voice; it's always a prelude to something unwelcome. And it is: his hand is stroking my exposed bosom.

I flinch, but he takes no notice. He may even think it's a response of pleasure. He does. 'Oh, Margaret,' he murmurs. 'May we try again tonight?'

Tonight? The giddy feeling rolls and swells through my body. The wedding night flashes before me in all its horror – and I am tense from head to toe. 'Please, Robert. Not quite yet. I'm not ready.'

I wonder, though, if I'll ever be ready. If it's not tonight, then it must be tomorrow, or the day after. And it must be done. It's like a high hedge that has to be painfully scrambled over, but, surely, once on the other side there should be smooth pastures – happiness and affection and the beginnings of family life. Everything I want, in fact.

I glance at Robert. He is less nervous than on our wedding night, and I am calmer too. Maybe now is the time to abandon myself to his touch, here at six o'clock on an autumn evening in our own room with an hour to spare before dinner. I can let my eyes fix themselves on the watercolours of the Lake District, the pretty brocade curtains, the fading light through the window – anything so I don't have to think about what he is doing with his hands and his lips – or the other, more appalling parts of his anatomy. I merely need to make the effort.

But even as logic is telling my mind to submit, my body is in a panic. Robert is breathing hard and doesn't seem to notice my distress. He's plucking open my chemise, murmuring things I can't hear. I know that they are words of love and desire. I'm sure that they are meant to melt me, make my arms soft and my lips ready – but I'm a piece of wood beneath him. I feel the old nightmare returning; the dark shadows, the hot sense of guilt. I cannot, *cannot* do this; I rear up from the chair and push him off. My strength surprises me. It surprises him too – he falls heavily against the dressing-table, striking it with his elbow, and then slides to the floor, making my eau de Cologne bottle topple over with a crash. He looks up at me. His shirt is open, the buttons on his trousers partly undone. He's lost all his dignity.

I feel instantly ashamed. 'I'm sorry,' I say. 'Dear Robert, I am *so sorry*.'

He shakes his head. He is perplexed and angry and sympathetic all at once. 'I'm not a demon from the depths of Hell, you know. Just a man wishing to make love to his wife.' He gets up, rebuttons his trousers and smoothes his sleek black hair.

I apologize again. 'You must think me unloving – but it's simply that I can't . . .' But I cannot explain. I'm shaking head to foot.

He takes my hand – tentatively this time, as if he fears I will hurl him to the ground once more. 'I know you're apprehensive. It is a natural thing in a modest and well-brought-up young woman. But you are perhaps taking such feelings to the extreme. There is nothing to fear – from me at any rate. We have known each other for eight years. Surely you trust me by now?'

His kind words hurt me more than harsh ones. All my attempts to pretend to myself that only time is needed, that I will habituate myself to the idea if I am left alone, now strike me as weak and self-deceiving. I squeeze his hand; notice how his sallow fingers contrast with my white ones, as if we are opposites never to be conjoined. 'Oh, Robert, you are kind and admirable and everything a husband should be. But I have an irrational fear. I cannot describe it. I cannot understand it myself.'

'You know I won't hurt you – at least not more than I can help.' He sounds as if he might break down in tears.

'I know you won't, Robert. And, anyway, I can bear pain.' I know that for certain. I've tested myself over and over, just to make sure. I've held my fingers over candle flames, and jabbed darning needles into my palm six at a time.

'Then I'm at a loss.' He puts his face in his hands, hopeless. We are silent for a while. Then he raises his head. 'Margaret, I hesitate to say this, but I feel maybe the time has come when we should consult a medical man. This antipathy of yours cannot be normal. It must be some sort of nervous condition.'

I need to offer him some hope. 'Yes,' I say. 'Maybe you are right.'

He smiles like a man who has been given a new life. 'I am glad you agree. I will ask Dr Lawrence to recommend a specialist. Someone in London – Harley Street perhaps. We will have this cleared up in no time.' His face is flushed and joyous, and I feel guilty for encouraging him along what I am sure is the wrong path. 'Now, will you come down for dinner – or shall I have something sent up?'

'A little soup, perhaps?' I am anxious to perpetuate the notion that I am in somewhat fragile health. I kiss his hand. My lips feel the little black hairs that cluster there and I have to suppress a shudder. 'You are so kind, Robert.'

He looks gratified. 'Nonsense,' he says. 'You are a dear girl and I love you. It's simply that I wish to love you more *fully*. As is right for man and wife.' He bends and kisses me on the forehead, a kiss of forgiveness and absolution. 'I will sleep in the dressing-room tonight. Let you rest with no fear of – well, you know.' He backs away to the door and gives me a parting smile. 'Goodnight, dear.'

'Goodnight, Robert.'

He's forgotten all about the journal. But I can feel it against my thigh, an insistent presence, and now (maybe) my salvation. Memories are emerging in small and elusive flashes. Robert won't come back tonight, so I can read as much as I want. I draw it out and open it again, skimming over my innocent prattlings about teatimes and theatre visits, finding where I left off. There is a storm to come, I feel sure.

Yesterday I cut my hair short and now everyone is cross with me, except Mr Jameson, who said it made me look prettier than ever. (I know I shouldn't write down compliments, but he did say it.) I am very pleased with the result, which was mainly thanks to Mr Jameson in the end.

Mama looked really cross and said, 'Really, Mr Jameson, you should have stopped her,' but I told her Mr J didn't know I'd done it – so she didn't say any more. My sisters are being spiteful as usual. Sarah said it wouldn't grow back for ages, so I said I didn't want it to, as I wanted it short for ever. Christiana said she thought fringes were very common and it made me look as if I had lice and she'd be ashamed to go out with me now – not that she often does. Papa said he didn't mind what hairstyle I wore except that there was deceit involved and he was disappointed in me and that I would need to ask forgiveness and learn suitable verses from the Bible. I thought this was a quite lenient punishment for Papa, but I'm not sure that I can ask for forgiveness as I am still pleased that I did it. I hope this will not affect my outings with Mr Jameson. It was truly not his fault, although I did it in his rooms. I hadn't intended to do it, it just happened on the spur of the moment after we had come back from the Botanical Gardens, which was very interesting as I saw the monkeys again and fed them on bits of fruit. Mr Jameson pointed at one and said, 'How would you like it if you had that fellow for your great-great-grandfather?' And I said I wouldn't like it at all. And he said some people thought we had monkeys for our ancestors but of course that was foolish talk because the Bible says we are all descended from Adam and Eve, and that was far more logical, wasn't it – at least Bishop Wilberforce thought so. And I said I thought the bishop was right, and Mr Jameson said that was sensible of me, as bishops were always supposed to be right.

Then we went back to his rooms to have tea, and he said he'd like to take some more photographs of me if I didn't mind. Then he said, 'How would you like to dress up as a gypsy girl?' And I said I would like it very much but I didn't have the costume. And he said Aha, and opened his bedroom door and there it was already waiting for me, laid out on his bed. He said he had had it sent post-haste from Nathan's, and he hoped it would fit, as he'd had to guess my size. I don't know what we would have done if it hadn't fitted, as Hannah wasn't there to help and I am not very good at sewing except for plain seams and cross-stitch.

However, the dress was just right and was very pretty although the top of the sleeves kept falling down over my shoulder, but Mr Jameson said that bare shoulders looked right for a gypsy girl, and went with my bare feet. He said the way my hair was untidy was right too. That was when I told him that I hated my hair and wanted to cut it short like Miss Garfield had said, but I was afraid Mama would not allow it. I said I wished Miss Garfield had had some scissors with her because it was very difficult to cut your own hair especially with embroidery scissors. Then Mr Jameson said, 'Have you been trying to do that?' And I said I had snipped a bit off but I was afraid I'd make a mess of it so I'd stopped. And he came and stood behind me and lifted my hair in front of the looking-glass and asked how short I wanted it, bringing his hand higher and higher until it was up to my chin. And I said yes, and as well as that I wanted to have a fringe like Enid and Emma, so that my hair didn't fall over my face and make me hot. It is so horrid to be hot all the time and I just want to be cool and free. And he stood there holding my hair in his hands and looking at us both in the glass as if we were a photograph in a frame. I asked him if he would be so kind as to cut it for me but he shook his head and said it was Quite Impossible, and I was a bit cross and said it was not impossible at all, and anyway he always said it was important to think the impossible. Then he laughed and said, 'Don't you know that a thing can be possible and impossible at the same time?' And I said that was silly, it had to be one or the other. And he said no it didn't and that cutting my hair was possible *because he knew how to use a pair of scissors – but* impossible *because it would be wrong. I said it wasn't wrong as Nettie always used to cut an inch off every month, but Mr Jameson said that was different as Nettie was my nursemaid, but he was a batcheler don and as such he came under the Eye of Society. I wasn't sure why the Eye of Society was interested in who cut my hair but Mr J said Society was interested in a lot of things it had no business to be, including kindnesses that might pass between a little girl and a gentleman who was not related to her (meaning him of course). Mainly he was afraid that my mother* would disapprove and stop me visiting him – which would make him miserable. Well, of course, I didn't want that to happen but I thought all the same that he was giving in too easily. Surely Mama would not be cross with him as he was a grown-up person and had saved Benjy from drowning? But he said mamas could be very particular about some things and this was one of them.

Then he stood back from the glass and said it was time to take the photograph and then he noticed that I was still wearing my pantalettes and he said that, if it was not too delicate a matter to mention, he feared I would need to remove them, as all the frills and ribbons were showing through the rags, which would not do at all. I asked him what real gypsies did when their drawers showed through their rags, and he said, 'Oh, I think you'll find they are very free and easy in such matters.' He then went back into his sitting room and I took off my drawers and folded them up with my petticoats and dress. Then I saw there was a pair of very large scissors on the dressing-table that seemed to be asking to be picked up, so I did, wondering what Mr Jameson did with them. They were very heavy and had big black handles. They were so big that I knew they would cut my hair in no time and once it was done it wouldn't matter what Society or anyone else said. I stood in front of the looking-glass and put them across my forehead and let the blades crunch through my hair. I couldn't see what I was doing because my arm was in the way but I saw great long bits of hair fall onto my chest and when I put my arm down I saw my face looking quite different, and I felt quite airy and nice. Then I noticed that the fringe was very crooked so I tried to take a little bit more off one side, but the scissors were so heavy, I couldn't hold them straight. I began to feel very hot and panicky and was afraid I might end up with no front hair at all like Enid's sister who had allopeasha and couldn't go out for a year. So I went back to Mr Jameson in the other room.

He was so astonished when he saw me that his eyebrows went right up. 'Dear, dear,' he said. 'You have put the cat among the pigeons! But what a very disagreeable job you have made of it. I cannot take *your photograph like that.' I said that his scissors had been too big to do it properly. 'Oh,' he said. 'I daresay. They are Benson's scissors as it happens. I asked him to take a couple of inches off my gown as the hem had come undone and I was treading on my tail. But you cannot go back to your mama like that. We'll have to improve it somehow and you'll need to stand very still while I do it.' I was relieved that he was going to help me but I said, 'What about the Eye of Society?' And he said, 'Well strictly speaking I'm not cutting your hair, just trimming it to make sure you're not too much of a fright when your mama sees you, which is as different as a peach from a perambulator. Now you'd better stand on a chair while I do it.' And he got a wooden chair and put it in front of the wardrobe mirror and picked up the scissors. I climbed on the chair and said that I was as tall as he was now and he smiled and said in this world it was easy to grow larger but very difficult to get smaller which was a pity as he would rather like to be as small as me sometimes. And I said I hated being small and wanted to have long legs like Christiana and Sarah, so I could wear long skirts and petticoats and swirl them around. And he said don't wish for that, enjoy your childhood while you can. Then he lifted the scissors and started to make neat little snips to my fringe and I could feel his fingers against my forehead and they were so shaky I was worried that he would make things worse but in the end he cut it what he called a Perfect Horizontal at ninety degrees to the plum although I couldn't see a plum anywhere. When he finished, he said I looked very pretty now and when I looked in the glass I thought I did too and I could imagine myself on the stage with all the other gypsy girls and everybody clapping. Then Mr Jameson brushed the little bits of hair off my cheeks and neck, and his fingers tickled me and I laughed and tucked in my chin and he said he could see I was ticklish which was a sign of a Sensitive Nature, and he was rather ticklish himself and his sisters had had no mercy on him when he was a boy. And I asked him how many sisters he had had and he said seven (which meant a lot of tickling!). And then he said we must get on a little faster as Benson would soon be getting the tea ready and*

would be in a bad temper if we were still in the dark room when it was
time to sit down. So we went into that little studio and he lit the lights
and told me where to stand and how to turn my head. I was a bit cold
without my drawers, but Mr Jameson said it was all in the cause of
Art, and Art is very important. *DEB.*

I have goose-flesh now, just to think of it – me in my skimpy
outfit against a painted background of sky and clouds, carrying
a basket as if I'm selling nosegays, and standing on a make-
believe rock with my hand on my hip. It's very clear in my head,
because I saw the photograph many times, as Mr Jameson kept
it proudly on his mantelpiece in a silver frame. 'I will always
remember you like that,' he said. 'Even when you are grown
up, you will always be a little gypsy girl to me.'

9

JohnJameson

I HAVE ALWAYS LOVED THE THEATRE. I HAVE NEVER BE-
lieved, like many men of the cloth, that it is a place of impropriety. To me, a theatrical performance, when done properly
– without oaths or coarseness, I mean – represents the best
and truest spirit of fancy, and is the means of touching what is
closest to our hearts. When I was a child, and even as a youth,
there was nothing I enjoyed so much as joining with my sisters
in performing anything from charades to melodramas – to the
great amusement of our parents and all concerned – and it has
remained my habit as an adult man to frequent the stage as often
as I can. I will always make it my business to see a Shakespeare
play, particularly if it is a comedy, and I am drawn by anything
of a light, fanciful nature. I especially like dancing when it is
done by young ladies or children. It is so natural and free.

I have to confess that one of my particular enjoyments is
watching the faces of the children seated in the audience; and
indeed at times I am guilty of watching them in preference to
what unfolds on stage. How I love their round-eyed sense of
wonder as the curtain rises and a magical scene is displayed: a
wood, a fairy castle, a baronial hall or a rose-covered cottage –
the colours so intense in the limelight. And here comes a princess
in a floating white dress with spangles! And there is a monster
with a head like a bear! And, ah, there is the young girl in a
short tunic and pink tights, who pretends to be a boy and shows
her shapely legs in all their beauty! How the little audience is

transfixed! How it opens its mouth in astonishment at the moving scenery! How it hides its head in horror as the villain comes up from the depths, or fairies fly down from the sky! How it laughs at the antics of the clownish servants and their acrobatic tricks! I think I would not enjoy myself half so much if the little people were not there with their unreserved and spontaneous response.

So the prospect of taking my own little member of the audience with me has been exciting me for days. Daisy, bless her, wrote an extremely formal reply to my invitation, so I replied with equal formality: *My dear Miss Baxter, Thank you for your excellent reply. But you will be getting tired of my long letter, so I will bring it to an end and sign myself, Yours afft, John Jameson.* She said the letter had made her laugh. She also said her sisters were envious of her trip to London and when they had complained, her father had chastised them for not paying me more attention. Thank heavens they did not, or I would have been obliged to arrange an outing for the three of them, which would not have been half so delectable.

As it was, Daniel brought Daisy to meet me at Carfax. As he had business in St Ebbe's, he took his leave of us there, and the two of us walked on to the station. It was raining lightly and I had to draw Daisy under my umbrella to protect her from the splashes. Her waist was so tiny, I could hardly believe it. She seemed like gossamer under my fingers, and to have her so close – bobbing along with her head just above my elbow, and the faint smell of her damp hair wafting up towards me – was supremely delightful. I imagined how it might have been were I her father; how proud I would have been of her, seeing old ladies and nurse-maids giving us approving glances as we walked and chatted.

'Is it a long way to London?' she asked, clinging to me as she daintily avoided a puddle. 'I have looked in my atlas, but it doesn't say.'

'It can be long or short. It depends where you start from,' I replied.

'Well, *here* of course,' she said with a laugh.

'Well, there's no "of course" about it. If we were in Birmingham or Chester, we would have to start our journey *there*, and it would be a lot longer.'

'But we're not in Birmingham or Chester!'

'How very to the point you are! Let me see, I reckon it will take us an hour and three-quarters provided it is not a very slow train. Some trains are dreadfully slow, you know. Some are so slow I think they might even go backwards, and you'll end up in Newcastle the day before yesterday.'

She looked a little alarmed. 'Can trains really go backwards?'

'Well, some are pulled and some are pushed. The locomotives may go backwards, but, rest assured, the carriages will always go forwards – relatively speaking, that is.'

She wrinkled her forehead. 'I think you are just making all this up! I shall take no notice of you.'

'Quite right. I am a foolish old thing.'

She gave me a sharp look. '*Are* you old, Mr Jameson?'

'Depends on what you mean by "old", Miss Baxter. I'm younger than your pa. But age is as age does. I'm only eleven at heart.'

'That's *my* age.'

'Yes. That's why we are such good friends.'

'And what will happen when I am twelve?' She laughed. 'Will you be twelve too?'

My heart sank. 'Sadly, no. I am destined to be eleven for ever. You will grow away from me, my dear. Soon you won't want to know me – just like Christiana and Sarah.'

'I will! I'll always want to know you!' She grasped my arm again.

'Bless you. You are a dear child.' But my heart was heavy at the knowledge that she was so dreadfully wrong.

*

The journey passed quickly. Daisy was so interested in everything. She said she had been on a train many times to visit her grandfather in Herefordshire, and sometimes to go to the seaside at Aberystwyth. As a result, she knew not to lean out of the window for fear of getting a cinder in her eye. 'I shall look at the cows and sheep instead,' she said, pressing her face to the glass. But the cows and sheep lost their charm after about fifteen minutes, and she jumped up and kneeled on the brown plush of the seat opposite and began to examine the pictures below the luggage net. 'Taunton sounds rather a cross place, doesn't it? But Dawlish sounds nice – a bit like dawdling. And it looks nice, too.'

At Didcot we were joined by a lady with a Scotch terrier and a small boy who made appalling faces at us when his mother wasn't looking. Daisy ignored him with an air of infinite superiority, choosing to talk only to the lady and the dog, but I assumed the most grotesque of faces behind cover of my newspaper and fixed my stare on the wretched child for as long as I could. The mother, looking up suddenly, caught her son with his tongue out, and slapped his hand sharply: 'That's rude, Tommy! Apologize to the gentleman at once!' In vain did he burble that 'The gentleman did it first!' His mother gave him another slap and said lying would only make matters worse, and she was so sorry and hoped I wouldn't be offended. 'Why can't you just behave?' she told the boy. 'Why can't you be like this nice young girl and sit still and talk nicely?'

Daisy looked very smug, and spread her dress out around her and sat plumb in the middle of it with her back straight and her little hat tipped forward and her neat little feet crossed at the ankles, all as if butter wouldn't melt in her mouth. The boy looked daggers at her, and Daisy in way of response turned round and said pointedly, in a grown-up way, 'Which theatre is it that we are going to, Mr Jameson?'

'Theatre Royal, Drury Lane,' I said. 'That is the best one for spectacle and transformation scenes, I think. And always the best for fairies.'

'Oh, indeed,' said the mother. 'How lucky you are to be going there, young lady. But then I expect you have deserved such a lovely outing. And your uncle –'

'Sadly, I am but a family friend,' I put in, anxious not to have the woman make any mistake in the matter, even though we were unlikely to meet again.

'– Well, your nice friend, then. I'm sure he has arranged this treat knowing you would sit still and listen to what is being said – unlike *some people* I know.' And she glowered so much that even *I* was compelled to feel sorry for the boy.

They got out at Reading, the dog yapping at their heels, and Daisy and I were alone again. 'When we get to London, will we see the sights?' she asked. 'Or will we go straight to the theatre?'

I said that we would go to the theatre, as the performance began at half past three o'clock. 'We'll just have enough time to get across town from Paddington.'

'What's Paddington?' she asked.

'It's the railway station in London where we get out.'

'But why isn't it called London Station?'

I smiled. 'Ah, because London is so big that there is more than one station. We are coming in from the west, on the GWR. Some people say this stands for God's Wonderful Railway – although if the Almighty had really designed it I don't think the trains would be late, which, I have to say, they often are.'

'Do you often come to Paddington, Mr Jameson?'

'As often as I can and provided, of course, that I may. A college man is not a free agent. But generally I make it to London once or twice a term.'

'Mama says London is very fine, but there is too much poverty in the streets. She says it breaks her heart.' Daisy looked thoughtful. 'Will we see much poverty in the streets today, Mr Jameson?'

What a question from the child! And how to answer? Frankly, I'm not well-acquainted with the city. My general plan is: arrive at the station; proceed to the Athenaeum Club in Pall Mall; visit the appropriate theatre on the Strand; then go back to the station. A round – or rather a triangular – trip of approximately sixteen and one-third miles that on most occasions I do not vary. Everything outside that acreage is unknown territory and there could be Red Indians engaged in open warfare in Hackney for all I know. I certainly had no intention of plumbing the depths of the East End with a small child in hand. 'You will see nothing worse than you see in Oxford,' I said finally.

'Papa says I have to give away all my pocket money if I see a beggar,' she went on. 'Especially if it's a child with no shoes on its feet.'

'On the contrary, I suggest you go into a fruit shop,' I said.

'A fruit shop?' She wrinkled her forehead. 'What for?'

'To buy the poor creature a pear.'

'A pear? What good would that do?'

'A great deal of good, if it were a *pair of shoes.*'

She laughed. I was glad to see her face clear, but I could see the prospect of ragged children holding out pitiful hands was still very much on her mind. This would not do; this was a joyful outing, after all. 'But you may keep your pennies safe,' I said, patting her hand through her cotton gloves. 'I doubt there will be any shoeless beggars on the London Omnibus, and that is where we are bound. We'll go from Paddington to the Strand for sixpence, with a half-fare for the little lady with the straw hat and nice smile, and no one will bother us.'

And once we'd arrived and were aboard the omnibus, there were indeed no beggars, but only soldiers and sailors and carpenters and clerks, and ladies with baskets, and nursemaids with children in their arms, all pushed up together willy-nilly on the wooden seats as if they were an illustration of the Day of Judgement when all souls will rise up in unison. I noticed that Daisy was paying special attention to the young nursemaid who was jigging a baby on her lap and talking to it in baby-talk. I could tell what she was thinking, and I was not wrong. 'Do you think we might meet Nettie while we are in London?' she whispered.

'I doubt it,' I said. 'For one thing, London, as you see, is very big. And for another, we have no idea of her address. It would be like looking for a needle in a haystack, and the odds against that are almost infinite. Now, come, my dear, this is meant to be a treat. You must put a brave face on and put your best foot forward and your shoulder to the wheel and, in spite of the contortions involved, simply *force* yourself to be happy this afternoon.'

And the dear thing laughed and said she was very sorry and would set about enjoying herself immediately. 'I am really so very excited. What is *Sylvie's Wish* about? And do you really know one of the actresses in it?'

'Yes, it's a young cousin of mine on my mother's side. It was she who kindly arranged for Nathan's to send me the fairy costumes. I will take you backstage to meet her after the play and we can all go to tea together.'

The Theatre Royal was full of children and mamas and nursemaids and not a few fathers and uncles. I had reserved a box, which almost seemed to hang out over the stage and commanded an equally good view of the auditorium. Daisy was quite overcome with all the cream and red, all the velvet and plush, all the gilt and the marble and the myriad sconces with gaslights flaring away in the half-dark. She loved our box, too, with its own set of velvet curtains tied back with swags, and its own two gilt chairs facing the proscenium. To complete her delight, I brought from my pocket a bag of chocolate limes which she viewed with relish: 'Oh, my favourites. How did you know?'

'I didn't,' I replied. 'But they are my favourites as well. That's why we are the best of friends.'

And with that, the curtain went up with a great swish, which sent a cold draught over our balcony as the bright stage was revealed in a wash of pink light. At the same time, the orchestra struck up a rousing tune and a dozen or so little girls in charming gypsy costumes began a scampering kind of dance in front of a canvas facsimile of a country glade. Daisy sat open-mouthed, clutching her gloves in her lap, and she never moved from that position for the rest of the first act, not even to partake of a chocolate lime. When the curtain went down, she turned to me, her eyes shining. 'Oh, Mr Jameson. How wonderful this is! Thank you so much for bringing me!'

'Not at all!' I replied. 'But will Sylvie run away to join the gypsies, do you think? They do seem to be such happy, carefree people – and her wicked Uncle Archibald is so very despicable!'

'*I* would run away if it were me,' she said.

'But then you are a very exceptional child,' I said, laughing, as I ushered her out for lemonade refreshment in the saloon.

As each act unfolded, Daisy was further entranced. She gasped at the changes of scenery: the *trompe l'oeil* painted backdrops, the bushes moving to reveal even deeper woodland scenes beyond, the translucent drapes hung with stars, and finally the working fountains at the Castle of Dreams. She cried aloud at the changes of light from bright day to sunset, and from red sunset to blue-green moonlight. And she was delighted even more with the character of Sylvie, escaping from the tedium of life with her uncle (which was all drudgery and punishment) to freedom with the dancing gypsies and the disguised Prince Florizel. Daisy even began to look a little like Sylvie, I thought, as her hair escaped its ribbons and fell in a higgledy-piggledy fashion all round her flushed and rosy face, and it was as much as I could do not to kiss her upon the spot. But, at the end, after we had clapped as hard as we knew how, she turned in her chair and gave me a kiss on the lips, entirely of her own accord. 'Thank you,' she said. 'All my friends will be so envious. It is much better than the seaside. Better than my picnic too. In fact, it is the best thing that ever happened to me.'

'To me t-too,' I murmured, my stammer coming back with a vengeance as the memory of her soft little lips on mine threw me into confusion. I hardly wanted to get up and walk through the crowds at that moment. I just wanted to sit next to Daisy with her hand in mine as if the rest of the world did not exist. But she reminded me that we were due to meet my cousin Ellen, and so I picked up my hat and we made our reluctant way out.

At tea in the Aldwych, Daisy could not stop talking about the play and the theatre and London itself, and how you could become an actress and how old you had to be to appear on the stage. I noticed people at the other tables looking across and smiling in an indulgent way as she prattled on, tucking into cucumber sandwiches, buttered scones and fruit cake. Ellen, who is by far my favourite cousin even when she is not impersonating young men in breeches, kept remarking on Daisy's looks. 'How very dainty you are,' she said, leaning back and surveying her. 'Quite the perfect ingénue. But you would do better with shorter hair, dear. There is such a lot of it and it hides your face. And it is quite the fashion now to have a fringe. You should ask your mama if you can be shorn more neatly next time she gets out the scissors.'

'Mama doesn't do my hair,' Daisy said, tears starting to her eyes. 'It used to be Nettie, but I've lost her and Hannah can't be bothered with it.'

'Well, someone can do it surely? I'd do it myself if I had some scissors. You've no idea what an improvement it would be.' She cocked her head to the side, imagining it, and I tried to imagine it too, thinking Ellen might indeed be right, and Daisy's perfect heart-shaped face would show more to advantage when not half-hidden. But, having planted this notion in Daisy's head, Ellen got up. 'I have to go, dear people, as we have another performance at half past seven. Far too late for the little ones, Uncle, but you know how things are. Needs must, and so forth. Thank you for the delicious tea, and goodbye, Daisy dear, and remember what I said.' And she gave me her usual kiss on the forehead, which I could not but reflect had nothing like the same effect on me as Daisy's.

By the time we got to Paddington, Daisy was beginning to get very tired, and once we were in the train, she fell asleep with her head against my arm and her straw hat falling sideways over her face. Her ringlets had almost completely fallen out and her ribbons had come undone. Had it not been for the gloves and neat little stockings and shoes, she might indeed have resembled a gypsy child. How I would have liked to capture her likeness at that moment, but it was beyond my pencil, even if I'd had one to hand: only a photograph would have done her justice. I sat, enjoying for the first time the pleasure of looking at her as long as I liked. For once, she was oblivious to my gaze; and there was no one else in the carriage to stare or misconstrue. I moved closer to her, dozing a little myself, allowing myself to imagine how it would be if we were lying in the same bed, perhaps, her little body nestling trustingly against mine, her arms round my neck, her cheek against my breast . . .

I do not know how long we lay there together, dozing, but, all at once, a train whistled past from the opposite direction, making the carriage shudder and shake, and it woke both of us with a start. She pulled away from me and took her warmth with her, so it was as if a cold breeze had struck suddenly all down my left side. 'Oh, I have had such a strange dream,' she said, sitting upright and setting her hat back on her head. 'There were kings and queens, and lovely gardens, and cakes and sandwiches all mixed together. And sheep and cows and dogs and cats all sitting in a railway carriage, and Dinah saying, "Tickets, please!"' She shivered a little. 'And I was in the middle of it all, but *very, very* small, and everybody was telling me what to do. Including the animals.'

'Animals are extremely opinionated,' I said. 'Especially cats – Cheshire cats in particular. And dormice, of course – when they are awake, which is only at teatime, in my experience. And oysters. Oysters are in a class of their own. Never have an argument with an oyster. If it disagrees with you, it can put you in bed for weeks – in an oyster bed, of course.'

She laughed and rubbed her eyes. 'You *are* funny.'

'Well, life is a comedy to those who think.'

'Don't we *all* think?' she said, trying to retie her ribbons.

'Not in quite the same way. Your papa, for example, would be inclined to view life as a tragedy.'

'Why?'

'That would be telling. Now, would you like to finish the chocolate limes before we get into Oxford?'

'May I?'

'By all means. They will fill you out as you are fearful of being so *very, very small*. In fact, if you go on eating them you will soon be twice your size, like a telescope opening up, or the old woman who shot up seventeen times as high as the moon.'

'One won't hurt, will it?'

'I think it is unarmed and of peaceful intent.'

And she took it and popped it in her moist little mouth.

*

I didn't want the day to end, but, like all good things, it did. Daniel came to meet the train, and lifted Daisy down from the carriage and gave her a kiss. 'Have you enjoyed yourself?' he asked.

She nodded sleepily into his chest.

'I hope you thanked Mr Jameson?' he prompted her.

'She has already been more than thankful,' I said. 'And she is the perfect child to be with. I have never had a better companion.'

'Is that so?' Daniel looked surprised. 'Well, I am glad. But it seems our family has increased its debt to you, John. Is there anything we can do in return?'

'Let me take Daisy out again. That is sufficient reward for an old bachelor such as myself.'

'There you go again, John! Anyone would think you were seventy, not thirty-five! Now, if you were to marry, you'd have children of your own to take out and about. Think how delightful that would be. And, my dear sir, marriage is to be recommended not only on account of the children. It is the –'

'I think you know my mind, Daniel,' I said, not wishing to hear another paean to the married state.

'You know me too, John, and I am not a man who gives up lightly. But now is not the time for discussions of matrimony. Daisy is almost asleep. I've a cab outside. May we give you a lift?'

'I'll walk,' I said. The afternoon's rain had gone and it was a fine night. And I had no mind to witness Daisy curled up contentedly in her father's arms for the mile and a half to my college. I felt almost angry at Daniel for taking the delights of paternity as so much his due – as if feeling Daisy's sweet head against his chest was so much a matter of course as to be of no account or value. Besides, I wanted solitude in order to think about the whole day. When I got back, I'd maybe write down an account of it. Maybe make it into a story I could tell her later.

I thought I might sleep a little first, though. I find that strange state between sleeping and waking can give me such vivid ideas. Sometimes I have to get up and strike a light and note it down straight away with half-frozen fingers. Sometimes, I don't even strike a light. I've invented a little machine that allows me to write in the dark if I wish. I don't want too much bright light on my imaginings. The darkness keeps the magic close.

10

I DON'T KNOW WHY, BUT I'M DISTINCTLY PERTURBED AT the thought of Jameson's involvement in this hair-cutting business. Daisy insists that she did the lion's share of the massacre herself and begged me with tears in her eyes not to hold him to account; but I wonder if she's telling me the whole story. I don't know why I find it so unsettling – the picture of Daisy sitting on his lap while he snips away. But this episode has set me wondering why he has taken such an interest in her: first the parasol, then the tea parties, and finally the visit to London. Daisy's a sweet enough child, but she is very young to be the companion of choice for such a clever man. And, as far as the photography is concerned, it's not as though she is particularly pretty – or at least I hadn't thought so up to now. But the new fringe is a decided improvement; one can see her face much more clearly.

I've said nothing of this to my wife, of course, as she is in such a state over the whole business, accusing herself of being too trusting and lenient with the child. Both of us are surprised to find Daisy so underhand and, what is more, so very unrepentant. Evelina blames the actress – Miss Garfield – for putting the idea into Daisy's mind, but I reminded her that many ideas may come into our minds, but we are not automatically obliged to act on them. 'That is where the exercise of Will is required, is it not?' I said. 'To combat the Devil's whispers. As I have to do myself *every day of my life.*'

Evelina ignored my clumsy attempt to confide in her, if indeed she even heard the words. 'It's high time Daisy was prepared for Confirmation,' she said. 'You've been very lax about it, Daniel, and I have allowed myself to become utterly distracted – first by Nettie's departure, then Mrs McQueen's arrival – and now all this business with Leonard Gardiner.'

She was right, of course; there'd been a great deal of upheaval in the family of late, and Evelina's delicate nerves had been put to the test in no uncertain manner. As far as Mr Gardiner was concerned, I regretted that I had not acted immediately it became apparent that Christiana admired him. But Evelina had insisted on dealing with the matter herself, fearful that my intervention ('your intimidating presence' was how she put it) would turn a small problem into a great one. However, in spite of her personal attendance at the archery lessons and her close observations of the young man, she had been unable to come to a decision on the matter. 'He is very good-looking, so it is hardly surprising that there is a certain amount of simpering when he stands close and adjusts the young ladies' arms and fingers,' she said, in a way that made me think that Evelina herself had not been immune to his charms. 'And he is particularly complimentary to Christiana. Yesterday he asked all the others to watch her draw the bow so they could copy her movements – and applauded in appreciation – which delighted her no end. All the same, I think that the attachment is more on Christiana's side. It will peter out, I'm sure, but you know how headstrong she is. I must continue to chaperone her. I cannot rely on Hannah; she is too young to judge what is seemly. And if I am with Christiana and Sarah, I cannot also be with Daisy. *You* must be the one to take her in hand, Daniel.'

I agreed, and indeed I'll do my best with Daisy's spiritual and moral education, which is by no means as neglected as my wife seems to think. But I can't help wondering what constitutes the greater impropriety – allowing a middle-aged clergyman, who is not your relative, to cut your hair in the privacy of his rooms, or permitting a young man to touch your fingers and pay you a compliment in the safe gaze of a dozen onlookers while he does what he is paid to do? I suppose Christiana's situation should be of more concern, as she is of an age to make a fool of herself, with all the consequences that might accrue. But I have to confess that I am more upset about Daisy. There is, I think, an intimacy between her and John that is somewhat unusual, and which I do not altogether understand.

And yet it now falls on me to set a punishment for the child. In spite of my misgivings, I think her transgression is very slight, and I truthfully do not mind whether her hair is short or long. But I must bow to Evelina's unexpected firmness in the matter. She is of the opinion that it would not do to let Daisy's act of defiance pass, for fear she might become more disobedient in future. 'And I suggest you stop all her outings with John Jameson immediately,' she said.

'Do you mean that as a penance for *her* or a punishment for *him*?' I asked. 'Such a course of action might lead him to assume that we are blaming him in some way, or don't trust him to care for her.'

'*Do* we trust him, though?' Evelina gave me such an odd look that I wasn't sure what to answer. But I attempted to make light of it, and laughed.

'You mean, do we trust him to keep his scissors safe from her prying hands?'

'No, Daniel. I mean do we trust him to keep her innocent? It was he who introduced her to – well, new ideas. And new people, too.'

'And should she not have the opportunity to experience new ideas and meet new people?' I said. 'I thought you approved of her extending her education. You have been saying for some time – even before Nettie left – that she needs to be more grown-up in her demeanour. You have brought her down from the nursery, given her her own room, and let her join us at supper – and you positively encouraged her to go to London with John. You seemed to trust him well enough then.'

'I thought it was a safe thing to allow her to meet Miss Garfield, as she was a relative of his and would therefore be a respectable young woman, but I feel he has deceived me.'

'Have you discovered that she is *not* respectable, then, Evelina?' That would indeed have put the whole outing in a different light.

She shrugged. 'I can't say exactly. But the way Daisy talked about her was – well, it sounded as though some of her language was not refined. And she certainly gave Daisy the notion that she could do what she liked without reference to her parents. Do you realize, Daniel, that she would have cut Daisy's hair herself if she'd had the scissors to hand?' She looked at me as if she had delivered the *coup de grace*.

But I wouldn't have it. 'I hardly think Miss Garfield meant to encourage disobedience. It's just that theatre people say what they think rather more frankly than we do. She thought Daisy would look better with short hair, and she made a joke about cutting it. I don't think she was attempting to undermine our authority.'

'All the same, I'm surprised at Mr Jameson taking her behind the scenes, eating in public with an actress, letting her be exposed to questionable remarks. She's always been such an innocent child, so sheltered from the ways of the world; I should never have exposed her to the fleshpots of London.'

I looked at Evelina in amazement. The Leonard Gardiner business must have shaken her more than I imagined. Never since our first meeting had she been obsessed with such narrow proprieties. 'Fleshpots? Surely, my love, you're not talking of the Theatre Royal and the jolly afternoon entertainments it puts on for children?' I asked. 'Even the best families patronize the performances, and Daisy adored it in the whole-hearted, childish way she was meant to. And just because of a few teacakes in the Strand and a passing remark from an actress, you are now convinced that she will never obey us again.'

'You have not seen the way she talks, Daniel. She is completely unrepentant about her hair. I have never seen her like this.'

For my part, I am rather heartened at Daisy's show of spirit. 'Well, what's done is done,' I say. 'The hair cannot be put back. And truly there is no harm in her having it short. In fact, I think it suits her.'

'You take her part against me, Daniel? You add to my distress?' Evelina put her hand on her heart in the way that has become more common with her lately. As if my behaviour pains her. As if she suspects the emptiness in my soul.

'I simply try to be practical, my love. You have to admit Daisy's hair has always been exceedingly untidy, and it's been far worse since Nettie went. And she was never told *directly* that she couldn't cut it, so we mustn't be unduly harsh.' I was determined to be fair with my daughter – not like God with His Eternal Damnation.

She sighed. 'So, what do you suggest?'

'I'll find a suitable text for her to write out. I suggest Ephesians 6:1–3. And I'll preach a sermon on the topic next Sunday. No one else in the congregation will know what I am referring to. But Daisy will; and if I am any judge of her character, she will come to beg forgiveness.'

'And John Jameson? Do we receive him as before?'

'Why ever not?' I gave her a sharp look. Even though she had given voice to something of my own uneasiness regarding John, her uncompromising attitude made me rush to his defence. I told myself that my discomfort about John's friendship with Daisy probably stemmed from the fact that she seemed to enjoy his company so much more than mine. And that seemed but a weak premise on which to deprive myself of his company, let alone deprive Daisy of it. So I told Evelina that I saw no reason to stop him coming to the house. 'To be honest, it seems his only crime was to make good what Daisy had already ruined. If she had cut her hair in her own bedroom, would you have banished Hannah, or Mrs McQueen – or even myself – because we were under the same roof? I think John cannot – and should not – be blamed for Daisy's action.'

'You are very logical. But I think your fondness for him affects your judgement. John Jameson is a clever man – but you must acknowledge that there are other things besides cleverness when it comes to bringing up children. You should not put your friendship above your child's good.'

I felt a little angry that she should seek to put me in the wrong in this way, and felt obliged to praise John more than I intended. 'My friendship with John and Daisy's interests as my daughter are not mutually exclusive, Evelina. In fact, they very much go together. John teaches her all sorts of things. I am astonished at the encyclopaedic information she has acquired since spending time with him – natural science, philosophy, poetry, all sorts. He is as good as a private tutor. And I needn't remind you how much we are in his debt. Think about Benjy – our only son, as near to death on that day as he (with God's grace) will ever come! I can hardly contemplate what would have happened without John's quick action. Just think of that, Evelina, when you seek to blame the man for negligence!'

She put her hands to her ears as if to stop out my words. 'I know! Oh, how I know it! That deed of his debars him from any criticism. I am grateful to him, I own it, and he is in my prayers every night as I thank God for his action – but he has become a sacred idol where you are concerned, Daniel! I sometimes think he is more important to you than I am!'

I saw then in her anger, the traces of her old passion, and – was it possible? – jealousy. I took her in my arms and kissed her fervently. 'No one comes before you in my heart, Evelina. Certainly not John. He is my friend and I admire him, but I will cast him off entirely if it will make you happy.'

She lay against my breast and seemed mollified. 'He is harmless enough, I suppose. And we do owe him so much – so very, very much. I am an ungrateful wretch to have forgotten it – ungrateful, and unkind. God forgive me! Will you forgive me too, Daniel?' And she lifted up her face and returned my kisses in the way that she used to do.

And now, bright and early on this Monday morning, Daisy is standing on the proverbial carpet, awaiting my judgement. God knows how many people have stood there in front of my desk and trembled – children, servants, even my wife at times. I think of poor Nettie and how desperately she pleaded for me not to send her away: 'I know I did wrong, though I never meant to, just my back turned for two seconds, but the little ones is innocent and shouldn't suffer for it! Lower my wages, Mr Baxter – stop them, if you like, I'll manage – but as God is good, let me stay!' But I was hard-hearted. The thought of my only son slipping down into the murky depths – frightened and alone, and breathing gulps of weedy water – was too strong with me. I couldn't forgive her, couldn't trust her. I was angry with myself, too, although I didn't admit it and, in my double-dealing way, I blamed Nettie for my own failings. I regret my harshness now. I cannot think Benjy is better served by Mrs McQueen and her unflinching system than he was by Nettie's loving hands. And, since Nettie has gone, Daisy has been a child adrift. No wonder she has taken so well to John, with his jokes and stories. He has been more of a father to her than I have.

She stands there, hands clasped and resting against her apron, feet neatly together in her little pumps, her shorn head rising from her neck like the delicate flower she was named for. She looks up and I can see how grey her eyes are, how clear and fine her skin. Her expression is so like Evelina's when she was young – so innocent, pure and limpid – that it shocks me with its force. And in this moment, I realize that I've never loved Daisy as I ought. I've always shown preference for my tall and graceful girls and, more lately, my son. Daisy has always been the least of my concerns. She's hidden herself modestly from my view, under her cloud of hair: an unremarkable presence, an easy, biddable, self-effacing soul. But now, as I gaze at her, it comes to me that she – honest, sincere, steadfast Daisy – might be the salvation I have been longing for. She will be my second angel, my new Evelina, the one to lead me up the mountain, out of my confusion and darkness, into the bright light of God's presence. I cannot wait to embrace her in the Lord, to know that Perfect Love once again.

But I cannot embrace her, not today. Today I am the stern voice of retribution. 'You know why you are here?' I say.

'Yes, Papa.' Her head is down.

'And that is because . . .?' I try to encourage her gently.

'I cut off my hair although I knew Mama wouldn't like it.' Her voice is just a murmur.

'And are you sorry now?'

She pauses. 'No, Papa.' Her voice is so low I can hardly hear it. But all the same, I am startled. I had expected at least the outward signs of repentance, even if her heart remained stubborn. But I see that Daisy is honest as well as brave. '*No?* What do you mean by that?'

'I'm very sorry to have upset you and Mama, and to have got Mr Jameson into trouble. But I'm not sorry to have cut my hair. It is so very nice short!'

'Yes, I think so, too, my dear. You look so very, very pretty.' I can't help the words, and I can't help the smile as I say them.

She gives me a surprised look. 'Oh, Papa – do you really think so? Then may I keep it like this?' There's such joy in her face that I want to pick her up and cover her with kisses and ask her forgiveness for all the times I have been harsh and distant.

But I frown instead, pretend to consider. 'I will speak to your mother about it. But, first, we have to consider your act of disobedience. That is a serious matter.'

'Yes, Papa.' She is downcast again.

'Your mother is most upset. She didn't expect you to be underhand. Neither of us did. It is not how we have brought you up. Haven't we always encouraged you to behave as if God were looking over your shoulder every minute?'

She begins to cry. 'I'm so sorry, Papa! I wanted short hair so very much, and when I saw the scissors I just did it! I didn't think about God at all! Although I did think a little bit about Mama.'

'And did you think she would be upset?'

'Yes. But I thought it would be worth anything not to have my hair about my face all the time.'

'Worth *anything*? So you expected punishment?'

'Oh, yes, Papa.'

Of course she did. We are all indoctrinated into the need for punishment. Yet it is Love that matters, Love that will redeem us, Love that is like the stream of living water, pure and clear; that washes us clean of our sins.

Daisy lifts her eyes and seems to be trying to read my expression. 'You will still allow Mr Jameson to take me out, though, won't you, Papa? He says he will be miserable if not, and he has been so nice to me and it wasn't his fault that I did it and I don't want him to be sad.'

Her words nearly break my heart, and I wish that I were the one whom she so compassionately desires not to be sad.

But I am doomed to continue with my required chastisement. 'You see how your foolish action has such ramifications? Your deceit has involved others – others who love and care for you. I hope I shall never have cause to speak to you like this again.' I bend towards her, allow my voice to soften a little. 'Do you give me your word?'

'Yes, Papa. I will try my best not to disappoint you. Or Mama.'

'I'm sure you will. You are a good child, Daisy. But as penance, will you recite this for me?' I hand her my New Testament and point to the text. I see to my surprise that my finger is shaking.

She reads it straight off in her high, clear voice: '*Children obey your parents in the Lord. For this is right. Honour thy father and thy mother that it may be well with thee and thou mayest live long upon the earth.*'

'Obey and honour, Daisy. And in order that you will take this verse to heart, you must write it out one hundred times. I wish to see it after lunch today. I expect every word to be written neatly and no blots.'

'Yes, Papa. I will do it immediately.'

'And every day I will give you another text and you will write that out in the same way and bring it to me. And we will do this until I am sure that you understand and fully repent.'

'Yes, Papa. Thank you, Papa. Dear, lovely Papa!' And she dips a quick curtsey and is gone. And I feel as much a hypocrite and traitor as Judas Iscariot. What is her peccadillo compared with my great and yawning sin? She is a child and has done a childish thing. But I have betrayed my own soul.

I feel a trifle awkward when John calls this afternoon. I need to speak to him candidly, but Daisy is in the study with me. I've been looking at the neatly written punishment task which she has carried out so punctiliously. She jumps up and goes to John when he comes in and, taking his hand, announces very earnestly that he needn't worry, that it's all right and she can still go for walks with him and have tea with him as well. 'Dear Papa has given me a penance and I've been very busy at it, so we still have the afternoon to go out.'

'So I see.' He takes one of the pages that she proffers him. '*Children, obey your parents.* I hope you have taken the lesson to heart.'

'Oh, yes, Mr Jameson!' She gives him rather a special smile and John smiles back in a way that transforms his plain features. And once more I have to admit feeling somewhat excluded from this closeness of theirs.

'Now, I don't want you to think we blame you in any way, John,' I say, leading him to the window and speaking in a low voice. 'But Evelina is somewhat upset that Daisy was disobedient whilst in your care. She feels you are perhaps a little too indulgent with her. You are not used to children, after all, and perhaps don't realize how contrary and wilful they can be.'

He turns. 'How many times must I tell you, Daniel – I was brought up with seven younger sisters! I am very used to all kinds of naughtiness.'

'But there is a difference between the responsibility of an older brother and the responsibility of a parent. When you were at home, your mother was always at hand, was she not? Always there to refer to and ready to be of help?'

'I was perfectly able to manage the girls on my own,' he says, somewhat stiffly. 'And, were my parents still alive, they would have borne witness to this. But I would certainly not wish to impose myself where I was not trusted. If Mrs Baxter thinks –'

'It's not that,' I say hastily. 'Please don't misunderstand. I simply want to ensure you are not compromised.'

'C-Compromised? Whatever do you mean?'

'I choose my words badly. I mean that Daisy's misbehaviour must not reflect on you in any way, tarnish your own high reputation.'

'I assure you that n-nothing Daisy and I have done together would tarnish my reputation. But if her parents have any d-doubts in the matter, I would rather end our acquaintance now.' He picks up his hat as if to depart. His face is pink.

I find myself apologizing and, in my agitation, I concede more than I'd intended. I'd meant to suggest as delicately as I could that the outings with Daisy might be curtailed – but I found myself instead insisting they went on not just as before, but more frequently, so anxious was I to avoid any hint of a slur. 'It was only for your sake that I spoke at all, John. You're not the most worldly of men. I simply sought to protect you.'

'Innocence is its own protection,' he says. 'The Engines of Evil recoil from it as from a rushing, mighty wind.'

'Well, we are not talking of evil,' I say, laughing. 'Just one small child, who has misbehaved herself. Let the matter drop, I implore.'

'You have confidence in me?'

'Of course, dear fellow. Of course.'

'Very well.' He puts down his hat. 'We will say no more about it.'

I become aware that Daisy has heard the end of our conversation and that tears are streaming down her cheeks. 'I am very, very sorry, Mr Jameson,' she sobs, turning her beautiful little head towards him. 'I never thought about the Eye of Society even though you had told me about it. I was very wilful and wicked and don't deserve to have such a nice friend.'

'What do you know about the Eye of Society, Daisy?' I say, surprised by her turn of phrase.

'Mr Jameson said –'

John interrupts her. 'I merely remarked to Daisy that innocent actions are sometimes misunderstood by the Mrs Grundys of this world. Which is why I wouldn't tamper with her hair in the first place.' He casts her a sideways glance. 'Although I would have made a far, far better job of it than she did with Benson's All-Purpose Scissors and a pickaxe.'

'I didn't use a pickaxe!' says Daisy, her eyes wide.

'No? Well, if you had axed, I'd have picked something better for you.'

At which, she dissolves into laughter and he smiles at her with his eyes, while keeping his mouth in a very straight and sober line. 'And now, if we are to go a-promenading in the Meadow, I suggest you put on your hat and gloves so we can make a start. You may care to bring your parasol too. The sun is very hot today.'

'I shall be no time at all,' she says, bolting through the door and nearly running into Hannah, who is about to knock.

Hannah curtseys. 'Mrs Baxter says she hopes you will excuse her, Mr Jameson, but she has some things to attend to with Miss Christiana and Miss Sarah.'

'Naturally. She need have no concerns on that score. I am anxious that my visits p-put no one to any trouble.' He looks down as he always does when Hannah is in the room.

As the maid stands there at the open door, I hear the faint wailing of the baby in the distance. And then Mrs McQueen's attempts to hush him, *There! There! There!* Followed by more crying.

'Still inconsolable, I see,' observes Jameson.

I'm nettled, and can't keep the sarcasm out of my voice. 'Perhaps *you* will be able to soothe him, Jameson. After all, you have such a *wealth* of experience with children.'

'I generally prefer the ones who can talk,' he says. 'They are so very much more interesting. But if you wish me to distract the child, I'm willing to try. After all, a cat may look at a king.'

'Mrs Mac won't thank you for interfering,' says Hannah impudently, but I glare at her and she drops her eyes and says, 'Beg pardon for speaking out of turn.'

John is game to try his hand, though, and so we mount the stairs up to the nursery. The sobs and cries become louder, and Mrs McQueen's injunctions for Benjamin to 'be a good boy' also increase in volume.

'Dear, dear,' says John, as we go up the final winding flight. 'What a pair of lungs! How do you manage to sleep at night?'

'Sometimes we don't,' I say. 'We are often tired and frazzled these days. That's why we sometimes say things we don't mean to our very best friends.'

'Oh, we should all say what we mean. Even though we may not always mean what we say.' He laughs.

I open the door. 'Mrs McQueen,' I say. 'I have brought Mr Jameson to entertain Benjamin.'

I haven't been up to the nursery since the night of the accident, and I'm shocked at the change in it. It had always seemed to me such a cosy place, with its big brass fender winking in the firelight, and its little table always laid with a pretty flowered cloth and cheerful cups and bowls. I remember Evelina and I watching here all night when Sarah had influenza, and praying over her when I thought she was lost to us. I remember Nettie's quiet, bustling presence through the small hours, her calm voice, her anticipation of our every need, the way she kept the kettle singing on the hob, soaking cloths in hot water and then cold, lifting the child's head to soothe her brow and, once the fever had broken, tempting her with chicken broth. The room has the same furnishings, the same beds and chairs and crockery, but somehow it has lost its heart. It reminds me more of a barracks – beds neatly made, floor neatly swept, everything orderly, but nothing to raise the spirits.

Mrs McQueen rises as we come in. She has been sitting at the side of the cot where Benjamin lies in a bundle of tangled sheets, looking hot and sweaty. 'Reverend Baxter! I'm sorry if you've been disturbed. I've been trying my best to stop his noise. But I think he may have a bit of a fever.'

I'm alarmed. 'Fever? Why wasn't I told of this?'

'It's only just come on, sir, and, even now, I'm not sure if it isn't just his temper. He gets himself in a state sometimes and you just have to let him cry it out. I didn't want to worry Mrs Baxter for no reason. I like to get on with things myself, and she – Mrs Baxter, that is – trusts me to do so. My methods have been pretty good up to now and no one has ever found fault with me so far. The Lindemanns and the Crawleys were quite –'

'Enough!' I know the woman came with excellent references, but now is not the time for self-justification. I go to the cot. Benjamin casts weary eyes at me. He isn't crying any longer; he looks as if he has lost hope. I stroke his cheek. It is hot and damp. His hair sticks to his scalp and he seems to have tiny white pimples all over his skin. 'I think we should call Dr Lawrence,' I say.

'You must do what you think right, of course,' she says, making it clear that she is not of that opinion.

'Indeed, I will do exactly that, Mrs McQueen,' I say, my anger rising. 'This is my house and you are my servant and Benjamin is my son.' I turn to Hannah, who has followed us up the stairs, ready no doubt to witness any discomfiture on the part of Mrs Mac. 'Please run to Dr Lawrence immediately,' I say, and she is off like a shot, picking up her skirts almost to the knee as she gallops down the stairs, showing a flash of her black-stockinged calf and the undersides of her white petticoat.

As she goes, I spy Daisy poking her head around the corner of the landing below. She has on her straw hat and cotton gloves. Her face is full of alarm. 'What's the matter, Papa? Is Benjy ill?'

'I hope not. He may just be hot and bothered. It's very warm today. But I don't wish to take the slightest risk.'

She runs up the stairs. 'Oh, let me see him!'

'I think there's quite enough people milling about in this room now,' says Mrs McQueen. 'I'd be obliged if Daisy stays downstairs, if it's not too much to ask.'

But Daisy is already in the room and has Benjamin in her arms, his hot cheek against her pale one. Benjamin seems to rally at the sight of her and gives a little smile. 'There!' she says. 'He likes to see me. He misses me. Don't you, dear?' She looks up at me, her hat askew. 'I don't have to leave him, do I?'

'Of course not,' I say. 'It seems you do him good. You'd do anybody good.'

'If it's anything catching, I won't be held responsible,' says Mrs McQueen. 'That's the first law of nursery life; isolate any child that's ill or you'll have sickness right through the house.'

'Considering that until a few moments ago you didn't even feel it necessary to inform Mrs Baxter or myself, I think you are being over-particular,' I say. 'Daisy may stay if she wishes. I will take the responsibility.'

'Oh, thank you, Papa!' And she lifts Benjamin's face to hers and kisses him over and over. He grasps a strand of her fringe and seems to be considering what it is that is different about his sister's looks today.

John has been very quiet during all the fuss. 'I think I had better go,' he says. 'Clearly my outing with Daisy is forfeit for today and I doubt I could do better than she has done in calming Benjamin. I hope it is nothing serious, Daniel. I myself have a horror of fever and am no good about the sickbed.'

I could see that he was anxious to depart. 'Yes, John, please feel free to go.'

'Please send word if there is any development. I will come myself tomorrow to see if there is anything I can do. Take care of your brother, Daisy!' And he is gone.

'Is that the gentleman as saved him from drowning?' asks Mrs McQueen.

'Yes,' I reply. 'The very same.'

'They say that the person you save will do you a bad turn later on in life.'

'You mean Benjy will do a bad turn to Mr Jameson?' asks Daisy in horror.

I am furious with the woman. 'I believe that is an old seaman's tale, Mrs McQueen, and I don't countenance such superstition in this house. Benjamin will do nothing bad to Mr Jameson, either now or later.'

Daisy is aghast. 'But I opened my parasol in the house, Papa – and look what happened that day!'

'What happened that day was entirely due to Nettie's lack of supervision.' My heart recoils to think that the child may have been blaming herself all this time. 'And it was God's grace that John Jameson was among us that day, and his quick action was directed from Above.'

Daisy doesn't look at me as she busies herself diverting her brother with the ribbons on her hat, but says, 'Why was it Nettie's fault that Benjy fell in, but God's grace that he was saved?'

I hesitate.

'Fie, child!' Mrs McQueen interposes. 'You have to go by what's in the Bible. You, of all children, should know that.'

I ignore her, and address Daisy. 'We know it was God's grace because Benjamin being saved was a good thing, and all good things come from God.'

'But why did God allow him to fall in the first place?' She still doesn't look at me.

Why indeed? Why is there death and accident and sickness and misery and unbelief? If God loves us, why do we not all dwell perpetually in the Garden of Eden in perfect bliss and naked innocence? Why did God let ugly Sin slip in and damn us for ever? If God is both omnipotent and good, we can only hope there is a larger purpose in His permitting the suffering we see around us; that the temptations and deprivations of this life are there to strengthen us and make us fitter for Heaven. I do not believe it, though. Like Benjamin, I am slipping into dark water, but in my case, there is no one to haul me up. I want to cry out in anguish, but I can't: Daisy is waiting for her answer. I call up the familiar words. 'We fall because of our own actions, my dear, the sin that is born in us and stalks us day and night throughout our lives. But we are saved by the love of Christ.'

'Is everyone saved?' She gives me the most transparent of looks and I can hardly bear to hold her gaze.

'Everyone who has faith,' I say.

She nods as if she is satisfied and, in her satisfaction, I gain a kind of peace. The child is good for me. She takes me back to a better time. If I take her spiritual education in hand, she may indeed save my soul.

11

John Jameson

Every time I see Daisy, I feel twenty years younger and twenty-five years happier. She has only to walk towards me and I am back in the golden time of my own childhood; a time when the dull concerns and expectations of the adult world did not impinge; when choices were simple, when learning was easy and faith ran through my body as easily as my own blood. Of course, it is the perverse way of things that none of us appreciates our happiness until it is taken away. Had I known then what I know now, and had I had it in my power to stop the clock once I had arrived at the age of fourteen, I would have done so without a second thought. Childhood, as I had experienced it up to that time, was complete enchantment. Manhood, as it came rushing upon me, seemed a dreadful, tragic joke.

I'd been a good-looking boy – indeed I'd often been mistaken for a girl; but as soon as I had entered the adolescent state, I'd endured a sad falling-off in my good looks. Overnight, it seemed, the top of my head set sail for the ceiling and my neck had to stretch up after it. My feet suddenly seemed a long way down and my hands became awkward appendages that seemed to have lost connection with my arms, so that the simplest of tasks (like putting on a waistcoat or buttoning my boots) made me into a bumbling idiot. My hair lost its softness and became lank and straggling, and my voice was not to be relied upon, which (added to the stammer that already afflicted me) made me frequently prefer not to speak at all. I could hardly believe what was happening; I felt as though I were no longer myself. 'You are just growing, dear,' said my mother when I complained of the changes. 'You'll be a fine young man in no time.' But I did not feel fine. I felt clumsy and ugly and ridiculous. If that was what growing up was all about, I wanted none of it.

And then, one day, to my absolute horror, I found that I had hair in places where no hair had been before. I cannot say what dread and shame I suffered at this discovery. I felt that I had become a kind of Caliban – half-man, half-beast – and wondered what I had done to be so afflicted. I fell to my prayers with increased fervour, asking forgiveness day and night. But my body continued to change in ever more disgusting ways – and I feared that I might be eternally cast out from God's love. And then, as if all these torments were not sufficient, I became aware, for the first time in my life, of my own odour. However rigorously I washed myself, it was never enough, and I was forced to change my small complement of shirts as often as three times a week. Washday could never come quick enough and, in my eagerness to don fresh linen, I was often guilty of wearing it unaired, fearful that otherwise all might sense the smell of growing boy. I began to avoid anything that might bring me in contact with those I did not know, withdrawing from simple handshakes and eschewing physical closeness in any form, even shrinking a little from the embraces of my parents. Parish tea parties were anathema, particularly if I were given a seat near the fire; and even in church I hesitated to raise my eyes in case they encountered someone to whom I should be obliged to speak later. Old ladies, I found, were the very devil to avoid, and every Sunday, at Morning Service, I spent much of the time I should have been attending to my prayers working out ways to exit the congregation before they had time to waylay me.

At that time, my father was my sole teacher, and we had thoroughly enjoyed the many hours we spent together with our books, breaking off only if he needed to attend to his parish duties or reprimand the little ones if they were careering about too loudly in the flagstoned passage outside. And once we had completed our set tasks in algebra and geometry and translated the appropriate pages of Latin and Greek, he simply followed his preference as to what we would study next. He was not by instinct a sedentary man – and by no means a sedentary teacher – and almost every day we set forth on a voyage of exploration in the fields and lanes of the parish, examining flowers in the hedgerows, bending to observe fish in the streams, finding birds' nests, capturing butterflies and moths, sketching the shapes of clouds, and generally watching the unending panorama of the seasons. He particularly liked reciting passages from the *Christian Year* and relating it to what we could see from our own vantage-points on high ground. 'All this, John!' he would say, turning in a great circle with his stick upraised. 'All this shows us the might and power of the Creator! Does your heart not leap up when you behold such grandeur?'

'Yes, Father,' I would say. I often tried to reproduce, with my pencil and watercolours, the clouds and the hills, and the distant river flowing down to the sea; but when it came to finding the words to describe the scene, my mind would instantly come up with some irreverent line about tea trays in the sky, or turtles singing at twilight. I never spoke the lines aloud, of course. It was not that my father was a solemn man – indeed he often made play with words, saying every Sunday lunchtime, 'Mary-Ann, where's the boast reef?' or 'Why have custard when you can have mustard?' and he'd always written comic sentences in the margins of my work to lighten the task in hand – but God's creation was not a subject to be jested about.

But about a month before my fourteenth birthday, when we were about to set out on one of our expeditions, my father laid his hand on my shoulder (which was already almost of a height with his own) and said that I was so far outstripping him in my skill in philosophy and mathematics that I needed a better tutor than he. 'You are also too much among women,' he said. 'You need to experience the rougher habits of young men if you are to succeed in life. You have had a gentle upbringing in this house – and one that I approve of. But the generality of men in this world will come to judge you far harder than I, and certainly more than your sisters or your mother do.'

He thought I was in danger of becoming a milksop whereas I was afraid of the opposite; that the turmoil of passions within me might break out at any time. My peaceful child-body was no more. In its place, a loathsome, clammy, hirsute creature, which began to intrude itself on me at the very time I hated it most. But I would not submit to it. I prayed even harder, and spent even longer at my books, where I found the rigours of mathematics helped free my mind from vile alternatives. In between times I helped my mother and sisters as always, reading with them, making up spelling games, checking their arithmetic, and devising poems and puzzles that amused us for hours. I invented a folding pin-holder for Mary and a little bird-feeder for Ruth's canary. I never passed a moment in idleness, and exhausted my body by giving endless piggy-back rides along the passageway to the kitchen, playing numerous games of skittles in the dining room with the rug rolled back, turning skipping ropes on the grass for what seemed like an eternity, and hopping in the hopscotch chalked out in the kitchen yard (where I, with my long legs, was always pronounced the victor). As ever, I was looked to as the arbiter in my sisters' petty disagreements, and was required to compensate the injured parties with kisses and sweetmeats. In those two months before I was sent away, anticipating the loss of my dearest company, I felt most strongly the true wonder of being a brother – and so beloved a brother, too. When I looked at my sisters playing so trustingly with each other and approaching me with such sweet confidence, putting their chubby arms around me or lifting their faces to be kissed, I could not imagine how any gross and putrid thoughts could ever cross their innocent minds. Their company was my only consolation, and the sole means by which my inner demons could be subdued.

But inevitably the day came when my father told me to prepare my books and belongings, as my place at boarding school had been secured. Milburn House was at the other end of the county and had a good reputation for educating the sons of clergymen, but I was in dread of what awaited me. I knew remarkably little of other boys. I had always been somewhat shunned as a playfellow by the sons of the parish in spite of our being obliged to sit together in the choir every Sunday and say our catechism in unison once a week. They were all robust, red-faced Cheshire boys who seemed to find it hard to stay still for more than five minutes, and had funds of catapults, stones and horse chestnuts in their pockets which they brought out to admire at low points during the service and always covered up when they saw me look – fearful, no doubt, that I would tell tales. My only triumph with them had been when I played the part of St George in a Christmas mummer play and added comic dialogue of my own to make it more amusing. For a few brief days I was popular. But I never pursued my advantage or sought to ingratiate myself. I did not need friendship outside the family. I had all the companionship I wanted within it.

So it was with a heavy heart that I accompanied my father on the stagecoach to Chester, whence we were to travel on to Milburn. When I saw the diminishing sight of my mother and sisters as they waved us off at the parsonage gate, I wished that

I could weep half as openly as they; but I knew Father would see it as confirming my milksop ways, so I simply stared out of the window feeling like the prince in the fairy tale who had iron bands placed about his heart.

In Chester we were met at the Feathers by a servant in a pony and trap, and within another half-hour we had arrived at our destination: a pleasant brick house with very tall and elaborate chimneys. I remember thinking that they were not the kind of chimneys you would want to get stuck in if you were a chimney sweep – or anyone else for that matter. The headmaster, Dr Lloyd, to whom I was introduced in a small drawing room with an exceedingly large fire, reminded me of a stork, and throughout our conversation I half expected him to fly up the flue and make a nest at the top. He was kindly enough as he explained the rules, but everything he said had to do with 'boys' and 'masters' and I felt I could never be happy in a place with so little female company.

'Our aim,' he said, stooping low and seeming to flap his wings at me, 'is to develop the mind and to turn out Christian gentlemen. However you may shine in your studies, you will be judged above all by the quality of your character. I hope, John Jameson, that you will not be found wanting in that respect, and that you will be a credit to your family.'

'I will,' I said. Then, seeing my father take up his hat in preparation for departure, a terrible sense of desolation gripped me and, in spite of my fourteen years and my sixty-eight inches of height, I allowed some tears to drop down my cheeks.

My father looked embarrassed, and Dr Lloyd somewhat taken aback. 'Dear dear,' he said. 'I think a little firmness is called for now. A little manliness, too. This won't do at all. No, no, not at all. I suggest you stop this now before the other boys see you or you will have no reputation with them.'

I was used to making efforts of will, and I made a supreme effort then, breathing slowly and drawing myself up to my full height. 'I'm sorry, sir. I'm sorry, Father. I'll be strong from now on, I p-promise.'

My father came towards me. 'Let me be proud of you, John. Let me have good reports of you in every way. Now, God bless you and keep you.' And he pressed two half-crowns into my hand and was gone. I watched through the old-fashioned window as the pony and trap disappeared out of the gateposts, and Dr Lloyd, myself and the roaring fire were all that was left of my world.

Dr Lloyd then took me quickly up the stairs and introduced me to a boy of about the same age, somewhat shorter and plumper, whom he said was to be my 'pair'. He was called Frank Haywood and seemed of a very amiable disposition. He, too, was a clergyman's son, but had been at the school for two years already and had a fund of good advice as to the various 'dodges' it was necessary to employ in dealings with boys and masters alike. 'If you are the proud possessor of a florin or a half-crown, I'd advise you to keep quiet about it,' he said, opening the small bedside cupboard into which all my clothes were to go. 'We're all pretty skint at this time in the term and any new boy turning up is sure to attract attention as an easy source of revenue.'

I'd never heard the word 'skint', although I guessed what it meant. It was the first of many lessons I learned that day, not just about the prevalence of slang in the society of schoolboys, but also about the importance of keeping things to myself and not presuming on the good nature of others. 'I don't mind sharing what I've g-got,' I said, conscious of my stammer and fearing he would mock me for it.

'Well, Jameson, old fellow,' he said, putting his arm on mine. 'You may be ten feet tall, but you're pretty green. It's a good thing I'm here to look after you. You almost had Munnings as your study pair, but he's a complete toad, and the moment I saw you get out of the pony-trap I gave him tuppence to swap with me.'

'That's very g-good of you,' I said.

'Not at all,' he said airily. 'Although if you could see your way to giving me back the tuppence in due course, I'd be very obliged. I'm down to my last halfpenny.' And he looked at me with a very comical face, and we both laughed.

'Now for the clincher. Do you like riddles, Jameson?' he said, sitting on my bed and taking a piece of paper from his pocket.

'Oh, indeed,' I said. Riddles were a favourite family pastime and I warmed to the idea of starting out in my new friendship by solving this one.

'This is an easy one. Why is a raven like a writing desk?' he asked.

Why indeed? I cudgelled my brains for a good five minutes, but could not think of an amusing point of comparison. 'I g-give up,' I said at last, annoyed with myself for this failure.

He chortled, threw himself back on the counterpane and said I was quite right – as I'd have to be 'raven mad' to know the answer. I laughed too, knowing at a stroke that I had found a soulmate, and that my schooldays might not be as bad as I had feared.

I never ceased to long for home, but my experiences at the school were salutary in several ways. The main benefit, of course, was the advanced nature of the studies. There were two young masters newly come down from Oxford, who introduced me to mathematical concepts that my poor father had no knowledge of. It was exciting to discover the principles behind Euclid's geometry, rather than merely learning them by rote, and I could not wait to be back at my desk each day, fathoming out new problems and solutions. Most of my classmates seemed content to go about matters in the old way, but I was fired with the joy of discovery and I was soon in high favour with my masters for going beyond the tasks they set me. It was comforting to hear my teachers speaking so well of me and knowing that good reports were going back to my father and mother.

I'd also been mightily relieved to discover, on meeting the other boys, that they were by no means the beauteous young gods of my anticipation. On the contrary, they were in general rumpled, soiled and greasy individuals who seemed so happy in this state of dirty moistness that they hardly bothered to change their linen, and seemed to comb their hair only once a day before morning prayers when Dr Lloyd made his inspection. I was a paragon of freshness by comparison, and I began to entertain a higher opinion of myself than before.

I also learned, rather more slowly, that in addition to the slovenly nature of their outward appearance, there was much that was low in the inner thoughts of boys, and much that was impure in their conduct. What surprised me most was how little they attempted to hide it. I was horrified to find drawings of unclothed females, crudely labelled, circulating from hand to hand in the dormitories, and even more horrified when the act of procreation was similarly travestied. I averted my eyes when these images passed near my sphere of vision, wondering how the sons of clergymen could have so little regard for the holiness of God's image in human form. As a result I gained the reputation of a prude, and was mocked accordingly. But, if it prevented me having to look at such sickening pictures, I was happy to be so mocked. Munnings, thinking perhaps that I would bring the matter to Dr Lloyd's attention, held his penknife hard against my wrist and made me swear never to divulge what I had seen. 'I do not even wish to think about it,' I replied. 'Such things are loathsome to me, as they should be to you.' But a thing once seen remains in the mind, and sometimes I hated myself for allowing my thoughts to dwell for the briefest moment on what I had glimpsed, and experiencing the old, tormented feelings such glimpses had aroused. I could not imagine how love – pure, innocent, warm and holy love – could descend to such carnal couplings. And yet it had to be so. My father and mother had conceived eight children. We had not arrived on the wings of the wind.

But the best thing about Milburn was undoubtedly Frank Haywood. He was less prone to grossness than the others, and laughter bubbled up in him at every opportunity. He encouraged the lighter side of my nature and we spent all our recreation time making up silly rhymes and even sillier jokes. Naturally our schoolmasters were the butt of most of our juvenilia and each one was given the name of a bird or animal – Dr Lloyd being the stork as I had first imagined him, Mr Molloy (who had long and crooked teeth) a crocodile, Mr Walsh (with wild and wobbling eyes) a lobster, and Mr Melville (slow of pace) a tortoise. We kept pieces of paper in the leaves of our exercise books and created comical verses about them which we passed about under our desks. Frank would always start me off, and I would add the second line. I also shared with Frank the private language I had made up for my family magazine, and we would shout out 'brillibox!' if we found a solution to a problem – or 'stormish!' if we made an unexpected run at cricket. We found this all highly amusing and the fact that the rest of the school found it highly annoying only encouraged us more.

But, in spite of his readiness to laugh, and in spite of his rotund appearance, Frank was a boy who was prone to the very serious matter of falling in love. One time he mooned for a whole term over Dr Lloyd's pretty niece who came on a day visit, dressed in blue. And then he became enamoured of the bootboy's sister, followed by the gardener's daughter.

He often bought little presents for them – a handkerchief, or a bit of ribbon – which is why he was so often 'skint'. In our second year of friendship he fell in love with the bold, brown girls who sold apples and nuts in the village. He was always talking about them and writing love poems, which I enjoyed lampooning.

'Isn't it awful that we'll both have to wait so long?' he said one day as we took a walk in the walled garden, attempting to memorize lines from Pliny's account of the Punic Wars.

'Wait for what?' I said, my mind on the tribunes and the senate and the lack of foresight they were showing.

'Marriage and – you know – all that goes with it.'

'I hadn't thought,' I replied, truthfully. Marriage was something that I had never allowed myself to contemplate. The possibility seemed a hundred years away.

'Don't you? I think about it all the time,' he said gloomily. 'In fact, I'm afraid I might actually die of love before I have chance to find a wife.'

'No one dies of love. It's a p-pathetic fallacy.'

'I might be the first case. I'll go down in the medical books and my name will live for ever: *Haywood's Melancholy Disease of the Heart*. They will paint pictures of me on my deathbed!'

'You'll survive. Everyone does. And you'll marry in God's good time.' Frank had such an easy-going, loving nature that I was sure that would be the case.

He stopped in his tracks. 'You're very cool, I must say. My father was a curate for a dozen years before he got a Living and enough money to marry. That's twelve years added on to, say, three at Oxford and I've still two more here at school. Seventeen years, Jameson! Seventeen years living like a monk! Seventeen years seeing beautiful girls dance about in front of you and knowing you can't touch them or kiss them or – anything really. And it might be longer!'

'And it might be shorter too. You have to consider the law of averages.'

'What's average, then? How old is *your* father?' he asked, somewhat belligerently.

'Fifty-six,' I said sheepishly.

'And you are sixteen. So he was almost forty when he married. I can't imagine waiting until I'm *forty* to do the deed. It's bad enough *thinking* about it.'

I'd always avoided thinking about it. 'Things will happen when they will. There's no p-point in tormenting oneself. Now let me get on with P-Pliny.'

'Pliny? *Pliny?* I give up on you sometimes, John.' Then his voice took on a teasing note. 'I don't think you've even *tried* to kiss a girl, have you?'

'Well, have *you*?' I retorted, recalling that his passions had so far been unrequited.

'Yes, I have.' He looked at me triumphantly. 'I kissed my cousin, Jane Freeman, last Christmas during hide-and-seek. She had very soft, cushiony sort of lips. She was cushiony everywhere, in fact. I thought about her all the holiday.' He adopted the dreamy look I knew so well.

'Well,' I said, emboldened. 'I kiss my sisters all the time. And there are seven of them.'

'Oh, sisters don't count.'

'And cousins do?'

'Of course. You can marry your cousin, but not your sister.'

It occurred to me that if kissing my sisters was delightful, perhaps kissing a cousin – or a sweetheart – would be even better. Of course, I had not yet met anyone outside my family whom I wished to kiss. Perhaps I was simply very choosy. Perhaps, like my father and Frank's father and many hundreds of others, I simply had to wait for God's good time.

He lowered his voice. 'What do you think of Gypsy Susan, for example?'

This was a name he had given one of the nut-brown girls. She was not a gypsy at all, but it suited Frank to romanticize her a little. 'I think she's rather dirty,' I said.

'But beautiful, don't you think?'

I'd never really looked at her. To tell the truth, I'd never dared to. I'd just been aware of her bold eyes making me drop my gaze to her filthy, unshod feet. 'I don't know. Nice enough, I daresay. To other gypsies.'

Frank put his face close to mine. 'I dare you to kiss her.'

'Dare not accepted. And if we don't get this speech of Scipio Africanus translated in half an hour, we'll be in trouble with the Croc.'

'You're too scared to do it!' He did a little dance of joy.

'Not at all. It's just not polite to go around kissing young ladies without asking them.'

'But supposing you did ask, and she said yes?'

'Too many hypotheticals.' And I closed my mind to the topic and went back to my Latin.

But Frank was not a boy to be thwarted. Our next half-holiday, we went walking down towards the river. I could tell he was on the lookout for Gypsy Susan, living as she did in one of the hovels where the people burned sticks for charcoal and did a bit of fishing. There were always old women sitting on broken chairs outside their doorways, waiting for the children to bring back what they had scavenged. The old women nodded at us as they puffed away at their clay pipes, and the children rushed up holding out their muddy hands in begging welcome, but Gypsy Susan was nowhere to be seen. I was greatly relieved. But as we headed back along the woodland path, suddenly there she was, standing in a patch of dry earth under a chestnut tree, kicking a small stone about with her bare feet. I attempted to keep walking, head down, but Frank pulled me by the arm. 'Here's your chance!'

'No!' I said, wresting my arm away. She went on playing with the stone, ignoring us grandly. She was wearing some sort of dark red skirt, short enough to show her calves.

'Good afternoon, miss,' Frank said smoothly, pulling off his hat.

She went on kicking the stone, then sent it skidding into the undergrowth with one deft movement. I watched her graceful limbs and the toss of her black hair as if in a trance. 'Leave her alone, Frank,' I said, my voice choked.

'Would you like to earn sixpence?' he said to her then. His words were like a shard of glass through my heart as I anticipated his strategy.

She looked up warily. 'Wha' fer?' she said. Her voice was rough and cracked.

'For being so pretty.'

She laughed. She had bad teeth behind the rosy lips. 'An' whar' else?' She stood firm, legs set apart, eyes narrowed.

'Just a kiss. We've walked all the way hoping to see you. It's two miles, you know, from the school. Two miles for a kiss. Thruppence each one. Is that a bargain?' He gave her his most winning smile.

'Let's see yer monay, furst.' Her speech had a strong local burr.

Frank drew out a sixpenny piece from his waistcoat pocket. She looked at it hungrily. 'Just two kisses, mind?' she said. Then, looking at me, 'Your friend doan't seem too keen.'

I was stunned. 'You can't p-pay her, Frank!' I said. 'That's wrong!'

'No it ain't,' she said, turning on me. 'You don't need to poake yer nose in, beanpole.'

'Well, I'm having nothing to do with it.' I walked away, shocked at Frank's behaviour, my head reeling from the look of her taunting eyes, her maddeningly graceful limbs. Once out of sight I leaned up against a tree, my blood racing. All was quiet. Seconds later, Frank appeared, looking rather white and shaken. I thought perhaps she had stolen his money without completing the bargain. 'You shouldn't have done that,' I whispered. 'P-Paying her – it's making her a harlot. Kisses should be given freely.'

'She kissed in a very funny way.' He licked his lips, doubtingly.

Before I'd had time to ask him what he meant, she came prancing back along the path, her dark mass of hair swinging back and forth. She stopped when she saw us both looking so nonplussed. Then, before I had time to avoid her, she pushed me back against the tree trunk. Her hands were hard, her whole body was hard: bone and sinew rather than soft flesh. I smelled her overpowering sweat, felt her lips up against me, salty and dirty. I closed my eyes, half of me yielding, half resisting. Then I felt her tongue, lithe like a serpent. To my amazement, she tried to push it into my mouth. I gagged and thrust her away in horror. The she laughed again and let me go, and walked off. 'There y'are, lads – two fer a tanner,' she called out over her shoulder. 'I doan't cheat.'

I spat on the floor, trying to rid myself of her sour smell and fishy taste. I rubbed my mouth and my nose and my cheeks with my handkerchief. I felt I wanted to wash myself, cleanse myself, douse myself for ever in the stream of Living Water, purify myself of this horrid deed.

Frank seemed amused at my antics. 'What's the matter?' he asked. 'Anyone would think you'd swallowed a frog.'

'I feel I have.' I couldn't help shuddering. 'Ugh, ugh, ugh!'

'Her mouth was a bit wet,' he said. 'Not at all like Jane Freeman's. But still.' He smiled. 'It was well worth thruppence.'

I looked at him aghast. 'So you enjoyed it?'

He looked at me. 'Yes, of course I did. And she has her sixpence. You're the only one making a fuss.'

I could not tell him how loathsome I thought him, how I felt betrayed by him, how immoral the whole procedure had been. I could not understand how any decent person could indulge in such grossness, and I determined I would never again put myself in such a position. Kissing, for me, would always be confined to my mother and sisters. Let Frank look forward to the marriage bed; I had no such ambitions.

And I have not changed my mind. Even Daniel's blissful marriage does not tempt me. Even the prospect of begetting children of my own does not shake my resolve. It seems to me that I am supremely suited to be an uncle and a friend; to share a particular part of my life with others, but no more. I should, for example, utterly dislike to give up my life as a scholar, in which I have no one to be responsible for, save myself (and Dinah, of course). When you really love the subject which is your livelihood, no effort is too much. But I would hate to have dealings with a wife, as Daniel does, on the subject of What Shall We Have for Dinner? or Should the Cook be Given Notice? Or Can We Afford a Carriage? It is much more pleasant to know nothing of domestic matters except that I will find a four-course meal waiting for me at seven o'clock each evening, of which I may eat as little or as much as I please, and converse with my curmudgeonly fellow dons in like degrees. I may drink a little brandy without censure, and I may retire to bed as early as suits me. I may wake in the night and thrash around in the bedclothes without disturbance to a living soul except myself. If I have a mind to attend to algebraic geometry at two in the morning, I can do it. This is selfish, I own it. Whereas, in most people's minds, there is a sofa marked 'Kindness' to welcome all comers, in mine there is but one chair, marked 'Selfishness', and other people can't come into it to bother me, because there is nowhere for them to sit. And where most people have a little stool called 'Humility', in mine there is a great one called 'Conceit', and it is so high that, were you to sit on it, your head would knock hard against the ceiling. Fellows like Smith-Jephcott like to think that is all I am about; that work and self-importance are what I am entirely made of. He is wrong. I have a heart, of course, ticking away like a pocket watch. But I am only tempted to open my heart to children.

12

I'D FORGOTTEN THAT I'D TAKEN MY DRAWERS OFF FOR Mr Jameson. It seems very peculiar, now as I look back – how I'd dared to do it, and what a strange request it had been. I know Mama would have been scandalized, but it seemed natural enough at the time and I wasn't in any way embarrassed. I always felt safe with Mr Jameson. Yet all the same, I know he's connected with the dark events that have slipped so completely from my mind. Perhaps Daisy will shed some light on them soon.

I turn the page, and to my surprise, there she is, smiling up at me – Daisy Baxter with her gypsy dress and shorn locks. The photograph is worn and battered, but I smile back, thinking how very young she is. It's rather foolish of me to imagine such a child will have the answer to a problem like mine. I begin to think I'd do better to put my faith in the Harley Street man.

I close the book. But as I stretch forward to put it down, I catch my reflection in the looking-glass on my dressing table and, not for the first time, I'm shocked to see how different I look from what I expect to see. I'm well-dressed and my hair is elaborately curled, but I'm deathly pale and there are dark patches under my eyes. I've hardly slept since my wedding day. And I've become so thin that my rings slip off every time I wash my hands. I can't go on living like this. If only I could remember what happened in those four years between the ages of eleven and fifteen that are such a mystery to me!

I've never dared speak of this queer hiatus to anyone, afraid I would be ridiculed, or worse. But the fact remains that I awoke, one summer afternoon to find, quite suddenly, that I had become someone else. At first, I was only aware that my heart was beating rather fast and I seemed to have recollections of some unpleasant encounter. So it was a relief to see the grass and the flower beds and realize I was, after all, sitting safely on the lawn in the vicarage garden. But at the same time it seemed as though the bushes were unaccountably bushier, and the trees taller. And my body felt strange — as if it had suddenly become a great deal heavier. I looked down, and to my surprise, there in my lap was a pair of gloved hands clasping an ivory fan. But the hands weren't mine — they had elegant, long fingers and were altogether far too grown-up to belong to me. Yet they responded when I tried to move them and wiggled delicately inside their net gloves — gloves of the sort I'd coveted for a long time but had never been allowed to have. And I could see that my body was clothed in a very grown-up silk dress, and had, of all things, a bosom. It swelled out in a confident curve as I looked down, and it alarmed me in no small measure to think how — if it were mine — it could have grown so decidedly large while I was asleep. Then, as I tried to get up, I found my legs were encumbered by layers of long petticoats, and my waist was constricted painfully by something hard and rigid — undoubtedly a corset. It was the most curious thing ever, as if I had sloughed my old skin and suddenly become a different creature.

I looked about myself rather wildly, expecting to see my astonishment mirrored in the faces of others. But although there were over half a dozen people in the garden, nobody took the slightest notice of me, and everyone went on talking and handing around sandwiches and lemonade as coolly as if my metamorphosis were perfectly unremarkable.

Sitting next to me on the lawn was a slight young man, with a dark, serious face and glossy, straight, black hair. He was dressed in clerical black, but was wearing a straw hat with a green ribbon. 'You've been asleep, Margaret,' he said in a pleasant voice, tickling my neck with a blade of grass. 'Have you been dreaming? You don't seem quite yourself.'

He was smiling at me in a familiar way, as if we were in the habit of sharing confidences, but I had no idea who he was or why he was calling me 'Margaret'. Perhaps I had strayed into Margaret's body? If so, I wanted to be out of it as soon as I could. I didn't feel at all right in her silk dress and net gloves. I certainly didn't feel right with her curving bosom and languid limbs. I wanted to be myself again. But who, exactly, *was* I? I started to panic. I'd thought I was a child called Daisy; in fact, I'd been certain of it. But now, every time I thought of her, the fainter she became in my mind. She seemed to be rapidly disappearing down a long dark tunnel, leaving this grown-up person in her place.

I stared at the young man. It was clear that he knew me well. And it was clear that the people sitting around us knew *him*, as they left us to our own devices and murmured away in their own conversations. My sisters were looking more than ever like twins in matching dresses, with large sun hats tied fetchingly under their chins. They were grown-up women now, and were paying attention in a very ladylike manner to two young clergymen who lounged on the lawn beside them. One of them I recognized as Papa's curate, Mr Morton. He was very intimate with Christiana, laughing and smiling with her, and she was returning his smiles in quite a kind way instead of being haughty and sarcastic, as she usually was. Sarah was reading a poem aloud and I knew for sure it was in German, although I had no recollection of learning the language. And there was Mama, sitting on a folding chair, dispensing tea in her familiar way, but looking more anxious than I remembered her, with grey strands threading through her hair. And there in the distance was (surely) Benjy, nearly three foot tall, already breeched and running around in a sailor suit and throwing up the very same rubber ball which Nettie had given me. Running after him and calling out his name was a servant I didn't recognize at all. But there was no Papa. And Mr Jameson was absent too.

I thought about making a declaration of my strange situation to the assembled company, but I felt too too ridiculous. What could I have said? And what would they have thought of me? I would undoubtedly be taken for a mad girl, or perhaps they would say – like this pleasant young man – that I was dreaming.

Indeed, the only explanation for all the strangeness around me was that I was still dreaming, and sooner or later, I'd wake up. To hasten the event, I closed my eyes tight and counted to ten. But when I opened them, everything was exactly as it had been before. In fact, it seemed even more real. I could hear the crickets in the grass and smell the roses in the rose beds, and see the long shadow of the cypress tree across the lawn. I could even see the intricate braiding on my sisters' dresses as they rose to play croquet, and I could hear them laughing delightedly as they swept their great skirts around and clicked their mallets elegantly against the ball. 'Good stroke!' someone called out, and 'Well done!' Surely I was not imagining that? Then I felt a great thump as Benjy climbed onto my lap, his hot and heavy body crushing my frock and making moist stains on the silk as he wriggled about before leaping up again to chase a tabby cat I'd never seen before. Benjy was real too, smelling of sun and sweat and sugar. Even the pages of the novel lying next to me smelled of warm paper as they turned in the breeze and I stopped them with my unfamiliar hand in its unfamiliar net glove. All the time I was aware of the dark young man as he lay on the grass alongside me, attempting to draw me into conversation. As he spoke, he made a little garland of buttercups which he placed on my head. 'Made with the best butter,' he said with a laugh.

Hours and hours seemed to go by during which I said as little as possible. I smiled at the young man and drank the tea he offered, holding the china cup with my new, slender hands and daintily eating the sandwiches that were brought around, thinking – believing – hoping – that at any moment I would wake up and my everyday memories would return and rescue me. My whole head ached with the effort.

Then Mr Morton rose and said he had to get ready for Evensong, and the tea-party broke up. At which point, the young man with the straw hat took my hand very earnestly and said, 'I've hardly had a word from you today, Margaret. Have I done something to offend?' I hastened to reassure him, saying (in a grown-up voice that seemed quite foreign to me) that I'd foolishly given myself a headache through sleeping in the sun. 'Take care not to do it again, then,' he said. 'Or perhaps use a parasol.'

Soon it was time for church, and I put on Margaret's elegant hat, which was handed me by the new maid, and I walked across to St Cyprian's with my mother and sisters, feeling strangely tall. I sat in the front pew where I had always sat, with Margaret's silk dress taking up a great deal more room than I was accustomed to. And I listened, not to Papa's thrilling tones, but to Mr Morton's mumbled ones. And then I came home again. But Papa was still not there. And Mr Morton stayed to supper, sitting in Papa's chair at the head of the table. And no one seemed to feel it at all out of the ordinary. After supper he read to us from the gospels, but didn't explain why my father was not there to read to us himself. 'Goodnight, Margaret dear,' he mumbled, pressing my hands in blessing as I went up to bed.

The stairs were the same as I trod the thick patterned carpet to the first floor, and my room was the same, with its blue curtains and bedspread. But the person I saw in the looking-glass, with her grown-up hair and grown-up frock, was not at all the same; in fact, it shocked me to see that she bore a marked resemblance to my mother. And when I carefully took off her fine frock and her rather complicated underclothes, I found that the contours of her body were more like Nettie's than mine. It was all so very perplexing and upsetting. But, for the moment, there was nothing to be done except put on the lace-trimmed nightgown that was folded on the bed, and attempt to go to sleep. Maybe in the morning, I thought, things would be different. I closed my eyes and prayed that God would have mercy and restore me to myself. Yet when I woke the next morning and looked at my shape under the bedclothes, I could see I still had Margaret's long limbs and her fine bosom. What had happened to me was real and I would have to make the best of it. There seemed one course of action open to me.

So I got up and dressed in Margaret's clothes and pinned up Margaret's hair and went downstairs to live Margaret's life. And I found that she was such a quiet figure in the household that her curious ignorance of what had happened the day before (or even at any time in the recent past) was unremarked upon; if, indeed, it was noticed. I discovered that she could play the piano almost as well as her sisters, and could draw and embroider and do all manner of things that Daisy had never attempted; but that above all she was renowned for always having her nose in a book. I learned from the servants that the dark man with the straw hat was called Robert Constantine and that he was a friend of Mr Morton's, destined to take Holy Orders himself; that Hannah had left two years before to be married to the haberdasher on the High, and now turned up at church in the very latest fashion, to the disgust of both my sisters; that Mrs McQueen had long ago given notice, which nobody regretted – and that pink-faced Jess had come instead. I learned that Christiana, now much graver and more subdued, was engaged to Mr Morton, who now seemed to be doing all Father's work in the parish, and occupying his study. However, there was still no sign of Father himself, and I had such strange feelings when I thought of him that I even feared he might have died. But no one in the house wore mourning and there was no black drapery to be seen on any picture or looking-glass. So I kept my counsel, and waited, thinking he must soon return from whatever business had taken him away. I thought maybe the bishop had appointed him to an important committee to do with the conditions of the poor, and that he was away in London or even Manchester. But, all the time, I could not shake off the notion that he had been unwell and was convalescing somewhere. I was surer of this when Mama once or twice let slip a reference to 'your poor papa', and when I realized that Mr Morton prayed for father's health and well-being at every service. But although there would be a murmur of sympathetic approval when his name was mentioned, no one asked directly after him. Even Mrs Carmichael was silent. I thought this strange, but I could not say that I wished to hasten his return. The household seemed calmer without him.

The real truth came out bit by bit. One day, when I was in the drawing room quietly enjoying that fact that I could now understand quite difficult books in French and German, Jess brought Mama a letter. She looked at it. 'From the superintendent,' she said, shortly. And suddenly I had a brief picture of white walls and wooden doors and a general sense of distress and clamour before the image disappeared just as quickly as it had come. I watched as Mama opened the letter, and read it to herself. 'No better,' she said, shaking her head. Then she began to sob. 'Dear God, will it never end?'

Christiana went to her, and put her arm around her, but Sarah rose and ran from the room saying that it 'wasn't fair' and 'my life is blighted'. I could do nothing but sit like a stone, trying to make sense of it. If Papa was under the care of a superintendent, he must surely be in a hospital of some kind. A sanatorium, I reasoned. Somewhere a distance from Oxford — maybe near the sea. But why did we not visit him? For some reason it came into my head that he might be in isolation, like a leper, although I'd never heard of anyone having leprosy in England. All the same, notions of illness and fever now seemed to attach themselves more distinctly to my memories of him. I could picture bowls and jugs and towels and the spooning of medicine. Had I nursed him? Brought him food and drink? Even — it seemed unlikely — washed him? But when I tried to recall it more clearly, all that would come into my head was the fateful picnic, and Nettie's dismissal, and the seemingly endless summer jaunts with John Jameson. If I thought of Papa's face, I could only see that big brown oar in his study, and feel his warm breath as I sat with my cheek next to his.

I must have seemed the most unfeeling of girls as I affected an air of calm to hide the depths of my despair and ignorance. I desperately wanted to remember what had gone before, but I had no means of doing so. I couldn't refer to Daisy's journal to jog my memory, as I had no idea where she'd hidden it. All I could do was let each day help me to the next, as I pieced my life together and built up a picture of myself as the Margaret that everyone knew. I found that I enjoyed the many talks that I had with Robert Constantine, who came to the house nearly every day and was very attentive to me, although in his presence I felt stupidly childlike and naive. I warmed to him the more because I felt strangely separate from my mother and sisters, as if I'd done something to upset them. And when it finally became clear to me that Papa was not in a sanatorium at all, but an insane asylum, I could not get it out of my head that it was somehow my fault.

And now, as I sit here in my comfortable new house, I know that I'll need courage if I am to go back to those forgotten years. But Papa always said I had courage. *Brave little Daisy*, he called me, his hand on my shoulder. I feel his hand now, heavy and comforting. *Don't be frightened*, he's saying. *Just remember that I love you, and Love driveth out Fear.*

I close my eyes and concentrate hard. It makes me think of those séances when people sit in the dark and call up the dead. My heart is beating fast to think I may be doing what is forbidden. But I don't want to raise spirits, only memories – surely that cannot be evil. Nothing comes at first; I am too aware of being in this heavily draped room, with its oak furniture and patterned carpet, with the sounds of the birds in the garden outside, the faint clash of dishes in the kitchen below. Then suddenly it begins to come back – my blue bedroom, my father's study, Mr Jameson's camera, the buzzing of a fly against a window, white silk stockings, prayers by a bedside, tangled sheets, a low candle; lessons in a book-lined room; the sound of weeping. I feel my heart beating double time. But before I can make sense of it all, the pictures flicker and disappear, like candles going out, one after the other. I try again, emptying my mind of all mundane thoughts, but this time nothing happens. I feel ready to cry.

I grasp the journal roughly in a kind of desperation and almost tear it open. Even a child's words are better than nothing, I think. Daisy must have written something that will help me. I see that the handwriting is more hectic now, the letters less well-formed. Perhaps she knows she is hurtling towards some awful fate.

Monday 7th July

I cannot believe how kind Papa has been to me! I thought I was in the most terrible trouble and no one would ever *trust me again. Hannah said, You're in for it this time, miss, and Sarah said I'd probably never be allowed to see Mr Jameson again if that was what I got up to in the afternoons. I was so miserable because it was not Mr Jameson's fault at all, and I cried all night – very quietly so as not to make Christiana come running in – and I had to bathe my eyes with cold water three times before prayers this morning and could hardly eat my breakfast with Papa and Mama both sitting there in silence. Then Papa got up and said, Daisy come with me, and I thought he was going to tell me how wicked and vain I was, and I could hardly speak for the tears stuck in my throat. Whenever Papa is cross with me, I can never say what I mean and I start to cry instead. Papa says it's not the words that matter as Vain Repetition is Heathen but you have to be* really sorry *from your heart if you have done wrong and that you must show your repentance in everything you do and I thought perhaps I would kneel on the hearthrug to beg for forgiveness. But the worst thing was that I was still glad that I had done it, and I couldn't repent. I stood very still trying not to look at him but peeping up through my lashes, and he sat there staring at me and then he smiled and said he liked my hair short and would speak to Mama about it, which made me so releaved and happy but he said he still had to give me a penance for being disobediant and not caring about Mama's feelings and other people's – but it was only to write out Ephesians 6:3 which took me less than half an hour although it went over six sheets of paper. He looked at me so kindly that I knew he truly loved me in spite of my wickedness, and I am now determined to love him properly in return.*

Mama is still cross, though. I've hardly spoken to her since yesterday. Even in church she wouldn't look at me and when we walked home I had to walk next to Hannah who said Mama is of the opinion that I look like a ragamuffin. I said Mr J told me I looked more like a gypsy and that he had taken a photograph of me in gypsy costume and

Hannah said, Did you undress all by yourself? And I said of course I did as I was quite good at it since Nettie had gone – and she didn't say anything more. She wasn't in a very good mood because Mama has stopped her going with my sisters to their archery lessons. I wouldn't have known this except Christiana and Sarah came into my room yesterday evening, pretending to tidy my dressing-table as a favour and check my handkerchief drawer to make sure I had none of theirs. Christiana looked at my bookshelf and said, 'The child has enough story books to open a public library!' And I said Mr Jameson had given me some and Miss Prentiss had lent me two for the summer holiday. And Christiana said, 'But where's your diary, Daisy? Are you still keeping it? Do let us look!' And they both started to poke about looking for it and I was so dreadfully afraid they'd look behind the fire screen and all would be discovered, but that very moment Hannah came in to brush their hair, so they stopped. They said what a bore it was that Hannah wasn't accompanying them to Archery any more and Hannah pulled a face and said didn't she know it, and that she'd rather be Out and About in the afternoons than stuck in the house dusting ornaments and labelling sheets especially with Cook's bad temper in the basement and Mrs Mac's vile temper in the attic and not a pleasant soul in between. And we all laughed because sometimes Hannah is funny. Then Christiana said it was very demeaning of Mama to watch over her as if she were a child, but Sarah said: 'Oh, it's because you aren't a child that Mama is doing it! She wouldn't have bothered if it had been Daisy *that Mr Gardiner had taken a fancy to.' Then she laughed in that funny way that makes her sound like a horse and twisted my hair around her finger to see if it would still go into ringlets which it still will, a bit. 'Daisy leads quite a charmed life, don't you, dear?' she said. 'Mr Jameson is allowed to take you everywhere and cut your hair and do all sorts of peculiar things.' I said Mr Jameson had absolutely* not *cut my hair, I had done it on my own (which was mainly true). I think they are both jealous and it's their fault anyhow that Mr J doesn't give them tea or take them nice places. They kept asking, 'What on earth do you do at*

Mr Jameson's?' And when I told them about the games and puzzles, Sarah said it was the most boring thing she'd ever heard. 'Has he taken any more photographs?' she said, and I didn't want to tell her about it because of the way Hannah had looked at me before and because I remembered about the Eye of Society and knew Mr Jameson didn't like me to talk about our time together.

I've been very worried in case Papa would stop me going to see Mr Jameson especially when he said that Mama thinks Mr J is too lenient with me. But Mr J says he isn't lenient because he has a lot of sisters and is used to them and Papa said then that it was all right and I could go whenever I wanted and I was so pleased I hugged Mr J on the spot. However, Papa says I must start my preparation for Confirmation too, and he will undertake this himself. He said he thought he had neglected my Spiritual Welfare which was why I had been disobediant, and to that extent it was his fault. I think it's not his fault at all but my own wilfulness and I ask God to forgive me every time I think of it during the day and every night at bedtime – three times at least. However, I was very glad and releaved that I may still go on my adventures with Mr J. However I couldn't go with him today because Benjy wasn't well and Papa said I might stay with him until Dr Lawrence came, which Mrs McQueen didn't like but I didn't care what she liked as she is so horrid. Dr Lawrence said there was nothing wrong with Benjy and that he was probably only teething and to give him some Overdale's Syrup when he fretted, and Mrs McQueen was very pleased because it looked like she was right after all. But Papa said if it was only teething he didn't know why Benjy cried so much when he was with Mrs McQueen and was so much quieter when he was with me – and she gave him a very cross look and said something about never having had any complaints before and hoping he'd let her know if he wasn't satisfied as she didn't wish to remain where she wasn't wanted.

I was just glad to be with Benjy again. It was almost like it used to be except Nettie wasn't there. Benjy still managed to pull my hair *even though it was short. I sang to him – 'Tom the Piper's Son', and 'Lavender's Blue' and 'Little Nutmeg' and all our favourites – and Papa stayed to listen, which Mrs McQueen didn't like at all. I knew she was just itching for him to go so she could have the nursery to herself. But the funny thing was that Papa didn't seem to want to go. He kept looking around at the furnature saying he remembered this and that and he remembered when Nettie was here and how cheerful everything was. He asked Mrs McQueen if she'd moved things around and she said only the other small bed that had gone downstairs for me, and he said, 'Strange.' After a while she said she'd like a drop of tea and a bit of bread-and-butter and should she make some for him and for me, and he said he'd be obliged. Her tea was quite horrid and strong and she spread the butter too thick on the bread. But it was nice to be sitting down in the nursery having tea and not to be shooed away all the time. Papa said it would be a good thing if I could come and play with Benjy whenever I liked. 'Don't ever discourage her,' he said to Mrs McQueen. 'You know what the Bible says – Suffer the little Children' – and Mrs M said, Yes of course, although I could see she was* seething *underneath. I asked Papa why Jesus said little children had to suffer as it seemed unkind to say that, and Papa said 'suffer' in the Bible meant 'allow' or 'let', and that Jesus wanted the crowds to let the children pass so he could bless them. He said sometimes the words used in the olden days didn't mean the same as they mean in these modern days and we must be very careful as everything is open to interpretation, and Mrs McQueen sniffed so loud I thought her head would come off.*

Then Papa said that Luke 16:18 would be the exact text to write out for my punishment tomorrow. He said we would discuss it tomorrow afternoon. I said, What about Mr Jameson? And he said, What about him? He will not come if he thinks there is sickness in the house and I think, don't you, that you could spare one afternoon for your poor papa after all? And I said of course I would and I was so glad that I kissed him and he smiled very much and said, 'And of such is the Kingdom of Heaven,' which is actually my new text. DEB

Tuesday 8th July

I had my first lesson with Papa today. It was really strange being in his study but not being in trouble of any sort. He put a chair for me with a cushion on it so I could reach his desk on the other side, and he put his prayer book on top. It is quite old and battered and he said Mama had given it to him before they were married so it is very precious. He looked at my penance first and said it was very well written and he thought we had both learned our lesson now. He was nicer to me than he has ever been — even at Christmas and on my birthday — and it was easy to learn all the promises I have to make in front of the bishop. When we had been through it all, Papa asked me if I thought God would punish us if we broke a promise to Him and I said doesn't God forgive us all as long as we are sorry? And Papa nodded and said I was right and I saw with the eyes of a child which is the right way to see things. But it seems to me that children are always being told how naughty they are, which is a bit contradictery. Mr Jameson says Life itself is very contradictery and he wouldn't be surprised to see a pig flying backwards or a cat unwashing itself!

Then Papa asked me if I liked Mr Jameson, and I said I liked him very much and Papa said 'More than me?' and I didn't know what to say as I should love Papa more but Mr Jameson is nicer to be with and very funny — but Papa interrupted and said 'I see you do' — and I said 'No I don't — at least not all the time' and he laughed and said you are very honest, Daisy, considering it is a question I should never have asked. 'We all have to earn love, don't we?' he said. 'And I have not always done so.'

Then he asked me if I had written much in my journal and I said I had, and he asked if I would show it to him which frightened me and I said it was private and I shouldn't like anyone else to see it. He said he couldn't imagine that I had written anything very terrible, but then he smiled and said he understood my reluctance as there were thoughts he had committed to paper which were meant for his own eyes alone. 'Sometimes we work things out by writing them down,' he said. 'We don't always mean what we say.'

I must be even more careful to keep my diary hidden. DEB

I feel a cold wave ripple through me as I recall those lessons with Father, and how I'd been anxious about studying the prayer book alone with him. All through my life I'd half believed that beneath Papa's white surplice God Himself was lurking, with His eye on everything I said and thought and His hand ready to smite me if I did wrong. It was hard to forget the idea. Yet the more time I spent with him, the less frightening he seemed. Indeed, he behaved as if everything I said and did was delightful to him; as if he could not have enough of me. 'Is Daisy with Papa *again*?' I'd hear Sarah whisper outside the study door. 'She really must have a tremendous lot to learn.'

And I did have. He'd sit me on his lap and bring his cheek right next to mine as we read together, and I remember feeling almost rapturous that I had at last found such a place in his heart. And he seemed to share my rapture. Whatever we discussed, he would always come back to the same thing – Love. 'Love is the keystone, Daisy,' he would say. 'I love you and you love me, and Christ loves all of us. Love, in my experience, can never be wrong.'

But all the same, there is a deep uneasiness in my mind when I think of that study, with its brown books and its brown oar, and Papa with his thick brown hair and his watch chain with its sixteen links, and the whiskers that he let me comb if I especially asked. And the Bible open on the table, and his hand on top of mine as we read the verses together.

13

๛ JOHN JAMESON ๛

I CANNOT TOLERATE THE NOTION THAT ANYONE SHOULD think ill of me for my friendship with one of God's most innocent creatures. That it should be Baxter and his wife who have imagined something amiss in my dealings with Daisy fills me with horror. On reflection, I am sure that it is not Baxter himself who has jumped to this conclusion; he understands me better than that. But he is a married man, and is obliged to take his wife's views into account – and I have no doubt that it is Mrs Baxter who has misconstrued the nature of Daisy's headstrong action with the scissors, and my (imagined) part in it. Like many women, she is over-concerned with her reputation in society, and fearful that she will be blamed for not exercising sufficient supervision over her child, and by inference, not doing her utmost to keep her safe. But safe from *what*, I ask? From someone who can share with her that most precious of childhood gifts – the power of the imagination? From someone who allows her the freedom to pass the time as she wishes without fearing that her leisure time is but a dull extension of the lessons of Sunday School? From someone who takes such delight in the beauty of her presence that he would wear his shoes to tatters in walking with her to the ends of the earth? From someone who can instruct her about all that is marvellous in the myriad creations of the world? And, most of all, from someone who makes her laugh?

In my mind, there is no case to answer. My conscience is clear. And, if one examines it dispassionately, what is a few inches of hair in a child of Daisy's age? They are making far too much of it. But, of course, I am not so naïf as to believe that it is only the hair-cutting that lies behind Mrs Baxter's unease with me. No doubt she thinks that it is odd for a man of my mature years and undoubted intellect to choose to spend such a large proportion of his spare time with a child of eleven. Well, if I am odd, I am odd. But oddness is not the same as wickedness, and it grieves me to think that there is no Broad Church of love, where many kinds of attachment can be welcomed.

Of course, I recognize that in finding children more beautiful and appealing than their fully grown counterparts, I am in a minority. But being in a minority is not in itself wrong. So, while I am not planning to evangelize the world on behalf of my particular predilections, I feel I should not be censured for harbouring them. Or, indeed, for acting in accordance with those feelings, provided, of course, that no harm is done thereby. And what harm could be done? After all, compared with the fornicators and adulterers of this world – even the married men who keep their wives in thrall to their passions and lust – my gentle way of loving does no harm. So why should I be to blame for turning my back on fleshly sensuality and preferring what is simple, loving and good? Friendship with children is, for me, as great a sacrament as marriage.

But I recognize the precariousness of my position. The Mrs Grundys – for whom human conduct consists merely of a set of rules by which we step left and right or back and forth as if we were all participants in a universal game of chess – would undoubtedly choose to misunderstand the nature of my actions. All I have done is attempt, however unsatisfactorily, to fix on paper the transitory beauty of childhood; yet I cannot be as open about it as I would wish, and my unclothed studies have to be accomplished in conditions of secrecy, which imply a degree of guilt on the part of both the artist and his subject. This angers and distresses me. After all, I may walk through any museum or gallery in the land – indeed, in every civilized land – and view at my leisure representations of the naked human form. No blame is laid at my feet for that. Indeed, I have seen paintings in London and Rome depicting violent rapes and bestial couplings, which, because they have a classical provenance, are viewed approvingly by respectable matrons and unmarried ladies who examine the shocking details with interest. Yet, owing to the prejudiced views of the self-same respectable females, I cannot display, much less admit to making, a picture of a real, unclothed English child.

However, the crisis has been averted: Baxter has seen sense, and Daisy and I are able to continue our afternoons of leisure. I say 'afternoons', but I have been a little incommoded by Baxter's new-found determination to bring on Daisy's Christian education at this particular favoured time of ours, so that often when I call at the house, I find her ensconced in his study, inky-fingered and by no means ready to set forth at the time I have planned. Baxter has even gone so far as to ask if I would let him know in advance when I intend to visit, with the result that my free-and-easy ways as a privileged visitor to the home are somewhat curtailed. I have also formed the impression that Mrs Baxter is avoiding me, which confirms that she was the prime mover in the attempt to exclude me from Daisy's company. She is rarely at home when I call, although in mitigation Baxter says she is preoccupied with some matter to do with the older girls that necessitates her absence. We once met on the front garden path (I was arriving at the very instant that she and the girls were departing), and I sensed a faint *froideur* as I took her hand, although she was, as always, impeccably polite and gracious. She is certainly a very beautiful woman and I hope we will not be enemies, although it is doubtful that she will invite me to dinner again or send me any more presents.

Baxter himself seems to have some weighty matter on his mind, which makes him less genial company than usual. He talks in fits and starts and walks about pulling at his hair – or slumps in his chair with his hand in front of his eyes as if unaware of my presence. Several times when I have been in his study, waiting for Daisy to tidy herself for our outing, the pert maid has come in with an urgent message from some parishioner or committee member, and he has waved her away crossly, saying, 'Yes, yes, I'll attend to it later,' without even bothering to read the note. This is unlike Baxter. When I first made his acquaintance he would fly off to vestry meetings and parish committees the instant he was called, as if he were a fireman on constant watch for a fire which only he could put out. In fact, I would often tease him about his alacrity, saying he was travelling at such unconceivable speed that he was likely to return before he set out. But now he seems listless, and almost loath to leave the house. The only thing that seems to brighten him is the presence of Daisy. Sometimes I feel awkward about taking her away from him.

She is, of course, the same dear child, in spite of her shorn locks – in fact, even prettier on account of them – and I thank God I am able to have her company for at least a little while longer. Indeed, knowing that at any moment our outings may be brought to a close, sharpens my appreciation of each precious second we have together. And what delights we have had! Over the past weeks I have taken Daisy all over the city – by the Thames, admiring the college barges moored against the riverbank where I have taken her on board to sit under the awnings and watch the oarsmen go past, then up through the meadow, and along the water-walks of the Cherwell, enjoying the wonderful hot weather that seems to go on day after day.

Daisy has brought her parasol each time, and it gives me no end of pleasure to watch her twirl it back and forth in her artless way as we walk along. And, as we walk, I have taken the opportunity of making up stories about everything we see – fish, rabbits, frogs, flowers and small dogs – and many things we don't see, like fairies and talking sheep. It is easy to find subjects for my tales as Daisy asks so many clever questions, and each question seems to prompt so many foolish ideas in me, that my thoughts flow on and on through all the golden afternoon. Daisy, in spite of being critical of fact and tenacious with detail, is always very satisfied with my flights of fancy and says she will tell the stories to Benjy when he gets older. 'I don't believe anyone tells better stories than you, Mr Jameson. I shall remember them always.'

To entertain her further I introduced her to two of my practical inventions. On Wednesday, when we were resting on a bench near the cricket field, having admired the moorhens wading about in the pond near by, I showed her the little folding mirror and the collapsible cup I have now perfected. She held up the mirror in front of her face and looked at herself very solemnly saying she knew she had been *very naughty* to do it but she was so glad she was rid of all her horrid long hair. 'I should be so *very* hot now with it all around my neck,' she said, putting her hand up to her bare skin under the edge of her short bob and making me long to do the same, as I recalled how my hand had grazed her neck so lightly as I wielded the scissors that fateful day.

'No doubt,' I replied. 'If you still possessed your full head of hair, I daresay you would be quite melting away by now, and I should have had to catch you in my collapsible tumbler and take you home to your papa and mama with a label saying: *Daisy Baxter in Liquid Form*. I daresay they would have been terribly incommoded to have their child contained in a cup. They would have had to put you high up on the mantelpiece so as not to let any dog or cat lap you up in mistake for a drink of water.'

'But wouldn't I have become a solid girl again when I grew colder?' she asked in that earnest way of hers.

'Well,' I said. 'The laws of nature dictate you should; but sometimes the laws of nature surprise us by doing something perfectly contradictory, so they are not, on the whole, to be trusted.'

Then I asked her if she would like a cold drink and she said, 'Oh, yes please!' and I poured her some of Benson's homemade ginger ale from my double-insulated flask and she drank it out of the telescopic tumbler as if it were the greatest nectar in the world. 'I hope,' she said, looking soberly into the empty cup, 'that this was not the liquid form of any other living creature, Mr Jameson.' I said only if she thought that buttered crumpets and cherry jam were to be considered creatures, as that was what the drink was made of. She said she didn't believe me. And I asked her to have another taste, and poured her some more. And she drank it up and said perhaps I was right, as it was extremely nice and she thought she could taste a hint of cherry jam after all.

Yesterday it was so hot that we went to the museum to seek some shade. We looked at the remains of the poor dodo in his case, as well as no end of stuffed mammals, birds and insects. Daisy pressed her nose to the glass case and looked at everything with care. When we came to the beetles I explained that there were more of these than any other type of creature in the world. 'Over two hundred thousand, I believe. Can you imagine why that should be the case?'

She shook her head. 'Is it because they are so small and don't take up much room?'

'Perhaps,' I said. 'Or perhaps God simply has a fondness for beetles. Having created a stag beetle, He felt He had to go one better with a tiger beetle. And having created that, He was curiously inclined to ring the changes with the soldier beetle, and then the ladybird, and then the cockchafer and then the sexton beetle. Perhaps beetle-creating is a kind of hobby of His.'

'God doesn't have *hobbies*!' She looked scandalized and amused in equal measure.

'Why not? *We* have hobbies and we are made in His image. Perhaps when He rested on the seventh day, He wasn't resting at all but was secretly adding to His beetle collection and setting up a whole lot of bother for Noah a little later on. Can you imagine it – all that rain coming down and having to find two of each from all two hundred thousand species?'

'But wouldn't they have just flown around the ark?' she asked. 'And got mixed up with the flies and birds and maybe got eaten?'

'By no means. Noah was a carpenter, after all, and I daresay he fitted out the ark with hundreds of little drawers and put the insects carefully inside, two by two in cotton-wool beds to keep them comfy. I daresay they had a whole deck to themselves, drawer after drawer, with their names on the outside like the fittings in a haberdasher's shop, with Ham, Shem and Japheth coming around and giving each of them a thimble-full of milk three times a day.'

She laughed, then thought for a while. 'Papa says the story of Noah's ark isn't really true. He says it is really a kind of parable, like the ones Jesus tells, and it shows us God's grace towards those who try to lead a good life.'

'No doubt your father is right in the matter of theology,' I said. 'But I prefer to think of Noah sailing the high seas with all those beetles.'

'So do I,' she said, slipping her hand confidentially in mine. I felt so happy to feel its warmth and softness, I could have stopped breathing there and then, and accounted my life well-spent.

But Daisy was hungry, as I find small children often are, so we went back to my rooms and, while Benson made the tea and Dinah prowled about along the tops of the armchairs, we looked at a picture book I had just received from my London bookseller. There were coloured illustrations of many strange creatures, including sloths and anteaters and orang-utans. Daisy was particularly drawn to the flamingos on account of their colour, so I told her how that was caused by their terrible fondness for beetroot which they dug out of the lakes with their long beaks and swallowed whole in a manner too disgusting to relate. 'That is how their feathers become quite stained with pink,' I told her. 'And high-born ladies send explorers to Darkest Africa to catch the creatures, which they do with some difficulty by holding them under their arms in a kind of half-Nelson. Then they bring them back and take off the plumes so the ladies can wear them in their hair when they go to grand balls in London.'

Daisy looked up with a sharp expression and asked me if it were *really* true or just another story, and I had to confess it was just a story. 'Although high-born ladies *do* wear tall feathers in their hair when they meet the Queen.'

'How can you tell when things are true and when they aren't?' she said with something of a pout.

'You can't, always.'

'Papa says you can.'

'Then he is a most superior human being,' I said, adding quickly, 'which, of course, he is. That is generally acknowledged by town and gown alike. I hope you are making good use of his superior knowledge in your preparation lessons. We want you to astonish Bishop Wilberforce with your learning.'

'I am doing my best,' she said. 'Although I don't always understand why things have to be the way they are.'

I thought she was still fretting for her old nursemaid and the unfair ways of the world, and I was attempting to furnish an appropriate reply, but before I could do so, she surprised me by asking, 'What is Heaven like, do you think?'

It is a weakness of mine that I have always found the idea of Heaven difficult to imagine. I know *how* I should imagine it, of course: cherubim and seraphim bowing down; endless songs of praise; the community of saints; worship and glory illimitable: *Holy, holy, holy, merciful and mighty*. I say the phrases aloud every day of my life as I announce my credo in chapel and in my private prayers. But all the same, Heaven remains oddly unreal, and I have always felt the need to suppress a certain distaste at the monotony of it all. But seeing Daisy with her sweet little form standing in front of me, her clear eyes so trusting, her innocent soul so enticing, I found myself experiencing an epiphany. 'Heaven is when you are united with those you love,' I ventured. 'When you are intertwined with them, almost as if you and they are one. As if nothing else matters.'

'What about God and Jesus?' she asked. 'Isn't that the main thing?'

'Of course,' I said hastily. 'In Heaven, you will be in God's arms. We all will. And before you ask if there is room for everyone, I will remind you, as the earnest Confirmation candidate that you are, that God's arms are infinite. He is not confined to time or space. He is all around, past and present and future. He is here now. I can feel His Presence at this moment.' I smiled at her. 'Especially at this moment.'

She glanced around surreptitiously as if the Deity might be hovering near the tea table, but it was only Benson setting out the bread-and-butter, so she looked at me again, frowning. 'But if God is all around us, and Heaven is everywhere that God is, that makes Heaven and earth exactly the same.'

'Well,' I said, choosing my words as carefully as I could. 'Heaven *can* be with us on earth if we try very hard. We can have little glimpses of it, as if we are looking at a beautiful garden through a knot-hole in the fence. We can't get into the garden, but we can see that it's lovely, and we can enjoy its loveliness even though we are still on the outside.'

'Yes, I see.'

'And it's much easier for children to see into that garden,' I said. 'Because they notice things like knot-holes and don't mind getting down on their knees to look. I expect you've done that, haven't you?'

She nodded, slowly. 'So, Heaven is simply happiness – and beauty?'

'A special kind of happiness and beauty.'

'It sounds nice and simple the way you say it. When I'm with Papa everything seems very complicated. He says God is Imminent and also Transcendent, but I didn't know exactly how that could be until now.'

'Well, you will impress your papa with your new-found understanding. And you can tell him that it was Mr Jameson who helped you to it.'

She smiled. 'I will.'

That smile gave me courage to do what I have wanted to do for weeks. Daisy and I have continued our photography work on most of the days when we have taken our walks and I have been delighted at the results as they come into being in the developing tray. Daisy is an apt pupil and doesn't need telling more than once how to hold a pose. I have explained how important it is that she remains still while the image is impressed upon the plate, or else it will become blurred and of no use, and she understands perfectly. I always lay out in my bedroom the clothes she will wear, and she dresses herself in them very prettily, only asking for my assistance in pinning a flower to her hair, or tying a sash. I love her best when she is dressed at her most artless, in the simple shift of a woodland nymph or the rags of a beggar-maid. Her shape shows through in such a tantalizing way that I have long wanted to rid her of the artificial covering and reveal it to the world in all its natural glory. So now I decided I would broach the subject, at the risk of rejection or, worse, that my request would get to the ears of Mrs Baxter.

'Do you recall the story of Adam and Eve?' I asked, as I set up the tripod with Daisy standing obediently in front of me.

'Yes, of course. The Garden of Eden and the Serpent.'

'*Of Man's first disobedience, and the fruit of that Forbidden Tree,*' I murmured.

'That's not the Bible, is it?' she said.

'No, it's Milton,' I replied. '*Paradise Lost.*'

'Papa likes Milton. *They also serve who only stand and wait.* That's his favourite.'

I thought this preference strange. Baxter is – or was until recently – such an active man. But I had no time or inclination to ponder the matter. If I were to persuade Daisy to model for me without the encumbrance of dress, I would have to do it now, or I might never have another opportunity. 'Well, you see, Daisy, in *Paradise Lost* we are shown how happy Adam and Eve were as they wandered in the Garden of Eden like innocent children, naked, and without sin.' I could not look at her. I took out a new photographic plate and felt my hands trembling as I placed it in position.

'But that was before the Serpent came along and persuaded Eve to eat the apple,' said Daisy.

'The Bible just says "fruit". The Serpent brought the knowledge of nakedness to Adam and Eve through the fruit of the forbidden tree. As a result, Mankind is cursed with shame and we've made ourselves hideous with heavy and unbecoming clothes ever since. Think how free you feel now that your hair is shorter. Imagine how much freer you would feel without any c-clothes at all.'

I almost held my breath while Daisy considered this. 'I'm sure it would be very nice,' she said. 'But I'm not allowed to take my clothes off even when we are at the seaside – even when it's hot. I have to wear a horrid bathing dress and it gets very heavy when it's wet, and is not a bit comfortable. Some of the fishing-boys just wear their drawers, which I think looks very comfortable, but Mama and Papa say young ladies need to be modest at all times.'

'Oh, Daisy, don't misunderstand me,' I added quickly. 'I hardly meant that you should walk n-naked through the streets of Oxford. Mrs Grundy, I fear, would have something to say about that – and we would both be in trouble. No, I mean I would like to take your photograph in what is called a "nude study". There are many pictures done in this manner by many fine artists. I'd like to p-present you as a sea nymph, perhaps, lying on the ground as if it were the sea shore and you had just been washed up by the waves. I would maybe colour it too, to complete the effect.'

'I'm not sure. Mama and Papa might be cross.'

'That is why it is so essential to be secret – if you would do it, I mean.' My heart was pounding. 'There are so many people who cannot understand unconventional behaviour, even when it is perfectly innocent and proper.'

'Are you sure it is proper?' she said. 'Hannah said –'

'Hannah?' I was brought up unexpectedly at the thought that Daisy had inadvertently shared with the servant anything about our sessions together. Hannah is, I suspect, a flighty girl whose own coarse mind might have led her to coarse conclusions. I recall that she always seemed rather uneasy when she chaperoned the children in my presence, managing to be both smirking and sharp. 'What does Hannah know about it?'

'Well, she asked me if I undressed myself when I wore the fancy clothes for you. And she said it in a funny sort of way.'

'And what did you say in reply?'

'I said that I did it all myself.'

Relief flooded through me. 'And you will undress yourself this time, too. It will be perfectly proper. I will simply take the picture. Now, will you do it? You are free to say no, of course.'

She nodded.

And that nod sent the room spinning on its axis, so that I almost staggered in my joy. 'Good,' I murmured. Then I turned my back while she slipped out of her clothes. 'Now, when you are ready, lie down on the floor and rest your head on your elbow. Have you done that?'

'Is this right?'

I turned. There she was, my sea nymph, all pearly from the salt water, her hair in untidy fronds blowing in the breeze, her limbs so gentle and rounded, her toenails so tiny and rosy. 'P-Perfect,' I said, sliding the plate down with nervous fingers. 'Now I'll count to twenty. Stay as still as you can.'

The picture was so beautiful I could hardly believe it. The light fell on her skin as limpidly as it might have done in the Garden of Eden. Her limbs seemed to have just that hour come forth from the creating hand of God, her body as crisp and new as a perfect nut lying in its shell. Her shape was remarkable, ineffable, glorious. Who, I said to myself, could look at this and not feel the very essence of God's love? Yet this image of pure beauty is worlds away from liturgies and catechisms, rubrics and responses and all that categorizes our religion now.

14

THEY SAY THAT SORROWS COME NOT AS SINGLE SPIES but in battalions, and certainly that has been true of us these last weeks. First, my darling Benjy's near-fatal fall, followed by all the dreadful upset of Nettie's departure; then the lack of a nursery maid for weeks, with Hannah threatening to give in her notice, and Cook throwing the pans around in the kitchen to express her vexation; followed by Christiana's infatuation with the wretched Leonard Gardiner, and finally Mr Jameson (whom I had thought a reliable man) allowing Daisy to run wild when we had entrusted her to his care. But now the poor child has been afflicted with scarlet fever and the whole household has been broken up.

It was Mrs McQueen who alerted us to the illness. She brought Benjy down to me late one afternoon and said she was of the opinion that Miss Daisy was sickening for something. She said she knew Daisy wasn't her responsibility, but as she'd previously been chastised by my husband for not speaking out on a medical matter when he thought she should have, she felt the need to bring the situation to my attention.

'What makes you think she is ill?' I asked, instantly frightened out of my absorption in Mrs Browning's sonnets. 'I saw her only this morning and she seemed perfectly well.'

'Well, fevers often waits until the afternoon to make themselves known,' she said. 'And Miss Daisy was out again with the Reverend Jameson in the heat walking everywhere about the place as usual. But when she came up to see Master Benjy just now, it struck me as she was very hot and, well, clammy – if you don't mind the word. And then she says she don't feel so well, so I told her to go to her room and take a glass of water and lie down while I come to tell you. I didn't want Master Benjy to catch nothing.'

My throat tightened. I have almost a superstitious dread that the Angel of Death, having been once cheated of my son, is ever hovering over him eager to swoop again. 'No, of course not,' I said hastily. 'You did right, Mrs McQueen. I'll get Hannah to run to Dr Lawrence's immediately. Please keep Benjy up in the nursery, well away from Daisy's room.'

I rang the bell and dispatched Hannah for the doctor, then ran upstairs. Poor Daisy looked very red and hot and her forehead was burning. 'Oh, Mama,' she said in a whisper. 'I have such a sore throat.'

'When did it come on?' I asked, loosening her little collar and wiping the perspiration away. 'Why did you not say something earlier, you foolish child?'

'It wasn't very bad then. I had a headache, but I thought it was just the sun. It seems to have got much worse since I lay down. Oh, Mama, I hope I haven't given anything awful to Benjy.'

Anything *awful*. My heart thudded against my ribs. I'd heard scarlet fever was rife again in the poorer parts of Jericho and that a number of infants had recently died. But I'd always felt safe here, in the better part of town, among trees and gardens and away from bad air and open drains. But nowhere, of course, is ever really safe. It took me all my self-control to appear calm to Daisy. 'No, I'm sure he is quite well. Even if you have some sort of fever, you've hardly been with him any time, according to Mrs Mac. Now, let me undress you and put a cool flannel on your head. Dr Lawrence will be here very soon.'

Her little limbs were burning hot as I chivvied her out of her petticoats and drawers and put on a clean nightgown, and as soon as I was finished, she lay down quietly, her eyes closed. She made no fuss at all, and I thought what a sweet child she was, and how Daniel was right, after all, to have sung her praises. And as I gazed at her face, straining for any sign of the scarlet rash, I couldn't help thinking how much the new way of having her hair suited her. I felt sorry that I had made so much fuss about it. I placed my hand on hers, and she clasped it softly, and held it until the doctor arrived.

Dr Lawrence said there was clearly a fever, but he couldn't be sure as to the cause. 'If a rash appears tonight or tomorrow, it will be scarlet fever, a hundred to one, so it's important that she's kept in isolation. Young Benjy's the one you need to look to, given his age. In fact, if I were you, and if you have the means and opportunity, I would take him away from the household completely. I would suggest three weeks at least to be sure the infection has passed.'

'Yes, yes,' I cried, running through all the possibilities and coming to the solution before I had fully weighed things up. 'We can go to my father's in Herefordshire. The air is very fresh there. We can go tomorrow.'

Then Daisy's voice broke in. 'Will you be leaving me, then, Mama?'

And I experienced a sudden rush of guilt that my first thought had been for my son and not for my poor, sick daughter. I should be with her, of course. Yet Benjy needed me, too; I could not abandon him to Mrs McQueen for a whole three weeks. I turned and stroked Daisy's shorn locks. 'We'll see. If I do have to leave you, it won't be for long, I'm sure,' I said. 'And I'll see you get the best care in the world.'

'Thank you, Mama,' she said, closing her eyes.

But how was I to manage her care if I were in Herefordshire? Sadly, I had no mother or aunt to turn to, and Daniel's aunts were elderly and too far away to help. Naturally, Daniel himself would supervise the servants in my absence, but he could not be expected to sit by Daisy's bed and do all the womanly acts required in these cases. I needed someone who could nurse Daisy in a proper, motherly fashion. But who? Mrs McQueen was out of the question, and I could hardly leave Christiana and Sarah in the house unchaperoned. What if Leonard Gardiner took it upon himself to write letters or pay visits when Daniel was not at home? I knew Christiana was not above encouraging his attentions, and there would be no competent person to prevent her (Hannah naturally being excluded from this category). And, of course, they might find occasion to set forth into the town unaccompanied. They had no idea of the dangers of the world and did not appreciate that even respectable Oxford was not always what it seemed. No, they would have to come with me. It was high time they saw their grandpapa, and a change of scene would suit them, as well as placing them at a distance from Mr Gardiner and his syrupy smile. But that still left Daisy with no one to nurse her. Not for the first time I bitterly regretted that we had been so hasty in dismissing Nettie: I knew her to be utterly reliable in the sickroom, and, had she still been with us, I could have travelled to Herefordshire in the full knowledge that Daisy would be both loved and cared for. As it stood, Hannah was the only household member in a position to tend to the child, although I feared she was too flighty for such a task. On the other hand, she had been her nursemaid before, albeit reluctantly. And Cook and Matthews, relieved of their habitual duties, would have to help with any other tasks. And, if all else failed, Daniel would have to hire a fever nurse.

I began to breathe a little more easily. Sickness is always such a cause for panic when there are small children in the home. I remembered how dreadful it was among the poor families in Poplar when sickness came. They could not afford doctors, of course, and all they could do was watch and wait. Every family put at least one child into its grave, and most had seen a good many more taken from them. *What will be, will be*, they said. They were so stoical, it made me ashamed. I was the clergyman's wife, the one who should have uplifted them with hope of Heaven and Eternal Life; but it seemed as though it were they who were giving *me* a lesson in accepting God's will. Yet the more I thought about it, the more I felt it could not really be God's will that such little ones should die. It occurred to me that God had placed me there in the midst of them in order to fight against the dirt and poverty that caused such deaths. I was as angry as Daniel to think that such conditions existed within a mile or two of the Parliament building, and that none of our legislators were moved to lift a finger to prevent them. I sat with him as he wrote his pamphlets in the evenings, his tirades against the lack of schools, lack of honest employment, and the iniquities of child labour; and I even added a sentence or two of my own describing the plight of the poor people in our parish: the lack of clean water, the condition of the houses, the daily presence of rats and fleas. I was passionate in those days, and not averse to tucking up my skirts and scrubbing the floors in the worst of the hovels. My knuckles, I remember, were often red-raw, and our bishop once remarked on the fact when I sat drinking tea with his wife on the occasion of the annual diocesan Christmas party. 'My, Mrs Baxter, you have clearly been practising what the rest of us only preach!' And he'd laughed as if I was an embarrassment to him. I'd said it was only what Our Lord would do, and he'd looked at me very directly and said, 'Ah, you know the mind of the Almighty, do you?' and turned away. His wife had patted my wrist and said, 'I used to be like you. But it is impossible for one person to put everything right in the world. Wait until you have children of your own, my dear. You will find your view of things will change.'

I am afraid to say that she was right. After Christiana was conceived, both Daniel and I vowed that we would stay in the parish and continue to fight the good fight. But I was not well when I was carrying her. I was often unable to eat, and liable to faint as a result – and, even with a maid-of-all-work in the mornings, I found it hard to do my own domestic chores, let alone shoulder the burden of others. Nevertheless, once she was born, I bound her close to me in a big plaid shawl, and went out on my visits as usual – tramping up broken staircases to mouldy little attics with holes where the rain came in, and where the bedclothes were live with vermin; helping with the cleaning and washing when the women were laid low; teaching the children simple hymns and prayers on the wash-house steps, with the smell of melting tallow and boiling tripe drifting over from the factories and almost stifling me; and, not least, learning to avoid the drunken embraces of men who had found day-work on the dockside and spent their wages in the public house before returning to take a poker to their wives. At the end of one particular day, I was so overcome with exhaustion that I fell down in the street and was picked up by a passing chimney sweep and carried home on his cart. 'This is no life for you, missus,' he said, and I began to fear that it was not. And yet I had dedicated my life to such work: I could not let God down. I could not let Daniel down, either. Day after day, I hid my weariness from him. Day after day, when we had both toiled in the parish until our heads ached, I would settle Christiana in her cradle and continue to work by candlelight. There were always threadbare sheets to be mended, and I had to keep detailed accounts of my expenditure in the parish: bandages, sewing needles, pocket-handkerchiefs, tin bowls, enamel jugs, carbolic soap and combs. Then, when all was accounted for, the books balanced, and the candles burned down, sometimes all I wished for was to fall into bed and sleep. But every night I had to pray with Daniel in the way he liked best. I had once found this so uplifting, and had entered with joy into our naked intercessions; but at that time I found it hard to match Daniel's ardour. He never seemed exhausted, in spite of a day as hard as mine, and was always anxious to do more than his duty as a husband. As a result, it was often two o'clock when we fell asleep. Such nightly bliss, I feared, would have its consequences, and indeed it was not long before another baby was on its way. I recall leaning my face against the greasy wall of the kitchen and nearly despairing. I did not know how I would manage, and I wondered how the poor women I ministered to could give birth to child after child with no one to assist them – no kind mother or considerate husband – and still could endure with simple fortitude the filth, violence and drunkenness that were all around them. I began to admire rather than pity them. I began to wonder what right I had to preach to them – I, who was broken down by my encounter with so much lighter a load.

Daniel was always so fresh and strong, up every day with the lark and whirling around the parish like a dervish – from the ragged school to the workhouse, from a funeral to a baptism – but he was not blind to my smaller struggles. When Christiana was just taking her first steps, and Sarah still not weaned, he decided the time had come for us to move to a more genteel parish. 'You are not well enough for this, my darling. The work is too hard, and rubs against your gentle spirit. If I am not careful, you will begin to wish you had taken yourself off to the Lay Sisterhood and had nothing at all to do with me.'

I told him I had never regretted the life at Caerwen House, and that nothing would induce me to go back or separate myself from him. I pressed myself to him in a rush of ardent spirits. 'Give me another year, I beg, to show you my worth. I am getting stronger, and there is so much to be done.'

But Daniel was adamant. 'You must have proper servants,' he said. 'Not just a girl from the workhouse. You must have proper help with the children. We must all have better surroundings. You must let me do what is best.'

What he *did* do (unknown to me) was make his case to my father; and within the week I received a letter from Papa insisting that I bow to my husband's wishes and move to a more congenial parish.

In my humble opinion you have done your share with the Poor, and you now deserve a Reward. You will say your Reward will be in Heaven, I know that, Evelina, and I commend you for it. You have chosen a hard path and I have until now stood back and let you tread it, knowing your dedication – and if I may say – stubbornness. But you must think first of your two girls, and of course of any son who might follow them. Who will your children meet, and who will they play with in that most confounded place? If you do not see them properly brought up, I shall be obliged to see to it myself. I shall have them made over to me as my wards unless you come to your senses. Daniel is with me on this, and I hope that if you do not yield as a daughter, you will do so as a wife.

With my father and husband in league with each other for the first time in our marriage, and with the threat to separate me from my children, I knew that I could no longer hold out. For the first time, I felt a sense of estrangement from my husband. Daniel had always been my other soul, and shared with me everything he thought and did. But now he'd shown me that he could be secretive and separate, and could, if it were in his interests, treat me as if I had no more power to decide matters than a child. And, in a matter of weeks, I was aghast to find that he had, again without my knowledge, used my father's influence to procure the parish of St Cyprian in Oxford.

'I thought you believed in preferment through *merit*,' I said angrily, when he announced the news. 'You said you'd never accept a Living on the whim of a rich man.' And he laughed and said, 'Who has merited such a parish if not us? We have toiled in the vineyard and it is time to enjoy the grapes.' It was indeed the kind of opportunity he had longed for: a thriving, active parish, although with a congregation much divided between an enthusiasm for the ancient traditions, and a fear of popery that ran very deep. He thought that God was calling him to blaze a trail through the dissent, to reform and reconcile from within. 'I will be in the thick of things,' he cried. 'At the very centre of God's work!'

Daniel may have been enthusiastic for the change, but I felt wretched at leaving the women who had become, in spite of the differences in our stations, my friends and companions. And they were sad to see me go, which I found affecting in the extreme. Some of them made me a small sampler with the embroidery stitches I had taught them, saying I could hang it on the wall in my new home and think of them. I wished I could have written to them afterwards to show they were still in my heart – but they could hardly read, even after many efforts on my part to teach them their letters. They could decipher 'Keep Out' and 'Private Property' and 'No Trespassers', and they could tell the difference between 'laudanum' and 'poison' on the chemists' bottles, but they could barely decipher the clear print of the prayer book, let alone the cursive scrawl of a quill. So when our belongings were loaded onto the wagon and I stood embracing them on the vicarage steps, I doubted I would exchange words with them ever again. The new incumbent had no wife to step into my shoes, and I felt I was leaving my little flock to their own devices – or, possibly, to the tender mercies of the Dissenters and the Temperance Societies, a prospect I did not relish. I have to admit that, in spite of our best efforts to keep them in the Church of England, some of the women – drawn by the vociferous hymn-singing and condemnation of liquor – had been tempted into the dreary little brick chapels with not an altar flower in sight, to be preached at until they were roused to fury. Such preaching was too full of hellfire and damnation for my taste. It was certainly anathema to Daniel. *There are those who would bend the Bible to their own ends*, he'd raged in yet another pamphlet. *They spout a testament of death and destruction and fly in the face of our Lord and Saviour, to whom LOVE was All.*

So, as I sat there, holding Daisy's hand and praying so hard that sickness should not come to our house, the thought of those not-so-distant days – when every week I helped to lay out little corpses – filled me with panic, not to say despair. If Benjamin were already infected, removing him to Herefordshire would make no difference. Perhaps, after all, I should show my faith and submit to the will of God by staying in Oxford. If God spared my son, it should strengthen my faith and increase my love for Him. But then I thought of the parable of the talents: I had to use what resources God had given me. I did not need to let my son sicken. It would be wrong of me not to take him away to safety.

Daisy was looking at me now with such pathetic earnestness that I felt I was the worst of mothers even to think of deserting her. But she was older and more robust than Benjy. Indeed, it was undoubtedly owing to her relentless gallivanting with John Jameson that the illness had come to her. Goodness knows where he had taken her – the slums of Jericho itself, perhaps, with sickness in every door and window, in every foetid puddle and stagnant gutter.

Daisy stirred. 'I wish Nettie were here.'

'So do I, my dear.'

'Could you not – send for her?' She licked her dry lips.

'Unfortunately, we don't know where she went.' I'd supplied her with her reference the day she left and I hadn't heard from her since. I could hardly blame her.

'I expect she's with that London family.'

'What London family?' It was the first I had heard of such.

'The ones where – the ones where she wouldn't be able to – have time – to come and see me.'

The child seemed incoherent. My heart beat even faster. I knew it was the fever. I could see her skin darkening and flushing red as I watched her. I had seen it before in the slums. I had seen it far too often. 'I'm sure she thinks of you, wherever she is, and prays for you too. Now do your best to sleep.'

'Yes, Mama.' She closed her eyes. And I sank onto my knees and prayed as hard as I could.

I met Daniel at the door on his return from Evensong, and imparted the news. He turned quite ashen. 'What?' he said. 'A fever? My darling Daisy?'

He threw his hat onto the hallstand and, still holding his prayer book, prepared to mount the stairs. I restrained him only with difficulty. 'She is asleep,' I said. 'Hannah is with her and will tell us the moment she wakes. But I must take Benjy away. Dr Lawrence says it is imperative. And Christiana and Sarah must come too. I cannot leave them unchaperoned. We'll go to Herefordshire. I have already telegraphed The Garth.'

'You'll leave Daisy here?' He looked horrified.

I felt guilt rise in me all over again. 'What else can I do?'

'Who will nurse her? I won't have that McQueen woman.'

'Mrs McQueen will come with me to look after Benjy. Hannah will stay with you and Daisy.'

'*Hannah?* You'd leave our dear little girl to be nursed by an inexperienced servant who has no aptitude for children?'

I flushed at his criticism. 'You were the one who was so warm for Nettie to be sent away.'

He glared at me. 'So you would have preferred Benjamin to be cared for by the person who nearly let him drown?'

'It was her only mistake in twelve years, Daniel.'

'It was rather a serious one.' He glared at me again. 'I thought we were at one on this matter, Evelina. I am surprised that you now take a different view.'

'I was upset at the time – and angry. Looking back, I think that you – I mean we – were too precipitate.' I put my hand on his arm to calm him. 'But why are we arguing, Daniel? That is all past, now. Nettie is gone and there is no help for it. But I've spoken to Hannah, and we have come to an agreement. She's prepared to tend the sickroom for an extra five shillings a week and no waiting at table, which I'm sure you won't mind as Cook has agreed to serve you herself. And,' I added, 'I daresay that once your plight is known, half the ladies of the parish will be inviting you to dinner.'

'You think I will go out to *dine* with my precious child at death's door?' He gave me that same uncomprehending look. 'Are you so cold as to think me capable of that?'

I reddened. It seemed everything I said only incriminated me further. 'Well, then, Daniel, perhaps *you* will go to Herefordshire with Mrs McQueen and the children? In that case *I* will stay and look after Daisy.'

'You know that is not possible. I have too many duties here.'

'Then what I have suggested is the only solution. Unless we get in a fever nurse from the hospital.'

'I will not have a stranger caring for our child,' said Daniel.

'She would be a trained nurse,' I argued. 'Dr Lawrence would be sure to recommend a good one.'

'What can a fever nurse do that a loving parent cannot, and a thousand times more carefully at that? Don't you remember when Sarah was so ill? How both of watched at the bedside all night until the fever broke? How neither of us could sleep, or would have done, until we knew she was past danger? How would you give less loving care to Daisy?'

His words stung me with their truth, but I was angry that he could not see my dilemma. 'What is the point of John Jameson having saved Benjy from drowning if we expose him to scarlet fever instead? Daisy is eleven, and with God's grace will survive it. But Benjy is young. Dr Lawrence himself urged me to take him away. The risk is too great.'

He turned to me, and for a moment there was something like hatred in his eyes. 'You've never loved Daisy, have you? I was blind to it until now.'

I was appalled. 'Daniel! How can you say that?'

'Because it is true. I see it now as clear as day. I think you blame her for separating us in the flesh. But she shall have one parent at least who will do his duty. I will nurse Daisy myself. She shall lack for nothing while I am here. And now I will go and see her.' And he sprang up the stairs and I heard him go into the sickroom and shut the door.

I hardly had the desire to pack our belongings after that, and Christiana, Sarah and Mrs McQueen were left to their own devices as I lay down on the sofa in the dark, and tried to fathom Daniel's meaning. Did I really blame Daisy for putting an end to the happiest part of our married life? It's true that I'd suffered dreadful pain when she was born, and in the weeks that followed, it was hard for me to look on her with love, when all I wanted to do was to die. She was so small and thin, and yet she seemed to suck the life out of me. So when Daniel told me that we must have no more children, I think at first I was glad. And later, if anyone blamed Daisy for our straitened love-making, it was surely Daniel. It was he who found celibacy almost beyond endurance. It was he who tried to exhaust himself with more parish duties than ever clergyman attempted, as well as lengthy night-time Bible readings and long vigils of prayer. He also doused himself in cold water, and mortified his flesh with cords, but these chastisements seemed only to add to his excitement. And that dreadful night of Benjy's conception – I cannot say he forced me – that is too strong a word – but he tempted me beyond my will to resist. Afterwards, when we lay naked on the dishevelled sheets, he looked at me and quite broke down: 'Oh, Evelina, I am a wicked, wicked man! I have risked what I love most in the world and I deserve to be punished. I cannot undo what I have done, but if God sees my true repentance, He might have mercy on me!' And he made me take the cords and scourge him there and then. And when he was satisfied, we both kneeled quietly and prayed.

It seemed at first as if God had decided to punish us. I did indeed conceive a child, and was wretchedly ill for the entire nine months. And when it came to my labour, my nightgown and bedsheets were saturated in scarlet, and the baby himself seemed swaddled in my very flesh as they pulled him from me. But God was gracious, and we both survived; and since then, Daniel and I have kept ourselves strictly apart. And yet Daniel seemingly believes that it is I who harbours resentment against poor Daisy for what was, after all, the outcome of his own lustful desire.

15

ᴄ⸱ᴄ⸱ DANIEL BAXTER ᴄ⸱ᴄ⸱

T HE FAMILY HAS GONE, AND I'M ALONE WITH DAISY.
Hannah is here, of course, but she's happier being sent out
on errands or doing the cleaning, than sitting patiently by the
bedside. That particular occupation is a labour of love, and one
I keep jealously to myself. In Daisy's presence, I feel my doubts
being set aside, my soul-sickness assuaged. And although I am
in agony that this fever may bear her away, I feel blessed that
I am able to watch over her like this, touching her fine, pale
skin, kissing her sweet eyelids. With every touch, I find myself
praying more devoutly. The prayer comes up from nowhere,
like a fresh mountain spring, and I am bathed in its healing
powers. I pray as I lean over her in the fading dusk; I pray in
my sleep as the candle gutters beside me; I pray on my knees
by her bedside at dawn. But, even as I prostrate myself on the
floor, I know it is not through these my own efforts that I will
be heard. I am a base sinner. But Daisy's grace and innocence
may yet wash me clean.

She has the prayers of others, of course, and maybe the weight
of their united voices will tip the balance of divine mercy. Mrs
Carmichael arrived at the front door with a bottle of soothing
medicine the minute she heard, and messages have poured in
from people offering to undertake duties of every kind. The
bishop has arranged that my curate should officiate at Divine
Service during the week, and the churchwardens have given
me temporary dispensation from my other duties. It's not long

since scarlet fever last swept through the city and everyone on the vestry committee knows of a child who was afflicted, or indeed, who perished. 'We will pray daily for her, and for you,' said Mr Attwood, the senior churchwarden, grasping both my hands, as the good fellow he is. 'I know what it's like, sir; Louisa and I have lost two of our dear ones. It really shakes you about.' I tried to thank him, to appreciate his sincere fellow-feeling, but the thought of his children's deaths did not console me and I fear I may have been abrupt. Mr Attwood makes me ashamed. He's a simple ironmonger and has never stood in the pulpit sermonizing on the importance of the Apostolic Succession, but I have no doubt that of the two of us he is the morally superior man. And that awareness makes me quail. If a man of such exemplary life has not been spared the loss of a child – then surely I, with my sins so heavy on my head, will not escape punishment.

But as I look down now on Daisy's flushed and fevered face, I wonder why, if there is indeed a Divine Being, He should, of all things, choose to punish me through a little child? Why should my sins mean that Daisy should be the one to suffer? She is the one who brought me love and hope when I was in despair. I stroke her lovely face and take her in my arms. 'Please, God, let her live.'

At lunchtime, Hannah comes up with a letter from Evelina. I stare at it, blankly; it's like a missive from another world. Once I would have torn open any letter from her, eager to devour every word. But a shadow has fallen across the open landscape of our love. It is my fault, I own it; but although it seems that God has forgiven me for my error, Evelina has not. She turns from me every night, and won't listen to my entreaties that we might enjoy at least a chaste embrace. 'I cannot trust myself,' she says. But I know I am the one she cannot trust.

I read the letter. She writes that Benjamin has shown no sign of fever and that she intends to come back to Oxford very soon.

You do not write and I cannot sleep for worrying about Daisy. She is very dear to me, and I assure you that I have never held her responsible for any change in our married love. We must both acknowledge that God is now asking for a different sacrifice from us. We are not the same people we once were, and we cannot return to the heady days of our youth – but I hope I have never given you reason to think I am not a good wife and mother.

So, she is repenting, as well she might. But I don't want her disturbing the calm and loving routine that Hannah and I have established here. I don't want her fussing at the bedside with jugs and bowls and kettles and lists of linen and banishing me to the emptiness of my study like an Adam cast out from Eden. I don't want Evelina to be the one to mop Daisy's brow and comb her tangled hair, or kiss her sweet neck and soft eyelids. I want Daisy to myself, just the two of us in peace and quietness, in the heavenly blue of her own little room. I'm nursing her as gently as any woman; better, I believe. Daisy doesn't need Evelina, I am sure of it. She only needs me.

I write to my wife exhorting her to remain where she is. It is too early to return, I say. She needs to think first of our son, and her own aged father. I am caring for Daisy in every way she requires.

I've been watching over her for two days, now. Two days in which she has lain almost motionless on her pillow, her short hair damp and matted against her brow, her cheeks flushed, the skin around her mouth eerily pale. The rash is everywhere on her body, like sunburn, but it feels as rough as sandpaper to the touch. 'The rash will last for six days,' Dr

Lawrence said. 'But the fever is what I fear, and the closing of the throat. Keep her cool. Open the windows to freshen the air. Change her clothes as often as you can and wash everything in chloride of lime.'

Hannah has duly rendered the sickroom as spotless as a farmhouse dairy. With the utmost quietness and industry she has washed the walls and the windows, taken up the rug and scrubbed the floorboards. She has even rubbed a disinfectant cloth over Daisy's books. 'Dirt gets itself in everywhere,' she said, and I nodded. I have always been very much against dirt and very much for the invigorating moral virtues of cold water, and I liked to see her so well-employed. She has a shapely form as she kneels and bends with her brush and pail.

Today she is bustling about again, wiping a carbolic rag around the grate. 'Oh, my, what's this doing here?' she says, lifting up a red object from behind the fire screen. 'Isn't it Miss Daisy's writing-book?' It is indeed the journal which Evelina and I presented to her on her birthday. That day seems more like a century away, yet at the same time I can recall it in perfect clarity – everyone in their finery, Benjamin in Nettie's arms, John in his dark suit, and Daisy in her white summer dress, eager to receive her gift, then disappointed with it, and bravely pretending all was well.

Like Hannah, I wonder what the journal is doing in the grate. Perhaps Daisy has abandoned it; after all, she'd been much more delighted with the parasol. But she isn't a careless child. If it was behind the screen, she must have put it there deliberately. Perhaps she hasn't written a word and wanted to conceal the fact from her prying papa. She seemed quite alarmed when I asked if I could read it.

'Put it here,' I say, indicating the small table by the bedside. I don't wish to open the book in Hannah's presence. In fact, I know I shouldn't open it at all.

– 233 –

'Oh, look, there's things inside it,' says Hannah, nearly letting slip a sheet of paper and what looks like a photograph or two, before pushing them back where they came from. 'Be careful, Mr Baxter, it's all a bit loose.'

'I'll be careful,' I say, taking it from her. 'Now, isn't it time we changed Daisy's sheets?'

That is something we do twice a day. Nothing can be too clean for Daisy. I carefully take the child's limp weight in my arms and carry her to the open window where I sit with her on my lap so that the breeze is in our faces, while Hannah strips the bed and puts on the new, bleached linen. I can see the sheets billowing out from the corner of my eye as Hannah shakes them onto the bed, but my gaze never wavers from Daisy's face. The summer daylight seems to make her skin almost transparent, and as pure as the holy wafer. I kiss her again and again, feeling I might almost consume her loveliness, just as I consume the body of Our Lord in the Eucharist. I hardly want the moment to end, to relinquish her soft limbs to the uncaring bedstead. But relinquish her I do, and lay her back on the mattress so that Hannah can wash her. She inches off Daisy's nightgown, sponging her skin on her chest and belly, and then along the inside of her legs. She is flesh of my flesh; it is not wrong to gaze upon her. But she is so touchingly beautiful, even with the rash upon her, that I am conscious of a tremor that I cannot control.

Then, when Daisy is newly clothed and freshly covered with a clean sheet, Hannah departs with the bundled-up linen and I draw up my chair to the bedside once more. I take a comb and gently part her hair, drawing it back from her forehead and cheeks. She must have felt the touch of the comb, because she opens her eyes slightly, and murmurs, 'Are you still cross with me about my hair?'

I'm overcome with shame that, even in her fever, she is preoccupied with such a trivial matter. 'Oh, no, my dear one,' I say. 'Not cross at all. Never think that. Never, never, never.' But she closes her eyes again and slips back into that feverish state when she can neither hear nor speak. And once more I fall to the prayers that I hardly believe in and yet dare not let lapse for a second, in case the Devil creeps in and confounds me. *Dear Lord, let her live. Dear God, let my little child live! Don't let my sins lie upon her. Don't visit my sins unto the next generation.* I pray, and pray again, opening my eyes only to make sure that Daisy is still breathing, watching the rise and fall of her chest, so slight that at times I am almost persuaded it has stopped, and I have to bend low against her to sense the tremulous flutter.

From time to time, my eyes fall upon the journal sitting on the bedside table, its bright red covers contrasting with the scrubbed bareness of the sickroom. It has been well used, that is clear. And, as Hannah noted, there are loose papers placed between the pages. Perhaps I should tidy it. Glance at it a little, maybe. But before I can lay a finger on it, I hear the door knocker and the sound of voices downstairs: Hannah and – yes – John Jameson. I get up as quietly as I can and go out onto the landing. John is standing in the porch, his hat in his hand. 'I won't intrude,' he's saying. 'But I am desperate to know how she is.'

'It's the scarlet fever, sir,' Hannah replies. 'Dr Lawrence said it's definite. All we can do is wait and hope for the best. Mr Baxter's up there now.'

But John has spotted me. 'T-Tell me I am not to blame, Daniel,' he says in an agitated fashion, moving forward into the hall. 'I am overcome with the fear I may have exposed her to some malign influence. There are infective p-particles you know, in the air and in the water. Goodness knows what harm they may do.'

What things the man thinks of. 'I don't know about particles,' I say somewhat sharply as I come down the stairs. 'But have you taken her near Jericho? Mrs Baxter says it is the only place where the disease is rife.'

'Why would I go there?' he asks with astonishment. 'There is nothing in those streets except for poverty and the Iron Works. But we have been to other places where *hoi polloi* has been much in evidence and maybe I have not been as careful as I should. Picture galleries and museums can be very crowded. Bad air cannot be avoided. And there is always ordure in the streets no matter how careful one is.'

He looks so disconsolate that I feel obliged to say, 'I don't blame you, you know, John.'

'And Mrs Baxter? I hear she has taken the others away.'

'She has to protect Benjamin. And it was best for the older girls to go too.'

He raises his eyebrows. 'So who is nursing Daisy?'

'Who else but her father?' I reply, conscious of some pride. 'With some help, of course, from Hannah,' I add, seeing the servant's quick glance.

'And there is no improvement?' He looks upwards as if to see her through the ceiling.

'Still in a fever. But, thank God, no worse.'

'Would you give her this when she is well again – and I am sure she will be well again very soon. In fact, I am quite convinced of it.' He hands me a sheaf of papers in his awkward way. 'It is a story I have written. Something to amuse her and to remind her of me and to know I am thinking of her, although I am not with her. I have illustrated it, too, although it is not quite as good as I would like. But I felt I should not delay by making a second draft.'

I take it. I suppose it is his odd way of showing concern. He clearly doesn't understand how weak she is, how incapable of listening to a story. 'Now, if you'll forgive me, Daisy must always have someone with her. She may wake, and need something.

Or she may . . . well, she may suddenly . . .' I cannot finish the words.

'Of course.' He looks very miserable.

'If there is a God of Mercy, she will not die. Pray for her, won't you, John?'

'With all my heart.' And he turns and walks despondently down the path.

I have been with Daisy ever since. She has moved a little, and opened her eyes, and has swallowed a mouthful or two of water, but is otherwise the same. My eye keeps being caught by the red covers of her journal. It's almost full, if the amount of well-thumbed pages is anything to go by, and there is no small quantity of additional memoranda inside. I can't help thinking what a conscientious and hard-working child she is, even in her leisure time, and I wonder what she has chosen to write about at such length. Her school friends? Her family? Nettie? Her outings with Mr Jameson? Even her father, perhaps? Or has she made up stories to amuse herself? I hope she has not felt constrained to keep an account of her good and bad behaviour as I suggested at the outset, sanctimonious fool that I am.

I am tempted to take a peek at it. I feel it might bring me closer to her, help me to understand her thoughts and feelings and what interests her in the wide world. But I know the journal is private, and I hesitate to intrude on her girlish thoughts and feelings, harmless though I am sure they are.

I lean over her as she sleeps on the bed. Her mouth has fallen open a little, and I can see her tongue is dry. 'Daisy, my darling,' I say in her ear. 'You must drink some water.'

She opens her eyes. I lift her, cradling her shoulders as she sips from the tumbler. I can see it is agony for her to swallow. 'Thank you,' she murmurs, falling back on the pillow, as if exhausted by that one simple action.

'Drink a little more,' I urge. 'Dr Lawrence says you must.'

She makes another effort, but this time the water spills from the corners of her mouth, so I put the tumbler down. I lay the back of my hand against her neck. Very hot still, and with small swellings each side. 'Can you hear me?' I ask.

She opens her eyes.

'Do you know who I am?'

'Papa.' She smiles her strange, sad smile.

A wave of love floods over me. 'You know you are dear to me, don't you?' I whisper, cradling her again and kissing her over and over.

She nods. Then slips back into sleep, her head against my waistcoat.

Is she a little better? I cannot tell. The changes in her are so small. But I offer up the same prayer. *Let her live, dear Lord, let her live.*

It's evening now. I've dipped in and out of sleep all afternoon. I can hardly believe how tiring it is, simply sitting and watching. I'm used to being active. In one day I can do my parish rounds, take Holy Communion to the sick, attend a lesson or two at the school, chair a board meeting of the Charity Committee – and still have plenty of time to read or take a stiff walk along the riverbank, meditating on what occupies my mind the most. I almost never feel tired. But this watching and waiting has sapped all my energies. I feel almost as though I am becoming drawn into Daisy's very body, sharing her sickness and lethargy.

And in this moment, it comes to me like a sign from Heaven; I can take on her sickness myself. That is what is required of me. That is the sacrifice God demands for my pride and my lust. I drop to my knees. *Take me, O Lord*, I pray most earnestly. *Take my life, take my health, take my sanity – but save Daisy.*

I am still on my knees when Hannah comes in with my supper and a bowl of chamomile tea for Daisy. 'Oh, beg pardon, Mr Baxter, I didn't mean to disturb you at your prayers. It's just that you've had nothing all day and Cook says she might as well hand in her notice.'

I get to my feet, a little shaken at her matter-of-fact manner and the sudden intrusion of simple material concerns. 'Cook is right,' I say with an effort. 'We must nourish the body. It's the temple of the spirit, after all. But let me try to get Daisy to drink a little first. I'll hold her up if you will manage the spoon.'

I touch Daisy's cheek with my finger and she lifts her head slightly towards me, which I think a good sign. 'Come, dearest,' I say. 'Have some chamomile tea. Cook has made it specially.'

'There's ever so much sugar in it,' says Hannah encouragingly. 'Cook says sugar gives you strength.'

Between us, and very slowly, we administer at least half a cup of the sweet, warm liquid. Daisy's head lolls a bit, and in spite of Hannah's care, some of the tea dribbles down onto her nightgown and sits there damply around her neck. 'I'll wipe it in a minute,' says Hannah, opening the collar. 'You've done well, though, Miss Daisy. Cook will be ever so pleased. And now you, sir,' she says, holding out the tray with its covered plates and a glass of wine. 'I'll watch Daisy for you while you eat – that is, if you don't mind.'

'Thank you, Hannah. You're a good girl. I shall tell Mrs Baxter what a help you've been.'

She smiles and I think what a nice-looking young woman she is, and not nearly as sharp and flighty as I'd imagined. It seems to me that I have been inclined to judge people harshly, and that there is more common humanity in my servants than I have given them credit for. I except Mrs McQueen from that view, of course. I can hardly believe that we have allowed such a woman to have the care of our son. What was Evelina thinking of? But sufficient unto the day . . . Daisy must have all my attention now.

It's night time, and I've lit a candle by the bedside. I watch over her in its flickering light. I think she breathes more easily now. Sometimes she wakes and tries to speak. I think she's fighting the fever. At one point she throws off her sheet. 'Too hot,' she says. Then she asks for water, and I gladly give it to her. Then she sleeps again.

My eye keeps returning to the journal. It almost invites me to read it. I have prayed until I no longer know what to say, and my head is whirling with unanswered pleas and unimaginable punishments. I feel the need to rest my mind. Just a page or two, I think. Nothing more. I take the book onto my lap.

She's written her name on the first page in true childish fashion. Her pet name, of course. She never uses her baptismal name, and I've no quarrel with her there. I always thought Marguerite a little outlandish for a clergyman's child, but after all the tribulations of Daisy's birth, I had to allow Evelina her way, and she had a fancy for the name. Yet, by some subtle process, this name has never been used. To all of us, Daisy is – well, Daisy. And it suits her. It's as fresh and simple as she is.

I turn the page. I see that she's written about the birthday party. So much excitement beforehand and so nearly a tragedy at the end. And John's parasol has a mention, naturally. I see too that she got up early to record her thoughts. It's an excellent practice – and one I followed for years myself; the hours before dawn have such clarity. And I see she's been turning matters over in her mind, speculating why God allowed such a thing to happen to Benjamin. Unfortunately she also sets down my dismissive answer about the ways of the Almighty. Did I believe it when I answered her in that way? Sometimes I believe that God's infinite mind cannot be comprehended by mere mortals; and at other times I think such a glib explanation is a mere excuse.

What a deal she's written – and how observant she is. And forthright, too. I am ashamed to see that, in her eyes, I am a man with a temper, and even those I love are wary of me. She says – oh, what pain it is to read this – that Nettie's departure is the *worst day of her life*. How could I not have seen that? Nettie had looked after Daisy all her life: she was a second mother. Yet I was more occupied with asserting my moral superiority than with Daisy's welfare.

16

❧ MARGARET CONSTANTINE ☙

IN SPITE OF MY EXHAUSTION, I'VE HARDLY SLEPT. I KEEP hearing fragments of conversations I can't quite place, with people I can't quite see. I've tossed and turned so much I've been tempted to take some laudanum – but Robert says one can come to rely on it, so I've refrained. But it's seven o'clock now, and I'm fully awake. In spite of my earlier misgivings, I can't wait to take the diary from under my pillow, and immerse myself in it once more. But I can't risk Robert coming in and finding me, with a repetition of yesterday's embarrassing hunt-the-parcel.

I wash and dress, not waiting for Minnie, and I'm almost completely ready when she knocks at the door. She's aggrieved to find I have done without her, and insists on my sitting down by the dressing-table while she finishes my hair. 'You've got such lovely hair, Mrs Constantine,' she says, not for the first time, as she brushes it out.

'Oh, there's far too much of it,' I say. 'Sometimes I've a mind to cut it all off.'

She's horrified. 'Oh, no, ma'am – you'd lose half your beauty.'

I smile at the thought that my beauty is so resident in my hair. 'I did cut it once,' I tell her, with the memory of my childhood transgression still fresh in my mind. 'And a very well-known literary gentleman thought it improved me no end.'

'Well, that gentleman couldn't have had no sense, begging your pardon. Any lady'd be glad to have hair like yours. I know *I* would.' And she glances wistfully in the mirror at the thin brown strands of her own hair, dragged back into a scrawny knot beneath her cap.

'You wouldn't say that if you'd had to live with it all your life,' I say. 'Just think how long it's taking you to make it halfway presentable this morning. You must have used up at least fifty hairpins.' I laugh. 'Perhaps Mrs Bloomer should advocate Rational Hair for women, as well as Rational Dress.'

She says nothing. Obviously she disapproves of Mrs Bloomer.

When my hair is at last done to her satisfaction, she lifts my nightgown from the bed, and pulls back the sheets. She bustles about, affecting not to notice that the pillow next to mine is pristine and untouched. But she's not a fool, and as soon as she goes to clean the dressing-room, she'll know for certain that her newly married master has once again spent the night apart from his wife. I don't know whether she thinks grand folk do things differently, or whether she pities us for a lack of passion. But I am brisk and lively in front of her, and pretend that all is well in my world. I don't have to pretend too hard. The thought that I might at last find the key to what is amiss makes me almost excited.

At breakfast, Robert senses my change of mood. 'You seem in good spirits, Margaret. Is the prospect of a resolution to our problem cheering you up?' He folds *The Times* over with a practised movement, and bends towards me to impart his usual morning kiss. His lips hover, and then just brush my cheek. I see he intends not to risk further rejection – until the Harley Street man is consulted, at least. 'On that very matter, I have already sent a note to Dr Lawrence,' he says. 'I was up early, and it struck me that there was no time like the present. I have requested an appointment at his earliest convenience and I hope we will hear something soon.' He helps himself to tea, and butters a piece of toast with a satisfied flourish.

'Thank you, Robert. I'm sorry for being such a trial to you.'

'All trials serve to strengthen us, Margaret. I pray every night that God will bring us together. And I am sure He will. In the meantime, I hope you will come with me to see Mrs Wentworth this afternoon. She's been asking after you these two weeks and I feel maybe it is time you started your parochial duties. The carefree honeymoon life cannot last for ever.' He stops, sensing the irony of what he has said. 'At least, in the eyes of the parish, it will seem that, now that you are established at the rectory, that, well . . .'

'Yes, Robert. I understand.'

'I don't expect you to overtire yourself, my dear, but you need to settle into your new responsibilities and – whatever our private troubles – you and I need to set an example to the congregation. We must appear together, in step, and in good heart.'

'Yes, Robert. I really do understand. I am not a clergyman's daughter for nothing.' God knows Papa's situation made me only too aware of the need to keep up appearances.

'Good. Good.' He grasps my hand and looks at me in the old, friendly way. 'We will conquer this thing, Margaret. I will not be beaten.'

He has very sympathetic eyes. That was what first struck me when I awoke to that seemingly unreal world – and saw him smiling at me. In fairy tales, sleeping princesses are always being woken by handsome princes, and in general both parties take the thing in their stride, being fated since time immemorial to fall in love on the instant. But when my eyes fixed on his I still had the mind of a child, and could only guess what romantic love was about. Yet there was something in his expression, and the way he let the blade of grass linger on my neck, that gave me the idea he might be flirting with me. And at the same time, his manner was jovial and comforting – almost as I imagined an older brother to be.

Of course, in the days that followed, when I was trying to piece my life together, it never occurred to me that Robert would one day be my husband. I may have been fifteen, but I was very childlike – and Robert was already a man of twenty-one. But I liked his kind eyes and the trouble he took to ensure that I was always comfortable and entertained. He reminded me a little of John Jameson, so I was glad to have him as a friend. We walked together and talked together and went to church together, and when he was ordained and moved away for a while, I wrote to him every week – companionable letters of our everyday doings, and how dear Benjy was growing up. When he returned three years later and asked for my hand, I was completely taken aback; I had never thought of him as a lover. But everyone said we would make an excellent couple, and Mama was beside herself with relief. 'Not every man would take a wife tainted by nervous disorder,' she said, managing with one stroke to spoil any delight I might have had, while making me apprehensive for the future.

I take Robert's hand now, and place a kiss on it to thank him for all his past kindness to me – and his present patience as I struggle with wifehood. He looks surprised, but pleased that I have been the one to demonstrate my affection. 'Thank you, my dear.' And he rises and kisses me on the forehead in return. Then he departs for his study, humming 'Onward Christian Soldiers', and treading, I feel, more lightly than usual.

I feel guilty to be deceiving him, even in this most minor of ways, but as soon as the door shuts, I put down my breakfast cup and hasten upstairs to retrieve Daisy's journal from under the mattress. I've put it well into the middle, almost at the full stretch of my arm. I know Minnie's less-than-rigorous bed-making won't have dislodged it from there. I take it to the window and open it where I've left it. I squint at it. Daisy's writing is becoming ever more difficult to read, as if she were working against time, or in fear of discovery.

Friday 11th July
Mr J did not come today as he was too busy thinking. He sent me a note which I have attached. (And there it is, in John Jameson's inimitable neat script):

My dearest Daisy,
My head is so full of mathematical problems that it has grown to twice its size and as a result I am not fit to be seen in polite company. Now, I know yours is not really polite company, Daisy my dear – nor, of course, conversely, is it impolite company – but all the same, the apparition of a man with a hot-air balloon for a head might put you in a terrible fright. You may, of course, be one of those young ladies whom nothing shocks and who walk about with their noses in the air thinking of archery lessons and cream teas, but even Dinah won't come near me, preferring to sit on the windowsill and glare. Can cats glare, do you think? I'm sure you would agree that they do, if you were here watching Dinah. She has SUCH a decided glare, that even were she to jump off and disappear down a mousehole in the skirting board, I think her glare would stay behind and hover about by the window all by itself, showing its teeth in a disconcerting manner. All this brain work is a dreadful bother and I would much rather be walking about with you and playing our little games (which I am sure you will agree are not silly at all, but very educational), but I have to do it, otherwise the Master of the college (who is a very ferocious man with a face like a Cheshire cheese) will come and knock my huge head off in front of the massed ranks of the SCR (that is the senior common room, you know) and then play croquet with it around the quad, with the Dean and Chaplain flapping about in their scarlet Convocation habits like so many flamingos – all of which I shouldn't like at all. So, you see, I shall be much obliged to you if you will forgive me from attending on you just now.
    Your very dear friend,
                John Jameson.

P.S. I shall make every effort to be with you next Monday. Please give my regards to your dear parents, and I hope your brother is quite recovered from his indisposition – although if I were he (which I'm not, otherwise I'd have to shrink to one eighth of my size) I'd carry on being poorly just so I could see your darling face next to my cot and hear you singing those sweet songs, and have – good heavens – a kiss or two from your sweet lips. But such thoughts are in vain, as the poets say – so, like a broken pencil, there's no point to it.

I see that John Jameson has put a little drawing of himself at the bottom. He's sitting at his desk with a big head like a turnip. It glows with ideas coming out in little bubbles called variously 'geometrical calculus' and 'Archimedes' principle' and 'algebraic trigonometry', and Dinah's teeth glaring at him from the windowsill. I can't help laughing.

Mr J always cheers me up, especially after I have been working hard at my Confirmation lessons with Papa. I am doing that every day now. He always praises me and says how well I have done but sometimes he looks at me so oddly that I feel I have done something to displease him. I think he must still be blaming me for cutting my hair, although he says no, he is blaming himself for something else entirely. Perhaps he is sorry that he allowed Mrs McQueen to come and look after Benjy because now he knows how horrid she is and that she doesn't love him like Nettie did. She is still horrid to me when I go up to the nursery and makes sarcastic remarks about young people who have time on their hands and nowhere to put it, but she doesn't dare tell me to go away. I know it is wicked, but sometimes it is quite nice being annoying to her. DEB

Monday 14th July
I have had a very busy day with Mr J who came as promised and brought me a very nice story book by Miss Catherine Sinclair, which I

*can't wait to read and we walked to lots of different places and he took
some more photographs of me but the sun was very hot and now I have
got a headache and a sore throat. Mrs McQueen saw me on the stairs
and poked me hard in the back and said she thought I should go to bed
as I looked feverish, so I won't write any more in case she calls Mama.*

I turn over the page, but I see only blankness, and then loose
sheets of what looks like Mr Jameson's writing – some sort of
story – then a mixture of letters, drawings, photographs and
poems, all interleaved in higgledy-piggledy fashion. It's seems
that the narrative is finished. Or rather, it's unfinished. I'm in
a panic; I can't believe it. How can she break off now, leaving
so much unsaid, and me high and dry in my expectation? Was
the book confiscated? Or was something destroyed? I examine
it again. There are pages torn out, the cotton threads loose and
broken. And at the back, some of the photographs John Jameson
took. I don't want to look at them, and quickly thrust them back.
I look again at the last entry. Daisy has a headache, she says.
And a sore throat. And Mrs McQueen is concerned that she
looks 'feverish'. *Feverish*: the word reverberates around my brain.
And I know quite suddenly that this is not any passing childhood
indisposition, but the time I had scarlet fever and almost died.
   I don't at all remember being ill, but over the years Mama has
referred to *when you had scarlet fever*, as if to recall an anecdote, and
then she's pulled herself up short and changed the subject, as
if it were something shameful, something not to be mentioned.
How can a child's illness be blameworthy? It's hardly credible,
but I can feel the lick of shame even now. I see Mama's sad
face, her look of contained patience. *I forgive you*, she seems to
say. *Just do not mention it in front of me or it will be my death.* I strain
again to recall what happened, but it's like looking through a
window from bright sunlight into a dark interior: impossible
to make anything out except one's own reflection. Yet, when

I think of the words 'scarlet fever', it's not Mama's face, but Papa's that comes to me. The mysterious shame that attaches to it must have something to do with him. Perhaps it was when his madness first began.

Even as I think it, a door suddenly opens in my mind, and I see Papa – his broad, handsome face, his thick brown hair, and his abundant whiskers. He's saying something to me. But I can't hear the words. Then he comes closer, and puts his arms around me in a desperate way. 'You won't leave me, will you, Daisy? You won't go away and leave your poor papa?' And he holds me extremely tight for a long time. So tight I can hardly breathe.

All of a sudden, I'm back there, lying in my bed. There's some sort of rumpus going on in the house. But the only person I can see is Papa. He waits silently by the bedside, or moves in and out of the lamplight like a dark ghost. He speaks to me, but my throat is swollen and I can't reply. He looks kind as he bends over me and asks if there is anything I want. I nod. I want Mama; I want her to hold my hand and stroke my hair and say kind things like she did before. But she's going to leave me because of Benjy. Benjy's her favourite. He's everyone's favourite. The only person I know who loves me for sure is Nettie and I long for her to come back with her nice, warm, biscuity smell and comforting arms. But she doesn't come. Nobody comes. Instead I hear the sound of footsteps on the stairs. Up and down, up and down. Then someone calling for hush: *Think of poor Daisy!* Is it Mama? I think I see her in the doorway, and maybe for a moment at the bedside. But then she is gone. I hear the front door bang shut and the sound of the carriage departing. I have a wild idea that maybe I've been left abandoned in the house with no one to care for me. I'll be like a plague victim, and neighbours will leave my food outside the door in a basket soaked in vinegar and I'll die in solitude. Or perhaps not in solitude – perhaps Mama has left Mrs Mac to nurse me. I imagine her hard, square face and hard, poking hands as she comes towards me, and think I would prefer to be abandoned.

But I'm not abandoned. Dr Lawrence comes, and he and Papa stand over the bed. Dr Lawrence touches my neck. I can hardly swallow, and my skin feels hot and itchy and I can't hear what they're saying and they seem far off and peculiar. The walls and the ceiling are moving around and now Hannah is in the sick-room, cleaning the floor. And now she is holding me up to spoon liquid into my mouth. And Papa – can it be Papa? – helping me to drink. Combing my hair too, and wiping my face with a cloth.

Yes, it *is* Papa. I can see his eyes. Large and brown and sad, gazing intently into mine. Now he has his arm around me, now he is on his knees at the bedside, now he is praying aloud. Now I am on his lap and there is a cool breeze coming in from the open window. I watch the muslin curtains billowing out, then falling back, the sky beyond them pale and blue, the sun a hazy golden ball. I can't keep my eyes open. My throat is so sore, my head aches so much. I feel Papa kissing me. It's a very nice kiss, soft and tender, and I drift into sleep, comforted.

Someone is stroking me. I can feel hands on my face, my neck. It's dark, except for a little nightlight a long way off, so I can't see who it is. My heart leaps up for a moment when I think it might be Nettie – but it's not her hands. I know her hands – they have rough skin around the fingertips. From sewing, she says. And being in and out of water all day. The hands stroking me now are different. Mama perhaps, come back from Herefordshire? My heart rises again, but Mama always smells of lavender, and this smell is different. I can hear the sound of breathing, as if a wild creature is close at hand, hovering near me in the darkness. I think it's a lion; I can feel his mane, his thick, curly mane and the soft pelt of his skin. But the lion goes away, and suddenly I'm at the bottom of a huge and roaring waterfall. My ears ache, and my throat aches, and my head aches. I seem to be caught up in long, tangling weeds and I flail my arms and legs about. I scream but I can't make myself heard. I'm going to drown and no one is coming to rescue me. My body is sprouting with sweat as I shriek soundlessly against the noise. Then I'm carried out to sea, and I have forgotten how to swim: I think back to my lessons on the beach at Brighton – Papa holding me around the waist and making my limbs move back and forward like a frog. Suddenly there are all sorts of creatures swimming alongside me, rising and falling with the motion of the waves. They are making strange wailing noises and they bump against me, jostling me hard. 'So very sorry,' says a walrus with a huge moustache, before he changes into a crocodile. The crocodile opens his jaws very wide and I am inside his great red mouth with his white teeth gleaming on all sides. I know I am going to die, and I call for Papa to help me, but the jaws snap shut and all is dark. But there is sobbing somewhere. It's not me. There must be someone else beside me. The sobbing is very loud. It's right in my ear. I think it must be the crocodile, weeping crocodile tears. Now I think I am being sick. Now Hannah is taking off my nightgown: 'I'll put this in the wash.' And more weeping. Weeping, weeping, weeping. Papa's voice: 'Let her live, Lord. Let her live.'

Now I'm awake again. The bedroom seems paler and barer than usual. The blue of the walls is cool. It's like the sky, and I want to fly up and be an angel. I'm calling out for Nettie, but it's Hannah that comes. She's washing me all over with a sponge. The cool water trickles down my body and drips onto the sheets. Hannah says, 'Never mind, miss, it'll dry.' She's got a towel, now. She wipes between my legs like Nettie used to do when I was little. There's a crisp sheet over me now, lying lightly over my skin. My skin is itching, but I don't have the strength to scratch. I feel sick and have a pain in my stomach. The lamp is lit now, and Papa is reading something by its light.

Now he's down on his knees again, murmuring something. Now it's daytime again and he's walking around the room. I hear Cook's voice, and Matthews. They are moving some furniture. Cook says, 'She's past the worst.' And I sleep again.

Now I'm feeling cooler, and my head is lighter. There's a pale, early morning light creeping through the curtains. Everything in the room looks normal and the walls don't fly around any more. There's a little truckle bed next to mine, and Papa is lying on it in his nightshirt, his dressing-gown half open. He's asleep. I can't help noticing his bare feet, his rather large toes, and I find myself wondering whether I have ever seen his toes before. Even at the seaside he wears swimming shoes. And his face seems different too. He is asleep, of course, and I don't think I have ever seen him asleep either – except for a light doze in the garden on a fine day with his straw hat tipped over his face – and he strikes me as looking ragged and wild. 'Papa?' I whisper. My voice is so faint, I have to repeat myself. 'Papa?'

He wakes up and looks at me. Tears start from his eyes and run down his cheeks. He takes my hands in his and kisses them so fervently that, even in my weakened state, I'm taken aback. He doesn't seem like Papa any more, and not just because he's undressed and dishevelled. He seems different in a way I can't describe.

'The Lord be praised,' he says, his voice quivering. 'Oh, my dear, I have saved you. I have been cast down into the pit of iniquity, my sins heavy upon me, but the Lord is merciful and kind. We must praise Him, Daisy. We must praise the name of the Lord.' And he draws me to him, to the warmth of his chest, bare beneath his shirt. I can feel his heart beating, and smell his breath on my face. His smell is the smell of the lion. And I am afraid of him.

17

❧ EVELINA BAXTER ❧

I AM SITTING AT MY FAVOURITE WINDOW HERE AT THE
Garth. The Black Hills undulate in a dark mass against the
skyline and the grey clouds above them hint at rain, but I drink
in the fresh, sweet air as if it is tonic wine. Now I can breathe
again, free of the exhaustion that has weighed me down since
Daniel was first afflicted. Now I can I relive our happier times
as I take up my books again, and rediscover the country walks
that we both loved so much. But guilt still knocks at my door
because I know that I estranged myself when he most needed
me, and I allowed petty jealousies and unworthy thoughts to
come between us. If Daniel had not lived so long, I might
have found it in myself to be more patient and faithful. But
no one who has not endured it can understand how dreadful
it is to have undergone the same loss twice: not merely the
death of the body, but the death-in-life that preceded it. And,
in between – such horrors.

It is an irony to think that when I first married Daniel, I was
grateful that he was such a strong and vigorous man. When we
lived in Poplar, he seemed almost immune to the ravages of dirt
and disease. He once carried a half-drowned man all the way
from the river, setting him lightly on the kitchen table as if he
weighed no more than a loaf of bread, and he'd often dig graves
alongside the sexton, matching him spade for spade, yet come
home as fresh as if he had just risen from his bed. I was glad
then to think that our children would have a healthy father to

care for them if I were to depart this life, weak and worn out as I was. But now – and God knows it is dreadful to say so – I would ten times have preferred that he had dropped dead in front of me in the full vigour of his life, than to be delivered into the hell that we were later to endure. If he had died when our love was still new and full of hope, I would have torn my garments and kneeled in the mud at his graveside, imploring him to come out like Lazarus and not leave me alone in the empty world. But in the end I would have been consoled. I would have laid flowers on his grave, knowing that he lived the serene life of the Redeemed. But Daniel's vigour was our undoing. He lived on to torment me with changes that I could hardly have imagined.

At first, there was no end of people whom I blamed for Daniel's affliction. If only Nettie had supervised Benjy properly, I thought, none of this would have happened: she would not have been dismissed, and John Jameson would not have placed us under such an obligation by stepping into the breach. And if John Jameson had not taken an interest in Daisy and escorted her to the most unsuitable places, she might never have contracted scarlet fever. And there again, if Mrs McQueen had been a better nurse, I would have been able to entrust Benjy to her care and look after Daisy myself. And Daniel – well, if Daniel had not been so passionate and angry, sweeping aside all offers of help from the parish, blaming me for being a cold and unloving mother – maybe he would have been less prone to the dreadful brain fever that ensued. And if Christiana had not distracted me with her infatuation with Leonard Gardiner, perhaps I would have been more alert to what was happening to my youngest daughter, the one whom I thought safe and reliable, who, until then, had never given me a moment's anxiety.

But I knew that there was one blame that I could not apportion to others. It was I alone who was to blame for leaving

Daisy when she was ill. A mother's place should always be with her sick child. Yet God knows I was in a torment of indecision until the very moment of my departure, when, fearful that I might never see her again, I even unpacked my valise and determined not to go. But Daniel discovered me with my clothes all strewn around, and made me pack them up again. 'You've made your decision and everything is arranged,' he said, rather stiffly. 'Once Benjamin is settled in Herefordshire, that will be the time to return and take up your nursing duties.'

'But I can't forget what you said to me, Daniel. How you chastised me for not loving Daisy – or not loving her enough. I can't let you think that I don't care about her.'

He patted my arm. 'I think I may have spoken hastily last night. I was in a state of alarm. But Dr Lawrence is hopeful. He says she is healthy and well-nourished and will fight the fever well.'

I knew he was simply trying to reassure me. No doctor can tell who will live and who will die, and even princes fall to typhoid. But I was grateful that Daniel was making my decision easier. 'Do you promise to telegraph if she worsens?' I asked. 'Please, Daniel, promise me that. I can be on the train in an hour, and back in Oxford in two or three more.'

'I promise. But I am sure there will be no need. Now, make haste and give my regards to your father when you arrive.'

'Should we perhaps hire a nurse after all?' I queried, now lacking in confidence that any of my plans made sense. 'It is too much for you to do, and not a man's task – and Hannah may be unreliable at the sickbed. I could ask Mrs Carmichael if she could recommend someone.' But then I thought that Mrs Carmichael might recommend herself, and I selfishly did not want her spending even more time with my husband than she already contrived to do.

'Mrs Carmichael, good soul as she is, has already called and offered her services. But I feel that it's *my* duty to attend to Daisy. Don't forget Our Lord himself ministered to the sick, and humbled himself with mundane tasks. I can do no less. It is a test for me, Evelina, and I shall not fail in it.'

Daniel seemed so determined, and was so persuasive that I felt I could do no more than agree. My head had been aching all night and I began to feel I would be no use to anyone in that state. And Daniel was always so very good at everything he did, I was sure he would care for Daisy in the same way. So I pressed my lips to Daisy's moist brow and made my farewells, trying to imprint her face on my memory in case the worst should befall. All the way to Herefordshire, I kept wondering if I had done the right thing, and as soon as we arrived at my father's house I almost galloped up the front steps to enquire whether a telegram had come for me. Thankfully there was nothing, and I allowed myself to feel that I had, after all, made the right decision. My father thought there was no doubt of it: he felt my first duty was to my son. Ever since Benjamin had been born, he had been delighted at having an heir, and used to lift him up and point out the fields and farms that he would one day inherit. His main anxiety that day was that he had not brought the fever with him. 'Keep an eye on him, Evelina. I will call Dr Jenkins the moment there is any sign.' But there was none.

And so that day passed, and the next, and no urgent telegram from Daniel. And no symptoms of scarlet fever in Benjy, either. It was a relief, of course. Yet it was perplexing after two days to have only the most cursory of notes from my husband. *She holds steady*, he wrote, *and sleeps most of the time. There is no need to hurry back; she would hardly know it if you were in the room. And Hannah has proven herself a most efficient nurse.* The news reassured me, naturally, and I thanked God for it. But at the same time I was somewhat mortified that they were all managing so well without me. I kept reading the phrase 'would not know it if you were in the room', and wondering what lay beneath it. Perhaps Daisy was indifferent to my absence; but then I thought how tightly she'd held my hand that night, and how sad she had seemed when I said I'd have to leave her.

I replied in haste, saying I planned to return within the next two days, but Daniel wrote back immediately, saying that Daisy was not in danger and there was nothing more to be done by 'an extra person crowding at the bedside'. He urged me to enjoy my time with my father, in the countryside I loved so much. If he had been Satan himself, he could not have made a more tempting suggestion. There is no house quite like the one where you have been brought up, and The Garth has always held a special place in my heart. I loved to walk up Baycastle Crag, just as I do now, and I would gaze around from the summit, seeing the view just as it was when Daniel and I first made the climb, the day he had dedicated himself to God and to me. The magnificence of the scenery brought a sense of peace to me, and I realized how much I had missed it. Oxford always seemed to me so flat and enclosed. So I delayed my return, assuaging my guilt by sending little notes to Daisy every day and enclosing pressed wild flowers for her to look at. *I think of you every day, and will come back soon*, I wrote. More days went past and I continued to live in a fool's paradise. Although I was a little surprised that Daniel wrote so rarely, I assumed he was too busy to do more and Daisy, I assumed, was too weak to pick up her pen.

The first clear knowledge I had that something was amiss came when a letter arrived for me, addressed in an awkward, unschooled hand and directed like a signpost *To The Rev Mrs E. Baxter*. I smiled at the oddness of the direction, thinking one of the people from the village had written to me. Then I saw that it was postmarked from Oxford. A sense of foreboding came over me and I opened it quickly. To my astonishment, the writer was Hannah.

Dear Mrs Baxter,

I hope you dont mind my writing to you like this as Cook sais it is not my place to do so but as you put me in charge of Miss Daisy a long side of the Master I thought it right to let you know and I hope you wont hold it against me as it is only done for your sake and the families, to cut a long story short I feel there is some thing wrong with Mr Baxter and I hope you will come back as soon as is conveinant.

Hoping this finds you all well including Master Benjy and with kind regards and good wishes,

Ever your Servant

Hannah Potter.

Something *wrong* with Daniel? What on earth did the wretched girl mean? Why had she not explained herself more fully? And surely such a summons should have come from Mr Morton or one of the churchwardens – or even Mrs Carmichael? To be summoned by one's housemaid was rather invidious. I felt a curious mixture of impatience with the girl and anxiety about my husband. But it was clear I had to return home. By then I was content to leave Benjy with Mrs McQueen. She was somewhat in awe of my father, who took the greatest interest in his grandson.

I took the first train I could, and arrived in Oxford late in the evening. I'd had no time to telegraph, so there was no one to meet me, and I took a cab to Westwood Gardens. The house looked just the same, but it was Cook who greeted me at the door. 'Hannah's busy upstairs,' she said.

'And where is my husband?'

'Upstairs too,' she said, with a strange look in her eyes. For a moment, I had a picture of my husband and my servant in an adulterous embrace. I started up the stairs immediately, Daisy quite gone from my mind.

Cook put out her arm. 'I should just warn you –'

'What?' My breath was coming in sharp bursts, my imagination seeing a froth of white petticoats, two figures rolling on the bed.

'Mr Baxter is not quite himself.'

'What do you mean?' *Not himself. Something wrong with him* – the words went round in my head, confused with under-linen and stolen kisses.

Cook hesitated. 'I don't know how to put it, Mrs Baxter. You'd better see for yourself. Miss Daisy's much better, though.'

'Is she upstairs too?' I tried to cover the shame I felt for not enquiring about her the moment I set foot in the house.

'They're all in Miss Daisy's bedroom I believe.'

And indeed they were. Daniel was sitting in the little blue armchair, with Daisy on his lap, and Hannah was sitting on the edge of the bed, with Daisy's nightgown in her hands, stitching. The whole room smelled of chloride of lime.

All three looked up the instant I opened the door. Hannah rose with a look of relief and Daisy scrambled off Daniel's lap and stumbled eagerly towards me. I had forgotten that she had cut her hair, and was shocked to see it so short, although I suspected Hannah may have shortened it more on account of the fever. But it gave her a new, unfamiliar look – as if she had grown up a great deal since I'd been away. 'Oh, Mama!' she cried, embracing me around my waist and pushing her face into my bodice. 'I'm so glad you are back!'

'And I'm glad too, Daisy dear. And even more glad to see you so recovered. You look so well. I think Papa and Hannah must have been spoiling you.'

I glanced up at Daniel, who had not moved or made any gesture of welcome. In fact, he was frowning at me. 'So, you have seen the error of your ways?' he said at last.

'What do you mean, Daniel?' I replied, trying to smile, to cover my disquiet at his words and his abrupt tone. 'I would have come earlier had you not begged me to take my time.'

'Then why ask me what I mean?' he said, narrowing his eyes. 'Don't try to confuse me.'

I was dismayed. Not only were his words so brusque and odd, but he seemed not at all glad to see me. Generally, after we had spent time apart, even a day or two, he could not wait to take me in his arms, and would quickly contrive a reason for us to be alone together. But now he was looking at me as coldly as if I were his enemy. 'I'm not trying to confuse you, Daniel,' I said. 'If I have done something to offend you, let us talk about it later. Don't spoil my delight in seeing Daisy again.' I embraced her tightly, but could not help noticing Hannah's expression, her eyebrows raised as if to say: *See what I mean!*

All at once, Daniel clapped his hands to his head and cried out: 'Evelina, it's you! Forgive me, I didn't know you in that perked-up bonnet! I only know you with your hair all loose. They told me you had gone away. But I said you'd come back.' He crossed the room at great speed and embraced us both. 'I knew you'd come back. I said so, isn't that right, Daisy?'

I felt Daisy nodding her head against my corseted waist. 'Yes, Papa, that's right.'

'Well,' I said, trying not to show my horror at the incoherence of his words, 'now I *am* back, Daniel, you are released from your duties. I will see to Daisy myself from now on.'

A change came over his face. 'Ah, so that's it – you have come back to take her from me! You are subtle as a serpent, but I see through you, my lady, and I won't let her go.'

I half laughed, thinking he was play-acting, although for what reason, I couldn't think.

'Don't laugh at me, woman. Let me have her back.' He tried to pull Daisy away from me, grasping her shoulders quite roughly. I felt Daisy shrink against me, and she raised her eyes in a pleading way, as if to ask for my protection. For the first time in my life I was frightened of Daniel's superior strength, feeling we were in danger of a tug-of-war with our daughter being pulled asunder.

But Hannah put down her sewing and took his arm. 'Now, sir, you know very well that Mrs Baxter in't going to take Miss Daisy away from you. But she knows you're tired and she'll sit with Daisy while you takes some rest. You deserve it after all you've been through.'

He dropped his arms, as if suddenly distracted from his flare of anger. 'Ah, yes, rest, sweet rest. *Come unto me all that travail and are heavy-laden and I will give you rest.* Yes, I am tired. Very tired. It's all the sin weighing on me, you see.' He rubbed his eyes, and I could see that they were ringed with deep shadows. 'I will go and lie down. Upon the ground. Yes, upon the ground.'

'You'd be better off in your bed, I think. Come, sir, I'll go with you.' Hannah steered him gently towards the door, as if he were aged and in need of assistance. The absurdity of my previous imaginings struck me with force, but I thought I might even have preferred him to be dallying with Hannah than to be dependent on her in this dreadful, altered way.

'Well,' I said to Daisy when they had gone. 'Papa is in an odd mood, isn't he?' I tried to sound bright, not to let her see how hurt I was by his words. 'Fancy not recognizing me! I expect he's overtired. He'll be his usual self once he's had some proper sleep.' I hoped most fervently that would be the case.

Daisy looked down. 'I think it's my fault. He sat with me all the time I was ill. And prayed ever so much.'

I held her close. 'Oh, no, my dear, it's *my* fault. I should never have let your father take on so much. But I'll make amends now. Just let me take my hat and coat off and I'll put you to bed and read you a story.' I kissed her and sat her on the bed while I removed my outer clothes. Then I dressed her in a fresh nightgown. She was weak from days of bed-rest and leaned heavily against me as I pulled the sleeves over her arms and did up the tapes at the neck.

'Mama,' she said, as she lay down on the pillow. 'Will everything go back to normal now?'

'I hope so,' I said. Already the severe, scrubbed room was beginning to be more familiar to me, and I was feeling more like the mistress of the house. I even imagined that Daniel's strange words were not as strange as I had first thought. The effects of tiredness could be severe, I knew from my own experience, and Daniel had not expected me to arrive in the midst of things, unannounced, fresh and vigorous from my holiday walks. It had been a shock to him and he had become understandably confused.

I waited until Daisy was asleep, then I sat and watched her for a while, thanking God that I'd had the joy of seeing her face again. I pulled her poor, chopped hair away from her brow and gently stroked her eyelids. She was too deep even to stir. I wish we could have remained like that: I caring for her, and she in her turn trusting me. But it was the last time we enjoyed such closeness.

I eventually left the room in search of Daniel, only to find Hannah on the landing, sitting on a little wooden chair outside our bedroom.

'Just making sure,' she whispered as she got up. 'But I think he's asleep now.'

'Why are you sitting outside like this?' I asked, thinking she looked like a wardress at Bridewell.

She put her finger to her lips and walked me silently to the head of the stairs, as if we were conspirators. Then she stopped. 'It's all right. He can't hear us now.'

'Why shouldn't he hear us? What has been going on?' I demanded, feeling at a distinct disadvantage in my own home. 'This is all very irregular. I should have been informed the moment Mr Baxter was unwell.'

'I knew you'd say that. I told Cook you'd say that. I said, Mrs Baxter'll blame me if I don't tell her. But Cook said not to go behind the master's back or there'd be ructions. I nearly posted that letter three or four times, but every time Mr Baxter seemed to get a bit better, more his old self, so I held off. But in the end I said to Cook, "We can't take the responsibility." I was afraid he'd try to go out of the house, you see.'

'He is the master here,' I said, astonished at her presumption. 'He can come and go as he pleases. Why would you take it upon yourself to prevent him?'

'I'm sure I was only acting for the best, Mrs Baxter. I just didn't want no harm to come to him.' She hesitated. 'Nor any shame.'

'Shame?'

'Well –' She shifted, embarrassed. 'He's not always properly dressed. He forgets his coat and doesn't always put on his shoes. And he doesn't really talk sense – just seems to say what comes into his mind. I had an aunt like that – she'd suddenly start talking about Old Sugary Perkins, and no one knew who he was.'

I stared at her. 'Are you suggesting Mr Baxter has lost his mind, Hannah?'

'I'm only the maid, Mrs Baxter. You'd have to ask a doctor about that.'

I felt she was bordering on insubordination, but Hannah was always pert, and I couldn't afford to cross her now. I felt absurdly reliant on this nineteen-year-old girl. 'I think I know my husband,' I said. 'And I'm sure it's nothing serious.'

'I expect he'll come round now you're back,' she said, but not with a great deal of conviction.

'Yes. I'm sure he will. Thank you for your efforts with him in the meantime. And with Daisy too.'

'She's a good little girl when all's said and done. And Mr Baxter knows it. He's always quiet when she's around. He listens to her reading for hours.' She paused. 'It was him that saved her, you know.'

'Saved her?'

'By praying all the time and always keeping awake so that the Devil wouldn't take her.'

That sounded rather like medieval superstition to me, but no doubt Hannah had imperfectly understood the nature of Daniel's vigil and the substance of his prayers. But I was touched at this evidence – if I needed it – of his devotion to Daisy. No wonder he was tired, and drained of all his customary vigour. No wonder he had hardly recognized me and had been fearful that I was about to take Daisy from him after nursing her night and day. I had to admit that I had had no idea that Daniel would have shown his devotion by so continual a presence by her side. I had rather thought the burden of the bedside watch would have fallen on Hannah. But he had set himself a test, just as he said. And Daniel had never failed a test.

'I think I had better call Dr Lawrence all the same,' I said.

'He's away in Brighton, ma'am. And Mr Baxter didn't want any other doctor to see her.'

'I was thinking of Mr Baxter's own health. Some sleeping draught, perhaps. Or a tonic.'

She shook her head. 'It's hard to get him to eat or drink anything. Cook's at her wits' end.'

'Well, lack of food will have weakened him, without doubt. Get Matthews to run and see if old Dr Peacock can come instead.'

'Yes, Mrs Baxter.' She turned to go. 'I did right, though, didn't I? By sending the letter, I mean.'

'To some extent,' I said, curiously reluctant to give her credit for her unconventional action. 'But why did you not speak to someone in authority in the church? Mr Morton, for example?'

'Nobody from the church come near us. Mr Baxter was very strict in that: no visitors, he said. Even Mr Jameson had to wait on the doorstep. And I in't been out of the house for three weeks. Anyway, I don't know where Mr Morton lives.'

'You could have found out, though. You're not short of initiative, it seems.'

'I thought it weren't the thing to have the world and his wife involved, especially busybodies like Mrs Carmichael – begging your pardon. But maybe I was wrong.'

'No, you were right,' I said, thinking the girl had her wits about her after all. The last thing I wanted was for Daniel's plight to become the talk of the neighbourhood.

Daniel didn't wake all that evening. He lay on the counterpane, his boots off but his clothes still half on. Dr Peacock came, put his head round the bedroom door and said he should be left to sleep. 'He's a strong man,' he said. 'I daresay this tiredness of his will be over in a trice.' He gave me some purifying mixture to clear his system. 'Sometimes tired blood slows the workings of the brain.'

I didn't dare sleep in my usual place at Daniel's side. Instead I lay down in the room that belonged to Christiana and Sarah, leaving open the door to Daisy's room in case she needed me. But I could not sleep. I was too apprehensive about what I would find in the morning when Daniel awoke. Would he be his normal self or would he be this peculiar person I did not know?

All through the night I could hear Daisy's bed creaking as she turned over in her sleep. Then she started to mutter, so I got up and went to her. I had left a lamp burning low by the bedside and could see that she was moist with perspiration. 'No,' she said. 'I don't like it.'

'What is it that you don't like, Daisy dear?'

She woke up with a start at the sound of my voice, even though I had merely whispered. 'Papa?' she murmured, squinting up at me.

'No, it's Mama,' I said. 'I'm back now. There's nothing to fear.'

Her eyes looked very dark in the low light, her face a mere shadow. I put my hand on her cheek, but she shrank away from me as if my touch was a branding-iron.

'Daisy, what's the matter? Have you had a bad dream?'

This time she seemed to recognize me. 'Mama! Are you really back?'

'Yes, Daisy, I really am. I know it was wrong to leave you for so long, but I will make up for it now.'

There was a long silence. Then, 'Will you tell Papa to stop?'

'Stop what, dearest?

'Those – horrid things he does. I don't like it. I want everything to be as it was before.'

'Oh, my poor Daisy!' I said, taking her hand. To have seen her father rushing half-clothed into the street and babbling such nonsense as Hannah had described must have sorely frightened the child. I wanted so much to reassure her that Daniel would soon recover and that our happy family life would be restored – but I doubted that Dr Peacock's blood remedy would be enough to bring him back to us, and I couldn't give her false hope. 'I don't like it either,' I said. 'And I only wish I could make it stop. But some things are beyond my power. The best thing is to hope it will soon pass. Now, dearest, go to sleep. I'll wait here a while and say a prayer for you. And one for Papa too.'

She lay on the pillow, still staring at me. 'But can't you –?' Her voice died away, and it seemed that she was still half-asleep.

'Can't I what?' I bent over her to hear the words. I could feel her breath on my cheek like the palpitations of a little bird.

'I don't know. Never mind.' And she turned away from me so I could no longer see her face.

I slept badly that night, torn between worry for Daniel's state of mind and concerns for Daisy's anxious state. But the next day, when I peeped into our bedroom, Daniel was awake, and seemed almost his old self. He kissed me and stroked my hair and let me help him dress. 'I am so glad you are back,' he said. And I said I was glad he was back, too.

But my hopes were short-lived. I quickly found that for every good day when he was in possession of himself, there were two or three where he was quite the opposite. 'You don't seem to realize,' he would say, shaking off my restraining arm, and pacing about the house. 'I must work every minute to make sure we are all Saved.' He refused the medicine Dr Peacock had left, saying I was trying to poison him and accused me of keeping Daisy away from him (which, in the light of our bedside conversation, I'd felt it best to do). But, now it seemed that the weeks of nursing her had created a bond between them that he could not bear to be broken, and he became agitated without her, begging me to let her sit with him in the afternoons. 'She is my angel,' he said. 'She alone will save me.' I was reluctant at first, knowing how Daisy was unnerved by the changes in her father, but I sat her down and explained to her that her company would help him to get better. She nodded and said, 'I know.'

So it was arranged, and for a couple of hours each day, there was peace in the household. He'd read her stories and, in return, she would read to him from the Bible. He would always choose Corinthians: *Love suffereth long and is kind*. He could never hear it enough. I attempted to keep them company, to enjoy some of Daniel's calmer moments; but very often when I went into the room, he'd become agitated and even enraged. Once he threw the Bible at me, and when I remonstrated that he should not treat the Holy Book in that way, he looked at me very intently and asked if I had been baptized.

'Of course I have, Daniel,' I replied.

But he said I was wrong: 'You have a sin inside you that I can see clearly. I must wash it away.' And he took the jug from the washstand and poured the water all over me so that my hair and gown were utterly soaked.

Daisy looked at me with dismay, but I thought I detected in her face a touch of amusement at my plight. I think now that I was mistaken in this, but my mind was in such disarray that I was ready to jump to any conclusion. And I own that I was rather jealous that my husband should so insistently prefer my daughter's company to my own, and that they should enjoy things that excluded me. 'Don't laugh at me, child,' I snapped, as the cold water seeped into me. 'Hand me a towel. Can't you see I'm drenched?'

'I'm not laughing, Mama,' she said. And she fetched a towel from the washstand and began to dry my arms and hands in silence. I regretted my harsh words then, but was too angry to take them back. And she wouldn't speak or look at me, but simply went on patting at my gown until I took the towel from her and left the room.

After that, she became daily more and more mute. I know I should have reached out and asked her what was troubling her; but something held me back. We passed silently on the stairs, and I no longer went to her when she called out in her sleep. In fact, I kept the door between us shut so I could not hear her.

Perhaps Daniel was right and I never loved her as I should. Perhaps there was something from that time of her infancy which made my heart less generous towards her. But in the days and weeks that followed, my excuse – if indeed I can allow myself one – was that Daniel took up all of my attention. He made demands every minute of the day, whereas Daisy made none, falling in, it seemed, with whatever I proposed, never complaining in any way. But always giving me that mute, hostile look, as if she were deaf and dumb entirely at my behest.

When Dr Lawrence returned from holiday, he prescribed fresh air and activity, saying the Brighton air had invigorated his own mental capacities and would surely do the same for Daniel. As Oxford lacks sea air, Hannah and I began to take Daniel for short evening walks in the quieter byways of the neighbourhood. But it was very difficult to manage. We were always apprehensive about meeting any of the parishioners, and frequently had to escort Daniel down a back lane to avoid an embarrassing encounter. On one occasion he ran away from us completely, and had to be brought back by a constable. On another occasion, he managed to get out of his bedroom window before breakfast, and ran into the church, addressing the dozen or so gathered for Morning Prayers, clad only in his nightshirt. Charles Morton and Robert Constantine had luckily been witness to this incursion and had brought Daniel home before too much harm was done, but I understood that rumours had begun in the congregation as to the exact nature of Daniel's 'nervous exhaustion'.

After several months of this hole-in-the-corner existence, I realized that I could not manage my husband with just the servants to assist me. We were all exhausted with the effort of trying to keep him occupied and fully clothed. So in the end I had no option but to confess all to the bishop. He was most perturbed: 'Daniel is such a fine preacher; such a fine, God-fearing man. We must all pray for his recovery.' He agreed that Charles should continue to take the services, with help from the curate at St John's, until such time as Daniel's state of mind had improved. 'I hesitate to suggest it, Mrs Baxter, but there are excellent sanatoria for clergymen who are undergoing any trials of – er – a mental capacity.'

'You mean an asylum?' I said. 'God forbid that ever Daniel should be committed to a place like that!' I'd once visited a poor parishioner in Bethlem Hospital and I'd never forgotten it.

'I leave the matter with you, of course, Mrs Baxter. But the Church is anxious that there be no scandal. I must have your assurance that Mr Baxter will be kept out of the public eye.'

'Locked up, you mean?'

He tilted his head. 'Kept confined, I would prefer to say.'

'We cannot keep him in. We are all women – apart from the gardener – and my husband is strong.'

'Then I suggest you ask the churchwardens to assist you, or any member of the congregation that can be trusted.'

So, I set out to discover whom I might trust to help me. Mr Warner, the churchwarden, had in fact come to offer his help not long after my return, but he'd turned up with, of all people, John Jameson, so I'd refused him. I'd been incensed at Jameson's effrontery, having specifically written to him requesting him to cease all correspondence with both Daniel and Daisy, and yet he came in person asking to see Daisy, and making much fuss about a manuscript that he had left with Daniel. Maybe the purpose of his call was simply to retrieve it, as it formed the basis of that ridiculous fairy story, which later became so popular. However, much to my surprise, he used the occasion to end his role as Daisy's friend and confidant. I cannot say how much that contributed to my peace of mind. Daisy was upset, but she said nothing, and I was sure she would soon recover.

So I approached Mr Warner again, and, together with Mr Attwood, Mr Morton and Mr Constantine, we formed a kind of alliance to keep Daniel confined yet active; to distract him and to stop him accosting the general public with his revelations. We took it in turns to watch over him, and the men would bring new books to interest him and new subjects for him to write about, while Matthews taught him how to grow vegetables and clip the rose bushes. Sometimes he would be utterly absorbed in these occupations, but from time to time he would ask why he wasn't being allowed to preach at church. 'You are all preventing me from taking my message to the people,' he would say. 'You are of the Devil's party.'

This regime continued for the best part of three years. In spite of some terrible lapses, we always imagined that we saw signs of improvement – the return of Daniel's genial manner and more lucid conversation – and we continued to hope. Charles Morton carried out all Daniel's duties and the bishop gave what support he could, finally bestowing on Charles the title of Perpetual Curate *pro hac vice*, to be revoked on Daniel's return to health. The congregation prayed for him every day, and although his condition was formally attributed to overwork, most of them knew how badly his mind had been affected. Mrs Carmichael, calling to pay her respects, was distressed to find that Daniel did not know her before deciding she was the laundrywoman come to wash the shirt off his back, which he proceeded to remove. And he could be very insulting at times. He called me names that no woman should hear, and spoke harshly to Christiana and Sarah and made them cry. Dr Lawrence gave him copious doses of laudanum, which gave us respite – but, in the end, nothing helped. Even Daisy's calming effect diminished. She became increasingly reluctant to read to him, although he was always asking for her. I didn't exactly blame her; Daniel's often-stated love for her was more than a little suffocating.

And so, at last, I had to swallow my pride and consider a 'place of asylum'. It was not a bad place as these places go – but when I first visited Daniel there, I was shocked at the number of afflicted clergymen who skipped about and ranted to the heavens. Daniel came to me immediately, which was gratifying, but within minutes he accused me of being the cause of his captivity and caught hold of my skirts and begged me to release him. 'You are my wife, Daisy. They will listen to you.'

'It's Evelina,' I said. 'Not Daisy.'

'Ah, yes,' he said. 'Evelina. I see that now. You have long skirts and stars in your eyes. But where is Daisy? I've bartered my soul for her, you know. I have the right to see her.'

His delusions were clearly as bad as ever, and I had no intention that any of our children should see their father in such a place. In addition, it took the best part of a day to make the journey there and back. But the Superintendent said it might help Daniel recover if he could see his daughters. I refused at first, wishing to spare them more distress. Daniel could rarely be prevailed upon to wear anything more than a nightshirt; and he would often remove that. If I remonstrated, he would begin to unbutton my bodice or lift up my petticoats or – horror – pull down my drawers, and seek to lie with me in full view of everyone. I, who had once been so intoxicated with his body, now shrank from him as if he were a savage. And, every time, he asked for Daisy, and cried when I told him she could not come.

But, finally, my conscience got the better of me. None of the girls was anxious to go, but I insisted: 'He is your father.' Benjamin was left out of the expedition; Daniel seemed to have forgotten he had a son, and I did not remind him. But I was, surprised at how reluctant Daisy was, and how pale she looked when we set off. She was even paler when we arrived, and I thought she might faint as we waited in a little anteroom for him to appear. Daniel seemed to have grown much older in the course of a few months and I could see that the girls were taken aback. He was very scantily dressed and, as usual, seemed unaware of any impropriety. He pressed his half-naked body against us with expressions of great joy. Christiana and Sarah submitted graciously, but Daisy hung back, her stare fixed on the ground. In fact, she paid him little attention, and when he took her on his lap, giving her loving kisses and showing her special attention, she sat stock-still and glassy-eyed, and made no attempt to speak to him. At first, I felt it was somewhat unkind of her, given her father's obvious joy in her company, and I was annoyed that she made so little effort. It was as if the sweet little Margaret who'd sat with him every day and been the apple of his eye had completely vanished, and a horrid, cold girl come in her place. But then I realized that it must have been a shock to her, as it had once been to me, seeing her beloved papa in even more reduced circumstances, no longer the adored shepherd of his flock, not even the titular head of the household – but simply one madman among many. It was a great deal for a child of fifteen to bear, and I spoke gently to her then, and tried to ease her away from Daniel's smothering embrace. I knew that of my three girls, she'd been the one who had borne the brunt of the terrible changes in Daniel, and I could only suppose that after his departure, she'd comforted herself by putting all thoughts of him quite out of her mind. And now, this ill-advised visit had brought back memories she would rather have forgotten. I think I was right in my deduction: on the journey home she said nothing at all, and when I spoke of Daniel, she simply looked out of the carriage window. Indeed, I never heard her speak of him again. It was as if she had absolutely erased him from her mind.

None of the girls wished to repeat the visit, and not long afterwards, I put an end to my own. I could not endure being subject to such public humiliation. It was difficult enough that I had to endure all the curious and sympathetic enquiries at church every Sunday, and to stand in the pew saying the Creed and praising a God whom I felt had abandoned me.

Christiana was, to my surprise, my staff and comfort during this time. Indeed, she has turned out to be the most dutiful of our children. She lives just five miles from me now, across the Welsh border – where Charles has at last taken up a Living of his own. He is an excellent man, and the whole Baxter family owes a great deal to him. He was not the suitor we would have wished for our eldest daughter – and not the one she had dreamed of herself, I daresay, when she drew her bow with such grace in front of Leonard Gardiner, or danced with such feeling around the drawing room at Westwood Gardens. Charles, poor fellow, is rather pale and thin, with spindly legs and an indistinct voice, and I'd feared that she would ignore him much as she had previously ignored John Jameson – and for many of the same reasons. But she has been faithful and done her duty.

Sarah is still unmarried and likely to remain so, dedicated as she is to the life of an amanuensis in the household of a German theologian, crammed up, I believe, in an attic bedroom with pen and paper and dozens of Bibles. I have encouraged her to come home but she insists she is happy learning Hebrew and Greek, and hopes in time to attend lectures at the university under the auspices of Herr Doktor Fischer. She has set no date for her return. I tell her that we are no longer in Oxford to be pilloried and pointed at, but she only says that Dr Fischer cannot do without her.

Benjamin, of course, cannot remember his father and takes each day as it comes. But he is away at school much of the time, so I cannot count on his company. He can't bear to be called Benjy, which he says is childish. If I *have* to shorten it, he says, he'd prefer 'Diz', after the prime minister – which I think a good deal worse. He chafes at schoolwork and I fear he often neglects his prayers. Maybe Oxford will change him in due course, but he has no desire to follow his father's profession, and looks forward instead to inheriting his grandfather's estate when he is twenty-one. The tenants know him well and find him amiable and cheerful. Already he has Daniel's hearty manner and bonhomie. Sometimes, when he pushes back his hair and smiles at me, he is so like Daniel that I can hardly bear to look at him.

And then there is Daisy – or rather, Margaret. It is an odd thing, but it's the old name that keeps sticking in my mind. 'Daisy' was Daniel's name for her, but, as is the way of children, she decided one day that she didn't like it. Of course, a change of name cannot change a person's character, but it seemed to me that the alteration I had observed in her when I returned to Oxford at Hannah's behest, was reflected somehow in her decision to change her name. Once she was Margaret, she became even more unknowable and secret.

She is still unknowable, now. There is a *froideur* that keeps me at a distance. I feel I am about to say the wrong thing, or that I have already said it. She is such an awkward person to converse with that I am amazed that Robert Constantine was able to make any headway with her, especially as he is a shy young man himself. I had no idea, in all the years he was visiting the vicarage, that he was attracted to Margaret, or she to him. A mother likes to think that she has a sixth sense in such matters – or at least that her daughter will confess to her when she is in love. But with Margaret there was nothing – just silence, stillness and secrecy. She and Robert spent hardly any time alone as far as I remember, and she showed no excitement, no blushes, no sense of delight at being close to him. He might have been her brother – or indeed her father. As the wedding approached, I thought it likely that she was ignorant of the intimate duties of a wife, but when I tried to speak to her, she turned the conversation elsewhere, and so I let it lapse. Robert would guide her, I was sure, just as Daniel guided me. It does not do for a woman to know too much. It is the husband's place – and his pleasure – to instruct her.

I have not seen her since the wedding, she and Robert being on honeymoon, and I being so preoccupied with settling myself here at The Garth, although I have corresponded weekly with her, as I do with all my children. She writes of all the new things she is doing. She sounds quite animated, and I hope this means that married life is suiting her, although there is no mention yet of a child. I cannot help feeling that she is fortunate to have gained the love of Robert Constantine, who will, when his great-aunt dies, have wealth enough for a large family. With this thought in mind, I directed Daisy to the old toy-box that was left behind when I moved, and I believe she is going to investigate it. I warned her it was mainly dog-eared paper, but Daisy will make up her own mind.

18

⤬ JOHN JAMESON ⤬

I HEARD LAST WEEK THAT DAISY BAXTER IS MARRIED, and that she has moved into St Aidan's Rectory. I can hardly believe that my little flower now manages an entire household, and warrants being addressed as 'Mrs Constantine' every day of her life. At the same time, I feel sick at heart to think that her childhood is now so irrevocably past, and that I am the only one to mourn it as it should be mourned. I have many other child-friends now, a fact not unconnected with my small fame as an author; and I can pick and choose among the cream of those whom I meet or who write to me in their hundreds. I can even delight in the companionship of girls as old as fourteen or fifteen, provided they keep the freshness of childhood in their hearts. But once a young girl marries, she generally loses all capacity for enchantment. Still, it is the way of the world, and I hope Daisy is happy in her new life.

I think of her, of course, and imagine how delightful it would have been to take a photograph of her on her wedding day – a flower still in its perfect bloom. I would have had her look directly at me, her dark hair framed in its veil of white; orange blossoms massing in her hair; and that ineffable combination of purity and eagerness in her grey eyes. But this is mere foolishness. Far from taking any photographs of the bride, I did not even attend the ceremony. Mrs Baxter has not spoken to me for years and fails to acknowledge me in the street – and my relationship with Daisy was forfeit long ago. I have seen her at a distance, as I have seen them all; Oxford is a small place and we have been obliged to rub up against one another from time to time – at concerts or in the public parks, and occasionally at the cathedral – the eldest girls very tall and fine, and never looking in my direction, and the little boy Benjamin giving his arm to his mother with great ceremony, as if he were the paterfamilias. We never speak, but Daisy has always contrived to give me a shy smile before being hustled away in a flurry of petticoats. Naturally, I cannot help but hear the gossip that swells in their wake – the whispers, the commiserations, the questions. The family has had to put on a brave face since Baxter's downfall. That was a very bad business. A very bad business indeed.

I was as shocked as everybody else by his sudden descent into insanity, but having had a good deal of time to consider the matter, I confess there were some early signs that his mind was overwrought. He was ever a man of extremes and, since those first debates in college, he had struggled with doubts about the validity of his position in the Anglican Church. I could myself never warrant becoming heated over *Anglican Attitudes*, or even the famous *Tracts*. I did not entirely lack sympathy with Baxter, but while I had long come to the conclusion that logic has to be thrown to the winds where matters of faith are concerned, poor Daniel was incapable of taking such a pragmatic approach. He could not (like the rest of us) put his doubts in a separate and hermetic container, and trudge on with familiar habits of belief simply because they *were* familiar. He needed absolute certainty. I rather think he expected personal guidance from God Himself. And although I might be regarded as but a poor substitute for the Almighty, he would nevertheless catch me in the hallway when I went to collect Daisy, and, like the Ancient Mariner, draw me into his study and make me listen as he reviewed the whole basis of his faith. 'Suppose I have chosen the wrong path?' he would say. 'Suppose I am leading *others* down the wrong path? Perhaps Newman is right. Maybe a return to the traditional rites and beliefs is what we need. But I don't *know*, Jameson. I don't *know*.'

I always attempted to reassure him. 'Your parish does more good in Oxford than anyone has the right to expect. Think how many souls you have brought to salvation; how your church creaks at the seams on Sunday with eager worshippers who want to hear you preach. It's the Devil that makes you doubt, Daniel.'

I wish, in retrospect, that I had not mentioned the Devil. That fiery entity had been preying on Daniel's mind rather too much. He had allowed himself to dwell excessively on the question of Eternal Damnation and no explanation could satisfy him. But that was the other characteristic about Daniel: he could not hold his uncertainty quiet within him; he had to take up a Position. I urged caution, time to reflect, but for him there were no half-measures. And because I refused to become agitated in the matter, to – as it were – stand on the street corner with a tract in my hand, he accused me of *Laodicean lukewarmness*: *neither hot nor cold*. It was typical of him to have been poring over Revelations – a Book I am not fond of, I must say. And it was typical of him to find such a text.

Daniel was very extreme in other ways too. He told me he took a cold shower every day, rubbing and scrubbing until his flesh was raw: 'To keep the Devil away, John. To keep the Devil away!' And such ablutions were not just a prophylactic against sin; he took actual *pleasure* in the icy water, and expressed surprise that I myself took no similar daily refresher. I said I did not feel the need to mortify my body further; it was a poor enough thing as it was. But to be perfectly frank, apart from the unreliable workings of the college plumbing, I am rather like a cat, and hate to be cold or wet for any length of time.

I like to go about my toilette in a quiet, methodical way and nothing invigorates me afterwards so much as the prospect of a big fire in my room, and Benson coming in with a plate of toasted muffins. And as for the Devil – well, we have had our tussles, he and I, and continue to do so; but I don't feel cold water is much of an impediment to his temptations. So, in my lukewarm way, I took all these manifestations of my friend's excitable state of mind very much in my stride. I thought them not only native to him, but necessary to his equilibrium, in that they allowed him to let off steam. In that I was apparently both right and wrong.

I did not, in fact, witness the first signs of his breakdown, as I had decided to move to the seaside for the remainder of the summer vacation. The decision had been somewhat forced on me when I found all my hopes of attending on Daisy dashed. I'd called at the Baxters' house regularly throughout her illness, and once I had good news of her improvement, I hoped I would soon be reading a story at her bedside and encouraging her once more to take an interest in the world. I'd already sent numerous gifts of fruit and sugar biscuits, as well as a draft of a fairy story which I thought would amuse her. But each time I presented myself, I found the vicarage closed to me, and Daniel himself incommunicado. The servant Hannah would always answer the door, take the gifts, and give me reports on Daisy's progress; but she always added that Mr Baxter thought she was not yet well enough for visitors: 'Not for some weeks, sir, he says.' It was quite a blow; and I feared that I was being kept away as a punishment for not taking proper care of her.

Indeed, I blamed myself to some extent, recalling all too late an incident that had occurred and which had fallen from my mind with all the anxiety and hullaballoo. Just days before she fell ill, Daisy (who had a pronounced fondness for babes in arms which nothing could subdue) had enthusiastically embraced the infant of a somewhat uncouth family who had been waiting at the boating station alongside us. The child was rather dirty and wore a sticky residue around his mouth, and had coughed all over Daisy's face as she tenderly bent over him. Now, it is hardly to be credited that a sensible family would take a child with scarlet fever on a boating trip; but there again, some families are not just un-sensible, but insensible – and now I feared that this encounter may have given rise to Daisy's illness. But, with my guardianship of Daisy already under criticism, I felt discretion was advisable, and communicated nothing to Baxter of my post hoc suspicions. I might have written, I suppose, but Hannah, the servant, persistently stated that her master was exhausted by his duties in watching over Daisy night and day, 'and wasn't his usual self', so I felt such news would be an additional burden. With hindsight, I believe that he had already become caught up in his derangement.

Being, therefore, with time on my hands, I determined to make an exit from Oxford. I am used to decamping, as I generally take a holiday in July or August at one of the popular watering places, somewhere where there are plenty of little children to observe, and – if I am lucky – to talk to for a while. While trying to decide between the joys of Brighton and Bournemouth, I recalled that Daisy's friend, little Annie Warner, had mentioned that she was going to Ilfracombe for the summer, and it occurred to me that I might go too. I had never been to Ilfracombe, but had heard it had a bracing climate and picturesque cliffs and rocky coves, so I decided to take my camera and equipment and see what opportunities presented themselves. Benson had become a dab hand at packing my equipment and could do it in nine minutes flat. I have an excellent folding chest of a patent design, and I was able to fit myself, my clothes and my camera into the cab without the slightest problem, and thence onto the train. As we puffed out of the station, I breathed Daisy a sad farewell and turned my attention to the future, as a man must do when he is disappointed in love.

Ilfracombe is a very pleasant place, though very hilly when one has to carry around a portmanteau of bottles and wet-plates, so I decided I would reconnoitre without my camera before I attempted to capture any views. I also hoped I might meet Annie as I strolled about. I put on a suitably maritime straw hat, selected a walking stick, and set forth in the direction of the harbour. There were a great many people enjoying the sunshine: men, women, children – and also a great variety of dogs. The whole promenade seemed full of white crinolines and sun bonnets. Most of the ladies had frilled parasols as well as large, brimmed hats, and many of them were pushing perambulators with more frilled children inside. I half expected to find the dogs had frills too, in the manner of Dog Toby, but there was no Punch and Judy to be seen. A brass band was playing in a bandstand just under the hill, and a group of little girls was dancing in time to the music, supervised by a nurse-maid with a long, frilled cap. I smiled as I passed and one of the girls gaily waved her hand. 'Do you know that gentleman?' the nurse said – and, in response to something inaudible, she retorted, 'Then don't wave at strangers.' How sad my heart was to hear those words, to know how the natural friendliness of children was being shaped and curbed to the demands of an ignorant society.

I decided to walk up Capstone Hill and see the view. There was a telescope near the summit, and I hoped to be able to pick out some children who might make good subjects for a picture. I could see a group out on the rocks with buckets and nets, the girls with their petticoats tucked up, and the boys barefoot and bareheaded. They bent and peered into the pools, and fished things out and examined them with concentration before placing them in a bucket. I thought it a charming scene and resolved to strike up a conversation with them, if I could, with a view to drawing them, or taking their photographs if I could obtain permission. I find mamas are so flattered at the thought of having a photograph of their children that they are willing to give me carte blanche as to composition and length of sittings, with the only proviso that I must give them a copy at the end. I have had the occasional mother who has insisted on sitting and watching throughout the whole process, and this is most disconcerting – but such parents are generally in the minority.

I set off down the hill again, lengthening my stride along the winding path, but I was nearly knocked down by a child who was rolling down the slope at forty-five degrees to my own direction of travel. I bent and caught the child by the arm to prevent her rolling further. The hill is fairly steep and the deep sea lay below us with not a great deal in between. 'Good heavens, child,' I said. 'Have you no sense of danger?'

A face looked up at me from between the strands of delight-fully disordered brown hair. A child of about six, her rosy cheeks even pinker from her exertions. At the same time I became aware of a buxom nursemaid and two other children racing down the path. To my surprise and considerable pleasure, the older of the two children was Annie Warner. She threw herself at me, embracing my waist. 'It's Mr Jameson!' she cried, more enraptured than she had ever seemed when she had come to tea in Oxford.

The nursemaid swiftly picked up the child who had rolled into me. 'What was you thinking of, Lou?' she said. 'You could of fallen into the sea, and we'd never of seen you again!' Then she thanked me and, turning to Annie, she said, 'Do you know this gentleman, then?'

'Of course, Deedee. How else would I know his name?' said Annie, with her usual spirit.

I touched my hat. 'I am J-John Jameson, a tutor in mathematics at the University of Oxford,' I explained.

'Sir.' The nursemaid gave a quick curtsey, while keeping one hand on Lou's shoulder and the other around a boy of about four.

'Annie is a little friend of mine,' I went on. 'She has come to tea at my college several times, with her mama's permission, and I have taken her photograph.'

The nurse still looked wary, as if I might be about to doff my respectable suit of clothes and turn into a serpent, so I tried again. 'I am also the friend of the Reverend Baxter, of St Cyprian's.'

'Oh, Mr *Baxter*.' Her face softened. 'Oh, yes of course. We all know Mr Baxter. He gives a lovely sermon – the best in Oxford, Mr Warner says. Still, Lou's got no right to go rampaging into you like that, friend or no friend. I don't know what might have happened if you'd not been there to stop her.'

'I was slowing down,' said the child, crossly. 'He just got in the way.'

'Ah, young lady,' I said, bending down to her. 'What you don't know is that other forces may have acted upon you – a sudden gust of wind, for example, or the unexpected eruption of a rabbit from a rabbit hole – which may have changed your trajectory and sent you over the edge. Fortunately, it is a calm day and I have seen no rabbits; and, therefore, on balance, I conclude that it was not dangerous. But, because of all the variables and unforeseen possibilities, it was not undangerous either.'

'*Un*dangerous? That's not a word!' Annie laughed.

'You've heard of undignified? And undamaged? So why not undangerous?'

'You might as well say ungood, or unbad,' she added.

'You might as well say unspeak and hold your tongue,' I countered.

She looked abashed. Then, as was always the way with Annie, all was forgotten and she laughed. At which point Mr and Mrs Warner came round the corner with the rest of the family, and introductions were effected all round. And thus I achieved my entry into the Warner household. They were a rather boisterous family, who did not stand on ceremony in the slightest. Indeed, Mr Warner always said, when anyone came into the room, 'Don't stand on Ceremony – *sit* on Him,' before erupting into guffaws. Mrs Warner was also very good-natured and so very much on the portly side that I was unsure if she was or was not in an interesting condition. She had very dainty hands, like many a well-built person, and employed herself in crocheting every spare minute of the day. Her particular speciality was ladies' mittens and she must have netted dozens of them while I was there. The children consisted of two older sisters – Bella, shortly to be married and continually preoccupied with wedding arrangements, and Eliza, who was studying at the Royal Academy of Music and forever practising on the pianoforte. Then there was a fourteen-year-old brother of rather plain features, who was destined for a life at sea (and spent all his time looking moodily at it; sitting on the shore like a young Raleigh). Then, after Annie, were two younger children – Louisa, aged six and a boy aged four – who were under the supervision of Deedee.

The family had rented a house just beyond Hele, and I was given an open invitation to join them whenever I wished. I also received permission to take photographs of the children, which I availed myself of instantly. I took the whole family grouped in the drawing room, with the light coming from the left, and Annie and Lou with their little dog in a kind of bower in the garden – very pretty, I thought, and with quite an original composition. I also accompanied the three younger children to the seashore and drew sketches of them in their bathing dress, pottering among the pools or digging holes in the shingle of the quiet beach. They would bring me empty shells by the dozen, and any live creature they could find – spotted gobies and grazing snails, tube worms and periwinkles. We clambered on the rocks and I showed them three varieties of anemones and several small sponges, and was able to point out the solitary cup coral that Gosse had identified just seven years before. When the tide came in, we collected the backbones of cuttlefish and the light pieces of pumice that floated on the waves – and the small pieces of coal that came from the steamships that were forever crossing on the horizon: white-coloured pleasure ships from further up the coast, and black and red coal ships from South Wales. And the children took long pieces of seaweed – bladder-wrack and kelp – and adorned themselves with it, and tried to adorn me too. They piled on so much that I began to look like Jack in the Hedge, and I thought happily of my childhood, and Mary running in to tell us the mummers were come – 'and a whole hedge walking with them!' Usually Deedee was with us, but sometimes we were alone, and I couldn't have been happier. One day I paid a woman to let us ride her donkeys along the beach, and Annie was the first to be hoisted up. I felt her firm, stocky body under my hands, and could not help wishing it was Daisy's sylphlike form.

I hadn't forgotten my little flower, of course. I wrote to her as often as I could, hoping she was better, and enclosing a picture or two of Ilfracombe and the little cove at Hele.

I wish you were here with me, my dear, to be enjoying the sea air and all the delights of the resort. Do you know there is an anemone here on the beach that is called a 'daisy anemone'? When I saw it, my thoughts immediately flew over the rooftops and all the way to Oxford, landing I hope, in your very own bed in your very own room where you were waiting to catch them. But your friend Annie is here, keeping me company, and she will have to do in your place. She can never really fill your place, of course – but I daresay by mentioning that we have been on Donkey

Rides the whole morning, I hope I can make you furiously jealous, so that you will be even more glad to see me when I return. You know you should really not have got scarlet fever at such an inconvenient time and I suggest you speak sternly to yourself on account of it. In fact, I suggest that you line up in front of yourself and put your hands on your head in penance, promising most faithfully never to do it again.

Please pass on my regards to your parents, and tell them I would be glad for a line from your father, even though I know he must be very busy.

To my surprise, and in spite of sending several more letters, I received neither a reply from Daisy nor any word from Daniel. I went so far as to go to the post office and enquire whether anything had been sent there by mistake, but the postmaster assured me that, provided the address of my hotel had been 'put down correct', any letter would have been delivered. I began to wonder then whether I *had* for some reason put the name down wrongly, or forgotten it altogether – and almost persuaded myself that I had done so – before remembering that I had used the headed notepaper thoughtfully provided by the hotel.

I remained a full four weeks at Ilfracombe, and during this time I heard nothing at all from any member of the Baxter family. I began to feel anxious and apprehensive and even contemplated cutting my holiday short, when a lavender-scented letter arrived, which I knew immediately was from Mrs Baxter. Why was she of all people writing to me? I opened it with some trepidation. It was very short.

Dear Mr Jameson,
Circumstances compel me to request that you do not correspond with either my husband or my daughter for the foreseeable future. Please honour this request as I shall have otherwise to return your letters unopened.
Yours sincerely,
Evelina Baxter.

Naturally, I was taken aback. In fact, I found my hands and fingers trembling as I held the note, my heart beating wildly as to the possibilities. The tone was so stern and uncompromising – yet there was no explanation. And why should I not write to Daniel? It was hardly Mrs Baxter's role or privilege to forbid such a thing. And why was Daniel not writing himself? If any offence or breach of etiquette had occurred, it should have been Daniel who admonished me. Once more it seemed to me that Mrs Baxter was using her influence against me as she stood as guardian to the domestic portals of Westwood Gardens, determined that I should be kept out. But what new thing had occurred to bring about such a sudden and drastic fracture of our relationship? Terrible fears consumed me as I thought of Daisy and the photographs, and what scandal might do to a bachelor such as myself. It did not, however, explain Daniel's silence

'Has anyone heard from Mr Baxter?' I asked, the moment I got out to Hele. I'd hoped Mr Warner, as a churchwarden and treasurer of the Indigent Widows Committee, the Sunday School Fund and the Working Men's Educational Union might have had some information to enlighten me. He had not, he said. He regarded a holiday as a holiday, and did not favour mixing it with parish business of any kind.

But as it happened, the eldest girl's fiancé arrived from Oxford within the hour and he was full of news. The vicar, he said, had been taken ill. In spite of having been spared his clerical duties to nurse Daisy, he had come unexpectedly into the church the previous day and had interrupted Mr Morton during Matins, mumbling and raving and trying to mount the pulpit although Mr Morton was already in it. 'I gather he had to be helped home by members of the vestry committee. The congregation, thank goodness, was very small on a weekday morning – but you know how bad news spreads.'

'Baxter mumbling and raving?' said Mr Warner. 'What do you mean, Bertram?'

'Exactly that, sir. Talking about the need for baptism and the benefits of cold water. And in a state of undress, too – Miss Bessemer was very frightened of him, by all accounts. I'm glad *you* were not there to see it, Bella.' And he took his fiancée's arm and pulled her towards him protectively.

I could hardly believe what I was hearing – although at the same time, in the light of Daniel's passionate recklessness, it seemed almost too possible. It would certainly explain Mrs Baxter's letter. And we had our old friend Cold Water again. My agitation doubled and then trebled.

Mr Warner was aghast. 'Good heavens, I can hardly credit it. Baxter of all people! Are you sure?'

The young man said he was absolutely sure. He had got it from Mr Attwood himself. 'He was going to write to you, sir, but as I was coming down in person, he thought it more discreet for me to break the news.'

Mr Warner shook his head. 'And dreadful news it is! We must all pray that he will be recovered soon.'

'Oh, yes,' said the eldest girl with a look of consternation. 'I hope he will be recovered by our wedding day. I'd hate Mr Morton to take the service. He has such a very apologetic appearance and speaks so very faint.'

Mr Warner looked sternly at her. 'I think your wedding arrangements will be the least of our concerns, Bella. I must go back to Oxford, see what I can do to assist. The parish will be in chaos without him; he is so much the *fons et origo* of every undertaking.'

'I'll come with you,' I added quickly, anxious to be on the spot if rumours of any kind were circulating. And so it was that Mr Warner and I found ourselves together in the first-class smoking carriage en route for Oxford.

'Known Baxter a long time?' asked Mr Warner, puffing meditatively at his pipe.

'Only eight months or so,' I responded, wishing he would put the wretched thing out, and wondering if I might open the window.

'Sound chap, would you think?'

'Very.'

'So what do you make of this behaviour of his?' He puffed again.

'Daniel is very conscientious in both his faith and his works. I do not need to tell you that. He works harder than any man. And as you know, his daughter –'

'Ah, yes, Daisy. We have had her to tea. A dear little thing, very sedate. Clara says she is one of those children who watches everything and misses nothing.'

'Well,' I said, bridling at this description of my darling. 'Be that as it may, she has had the scarlet fever, as I'm sure you know. Baxter himself has been nursing her night and day, with only a servant to help him. I expect it is no more than a form of nervous exhaustion.'

'Hmm. You may be right. I suppose every man has his limits. Even a man like Baxter. Still – *mumbling and raving*, Jameson. Does that not argue something more serious? Some form of – insanity?'

I shrugged my shoulders. I was beginning to think that pipe-smoking itself was a form of insanity, and privately wished I might oblige Warner to sit out on the roof until we arrived at Oxford. But I really could not think what might have occurred to my friend. If Daniel was mad – why, he was in good company. All the greatest men have been, in my view, a little mad. I think I am a little mad myself. And it is the reaching after the unknowable and believing the unreasonable that often puts churchmen and natural philosophers in the same boat.

That is – mad, but only 'north-north-west', as Shakespeare has it. I wondered if Daniel had been contemplating Eternal Damnation again, and the paradoxes of it all had driven him to the edge.

My mind seethed with a mixture of tobacco smoke and apprehension as we chugged and whistled through the Devon and Somerset fields. By the time we reached the panorama of 'dreaming spires', I was feeling almost sick.

19

Margaret Constantine

I SIT WITH MY EYES CLOSED. THE ROOM IS HOT, THE curtains are drawn and the lamplight is faint, casting shadows everywhere. The door is shut and the key is on the table. He's bending over me, touching my cheek, smiling at me with that special smile, the one I like and don't like at the same time. He pulls my head to him and I feel the rough hair of his chest rubbing against my cheeks. I don't like being so very close to him. But he says it's the holiest thing in the world and will save us both. He lifts his head and prays. I am always afraid when he prays. I shrink back and shut my eyes.

Now I am falling backwards: away from him, away from everything. Down I go, through the floor, through the room below, through the cellars, and into the deep, dark earth. Nothing stops me; everything melts away, and I pass through solid objects as if they are made of mist. I fall on and on, and it seems I might go on falling for ever, until I reach the centre of the earth. But Papa is falling with me. He grasps me tight and won't let go. I try to shake him off, but he grasps me even tighter. He says we must stay together always. He says I am his salvation. He is so close I am almost suffocated. Now there are sheets of white paper floating around us. 'They are the words of God,' cries Papa. 'Catch them if you wish to be saved!' There are so many of them, it's like a blizzard. I try to catch them, but however hard I try, they whirl out of my grasp. My legs and arms seem not to belong to me, and I feel giddy. Suddenly the ground rises up to meet me like a giant wave and I hit it with a jarring bump, so that all my breath is knocked out of me. My legs collapse, and my knees are suddenly somewhere under my chin. I'm folded so tight I wonder whether I'll ever be able to open myself up again. Perhaps I'll stay like this, small and folded up, so nobody will know where I am. I think that might be nice, to stay hidden, away from everyone. But I'm out of breath and panting very loud; Papa will surely hear me. Perhaps he can see me, too. I open my eyes carefully and jump with fright: there's a man's face right in front of me.

But it's not Papa. Relief seeps into me like warm water. But I don't know this man. And I don't know where I am. It's a bedroom, I think, because beyond the man I can see a dressing-table and a wardrobe. But it's not *my* bedroom. My bedroom is blue, while these walls have dark green wallpaper, and there are heavy brocade curtains at the window. The bedspread is brocade, too. It doesn't quite reach the floor, and from my crouched position I can glimpse a flowered chamber-pot beneath the bed. The bed is high and broad and has a big bolster and lacy pillows. It's a bedroom for married people, for a man and a wife. I can't think what I am doing in it.

Now the man speaks. He has a nice voice. I think I may know him, after all, with his soft brown eyes and sleek black hair. 'Margaret,' he says. 'Can you hear me? Can you speak?'

Suddenly I remember. I am not Daisy any more; I am Margaret. And the dark-eyed man who is leaning over me with such an anxious look is my husband, Robert Constantine. And the servant I can see over his shoulder is a girl called Minnie, who admires my hair. I try to move, but I'm wedged tight into a corner, as if I've been playing a game of hide-and-seek. There is loose paper all around me, the remains of some notebook. My husband kneels on the torn pages as he comes forward to grasp my shoulders. He shakes me gently, as if he is trying to wake me, although he must see that I am already awake. His face seems to grow larger, then recedes, like the tide. I close my eyes – then open them again quickly, frightened of what I might see: the heavy door; the key in the lock; the hands and fingers.

'For heaven's sake, what is it?' He looks distraught – and I know this expression all too well. I see an expanse of white bedlinen, and hear the sound of sobbing. I have made him unhappy, I think. And perhaps myself, too.

'Do I need to call a doctor?' he says, and I shake my head vehemently. I don't like doctors and there's a Harley Street man I am particularly anxious to avoid. 'Are you sure?' He rubs my hand briskly as if to warm life back into it.

I nod. I know I'm not ill, although there is something very wrong with the workings of my brain, and my heart is beating double-time.

'Then what is it? Tell me, Margaret, please.' Another kind smile.

I don't know if I can even breathe properly, let alone speak. The blood is hammering loudly in my ears and all I can think about is falling through the blackness and Papa touching me in that terrible way. And although it was only a dream, it feels real. But it can't be; it's too unspeakable. So although this husband of mine is looking at me so expectantly, I cannot explain to him what it was. 'A dream,' I say, finally. 'About Papa. Or rather – a nightmare.'

'Indeed,' he says. 'I could hear all your commotion from downstairs. And Minnie, too – look, she's come running all the way from the kitchen.'

I raise my eyes. Minnie's standing just inside the room, wiping her hands on her apron, her eyes wide. She holds up a little brown bottle. 'I've got some salts, if you want.'

I shake my head. 'I'm not faint.'

'Then what on earth are you doing on the floor?' My husband surveys the untidy mess of skirts and petticoats as I slump in front of him, my back against the wall, my hair, as always, finding its way out of its pins and coiling around my neck.

'I must have fallen. Off the chair. In my sleep.' I've never fallen off a chair in my life. And it's not my habit to sleep in one. But I've no other explanation for how I find myself in this position.

'But it's only ten thirty in the morning! And what about all this paper?' He indicates what I now see are the scattered leaves from Daisy's journal. The book has been pulled apart. Yet it was intact when I last saw it, when I was last reading it. Was it today – or yesterday? It must have been today; I remember catching sight of myself in the looking-glass wearing this same velveteen gown. I was reading Daisy's journal – but something made me stop. There was something that upset me, something that took me back to an unhappy time. A photograph, I think – one of those long-lost photographs, one of those little Daisies in the flimsiest of costumes. Maybe that was it. But it doesn't seem quite right; there is something uncomfortable about the photographs, but they didn't frighten me. Then the word 'fever' comes into my head and this time I feel the flush and the slight prickling of perspiration. I remember now – not the details, but the horror of it. How I had scarlet fever, and Papa looked after me. And how he was especially kind to me, especially loving, especially close. Those were the pictures that came into my head unbidden; that plunged me down into that dark well with such sickening sensation. The pictures that I wanted to get rid of for ever.

I stare at the scattered pages, the mangled covers. I'm surprised that I had the strength to dismember it so thoroughly. 'I suppose I must have done it.' I shrug, hoping my admission will end the matter.

'Well, yes. There is no other culprit that I can detect, hiding behind the wardrobe or under the carpet. But I cannot for the life of me see what possessed you.' I see that my husband is embarrassed at my behaviour, and most of all he's embarrassed that Minnie is witness to it. He turns to her with a smile. 'Well, it seems that, contrary to appearances, Mrs Constantine has not been attacked by wolves. Smelling salts are not required, nor any liniment for broken bones. You may go back to your work, now. I'm sorry you've been disturbed.'

Minnie hesitates, as if she is not any more convinced by my explanation than he is. And even though my heart is beating fit to burst and my head is still full of dreadful pictures, I can't help wondering if she always keeps the bottle in her pocket, ready to attend to fainting ladies. Or perhaps she is prone to fainting herself. She does not seem the sort, though, with her wiry little frame. 'If you're sure you don't need me, Mrs Constantine,' she says, her eyes fixed on mine.

'Yes,' I reply, though in truth I'm not so sure. I am even less sure that I want to be left alone with my husband and his soft, enquiring eyes. But she backs out of the room and shuts the door. I lean my head against the wall; I have no strength to raise myself. Robert, to my surprise, doesn't help me up, but eases himself down beside me on the floor. I smell the faint scent of camphor that permeates all his clothing.

'Now,' he says, with a patient air I recognize as his habitual manner with me, 'what is this *really* all about?'

He knows there is something. But I shake my head. I can't tell him about my dreadful, sinful thoughts. He would think me the worst kind of liar, if not completely deranged.

'Try, dearest,' he says, pulling me close. For a moment, I am tempted. It would be nice to sink into his arms as if he were Nettie and I were a child again. But my body won't yield; it is ramrod stiff. I feel the roughness of his serge waistcoat against my cheek as I lie against him, and the ridge of his watch chain pressing into my flesh. I can hear his watch, now. It's ticking against my right ear, just like Papa's did – that same *tick-tick-tick-tick* that seemed to go on all afternoon. A wave of nausea comes over me and I struggle away from him. But he holds me tight. 'Now, Margaret dear, I have a feeling that you are letting all that dreadful trouble with your father prey on your mind.'

All that *dreadful trouble*? My heart beats so fast that I feel I will vomit. He must know. Yet how can Robert know something that's so confused in my own mind? But perhaps all men know such things. Perhaps all men *do* such things. Maybe it's no great secret, after all, and I am making a dreadful fuss about nothing. I touch the chain of Robert's watch. It's heavy and smooth, just like Papa's. 'What do you mean?' I say, as calmly as I can. 'What do you mean by "all that trouble"?'

He strokes my hair. He seems awkward, at a loss as to how to begin. 'Well, Margaret, I don't have to tell you that there were things that you shouldn't have witnessed. Not at your age. Not at any age, in fact. But you need to put it from your mind. And you can, now, Margaret. Now your father is finally at peace.'

Yes, I think, he's dead, but he doesn't leave me alone. He's always with me; always at the edges of my mind, ready to move in and take up all the space with his brown hair and tickling whiskers and hot, dry skin. 'What things should I not have witnessed?' I say. The lump in my throat feels as large as a plum-stone now.

'Come now, Margaret. I think you know.' He gives me an encouraging squeeze, grateful, I think, that I cannot move away from him, trapped as we are in the corner of the room.

'I *don't* know,' I say. 'Everyone thinks I know, but truthfully, I can't remember.'

He sighs. 'Then you are fortunate, Margaret. Be thankful for it, and don't seek to know what can only give you pain. Your father was a great man; it dishonours him to dwell on the period when he was – well, when he was least himself.'

'But supposing – not meaning to – he did something wrong when he was "least himself"?'

Robert rubs his chin with his forefinger, up and down, on the same spot. He does that, I realize, when he is uncertain, when he is trying to be fair. He has done that a lot recently. 'We can all do wrong,' he says after a while. 'But your father was the best of men.'

'But just supposing . . .'

He frowns, displeased with my line of questioning. 'What is the point of this, Margaret?'

'Please, Robert. It would help me – collect my thoughts.'

'Well,' he says, considering. 'Admittedly, at the end, your father could be very eccentric, very difficult to manage, very strange, even –'

'Strange?' I can hardly say the word.

'You know what I mean.' Robert allows himself almost a smile. 'When he was pouring water everywhere and running about in his nightshirt.'

His words bring it all back – all the noise and confusion, with Cook running around after him and Mama trying to hold him back and Robert and Charles and Mr Warner marching him back to his study and closing the door. And yet it isn't all that pandemonium which frightens me. It's the closed door and the key and the ticking watch. And the rough feel of his nightshirt.

Robert goes on. 'But, of course, you were the only one who knew how to calm him. Surely you remember that?'

I can see the Bible on the table in front of us. I can hear a fly buzzing against the window. My stockings are lying on the sofa, the coals in the fireplace falling with a soft crash as the afternoon wears on. And I'm wondering why no one comes to rescue me.

'Yes,' he says, reminiscing a little now. 'He loved to be with you. And he loved your little room, too – the one where he'd nursed you. He said it was like heaven with its blue walls and blue curtains. And that you were the angel inside it. He'd let you read to him for hours, you know.'

I feel Papa's large, firm hands on my nightgown, and the wetness of his tears on my skin. *You're my special angel, the only one I can trust. Love is everything, isn't it, Daisy? It doesn't matter what you do if you do it for love.*

'I keep seeing him,' I say, knowing these are not the right words, but feeling that at least they will make Robert give me his serious attention.

'*Seeing him?*' He frowns. 'In dreams, you mean? Was that what frightened you just now?'

'It wasn't exactly a dream,' I say. 'It seemed almost real.'

'Real? I fail to understand you.'

'I hardly understand it myself – but I could see him and hear him as if he were alive – and I could smell and taste such rancid things. Yet all the time he was smiling and saying it would be all right. He always tells me that. He always says it will be all right. I want to believe him, yet I know it's not true. Oh, Robert, did it happen, or am I making it up?'

'You believe your father comes and *talks* to you?' Robert looks aghast, clearly thinking that the family madness is coming out in me. Then his face clears. 'But he smiles, you say. Perhaps he only intends to reassure you, Margaret. To tell you that he lives again in Glory and all is well.'

'Oh, Robert,' I cry. 'You don't understand! The smiles are the worst. As if he is being kind and gentle, when all the time –' My chest begins to constrict and I can hardly breathe as I think of it.

Robert encircles my shoulder and brings me even closer. I endure the smell of camphor as best I can. Perhaps now, at last, he will understand.

'Poor Margaret,' he says. 'I suspected that the burden would be too great for you. I said so to your mother at the time. Some days when I came to the house I thought you didn't even recognize me. But then it seemed, once your father had gone away, that you were like a new person and I was confident that all those anxieties had quite disappeared. You should have told me that it was not the case; we could have prayed together. And we still can. You mustn't mind it, Margaret; you mustn't mind any of it. It will go away in due course.'

'Will it?' I want so much to believe him, to know that it is only time and a little prayer that is required to shake off these waking nightmares and melt away all my dreadful imaginings. I tell myself it is my fault for reading Daisy's journal; it has inflamed my brain and allowed the Devil to do his work. I don't like to think that I could have conjured such images out of nothing, but if I *haven't* conjured them up, the prospect is far, far worse. I can't control the shudder that runs through me.

Robert feels it, squeezes my hands. 'Peace will come to you, Margaret. Believe me.'

'But supposing,' I murmur. 'Supposing *I'm* the one who is guilty of a sin? Maybe even a mortal sin? Supposing *I'm* the one who's spun wicked thoughts and done wicked deeds – things you won't forgive me for?'

'*You?*' He laughs. 'Nonsense.'

'I wish you wouldn't dismiss me in that manner,' I say. 'It's as if you think I'm incapable of judging my own faults.'

He starts at the sharpness in my tone. 'I did not mean to dismiss you, Margaret. I simply mean that I hold such a high opinion of you that I couldn't imagine –'

'I wish you wouldn't hold such an opinion, then. I'd rather you thought me a sinner. I'd rather you weren't quite so patient with me all the time!'

That has come out badly and he's disconcerted. He loosens his hold on me. 'You want me to be *less* patient? Forgive me, but it has been you who has asked – nay, begged – that I exercise that very virtue in respect of you. And now you blame me for it!'

He's right, of course. I am making no sense. 'You are too saintly for me,' I say in the end. 'I don't deserve it.'

'Saintly? Oh, Margaret, I'm a man like any other, as vain and venal as it is possible to be. Look how I just now chastised you in front of Minnie. I didn't intend to do it, but my pride was dented and I allowed it to overrule me.'

'But that's such a small thing, Robert. I wish a sharp word was all I had to confess. But I'm afraid there is something bad I've done as a child. I've been reading my old journal and –'

'Your journal? So that's what all this paper is!' He laughs and picks up a page at random. 'Good heavens, you must have been very young when you wrote this. Look, you still sign yourself "Daisy".'

'Even Daisy might have done wrong,' I say.

'In principle, no doubt.' He smiles. 'We are all born sinners, after all. But, in truth, what sins could you have committed when you were – what? Ten? Eleven? Cross words, perhaps? Little untruths, or failure to say your prayers? Well, I forgive you those, if you need forgiving.'

It's as if I am calling to him from a distant shore in a language he doesn't understand. I have to persist, though. I take his hand in mine. 'Robert, supposing – just for a moment – that I had committed sins that were much worse than you imagine? Sins that are preventing me being a proper wife to you?'

'I'd forgive you, of course.' It comes out so pat. 'But you've lived in the bosom of a God-fearing family all your life. How could you have committed any real sins?'

'But if I had – would it change your feelings for me?'

'There is nothing that would change my feelings for you, Margaret.' He gives me his most brilliant smile.

'Nothing? Are you sure, Robert? Absolutely, completely sure?'

His brilliant smile is somewhat fixed now. 'Good heavens, what is this catechism of "just suppose" all about?' he says. 'Truly, my dear, it's rather silly, and I think you should stop it straight away.'

I see that he is uncomfortable with the notion that I have sins; they spoil his idea of me. But if we are to start afresh in our marriage, I must speak what is in my mind, truth or not. 'Please, Robert, there are things I need to tell you. I'm not altogether sure about them. But you might wish you hadn't married me when you know.'

'I think that unlikely, unless – good heavens, you're not by any chance married to someone else, are you?' He pretends to think this very amusing.

But I won't be stopped. I warm to my theme now, the accumulated despair of seven weeks rushing to the surface. 'But supposing there *is* a part of me you don't know about – some secret I haven't told you? Supposing I am not quite as I should be? Supposing that's what's stopping me from being your wife in more than name?'

He laughs, uneasily this time. 'Come now, Margaret.'

'I won't "come now"!' My voice rises as the words spill out. 'Supposing there is an impediment, Robert? An impediment that cannot be overcome? Perhaps that is the cause of all our difficulties. Maybe I will never be able to love you. Maybe you should cast me off. You can annul a marriage that's not been consummated – there'll be no disgrace to you. You can say I am mad – just like my father.'

'Quiet, I beg you!' He glances at the door. In a low voice he says, 'Are you really telling me that you wish to end our marriage?'

'No, Robert, I don't wish to. But it may be for the best.'

'I see. I suppose the truth of the matter is that you find me repellent.' A flush creeps over his cheeks.

I want to deny it, to spare him more misery; but I cannot separate him in my mind from Papa – Papa with his ticking watch; Papa with his hands around my waist; Papa in his nightshirt, pulling me onto his lap. And I know it was the sight of Robert in his nightshirt that so horrified me on our wedding night. Even before the glimpse of his naked skin and bushy hair. And I begin to shake even now to think of his dark and secret body beneath his respectable clergyman's clothes; the waxy flesh under the thick layers of serge and linen. 'No, Robert,' I say, trying to find the words to console him. 'It is not exactly that.'

'Not *exactly*?' He laughs a short and mirthless laugh. 'Hardly an extravagant compliment. We men have our pride, you know. We like to think we are attractive to our wives.'

'You *are* attractive, Robert. You are kind and good and –' I cast about for what to say. '– And you are very nice-looking, too.'

'Nice-looking! Well, Margaret, forgive me, but when a man's had to watch his wife sheltering under the bed on her wedding night it's hard to believe that she finds him "nice-looking"! When she refuses to kiss him or even to hold his hand, it is hard to believe she finds him appealing in any way!'

My voice rises again. 'Why won't you *understand*? It's Papa. He's the one who's coming between us. Oh, please make him go away, Robert! I don't want him near me any more!' I start to weep, noisily. The tears gush down my cheeks in torrents and run into my mouth as I gasp and sob, gasp and sob.

He is alarmed now. 'Please, Margaret, take a deep breath. You are near to being hysterical.' He releases his hold on me and takes out his pocket-handkerchief. I watch him shake out the neat folds before he wipes my cheeks. 'Now, listen to me. You have allowed your imagination to get the better of you and have started believing the most ridiculous things. The "difficulty" in our marriage has nothing to do with any sins you may have committed as a child – except in your mind. That is where you are at fault. That is where your thoughts are disarrayed. *I* do not blame you, and therefore there is no need to blame yourself. If misplaced blame has been holding you back from loving me, I'm sure our problem can be resolved in no time at all. There will be no need for doctors.'

'It's not misplaced blame, Robert.' I sob, wishing he would listen before jumping to conclusions.

'Well, maybe that is not the only reason. You are young and fragile and your fear of the conjugal act is understandable. But I am sure the Harley Street man will set your mind at rest on matters of – well, on any matter of concern. And I have been reading some books on the subject – books I should have consulted earlier – and I realize a woman must not be pressed. She must be allowed to ready herself for her wifely duties in her own time. Preparation is necessary: a light diet, loose clothes, meditation. One should not rush into things on the wedding night so soon after all the exhaustion of the preparations: the ceremony, the wedding breakfast and so forth. And one needs to ration one's resources; abstinence should be practised even within marriage in order to protect the woman's health. I have been too hasty, I see. I have only thought of myself. If it is anyone's fault, it is mine.'

All the time he's been drying my tears, I've been obliged to study his face at close quarters. There are flecks of yellow in the brown of his irises, a small round mole near his eyebrow, and a patch of reddened skin where he has shaved too close around his mouth and chin. I'm shocked that I've never seen these imperfections before; it comes home to me that I have never really looked at him as a woman should look at her lover, with an eye for every detail of his face and body. I've drifted through our courtship like a dream-girl. And Robert never broke into that dream; content, it seemed, with soft words and shy smiles. And I suppose I must have imagined that married life would go on like that – that we would lie side by side in our bed-gowns and chatter inconsequentially into the small hours; that he would make buttercup crowns for me and place them chastely on my head before turning over to pursue an innocent sleep; or that we would kiss in bird-pecks like Hansel and Gretel in the wood. I must have kept everything else at bay – happy simply to envisage new clothes, wedding presents, and the pleasure of leaving my mother's house. Poor Robert, as he watched me come to him with orange blossom in my hair, could have had no idea what an unprepared wife I would turn out to be. And for my own part, I had no premonitions, no fears, no misgivings. I might have been setting out on a summer picnic. No shadow of the past even crossed my mind. But my ignorance is not Robert's fault, and I need to be the one to make amends.

'Dear Robert.' I put my hand up to his face, tracing the shape of the little mole. 'You are so good and patient. I will do whatever you say. I will forget my foolish thoughts. I will see the doctor and do whatever he recommends.'

He smiles. 'I am so glad. So very glad. We will triumph, Margaret. We will triumph.' He brings his own hand up to meet mine, running his lips lightly over my fingers – so lightly it tickles. I am surprised to find that, having no expectation that it will lead to anything else, I almost enjoy the sensation. A slip of fire threads through my abdomen. We sit in silence for a while, and I think that maybe things will resolve themselves as he says, with time and patience, with light diets and loose clothing, and the careful advice of the Harley Street man.

'Now, my dear,' he murmurs. 'If it is not too prosaic a point, I think we might allow ourselves to get up from the floor. It's unseemly to be crouching here – and a little hard on the joints.'

He rises, puts out his arms and lifts me up so we are both standing on the scattered contents of the journal. His heel almost skewers a piece of card lying face down, and he stoops to retrieve it.

But I have already seen what it is. As I catch sight of the scratched and battered backing with *Daisy 1862* written on it, I remember – oh dear God, I remember – the day I came into Papa's study, and all the photographs I'd secreted in my journal were laid upon his desk, like a dreadful game of patience. And there was Papa standing behind the desk, staring at them and then at me, as if to be sure that I was the same girl, in my cotton dress and pinafore, as the angels and nymphs and flower-girls that lay so artfully in front of him. I thought he would surely punish me most severely for keeping such a secret and I was unable to speak for fear. His face seemed quite flushed, but he put his arms around me and said, 'Well, Daisy, you have clearly been a beautiful angel for John. I think you must be an angel for me, too.' But, although he was not at all cross and said there was nothing at all wrong, my clothes seemed to burn me with shame as I took them off.

Robert must not see the picture. I try to pull it from his grasp. But he thinks I am teasing, and holds it away from me, laughing. 'Please don't look at it!' I cry.

But Robert laughs again. He wants to see, he says. He turns it over, full of delighted anticipation. He expects a shy little girl in a pretty dress. The shock almost floors him. 'Good God,' he exclaims, and sits down suddenly upon the bed. There is a long silence. His gaze seems fixed to the photograph, as if mesmerized. Then, after a long while: 'Who on earth took this?'

'A man called John Jameson,' I say lightly. 'He was a friend of Papa's.'

'I know who he is. He is the best-known man in Oxford. But he is a respectable man in Holy Orders.' He shakes his head, as if it is beyond imagining.

'But what is the matter?' I ask.

'You are naked,' he says.

'I was being a cherub,' I say, attempting lightness. 'You see, I have wings.' Although I can't help thinking that the feathers look rather forlorn, now.

Robert holds the photograph by the corners, as if it is contaminated. 'But why on earth are you *smiling* like that?' His voice is shaking.

'Smiling?' I'm surprised he thinks that. John Jameson told me never to smile when he was taking a photograph. He said smiles had the habit of looking fixed if they were held for more than ten seconds. I have a very candid expression, admittedly, and there is perhaps just the hint of a smile. 'I don't know, Robert,' I say. 'Perhaps I was happy. Mr Jameson usually made me happy.'

'Did he? Then he seems to have been successful where I clearly have not.' His voice has a hurt, angry tone that I have never heard before.

'What is the matter, Robert? It's only a photograph.'

'Oh, I think it is more than that, Margaret. That's why you didn't want me to see it.'

'I simply needed to explain the circumstances to you.'

'Explain? What explanation could you possibly give?' I see with dismay that he is near to tears. 'What a fool I've been! I imagined that you were innocent as the day. And yet, here you are half naked, *seducing* this man!'

I'm horrified by his language and by the anger that throbs through his voice. 'What do you mean, Robert – *seducing*? I was just a child!'

'But you have confessed it here in this very room – this very room, Margaret! You knew you were in a tainted state – a great sin, you said. Perhaps a mortal sin. You even suggested we should end our marriage on account of it.'

'But I didn't mean *this*!' I gesture at the photograph; Daisy looking up so brightly, insensible of the storm raging around her. '*This* is not what I meant. This is nothing!'

His face is a picture of misery. 'Nothing? You mean I'm *even more* mistaken about you?'

I'll have to confess it now. I try to keep my voice calm; it's Robert's voice that has been raised this time. 'Yes, Robert, you have been mistaken. And it all has to do with Papa.'

He cuts me off with a groan. 'Please don't try to blame your father, Margaret. That is a low and wretched thing to do.' Then, as if it suddenly occurs to him: 'Don't tell me the poor man saw this picture?'

'He saw them all.'

'*All?*'

'John Jameson said to keep them secret, but Papa found them somehow. Oh, Robert, that's what started it all – or made it worse. I can't exactly remember, it was all so confused –'

'There are more photographs? More like *this*?' He looks wildly around. 'Oh, Daisy, Daisy, Daisy, what have you done? No wonder your poor father haunts your dreams. Oh poor man, poor man . . .' He is lost for words.

I don't know what to say either. I'm horrified that Robert finds it so hard to believe that Papa was capable of wrongdoing, yet is so ready to think me a child seductress because I have taken off my clothes, and am trying to look pleasant for a photograph. And I see with a dreadful clarity how different the world is for a man and a woman, and how easily a man escapes censure while a young girl is condemned. Robert should be taking my part, I think. He is my husband. He said he loved me. He said we should step out together in good heart, and that we would triumph in the end. He should be up in arms now to defend and protect me against the world. But he looks already hopeless and beaten. I put my hand on his arm. 'Please, Robert,' I say.

He shakes it off. 'No,' he says thickly. 'Don't touch me. Go away.'

I see that his whole world is dissolving, just as mine once did. And he, too, is falling into a deep, black hole where nothing is as it seems and everything he once thought was true is now altered beyond recognition.

I go, and close the door behind me.

20

JOHN JAMESON

A FTER MUCH THOUGHT AND DELIBERATION, I HAVE written to Daisy asking if she will come to tea with me. I advised her that Benson is no longer with us and that Dinah, poor thing, has seen the last of her mousing days, but otherwise my set of rooms is much as it was when she last set her dainty foot in it. What I did not tell her was that, although many other little friends have passed happy afternoons here over the years – and some have been sweet and some have been clever – none holds my imagination like she does. She was the first and the best and the most enduring of my child-loves. And now that she is married (and happily beyond her mother's control), she may visit me here without any feelings of constraint.

I am already somewhat excited, although I don't know if she will accept, or indeed whether she will still have any of the qualities that so endeared her to me when she was a child. Maybe she will be bored at the prospect of a college tea with a dull and none-too-youthful mathematician, and will make a polite excuse. I shall be disappointed if so, but I am used to such disappointments: the irony of my life is that all children grow up, and most of them go away and leave me. But I have learned to enjoy my child-friendships for what they are: delicious, certainly – but transitory and brief. If Daisy declines my invitation, I shall have to make do with all the new Daisies who write to me and beg me to take their photographs.

In truth, there are more of them than I know what to do with and sometimes I wish I had a machine that could write letters for me, so I need only speak into an ear-trumpet in order to convert my thoughts to paper. That would save a great deal of my time. As it is, I have to labour conscientiously over each reply, not knowing if the Edna or Ellen or Esme I am replying to is a child who is worth cultivating or not. I wish I could see a picture of each of them before I reply; I would not wish to encourage the acquaintance of an ill-made child. And I cannot always gauge if a particular one is intelligent or not; frequently the mama will direct the child's pen, hoping to flatter me with some compliment, or engage my attention with some clever pun. I would far rather make the acquaintance of a child face-to-face – in the park, or on a train, or at the seaside. But since my books have become such a success, I am besieged with epistles from the length and breadth of the country, and I am obliged to reply. Sometimes they write to me as James St-John Clark, and over and over again I have to make it clear that no such person exists. When I write my narratives, I tell them, I use the nom de plume of St-John Clark; but in my real life I am the Reverend John Jameson, and it is in my real-life capacity that I keep up all my acquaintance. I should therefore be most obliged, I say, if they would address me in the correct manner. The lodge porter knows my views and says, 'Three letters for Mr St-John Clark, today, sir. Will you be so kind as to pass them on to him if you're not too busy – he's a devil of a man for not collecting his own mail.'

Smith-Jephcott describes my attitude as 'tetchy' and says it is a wonder that children are not put off by my fussy ways and hair-splitting. 'It is only your reputation that saves you,' he says. 'When you write your children's stories you are whimsical and witty, but in daily life you are a maiden aunt, and a vinegary one at that.' Smith-Jephcott has not improved over the years, merely become fatter and more slovenly. He still occupies the rooms below me and takes a delight in waylaying my little visitors and making impolite remarks as they climb the stairs to my door. 'Don't think you're especially lucky,' he calls out. 'You're the third Amelia to take tea this week and the other two were prettier.' I have been obliged to make use of my pocket-handkerchief on more than one occasion to staunch the tears of a disconsolate seven-year-old.

But I've a feeling my Daisy will come. I suspect that she feels like I do, that our acquaintance was rudely – even cruelly – terminated. If she comes but once, it will at least make a proper end to our friendship. She must have read *Daisy's Daydream*. She must know how much of our outings together I have put into that story. And I hope that, in spite of everything, she was able to read that first little fragment that I sent her when she was ill – a crude attempt, admittedly, and one I would never wish to see in print, but my first venture into literature, and inspired only by her. I hardly remember it now. I passed the only copy into Daniel's hands and it seems to have gone astray – but I like to imagine she was able to read it and recognize the ten-year-old child whose hair grows and grows until it fills the whole house. I like to think that she recognized all the creatures who came to live in it – all the animals and people we used to talk about on our walks – a talking cat, a crying baby, a cruel nursemaid, a not-so-dead dodo, hundreds of beetles, scarlet flamingos and the dons playing croquet in the quad. I so wanted to read it to her, to see her laugh and say, 'Why, that might almost have happened to *me*!' But of course that was not allowed.

It was indeed a dreadful day for me when I visited her for the last time. I'd returned to Oxford with Mr Warner, in turmoil as to what I should find. In truth, I was fearful as much for my own skin as for Daniel's state of mind, although the latter did cause me concern. Apart from our ties of friendship, I did not like to think of the office of clergyman becoming besmirched with scandal in any way. But selfishly (and I own I am selfish) I was preoccupied with what Mrs Baxter might know, and how I might explain myself. Once more I was finding myself obliged to exonerate myself from actions I did not in the least regret.

When we arrived at the station, I sent my luggage on to the college with a note for Benson, and accompanied Mr Warner immediately to Westwood Gardens. I argued to myself that although Mrs Baxter had urged me not to write to her husband or daughter, she had not expressly forbidden me to *visit* them, and therefore I was not disobeying her wishes in attending at the vicarage. I also felt the presence of the bluff Mr Warner would act as a conversational buffer; she could hardly snub me in front of him, and I doubted she would mention the photographs (if indeed she had found them) on the same principle.

The house looked the same as it had five weeks previously – the shrubs neat, the brass polished – and Hannah answered the door as usual. 'Oh, Mr Warner!' she said, surprised. And then, with more surprise, 'And Mr Jameson, too!'

'Is Mr Baxter at home?' said Warner, diplomatically.

'No, I'm afraid he's not well, sir,' she said, a distracted look in her eye. 'He's not supposed to have visitors neither.'

'Is *Mrs* Baxter in a position to see us?' Mr Warner asked. 'We have come all the way from north Devon to be of assistance.'

Hannah seemed undecided what to do, as if under strict orders to admit nobody, but chastened at the presence of two such urgent visitors who had come such a long way for the purpose. But seeing Mr Warner not standing on ceremony as usual, and about to step over the threshold willy-nilly, she took our hats and ushered us into the drawing room, saying she would see if her mistress could be disturbed. We both stood there awkwardly, in the centre of the room, among the potted plants and plush hangings, feeling the seriousness of the occasion prevented us from sitting down.

'Does well for himself,' said Warner, eyeing the furnishings.

'I believe Mrs Baxter has some money,' I replied, sensing the criticism implied. 'But I take it from your remarks that you have not been a regular visitor to the house.'

'Never had a need,' he answered. 'Did all my church business in the parish hall or at the vestry meetings. Annie used to visit sometimes to play with their girl, but Deedee would escort her back and forth. My wife has been here – the usual teatime calls and so on, but she found Mrs Baxter' – he lowered his voice – 'well, a little too refined and poetic. A little distant, to tell you the truth. Fine-looking woman, though.'

We were still whispering like conspirators when Mrs Baxter came into the room. She looked extremely agitated, and her costume was rather disordered. 'How good of you to come all this way, Mr Warner,' she said, taking him by the hands. 'And Mr Jameson.' She turned to me somewhat stiffly. 'I did not expect *you*.'

Warner blustered on. 'We heard, ma'am, via my future son-in-law, who only this morning arrived in Devon and informed us of the case, that Mr Baxter had been taken seriously ill and was unable to perform his duties. It seemed that there might be matters on which we could assist – at least on which *I* could assist. Mr Jameson is not a parishioner, of course, although as a friend of your husband he would not be dissuaded from coming with me.'

'I am sure I am obliged to Mr Jameson for his consideration,' she said in an even tone, not looking at me. 'But my husband is unable to see anyone at all at present. The doctor has given him a sleeping draught. He needs complete rest. He is overwrought, that is all.' She gestured for us to sit down, and we did so, but she remained standing, fretting a little, and casting glances at the door, as if expecting some sound – or person – to erupt from elsewhere in the house.

'I am very sorry,' Warner replied. 'Is this a sudden, um – indisposition of his?'

'I was not present when he was first affected. Indeed, I am at fault for being away when he needed me. Maybe if I had been more insistent in employing a nurse from the hospital to look after our youngest daughter, then matters may not have come to such a head. But Mr Baxter is a devoted father and insisted on nursing her himself. As a result, he is in a state of collapse –'

'We are none of us predictors of the future,' said Warner. 'You could not have known, when you went away, that such a situation would have come about. You cannot be blamed for taking a holiday. You might as well say I should not have gone on holiday myself, in case a crisis arose in the parish.'

'Indeed, you might as well say that no one should ever do anything at all, in case their motives are misinterpreted,' I said.

Mrs Baxter ignored me. 'I am sure there are many in the parish who will see me as remiss. But the servants did not keep me informed of what was happening. If I had been here, I could perhaps have prevented this – exhaustion.' She wrung her hands. 'I should have come back four weeks ago; I should have left my son in Herefordshire and returned immediately. But Daniel's letters were always so encouraging. He urged me to stay, to give my aged father the benefit of my company for another week or two. He said that Daisy was recovering, and that he was managing admirably with Hannah helping in the sickroom and Mr Morton taking the services. But it seems he was keeping the true situation from me. And now he is paying the price . . .' Her voice trailed away and I could see she was almost in tears. I was quite surprised to see her affected like this, and for a moment my heart went out to her. But I kept my counsel.

'I am sure you are not to blame, dear lady,' said Warner, gallantly. 'But it seemed from what Bertram – my prospective son-in-law – said, that Mr Baxter might need quite a little time away from the helm of the ship, so to speak. When the captain is stricken, it's a case of "all hands on deck". Hence, we are at your disposal.'

'Oh, I am quite sure his indisposition is temporary,' said Mrs Baxter, still steadfastly refusing to look at me. 'There was no need for you to interrupt your holiday, Mr Warner. Nor you, Mr Jameson; your presence is quite superfluous.'

Even Warner must have detected the barb beneath her words, and he glanced at me in surprise, but I affected not to notice. 'I am glad to hear it, Mrs Baxter,' I said, thinking of how, not so many weeks before, we were laughing together over a parlour game in this same room, and flirting lightly as our names were coupled in a comical way. There was nothing of the flirt about her now, but I was certain that her coolness to me and the cryptic content of her letters arose entirely from her concern for Daniel, and not from any revelation regarding myself. I tried to be emollient. 'I hope the rest of the family at least are well and that Daisy has recovered from her fever.'

'Thank you. Daisy is quite well. She has a lot to thank her father for.' She said this in such a way that implied Daisy was somehow to blame for being ill. I regarded this as very unfair, but people in extreme agitation are liable to see blame where there is none.

'May I see her?' I said. 'I sent her so many letters from Ilfracombe, and would very much like to know if she received them. I never had a reply, you see. Maybe she was too weak. I know Daisy is too well brought up not to have replied without good reason.'

I watched Mrs Baxter seek for some excuse as to why I should not see the child, but under the watchful eye of Mr Warner, she failed to find one. She went to the mantelpiece and rang for Hannah, who came looking ruffled, and departed again in a quest for Daisy. I could not but help noticing that the house seemed more than usually hushed, but I put that down to the absence of the infant Benjamin.

'Are you sure I cannot be of assistance?' asked Warner, clearly weighing the apparent normality of the household against the lurid reports of his son-in-law, and no doubt thinking his departure from the seaside had been a little hasty. Of course, he could not mention the alleged mumbling and raving, and nor could I. And Mrs Baxter would clearly have us believe that no such thing had ever taken place.

'Charles – Mr Morton – will continue to take the services for the time being,' she said. 'But you may wish to consult with Mr Attwood or Mrs Carmichael about other matters. I'm afraid I am not fully apprised of parish affairs.' As she spoke, I could see why the ever-busy Mrs Warner had found her distant and poetic. 'But I am sure,' she said, 'that you need have no concerns. My husband will soon be back at the helm.'

Warner again attempted to offer his help, and she again declined it, but I found myself paying only scant attention to them, as my anticipation of seeing Daisy again began to mount. Indeed, my ears were taking a walk into the hallway for any sound of her approach. But when she came through the door I was taken aback. She was like a different child. Her illness had left her extremely thin, and without that delicate softness of outline that characterizes the supreme beauty of childhood. And her eyes had an odd kind of sadness – a blankness almost – as if she was now privy to a more grown-up world than when we had last met. She seemed taller too, and more sedate. I knew then that she had already begun the journey to womanhood, and that she was fading from me even as I looked at her – like one of my ruined photographs, numinous and overexposed.

'Daisy, my dear,' I said, holding out my hands. 'It is so good to see you. You have been in my thoughts so very much.'

She curtseyed, like any well-brought-up young lady in front of a stranger, her once-bright eyes cast down. Not at all like Daisy with her eager enthusiasm – not at all like my dear Daisy of yore. 'I'm obliged to you,' she said.

Obliged! When had she started to use such an expression? And where had this new stiffness come from? I tried to steady my voice. 'I am glad you are recovered, my dear. Did you receive my letters from Ilfracombe? I took considerable trouble over them.'

She looked at me, startled out of her composure. 'No,' she said. 'I didn't even know you'd been to Ilfracombe. Isn't that where Annie goes in the summer?' Then she seemed to notice Mr Warner for the first time, and dropped another curtsey. 'How do you do, Mr Warner?'

'Very well, my dear. But you are quite right. We holiday in Ilfracombe every year. But this year we have had the extra pleasure of Mr Jameson's company. He is out all day with my children – donkey rides and beach-combing and sketching trips and all manner of entertainment. Mrs Warner and I have hardly seen our youngest three since he turned up. I think I shall strive to engage him for all our future holidays, as I have been able to read my newspaper without interruption and Mrs Warner has netted at least double the amount of mittens she normally manages in three weeks.'

Daisy turned accusing eyes at me. 'You have been at the seaside?' she said. 'With *Annie?*'

Of course, when I looked at it through Daisy's eyes, I could see that she might conceive it as a betrayal – my entertaining Annie and her siblings in riotous assemblage while she herself lay in a fever hundreds of miles away. And yet there would have been no logic to my remaining in Oxford when I had done all I could to speed her recovery. If she were not allowed to have visitors, it wouldn't have mattered if I had been at Land's End or John O'Groats, or even on the moon. And, though I was far away, I had persistently enquired after her, and written to her at great length and with many illustrations. But people do not always look at things logically, and it is a pathetic fallacy that a lover should show his nobility by pounding the city streets where his beloved lives, even though she has no notion of his presence and is happily playing cards with her best friend in a drawing room five miles away. What a waste of time and energy. But I was still anxious that Daisy should think well of me. 'I have simply been taking a short holiday from the demands of trigonometry,' I said. 'For fear my head will grow to an uncommon size and no hatter would be able to accommodate it. Besides, Benson always likes a week or so off during the summer and I think it would be unfair not to release him, don't you? He is so very good with the bread-and-butter for the remaining eleven months of the year.'

'But who looks after Dinah if you are both away?' she said. For a fleeting moment she was like her old self – quick and curious.

'Mr Bunch, who is a scout on the next staircase, sees to her. In fact, she is so fat after a fortnight or so in his care that I am convinced that he spoils her with mouse cutlets and buttered bats. There are many bats, you know, in our college – a whole belfry full of them – and we are enjoined to deplete the numbers whenever we can.'

'*Do* cats eat bats?' she said, half laughing like she used to. 'I never heard that!'

'Did you ever hear they didn't?' I replied, getting into my stride.

But Mrs Baxter was not about to allow us to have any fun. 'Mr Jameson wishes to know if you received his letters,' she said curtly. 'As it seems you did not reply.'

'What letters?' she asked warily, and not very grammatically.

'Mr Jameson claims he wrote to you from Ilfracombe.'

I interrupted. 'It is not a *claim*, Mrs Baxter; it is a fact. That I wrote them is indisputable. That they were received is what is open to doubt.'

'Perhaps Papa has them,' suggested Daisy, a little uneasily.

I thought this more than likely. He had probably put them aside for her convalescence and had not had time to give them to her before his own indisposition came upon him. 'But did you read the story I wrote for you?'

'A story? For me?' She put her hands together – but, in her new grown-up way she stopped short of clapping them, and merely held them to her chest.

'Not only *for* you, but *about* you,' I said, smiling at her delight. 'I gave it directly to your papa.'

'Well, no doubt, that is the answer,' Mrs Baxter said with some relief. 'Mr Baxter has undoubtedly put all your correspondence away safely. I will get Hannah to search for it later. You will appreciate, Mr Jameson, that things are very much out of joint in our household at the moment. I cannot be spending time looking for lost letters, particularly if they contain only humorous trivialities. Now, if you do not mind, I must ask you both to take your leave. My husband needs my full attention.'

'Of course. But I am ready to help in any way,' replied Mr Warner, pushing up from the big winged chair. 'I shall speak to the other churchwardens and see what needs to be done. Please do not hesitate to call on me. I shall remain at home for the next few days and you may send your servant at any time of the night or day.'

'You are very kind, Mr Warner, but I am sure that will not be necessary.' And with that she began to usher us out.

I knew that Mrs Baxter, having forbidden me to write to Daisy, would not easily allow me to see her again, and I could not rely on Daniel, in his current state of health, to overrule her. I did not wish the child to think I had abandoned her without a word, or to be told by some ill-intentioned person that I no longer cared about her, so I took the opportunity to fall behind Mr Warner and Mrs Baxter and clasp Daisy's hand. 'Goodbye, my dear. I'll never forget you,' I said. 'Don't forget me, either, will you?'

'Why? Won't I see you again?' she said, with something of a stricken look.

I could hardly answer her. 'I c-can't say. I think our time may be over. You are growing up now. Too old for my sort of nonsense.' I could feel the lump at my throat.

'I'm not! I'm not too old at all!' She clutched at my coat sleeve.

'You are getting older by the minute, Daisy,' I said, patting her shorn head. 'Time is rushing on for you. But Time has a wretched habit of staying still for me, lazing around and doing nothing in particular. I rather think we are fated to go our separate ways.'

'No, Mr Jameson, please don't say that! I still want to go walking with you and see Dianah and Benson and have my pho–'

I interrupted her quickly. 'Please, my dear – remember the Eye of Society. Young ladies cannot skip about with old bachelors for ever. They have to learn how to put on long dresses and sit sedately and make polite conversation with young gentlemen. It's the way of the world, my dear. Even though we may not want it.'

Mrs Baxter heard my words and turned, almost gracious now. 'Mr Jameson is right, Daisy. You'll have different matters to occupy you from now on. We all will. Now, say a nice farewell to him as he asks.'

'No,' she said. 'I don't understand why he has to go, why everyone has to go.' Then, rather desperately, 'I want to tell him something.'

Mrs Baxter looked me in the eye for the first time. 'Daisy is anxious about her father, that is all.' Then, taking Daisy by the shoulders, she said, 'There is nothing that you need to tell Mr Jameson, my dear. Family matters are to be kept to ourselves.'

I could see Daisy's lip trembling and I so much wanted to comfort her. But it was all too dreadfully late. I held out my hand. 'It's been the greatest honour to know you, Daisy. But your mama says I must go, so go I must.' I shook her hand. 'Goodbye, dear child,' I said.

'Goodbye, Mr Jameson,' she said at last, her grey eyes fixed on me. I thought I saw despair in them, and for a moment I hesitated to abandon her to the Scylla and Charybdis of her vicarage life – her clever, cold mama and her wild, distracted father. It could not be a happy situation for a child. But I could not force my way into the house, and I could not force Daisy out of it. I had no power at all. I was just a single man whom nobody listened to; as dead and flat and unimportant as a breakfast bloater.

'Perhaps we *will* meet again,' I said, kissing her little hand. And then, unable to stop myself, I put my arms around her, feeling the tightness of her chest as she tried to prevent the tears coming. Then I stumbled out through the grand front door and into the breezy afternoon. Mr Warner made as if to speak to me, but I put on my hat and walked quickly down the hill, unable to look behind me.

Sad to say, Daniel never recovered his wits and, apart from fleeting glimpses around town, I didn't see Daisy again, although she has lived with me this long time in the pages of my book, and of course in the pages of my heart. I never saw Daniel again either, although in the early days of his affliction I frequently haunted the environs of the vicarage, knowing that Mrs Baxter's writ did not extend to the pavements of the public streets. But he was kept close inside, guarded it would seem, by the servants, and I saw not so much as a glimpse of him. I retired to my usual day-to-day work, and in the evenings I consoled myself with the delightful occupation of writing *Daisy's Daydream*, hoping against hope that my old friend would soon be restored to health and a new regime instituted at Westwood Gardens. But news of his insanity began to leak out bit by bit.

I heard from Smith-Jephcott that he was seen in the Gardens dressed only in his nightshirt – and, on one celebrated occasion, stark naked. Smith-Jephcott could not disguise his delight at being the bearer of such news. He has always had an irrational dislike of Muscular Christianity in general and Daniel in particular, so he kept me fully aware of his distressing decline, even though it was painful for me to hear it. He told me of Baxter's attempts to sequester the communion wine, and his habit of sending petitions to the Archbishop of Canterbury by floating them on the breeze from an upstairs room. At the last it was he who gloatingly informed me that Dr Lawrence, after years of administering pills and lotions, hot poultices and cold compresses, soft words and harsh remedies – had been forced to resort to the straitjacket. 'The women of the household can't manage him – even with the curate and the churchwardens attending the house day and night. So he's off to the asylum where he'll have no option. The congregation is all at sixes and sevens; half of 'em believing their prayers will come true and holding out for Baxter's return to the pulpit; the rest clamouring for a new vicar in his place. Some say that Baxter overreached himself; that he let his pride come before his duty – and this is his punishment. Morton can hardly hold the vestry committee together.'

I was appalled and saddened to think it had come to this. I had always thought of myself as somewhat eccentric, and there were many Oxford dons who were, in my view, completely deranged – but we all managed to live in the world and not be too unkindly remarked upon. Daniel had unfortunately contrived to assault every social constraint by his naked ravings; and he could not be forgiven. I was grieved to think of him caged up in an institution, and once he had left the watchful eye of his wife, I several times wrote to him at the asylum, thinking maybe that a correspondence with an old friend would be good for him. But my letters were returned, unopened. Except for one, which came back with a scrawl over my name and written alongside, in an almost unrecognizable version of Daniel's hand, the words 'Corrupter of Innocence!'. I cannot say what a shock that gave me. It came to me that he must have seen the photographs and drawn the inevitable wrong conclusion. I wanted to see him, then, to explain that no corruption had taken place, that his darling Daisy was still as fresh as a flower. But, of course, he was mad, and there is no persuading a madman. I began to be angry, then. I could not think what the superintendent of the asylum had been thinking of – letting such a libel slip past, to be seen by the workers in the Post Office and by the porters at my college as they handled it and assigned it to my pigeonhole. I was minded to write a letter of complaint. Indeed, I composed one, so shaken was I by such public incompetence. But in the end I decided that discretion was the better part of valour, and that it was best not to stir up matters that were long dead.

As time has gone on, I am relieved that I distanced myself from him. It might have prevented other children being allowed to see me if it were known that the naked, ranting Daniel Baxter had once been my friend. The shame has fallen most heavily on his family, of course, but Mrs Baxter remained in the vicarage to the end, proving a good deal more resilient than she looked. And Daisy, bless her, has prospered. Smith-Jephcott, who is a mine of unsolicited information on all hatchings, matchings and dispatchings, informs me that young Robert Constantine fell in love with her the moment he saw her, and, casting aside all fears of hereditary taint, determined to make her his wife. He is now the fortunate incumbent of a well-established parish just beyond Oxford, and she his fortunate wife. I couldn't have written a happier ending myself. Indeed, I find endings difficult; the need to point up a moral for everything goes against the grain; yet it is required and I have to twist my narratives to accommodate it.

21

◈ MARGARET CONSTANTINE ◈

ROBERT AND I HAVE BEEN LIKE STRANGERS THIS LAST week. I don't think I can continue in this way, and I doubt Robert can either. It's far worse than before, when at least there was a glimmer of hope that we would find a resolution. Now, it seems, I've utterly broken his heart. I hear him in his dressing-room at night, tossing and turning for hours on end. I myself cannot sleep, and rise early every day. But whenever I go down to breakfast, he has always finished and already gone out on 'urgent parish business', not returning until late. And then he stays in his study until long after I've gone to bed.

I don't knock on his door; there is no point in trying to speak to him: John Jameson's photographs are my dumb accusers, and won't be denied. I've looked at them over and over again, but I fail to see what Robert sees.

Today, though, just as I arrive in the breakfast room, he comes to speak to me. I stand by the table with its white tablecloth and blue crockery; he stands just inside the room with a letter in his hand. Acres of red Turkey carpet seem to spread between us. 'Dr Lawrence has written,' he says, shortly. 'There is someone he recommends – an eminent specialist who is coming up to speak at the university this evening. He has kindly arranged an appointment for us at two o'clock tomorrow afternoon, when Dr' – he glances at the letter – 'Dr Franklin will be free. Naturally, I shall write to decline the offer. His intervention is not required now.'

It is not required, I think, because Robert no longer desires to touch me. That I may wish to touch *him*, and be grieved at my inability to do so, does not seem to occur to him. 'Then everything between us is at an end?' I say, holding on to the back of my chair for support.

He doesn't say yes, but he doesn't contradict me either. He looks through the window and seems to be considering something a long way off, out in the churchyard, or beyond the hedge. 'I don't know,' he says, eventually. 'I don't know what to think any more. I truly believe I would have given my life for the old Margaret – the Margaret I thought you were. But now it seems you are somebody else, and I don't think I can love that person.'

'But we are the same person, Robert. I mean, *I* am the same person.'

'Are you?' His voice sounds hollow. 'Are you really the sweet girl I courted? Is your mind as unpolluted as I always imagined it to be?' He turns and fixes me with his eye. 'Can you swear to God that is the case?'

I look down. The pattern in the carpet seems to swirl up to meet me. I cannot swear an untruth; I would be struck down in an instant.

'You see, Margaret? It is, admittedly, to your credit that you tried to confess to me – and to my considerable shame that I would not listen. But the fact remains – you are a different woman. And neither you nor I can change that.'

He turns to go, and I notice that the back of his coat is creased in deep horizontal lines, as if he has been sitting in it for a long time. Perhaps he has even been up all night, deciding what he is to do with this stranger-wife of his. I stare at his back, the way his shoulders stoop. Surely matters cannot end like this – here on a bright clear autumn morning in this comfortable little room, with its fire burning cosily and the table nicely laid with butter and jam and marmalade? I must make some sort of effort to preserve my marriage.

'Robert –' I say. And he turns back hopefully. Perhaps he thinks I'm going to take the solemn oath after all. I wish I could do it; I long to make him happy again. But I cannot lie; and I cannot defend myself except by adding to my shame.

He looks at me, but still keeps his hand on the doorknob to indicate his wish to depart and have done with all this unpleasantness. I step towards him, conscious of a long band of sunlight which suddenly falls across the carpet between us and seems to emphasize how separate we are. Maybe if affection for *me* doesn't move him, I can appeal to his love for Christ. 'Have you forgotten about forgiveness?' I say. 'That is Our Lord's commandment – even for the worst sinner, and for the worst sins. And I don't think I'm quite the worst sinner, am I, Robert? Even though I have made us both unhappy.' I consider sinking to the floor in front of him to show him how penitent I am, but I fear he may find me ludicrous; more like a slave girl of the Roman Empire than a respectable communicant of the Church of England.

'I *have* forgiven you, Margaret,' he says, his hand still on the doorknob. 'I bear you no ill will, no ill will at all. But forgiveness is one thing, and loving and cherishing you as a wife is quite another.' I see he has steeled himself against all appeals. He won't even look at me as he goes on, doggedly. 'As you pointed out, we have grounds for annulment. But I've seen what it's done to other men and women, even the highest in the land. We must find another way less painful to us both, a way in which we may keep our dignity at least.'

'Thank you, Robert.' I clutch at this small shred of comfort. An annulment would be dreadful. I'd have to move to Mama's house, and spend my life in shadowy corners; a woman with a doubtful past and no future. And Robert would have his manliness and judgement held up to ridicule, his position as a clergyman open to question, his ability to remarry damaged perhaps for ever. And then there would be the medical examination, the opening up of my most secret self for all to gossip about. I've wondered over and over what gruesome procedures that would entail. If I've shrunk from my husband, how much more would I shrink from the physician's touch? And, worst of all, I don't know what would be revealed; I don't know what a doctor is able to tell from mere inspection. But one thing is certain; it would involve shame for me. No woman can escape such investigation with her reputation intact.

'I am glad you agree about that.' He nods to himself in a distracted way, and I see that it is costing him a great deal to be fair and reasonable and not to break down under it all. His world is upside-down; but he is doing his best.

'Yes. Let us be friends, at least.' I cross the band of sunlight and put my hand on his arm. I can see now that his coat sleeve is flecked with crumbs of bread and pieces of thread, and that there is ink on his shirt cuff. His hair – usually so sleek – is unbrushed, and his shirt doesn't look very fresh. He has the air of a neglected bachelor and I feel a surge of new love for him.

He shakes me off lightly. 'No, Margaret. That only makes things more difficult.'

I recoil, feeling the chill of his distaste and thinking how our roles have been reversed in such a short space of time: I now the beseecher; he, the hard of heart. If only I hadn't rebuffed him quite so many times; if only I'd tried harder to overcome my repugnance. Perhaps if he came to me now, in this reduced state, I could bear his caresses; I could close my eyes and forget all about Papa's hot skin on mine, and live only in the moment. 'Maybe the London doctor can still help,' I suggest feebly, grasping at any straw now, any chance, any hope. 'Perhaps we should keep the appointment after all.'

He closes the door and places his back against it. He looks at me as though I am, actually, mad. '*Keep the appointment?* But, Margaret, what would be the purpose? You have admitted the cause of your shame. Do you really want to share it with others?'

Do I? I don't know. I can hardly find the right words when I try to describe to myself what happened. How could I find them in front of a stranger? And would not a stranger feel – as Robert feels – that I must have been in some way to blame; that there was something in my smile, or in my kisses, that urged my father on against all natural feelings? It goes against the grain to sit down mutely and say nothing, but would be even worse to speak and be branded as a young Salome. 'I suppose not,' I say.

'Quite so. The awkward thing is withdrawing ourselves after Dr Lawrence has gone to such trouble. I shall have to find a suitable form of excuse. I shall plead a change of heart on your part.'

'But that is not true.'

He turns beetroot red. 'Nevertheless, that is what I shall say. I simply wished you to know of my intention.' Then he pulls open the door, and departs.

I sit down heavily at the breakfast table and put my head in my hands. My elbows crash into the crockery, upset the milk; but I don't care.

Then I see it, level with my eye, half under my plate: a letter. The small neat writing is shockingly familiar. I can hardly believe it, and I half think he has got to know of my despair by some supernatural means; I cannot think how otherwise he would choose to write to me just at this moment in my life. I pick it up, thanking God that Robert does not know John Jameson's distinctive hand.

My dear Mrs Constantine (or may I still call you Daisy?),

Permit me to congratulate you on your recent marriage and to hope your life with your new husband will be a long and happy one.

It's some time since we last met over a cup of tea; in fact we did not strictly meet over anything in those days – except Mr Smith-Jephcott's rooms. However, I would take it as no uncommon courtesy if you would grace me with your company at four o'clock tomorrow. Dinah is no longer with us, and neither is Benson (O tempora! O mores!), but I am on the same staircase as ever, with a splendid new scout who keeps me in order and seems to produce jam tarts at the drop of a hat. Take care to bring your hat, therefore, or you may end up hungry.

Please reply to the undersigned, and not, under any circumstances, to that puffed up impostor, James St-John Clark,

Your dear friend, as always,

John Jameson.

I laugh. And then I re-read the letter and laugh again. I'd forgotten how happy John Jameson always made me with his incapacity to take anything very seriously. Just to read his words makes me feel young and carefree and full of vitality, as if I have escaped into another world and all the wretchedness of my life has vanished in an instant. He says nothing of my troubles – of course; he doesn't know them – but just the mention of tea and jam tarts and I am back in his rooms and remembering all the fun I had there. Robert is right in a way: he's never made me as happy as John did – and that happiness was untainted with any sense of sin or failure. And now that my spirits are soaring again, I realize that for much of my adult life I have not been fully myself. I've never been the Margaret that Robert thought I was; I was always Daisy inside.

And I suddenly want to be Daisy again, to go back to those wonderful afternoons; to have as much tea and jam and bread-and-butter as I like; to ask questions; make up rhymes, answer riddles, eat chocolate limes, and altogether worry not a jot about the Eye of Society. I want to laugh and be silly, and forget adult life and its disappointments completely. And I can do it. I get up hurriedly to pen an answer, to express my joy at the prospect of seeing John again.

But I stop dead. Far from seeing him, I cannot even risk a reply. If Robert were to find out, he'd assume we'd been engaged in some underhand connection all along and even the faintest hope of reconciliation would be gone. My sudden burst of happiness dies within me, and the clerical gloom of the past week returns like a wet fog. I slump back in my chair. It seems I'm now in the worst of all possible worlds. There's no comfort to be found in my husband, and certainly none from my family; and the only friend who might cheer me up is forbidden to me. I start to weep, overcome with the hopelessness of my position. Women who have lost the love of their husbands generally console themselves with their children. But I have none, nor am I ever likely to have.

Minnie comes in to clear the dishes, and sees me in tears. 'Oh, dear,' she says. 'Are you ill again? Shall I call the master?'

'No, no,' I say, indicating the letter. 'It's just the loss of an old friend.'

Minnie puts her hand in her pocket. 'Would you like a sniff?' she says. 'It always helps me if I'm feeling a bit down in the dumps.'

So that explains the bottle's permanent presence in her apron. 'Why not?' I say, and she brings the smelling salts out with alacrity. The pungent aroma knocks me back, but, as she says, I feel strangely the better for it. 'Thank you,' I say. 'I'll remember your advice.'

She smiles. She has a jaunty smile, in spite of her pinched appearance. Then she looks at the table and puts her hands on her hips. 'Oh, you've hardly eaten anything. It's been like that all week. And Mr Constantine the same, although he's usually a good trencherman. Mind, he says put anything that's not eaten into a basket and he'll take it to the poor, but Cook says she's not cooking for the poor and anyways scrambled eggs don't keep.'

'Have you already made up a basket?' I ask. Parish visiting is, after all, my duty. And it's something I'm used to. Mrs Carmichael used to let us accompany her around Headington, carrying her baskets while she held her Bible. And after Christiana married Charles, she and I would often go together to Jericho and St Ebbe's. People always said I was good at listening, and didn't make them feel 'preached at'. And there were always the children to pick up and nurse. I'd tell them stories sometimes – even take along *Daisy's Daydream* and tell them it was all about me. And Robert was only last week encouraging me to start my rounds.

'Yes, it's on the slab in the pantry, waiting for Mr Constantine to pick it up. There's some apples from the garden, and bread from the day-before-yesterday that's still quite nice, and a couple of oranges, and half a steak and kidney pie (because Cook and I won't eat kidney), and a ham bone with quite a lot of meat on it and some hard-boiled eggs.'

'I shall take it,' I say. 'Do you know who it's intended for?'

'Some family in Parsloe's Lane, I think. I'll ask Cook. If she knows you're going, she'll put in a few extras.'

Cook has indeed put in a few extras and the basket is quite heavy. I enjoy the pull of it, though; the physical nature of it, as I walk along. I haven't had a good walk for a long time, and I relish the exercise and the freshness of the autumn breeze. Parsloe's Lane is at the very edge of the parish, on the Oxford road, and it takes me quite a while to get there. It's a little, narrow, run-down row of houses giving straight on to the unmade street, and there are children playing in the mud outside, teasing a dog with a bone. They rush up to me as I approach, the dog wagging its tail. A little boy with bright eyes catches on to my skirt. 'Have you got any cake, miss? Have you got a napple?' He gives me the most brilliant of smiles, and there is something in his face that I take to straight away.

Before I can say anything, a woman comes out of one of the houses, shading her eyes against the slanting sun. 'Come here, Benjy!' she calls out. 'Leave the lady alone.'

I stare at her. She's very plump, now, and her hair is not nearly so neat, but her voice is exactly the same. Yet how can she be here – in a broken-down street on the outskirts of my husband's parish? I fear I have conjured her up from my imagination, but I see she is as real as the little boy by my side. She continues to look at me, hand raised. 'Sorry, ma'am,' she calls out. 'I hope he hasn't muddied you. He means no harm.'

I don't care if he has muddied me. I don't care if I muddy myself from head to foot either. I break into a run, splashing through the puddles and bits of broken brick that litter the lane, the heavy basket beating against my leg. 'Nettie!' I cry.

She looks startled. She doesn't recognize me.

I stop in front of her. 'It's me, Daisy!'

'Daisy?' She seems confused at the idea. Then she puts her hands to her face. 'Daisy *Baxter*! Oh, my dear Lord! *Oh, my dear Lord!*'

She is just the same. *Just the same.* I rush into her embrace, nearly knocking her over. She still smells of biscuits, and it makes me cry just to breathe in that old familiar scent. We hug each other for a long time. When we pull apart, I can see the tears coursing down her own cheeks. 'My, my!' she says. 'I would never have recognized you! You've grown up so fine.'

'You're just the same,' I say. 'Oh, Nettie, I've thought about you so often! But I never thought I'd ever see you again!'

'Me neither,' she says, hugging me again. 'Me neither. And how is my darling Benjy – my *other* Benjy, I should say – is he well? He must be – what – eleven or twelve now?'

'He's eleven. But he's ever so tall, just like Papa. He's away at school, now, spending all his time on the cricket field.'

'And your ma and pa? Are they keeping well?'

'Oh, Nettie, didn't you know? Papa died six months ago –'

She looks nonplussed. 'Mr Baxter? But he was always so fit and healthy!'

'– And Mama has gone back to Herefordshire. But,' I say, trying to change the subject, 'are *all* these children yours?' There are about nine of them, crowding round us, full of curiosity.

'Oh dear no. Benjy's mine, as you might have gathered,' she says, pointing to the bright-eyed boy. 'He's a terror. And this is my Daisy – my *other* Daisy, I should say.' She indicates a younger child, sucking at a piece of cloth. 'And there's the baby indoors. These two – Billy and Lizzie – I look after, and the others over there aren't nothing to do with me. But where's my manners? You must come in and have a cup of tea.'

'Oh, I will! But first I have to take these things to a Mrs Bunch at number nine. Do you know which house that is?'

'Indeed I do,' she says with a laugh. 'It's *this* house. Mrs Bunch is *me*, Daisy!'

I feel awkward to be bringing my one-time mother a basket of leftover scraps to celebrate our first meeting in over ten years. I can't help thinking of the picnic fare we had that day on the river, the largesse for a mere ten people, all the delicacies set out on the white tablecloth. 'Mr Constantine sent it,' I say.

'Oh, yes. He sends things most regular.' She takes the basket from me, and the little ones start to lift the napkin to see what's inside. 'He knows I have trouble making ends meet – five mouths to feed and Mr Bunch with a weak back. He's a kind man. I've always said that.'

'So you approve of my husband, then?'

She draws back in a fresh onset of amazement. 'Don't say you're the rector's new wife!'

'I do say,' I reply with a certain pride, but feeling all the same something of an impostor.

'Oh, Daisy, I had no idea! I knew it had happened – Mr Constantine getting married, I mean, and we all sent our good wishes. But I don't get to St Aidan's much these days and I seem to miss out on all the gossip – parish news, I should say. I knew he were marrying an Oxford lady, but my friend Agnes said his fiancée was a Margaret Bassett, although I suppose she must have meant Baxter and I never thought of it being you, as you were always Daisy to me. But come in, come in! You're even more welcome, if it's possible.'

And so I go in, and although the house is tiny, with only one room for all to live in, with a scullery beyond, everything is spick and span as I would expect it to be with Nettie in charge. The fire is lit and there are clothes drying in front of it, neatly folded, and there is a tea table laid with a clean cloth, and a bunch of wild flowers in a jar. In a cradle by the fire is a baby.

'She's called Maud,' says Benjy, pushing his way past us. 'Hello, Maudie!' he cries, waving a piece of bread at her. The baby chuckles.

'She's a fine baby,' I say, looking down at the infant. 'A really beautiful baby.' I feel a sob catch in my throat, and Nettie looks at me sharply.

'Don't worry. I expect you'll have one of your own soon,' she says. 'Now, Benjy, get out of my way so I can put more water in the kettle.'

'There's cakes,' says little Daisy. 'Ma, there's cakes!'

'Mr Constantine is always generous,' says Nettie. 'Now don't you dare touch nothing until I've cleaned your hands. That's right, isn't it, Daisy? – I beg your pardon, Mrs Constantine, I should say.'

'You should say nothing of the sort, Nettie – unless I call you Mrs Bunch in return. Anyway, it's lovely to be called Daisy again. Nobody calls me that now.'

'I used to look after this lady before I got married,' she says to the children, wiping their hands with a damp cloth while keeping her eyes on me. 'And look how fine she's got – although I wish she wasn't quite so thin!' Her eyes take in my gaunt face, my bony fingers. 'Tell Mr Constantine he'll have to feed you up.'

I think of the unfinished meals, the waste on the breakfast table. 'I'll do my best.' I watch her settle the children around the table. 'But why didn't you ever come to see me again? Why didn't you ever write? I thought about you all the time.' As I speak, I realize how the injustice of it still burns in me.

'I thought about you too – and my little Benjy (not you, my love, another Benjy). But when you loses your place there's a lot of things to do to get another one, and every time I thought about you I started to get weepy, so I put my mind elsewhere and just hoped and prayed you was being well looked after by the new nursemaid.'

'Oh, she was utterly dreadful.'

'Oh, don't tell me that, Daisy!' she cries, her face a picture of horror. 'That was my one consolation!'

'Well,' I say, modifying my words. 'The fact is that she didn't like me.'

'How could anyone not like *you*?'

I laugh. 'Easily enough, I think. Mama said I was secretive, and you know how horrid my sisters could be. You were the only one who was always on my side.'

We smile at each other, and the years drop away.

*

After Nettie has made the tea and cut each small cake into two and given each child a portion, she and I take the wooden armchairs next to the fire, the drying clothes having been deftly whisked away.

'So when did you come back to Oxfordshire?' I ask, as I sip my tea. 'I thought you were in London.'

'London? Why ever did you think that, Daisy? I've never been to London in my life.'

'But you said if you were looking after children in London, you wouldn't have time to come and see me.'

'Oh, I expect when I said it I just wanted to get as far away as possible – after all that terrible business on the river, I mean. No, I went home to Wallingford. I hadn't seen much of my ma and I wanted time to find a new position. I went to work for another minister, after that – a Baptist in Bicester.'

'A Baptist! Papa would have been annoyed.'

'Well, if your pa had kept me on, there'd have been no need for me to go there. I even offered to work for nothing, but he wouldn't have it. I don't blame him, really, but I did miss you so much! Mr Protheroe was quite different, very quiet, with a cripple for a wife and just one little girl of seven, very moody. It was a bit tedious to tell you the truth, but beggars can't be choosers. I was only there a couple of years, and then I met Mr Bunch at St Giles's Fair. We got courting, and then we married and I moved here with him. He used to be a servant in one of the colleges, what they call a scout. But it's not a job for married men. And anyway Mr Bunch weren't fit enough after he fell down the stairs. They're stone stairs in the colleges you know, Daisy, ever so worn and slippery –'

'Oh, yes,' I say. 'I've seen them. I used to go to tea every week with Mr Jameson.'

'Well then, you can imagine what it would do to your back to fall down a whole flight of them. Mr Bunch was off for weeks, and when he did go back he couldn't carry the coal scuttles or make the beds or carry the wine up from the cellars – and that's the main part of the job. He'd been at the college since he was a boy, but they still give him notice.'

'Oh, Nettie, how unfair!'

'Well, I have to admit they do what they can for him, casual work and such, and we're grateful for it. There's not much work round here except for the colleges – and he has to do all sorts to make ends meet – sharpening tools door-to-door and suchlike. But there's a big dinner tonight and so the Bursar has called him in to help wait at the High Table. That'll be a few extra shillings.'

'Oh, Nettie, how do you manage?' I say, thinking how easily I can spend a few shillings. 'But what about Billy and Lizzie? Don't you get paid for looking after them?'

'Not really. Their mother used to live in half a house around the corner, but she was put out on the street for not paying the rent. She come and asked me to mind the children while she looked for work, and I couldn't say no, not with those two poor things looking up at me. She promised to pay me regular as soon as she got herself some employment. That was eighteen months ago, and I've never heard from her since. She was a bit flighty, to tell you the truth, and I think the children are better off without her. The things they've told me – you wouldn't credit it! Some children are dragged up any old how. We should thank our lucky stars that we were both brought up right.'

I am sorely tempted to tell her. I take a breath, but I can't find the words, and the room is full of children. I glance at Billy and Lizzie, fighting surreptitiously over the last piece of cake. 'So, you're keeping those two for nothing, Nettie?'

'No, Daisy, I'm keeping them for love.' She looks across at them with the old fond look I remember so well. And I wish again that I could have kept her close through all my growing up. I'm sure she would have protected me from harm. I long to nuzzle into her shoulder, climb on her lap, have her tell me that everything will be all right.

But now she wants me to talk about Mr Jameson. She's saying she'd heard he was quite famous now, and that he'd written books for children, which everyone had read, including Queen Victoria, although he still went on living in those same old college rooms day after day.

'You seem to know quite a lot about him, Nettie.'

'I gets the news from Charley – Mr Bunch I mean.'

'And how does *he* know?'

'Oh, didn't I say? He used to work in Mr Jameson's college. He even used to help out Mr Jameson's scout –'

'Benson, you mean?'

'That rings a bell. Anyway, that's where he is today – helping get ready for the dinner.'

'So,' I say teasingly, 'all these years you've known about *Daisy's Daydream*, but never once come to see the real Daisy?'

'I *did* come once. A long time ago.' She looks down at her hands.

'To our house?'

She nods. 'You and Benjy was so much in my mind at first that I couldn't settle to anything. I'd just started with Mr Protheroe and as soon as I had half a day off, I took the train back to Oxford and walked up to Westwood Gardens.'

'Did Mama let you in?'

'I didn't go to the front door, silly goose. I went round the back and saw Cook and Hannah. They said Benjy was in the drawing room with your mama and that you had gone out with Mr Jameson. They said you were always out with Mr Jameson and that you talked of nothing else but what you had done and what you would do next. "Is she happy, then?" I said. And Hannah said, "Like a dog with two tails." So I was satisfied, and went home. I thought it better not to write, to bring up old memories.'

'Oh, Nettie, how I wish I'd known! I thought you didn't care about me!'

'Well, now you know I did. It's all water under the bridge now. You've grown up and got married and are as happy as you deserve.'

I flush. 'I'm not sure I am – deserving, I mean. *You* are more deserving, Nettie, and yet you have no money and your husband isn't well. Where's the fairness in that?'

'Oh my, you haven't changed. Always wanting to know why things are the way they are and not how they should be!'

'But it's true, isn't it?'

'We're happy, that's the main thing.' And I see that she is indeed happy, and that her children are happy, and I am sure her husband, in spite of his infirmity, is happy too. And I, with my nice clothes and nice house and healthy husband, am completely miserable.

'I haven't spoken to Mr Jameson since I was eleven,' I say, putting down my cup and watching as Nettie picks a piece of linen from the big pile beside her and starts to hem it. Her needle flies in and out like quicksilver, just as I remember. 'We went everywhere together that summer, and had such jolly times.'

'Oh, I read about them. Everybody in the world has read about what Daisy did on her summer afternoons.'

'Well,' I say, laughing. 'I didn't quite do all the things he wrote about – at least I never remember going to sea with the Fatted Calf. But I did enjoy Mr Jameson's company. I was so upset when he stopped coming to see me. Not quite as upset as when *you* left, Nettie, but at least I knew why you went. I couldn't understand why John Jameson gave me up.'

'Gave you up?'

'He simply came to the house one day and announced that I was getting too old for him.'

'Too old? At eleven? My, he's a strange one.'

'He was always very nice to me. But I don't think Mama wanted to see him any more.'

'Even after he'd saved poor Benjy's life? Dear, dear, I *am* surprised! But what did your pa think? Him and Mr Jameson was the best of friends – at least that's how it seemed to me.' She finishes the seam and breaks the thread with her teeth before starting again.

'But did you never hear what happened?' I ask, thinking that surely some rumour of it had got to her.

'Oh, you don't get Oxford news in Wallingford,' she says, laughing. 'And since I married Mr B, I haven't gone further than St Aidan's, let alone all the way into Oxford. And I don't go to St Aidan's as often as I should. Mr Constantine don't mind, though. He says I'm doing God's work with the little children and as long as we all pray every day – which we do – it's just as good as going to church.'

Suddenly I imagine Robert here in this house with Nettie's children around him, smiling and handing out apples. I imagine him taking Benjy – or Daisy – on his knee, and reading them a story. I imagine him thinking that one day he'll have children of his own to love. I see him full of optimism and joy. And now I have spoiled it all.

'What's the matter?' Nettie asks, quick as always to spot my changes of mood.

'Nothing. I like to hear you say nice things about my husband.'

She laughs. 'Well, you'll soon be hearing a lot more about him if you get out and about in the parish. I'm sure you don't mind me saying, but lots of people thought he was a bit solemn at the start, a bit bookish – but he's set to and no mistake. He's never afraid to get his hands dirty. But you were going to tell me about your pa. I don't hold him no grudge, you know, in spite of what he done.'

'He was ill, Nettie.' I take a breath. 'More than ill. He had to go to an asylum.'

Nettie stops sewing and looks up. 'An asylum? Oh, Daisy.' She lowers her voice. 'You don't mean – not a *lunatic* asylum?' I can hear the utter disbelief in her voice. 'I hope it wasn't for long.'

'Ten years, Nettie. He died there, in fact.'

She puts her hand in front of her mouth just as she did on the riverbank all those years ago, her face the same picture of horror. 'Oh, Daisy, how dreadful! Oh, poor man. And your mother and sisters and all of you – what a time you must have had! And me sitting here all this time and knowing nothing!' She shakes her head.

'And now there'll be a new vicar, and all new servants except for Matthews, and a new nurse in the nursery. Everything will be changed, Nettie. Everything.' A sob rises in my throat. 'There's nothing left of the old times – no curtains or beds or wardrobes or tables . . .'

'Beds and tables! You're not upsetting yourself about *furniture*, are you?' She laughs. 'Not when you've got a whole new life to look forward to.'

'It's not just the beds and the tables.' I weep, unable to control myself now. The sight of her neat frock and her kind motherly face is just too much for me. My words come out in a rush. 'If only you hadn't left us! Everything went wrong after that! Mrs McQueen came and Mr Jameson took the photographs and I cut my hair and was ill with scarlet fever, and Mama went away and Papa saw the photos and Mama wouldn't listen and then I forgot everything that happened and when I came to myself, Papa was locked away, and I married Robert thinking I'd be happy because he was so kind – but we're not at all happy – and now he's seen the photographs and thinks

I did something wrong and doesn't want to be married to me any more! And now I don't know what to do. I don't know what to do at all!'

I'm aware that she is getting up, and the children are disappearing from the room as if by magic. The next thing her warm, plump arm is around me. 'Tell me again,' she says. 'But calmly this time, Daisy. So I can understand.'

So I start to tell her about the summer with Mr Jameson, and how nice he always was, and how he seemed to understand me. 'Almost as much as you did, Nettie,' I say. I tell her about cutting my hair and how Mama hated it, but Papa seemed to like it. And then I tell her how Mr Jameson had taken my photograph, dressed in different costumes. 'And sometimes as a cherub. You know,' I say, watching her face. 'With no clothes on.'

She frowns. 'No clothes at all?'

'Well, wings and so forth. But it was art, Nettie. As if I was in a painting.'

'I see.' She looks dubious. 'But what did your mother think of this "art", then?'

I can't suppress the blush. 'She didn't know. Mr Jameson said she might not understand.'

'It sounds a bit peculiar to me. But then, you were only eleven. And he was a clergyman after all. He wouldn't have done nothing wrong.'

'I don't think that being a clergyman makes you always right,' I say. 'I think that clergymen are just like the rest of us. And some are worse.'

'Oh, Daisy, surely not. You only have to look at Mr Constantine,' she says. 'Or even your own father.'

'How can you say that, Nettie? Papa turned you out, and he didn't care how terribly I'd miss you and how Benjy would cry for you all that time. He seemed to think that as long as I had a maid of some kind it didn't matter who it was. As if being a child meant I wasn't quite a human being. As if I didn't notice things. As if I didn't feel as deeply about things as he did!'

'My, my, Daisy!' She gives a rueful laugh. 'I can see you're still angry about it after all this time. It don't do no good, though, keeping bad feelings alive like that. It poisons your mind. I've had to forget it. So should you.'

'I did forget it for a long time, Nettie. I told you. I forgot everything that had happened during *four whole years.*'

'Four *years*? But, Daisy, however can you forget four *years*?'

'I don't know, Nettie! But it happened. One moment I was ill with scarlet fever and Papa was looking after me – and the next thing I was fifteen years old and Papa was in the asylum, Mr Morton was in charge, and Robert was coming to visit every day. Robert was very kind to me, Nettie. Very kind indeed. And when he asked to marry me, I thought it was the right thing to do.'

'I can't imagine a better match.'

'Everyone said that. And I thought everyone must be right. And I do love him, Nettie. But when he comes near me, *in that way*, and holds me and kisses me – I feel almost sick. Our wedding night – oh, Nettie, it was dreadful! I wouldn't let him near me. And we still haven't – you know.' I start to cry again.

She pats my hand. 'Now, now, don't upset yourself. Many a bride's got herself into a panic on her wedding night. I was a bit taken aback myself. It's all so very *surprising*, isn't it? But Mr Bunch was good to me and things worked themselves out in the end. In fact,' she says with a little smile, 'I quite enjoy it now.'

I dry my eyes. I imagine Nettie and the unknown Mr Bunch happily embracing in the upstairs bedroom, and I know that it is the most natural thing on earth. But I also know that, when I saw Robert coming towards me that night, it didn't seem natural at all. It seemed like the worst kind of nightmare, and all I could think of was Papa coming towards me; Papa kissing me and showing himself to me and putting his hands in my secret places, so that I wanted to faint away with the fear and shame of it all. But I can't tell Nettie. Much as I want to, I can't find the words. As I look at her kind and honest face, I almost believe it didn't happen. 'I can't tell you the worst,' I say at last.

'Come now, Daisy, you've got this far. I'm sure you'll be all the better for getting the whole lot off your chest. It's about them photographs, isn't it?'

I almost welcome the diversion. 'Yes,' I say. 'It's the photographs. Robert thinks I was wrong to let John Jameson take them. He thinks I'm tainted.'

'*Tainted?* My Daisy *tainted?* Wherever did he get that idea? I mean, I can understand a man not liking to think his wife had showed herself to another man, even if she was a child – even if it was "art" – and I'm not at all sure Mr Jameson should have asked you, not without asking your Mama first. But to say you were *tainted*! It's like you were a piece of bad meat. Shame on him!' She pauses, bristling with indignation. But then she softens. 'But on the other hand, I suppose Mr Constantine had that high an opinion of you in the first place that he thought you could do no wrong. It'd come as a shock, then – this "art".'

'I didn't do any wrong, Nettie. At least, not –'

She interrupts. 'You see, men can be very touchy when it comes to – things like that. They gets put off their stroke. I wouldn't mind betting that Mr Constantine is regretting his words, now. All you needs to do is show him that you love him. Put your arms around him. Give him a kiss. You'll find he'll forgive you. And then things'll come natural after that.'

She makes it sound so easy. But she doesn't know the depths of the divide between us. 'It's not just the photographs,' I say. 'There's more, Nettie. It's much, much worse.'

But I struggle once more to find the words. It almost seems as if what happened with Papa took place in a different world.

A world where nobody could be trusted and nothing was as it seemed. Whereas now, with Nettie here in front of me, I'm in the ordinary world, the one in which everyone is kind and responsible and where such thoughts seem almost heresy. 'I'm sorry, Nettie, but it's too horrible to talk about!'

'Not too horrible for Nettie, surely? And you know a trouble shared is a trouble halved.' I can't help smiling at Nettie's affection for the proverbial: all the things that will come out in the wash and the inadvisability of crying over spilled milk. She sits beside me and draws me close, composing herself to hear my tale of woe.

'I'm afraid you'll blame me, and take Papa's side.'

'Now, when did I ever take your pa's side?' She hugs me again.

I know that if I'm ever to tell anyone, it will be Nettie. And if there is any time to tell her, it must be now. And so I explain how Papa began to act strangely; how he seemed to notice me for the first time after I cut my hair; how I had to go to him every day in his study to do my catechism and he'd show me all his sermons and the photographs of himself when he was young. 'He wasn't the least bit frightening – and he made me feel special. We were special to each other, he said. Our love was a special kind. And after I was ill, he told me I'd saved him and that he'd saved me in return. He said that we were bound together for ever. Nothing should come between us, he said – not Mama or Mr Jameson, and –' I whisper '– *certainly not clothes.*'

I sense Nettie's body stiffen. But I carry on, my heart thumping, my mouth so dry it is difficult to speak. 'I'd always sit on his lap when he read to me, and after a while he'd ask me to take my stockings off and sometimes my drawers, so we could be really close. As close as it was possible to be. I didn't like it, but he always made me. And he'd take some of his own clothes off – his waistcoat and his –'

Nettie stops me, her fingers pressed hard on my lips. Her eyes are fierce with horror. 'What are you saying?' she gasps. 'Oh, Daisy, think, girl, *what are you saying?*'

Indeed, what am I saying? Is this simply part of the nightmare in my head, without an ounce of truth in it? But hot tears roll down my cheeks as I feel myself back with Papa, back in the study with the door locked and the pocket watch ticking never-endingly.

Nettie pulls me to her breast, and I feel how wonderful it is to be touched and held by someone I trust. 'There, there, my dearest,' she murmurs. 'But are you, you know – *really sure?*'

The comfort of her arms drains away. 'Oh, Nettie, do you think I am making it up!'

She rocks me, now, and I can sense that she doesn't know what to say. 'Well, Daisy,' she says at last. 'I know you were the truthfullest child ever. But are you sure you're not remembering things wrong? You always had such an imagination. And to think Mr Baxter should do such wicked things – a Man of God like him – well, I can't credit it.'

My heart sinks. 'So you *do* think I'm making it all up?'

'I'm not saying that,' she says, although, clearly, she is. 'I knows such things goes on. Men can be very wicked, Daisy. Very wicked indeed. Even in respectable families. I've known servant girls disgraced by their masters, and babies born out of wedlock and all sorts. It's just that your papa was a clergy-man – and not at all *like that*, and I was in the house for nearly twelve years. I know he had his faults – but he was always most respectful of us women servants and never tried to do anything he shouldn't. And you'd have known straight off if he'd been that way inclined, with a girl like Hannah flaunt-ing her wares. And why would he have done such things to a child? To his own daughter, too? He had a lovely wife and he always spoke so wonderful about the little children on a

Sunday: *For of such is the Kingdom of Heaven*. And you knew he meant it.'

I start to cry again, mangling my handkerchief. And Nettie carries on rocking me, as if she might rock away all my evil thoughts. 'Maybe you mistook his meaning. After all, fathers can hold their children and love them, can't they? Mr Bunch has my Daisy on his lap most nights, playing and giving her kisses.'

'But that close, Nettie? Touching me *that close*?'

She's flustered now, out of her depth. 'Perhaps your papa was just a bit too, well, overpowering in the way he went about it. You were always very fussy about kissing people, as I recall. You wouldn't kiss your Uncle Bertie for love nor money.'

'He had a wet mouth and smelled of rum. And that was just kissing; don't you understand? This was *more than kissing*, Nettie.'

Nettie desperately tries a new tack. 'Well, maybe when you lost your memory that time, things came back all jumbled up. Perhaps it was Mr Jameson who did something he shouldn't have. Perhaps *that's* what you remember – Mr Jameson, not your father at all. I mean, he was the one taking pictures of you without your clothes on. Are you sure it wasn't *him* as touched you?'

I pull away from her. 'No, Nettie, I'm sure. My memories of John Jameson are quite clear.'

She ponders. For once she doesn't have the answer. 'I don't know, Daisy. This is all beyond me.' She rises and goes to the window, glancing out at the children playing piggy-back outside as if they don't have a care in the world. I am conscious that it is beginning to grow dark, and I know I must return home. But the thought of going back to that silent mausoleum with nothing to do but make another list, and no one to speak to but Minnie, fills me with despair. There must be something I can do. 'Should I try again to tell Robert the truth?' I ask her. 'Perhaps he will make sense of it. He's a man, after all.'

'Oh, no, Daisy!' she exclaims, turning hurriedly. 'You must never tell him. That would be the worst thing ever.'

I am startled at the vehemence of her response. 'But he already thinks so badly of me. It can hardly be worse.'

'Oh, it can, Miss Daisy. Believe you me. With Mr Jameson, it's only some photos when all's said and done, and art like you said, even if Mr Constantine has taken it bad. But speaking against your father like that, you could be sent to the asylum too.'

She's right. No one will believe me. My father may have been deluded at the end, but he served for twelve unblemished years in the parish and was worshipped by all. And even if I were to speak out, to whom should I go? The bishop? Mama? My sisters? And, even if they listened, what good would it do? But I fear they would not listen; it is too unthinkable.

Nettie goes on. 'No, whether it's true or not, you just got to forget all about it, Daisy. Just like you did before.'

But I don't know how I managed it before; it was certainly not an effort of will. And now there seems to be so much more to forget. 'Perhaps I should take some laudanum? Perhaps that will help me forget?'

She takes my hand. 'Now, Daisy, you don't need medicine. You just need to make your mind up to do your duty. Love your husband, Daisy. All these other fancies will go away then, I'm sure.'

Nettie is a simple soul. And I can see she doesn't want to lift the curtain into my nightmare world. But I've always relied on her for advice, and she has always been right. My best – indeed, my only – hope lies in making my peace with Robert. He's promised to do nothing precipitate; so there may yet be time for me to absolve myself in his eyes.

I'm home again, with my empty basket and my mud-splashed coat, and I find to my surprise that Robert is back before me, sitting at the tea table with his velvet slippers on. He sees me hesitate in the hallway, and invites me to join him, giving me a little smile of welcome. It's the first time he has smiled for over a week, and I've never felt so grateful. I return the smile in good measure, and, discarding my coat, I go eagerly into the room. I wonder, as I approach him, how close I can sit. We have not eaten together since he discovered the photograph, and I try to read his intention in the position of his body, the placement of his arms and legs. But he sets a cup and saucer next to him, and speaks as though nothing untoward has happened. 'I hear from Cook that you have been attending to your parish duties, and I'm very pleased. Mrs Bunch is an excellent woman and a true Christian. I hope that she and the children are all well?'

'Very well,' I say, wondering whether to tell him of my connection with Nettie, but deciding against it, for the present at least. 'They are a lovely family.'

He takes the silver teapot and pours me some tea, and adds milk and sugar for me, as if I am a child. He has never poured me tea before, and although I am a little full with Nettie's hospitality, I drink it down. It's lukewarm, and I think he must have been waiting here for some time.

He clears his throat. 'I'd originally feared – when I found you not at home this afternoon – that you'd gone to take tea with John Jameson. I hope you don't mind my referring to this, Margaret, but I would rather that you didn't reopen your friendship with him. This is no reflection on you, but I'd prefer it all the same.'

'Of course,' I say, wondering how on earth he could know about John Jameson's invitation. I hid the letter; he could not have found it. Anyway, the invitation to tea was for tomorrow. And 'no reflection' on me? How can he mean that? 'I will do whatever you say, Robert. I don't wish to offend you in any way. John Jameson is nothing to me, now.'

He nods. 'I simply think it would be wise. Under the circumstances.' He clears his throat, plays with the teaspoon. 'The fact is – I seem to have made rather a fool of myself with Jameson, and I think it will be less embarrassing for all three of us if we do not meet or correspond.'

'You surely haven't been to *see* him?' I am astounded. I couldn't have imagined that Robert would have the nerve to confront John Jameson about the photographs, and I wonder what on earth John said to bring about such a change in my husband.

He colours. 'It was foolish. *I* was foolish. He's an odd fish, and I can't say I like him. And I certainly disapprove of his taking photographs of you in an unclothed state. But I realize I may have been at fault in the conclusions I drew. I accept his word that nothing sinful took place between you.' He passes me a plate on which there is a slice of cake, already cut, and I take it. I see that he cannot ask me out loud to forgive him. But he is doing it by means of the tea and the new, emollient manner.

I don't think I can manage the cake after the feast at Nettie's, but I need to acknowledge the effort he's made, and the apology he's trying to make now. I nibble the edge. I think about taking Nettie's advice, but I'm afraid that I might shatter this delicate rapprochement by an untimely hug or kiss. It's enough for the moment that he's prepared to be my friend.

He pours himself more tea, and makes a great deal of fuss with the milk and the sugar, as if he is playing for time and cannot quite bring himself to say what he wants to. I think maybe he is going to tell me what he and John talked about and why he has accepted a stranger's word as he never accepted mine. But then, I don't suppose John incriminated himself as I did. 'I ran into Lawrence on my way back,' he says, finally.

'*Dr* Lawrence?' I didn't expect this. I feel a new, quick beat in my pulse.

'Yes. It was rather embarrassing. He said this fellow Franklin – the Harley Street man – was very put out that we no longer wished to see him. He'd been looking forward to it, it seems.'

'Oh.' It seems an odd thing for a doctor to have been 'looking forward' to, and I wonder what kind of man Dr Franklin is, to be so interested in what passes – or does not pass – between a man and a woman. But I'm glad, now, that I don't have to meet him and talk to him, and allow him to put his hands on me.

Robert drinks the cold tea he has fussed over so elaborately, then looks out of the window. The wind is tossing the dark line of yew trees along the drive and I think there may be sleet in the air. He clears his throat. 'Franklin's lecturing at the Sheldonian this evening; I might go along and see what he has to say. It won't do any harm, and may be of some general use.'

'Of course, Robert. Yes, indeed, you should.' That is what I must say all the time, now: 'yes', 'of course', 'indeed'. I must cultivate the art of pleasing him. I must agree with everything he says and does. If he thinks the lecture will be 'of general use', then I will not dispute it.

'You don't mind being left alone?'

'Robert, I have been more alone this past week than ever in my life. I have been almost out of my mind with loneliness. But now that you are not angry with me, you may go to the moon and I shan't complain.'

He smiles. 'I may be late, but I won't disturb you, of course.'

'No, *of course*. Thank you.' The very fact that he refers to the possibility gives me hope. But, at the same time, I have the old, anxious feeling that when the time comes – if it comes – I may repeat my fearful behaviour. I must remember what Nettie said. I must put my duty to my husband before my own feelings. I must forget Papa – push him away from me and bury him deep. I can't let him control me from beyond the grave.

'Do you think it is going to rain?' says Robert.

'Well, the sky is very dark.' Indeed, as we have been speaking, all the daylight has gone, and we can barely see each other.

'Perhaps I'll take my umbrella.'

'Yes, do so. There is nothing worse than sitting in a wet overcoat.'

'You are quite right. Nothing worse.'

'Are you teasing me, Robert?'

'I believe I am, Margaret.'

I think, in the dark, he may be smiling at me.

22

❦ JOHN JAMESON ❦

AND NOW, AT THE TIME APPOINTED, I SIT HERE waiting, although I know in my soul that she won't come. I find I can't enjoy the warm fire Donnelly has stoked up for me, or the sight of the kettle boiling on the hob. Even the tempting sight of the jam tarts on the sideboard does not lift my spirits. Her husband has prevented her; that much is clear. My little tête-à-tête with him yesterday was not of the most amicable kind.

I had not expected him to call on me at all. I don't know the man in the slightest, and my thoughts were all on Daisy. Indeed, the moment I had finished my morning lecture on plane trigonometry, I could not help looking in the lodge to see if there was a note from her. My pigeonhole was bare, but the porter advised me that I had a visitor. 'I've put him in your sitting room, Mr Jameson,' he said, passing me a visiting card. 'I hope I did right.'

It is unusual for me to have visitors in the morning. I always arrange for my little friends to come near teatime. Indeed, all my visitors are encouraged to come then. A visit just before noon is extremely inconvenient. So I took the card rather crossly, ready to dislike whoever it was who was now encamped in my sitting room. To my surprise, the card said, *The Reverend Robert Constantine M.A.*, and I assumed it could be no other than Daisy's new husband. My first thought was that something dreadful had befallen her, so I hastened across the quadrangle and up the stairs.

He was standing at the fireplace, staring at the mantel-piece. I could see him in the glass as I came in: a slight man, almost a head shorter than I, with very black hair. He did not have the appearance of someone who was about to impart news of illness or death; in fact, if anything, he seemed rather angry.

'Mr C–Constantine I believe?' I said, extending my hand as he turned to face me. 'I am John Jameson. To what do I owe the pleasure?'

He ignored my hand. 'I am not sure it *is* a pleasure, sir. I am here concerning my wife.'

'She's not unwell, I hope? I was so looking forward to seeing her tomorrow.'

'You expect to see her *tomorrow*? She is due to come *here*, to these rooms tomorrow?' He looked so aghast that I realized that he was unaware of my invitation. I could not imagine why Daisy should have kept it from him, but I was mortified to have blundered in this way.

'I was hoping I might see you *b–both*,' I said, feeling a small misdirection was required in the circumstances. 'But I only dispatched my note yesterday and I have not yet had a reply. So I must admit to being in the dark as to the reason for your visit now. But, pray sit down; it makes me uncomfortable to see anyone standing.'

He hesitated, then sat, keeping himself bolt upright on the edge of the armchair as if he were ready to launch himself at me on the slightest provocation. There was an awkward pause, and then he said grimly, 'Mr Jameson, how well do you know my wife?'

'I don't know her at all.'

He leaned forward. 'How can you deny it when there is a photograph of her on this very mantelshelf?' He pointed at it, accusingly.

'Oh,' I said. 'I don't deny that I know *Daisy Baxter*. That was, of course, ten years ago. But I have never met your *wife*; she is another creature altogether. Which is why it would be very pleasant to make her acquaintance in my rooms.'

'I see you are a casuist,' he said, as if 'casuist' were cognate with 'murderer'.

'I simply try to make words mean what they say.'

'Very well,' he said patiently. 'I will play your game. How well did you know *Daisy Baxter*?'

'I'm not sure I can answer that. It's a very open question. And to be frank, I'm not sure what it has to do with you.'

'I am her husband.'

'You are not *Daisy Baxter*'s husband, though, and it is Daisy Baxter we have established as the subject of this interrogation.'

He gave a groan of exasperation. 'Are you deliberately obfuscating? I want a simple answer to a simple question.'

'In my view, simple questions rarely have simple answers. For example, "What is the purpose of life?" rarely provides an answer of fewer than ten thousand words, and generally a great many more.'

He got up. 'I think you are avoiding answering me, Mr Jameson. And that is because you are guilty. Guilty of a heinous act towards my wife – or the child she once was. You are loathsome, sir. And a coward to boot.'

I have never had such words openly directed to me; I felt quite nauseous. I have been prepared for vilification from a number of quarters during my life, but did not expect it from the husband of Daisy Baxter. I stood up too, and felt glad that I was the taller man; it gave an illusion of superiority even though I felt weak as water. '*Heinous act*, Mr Constantine? What on earth do you mean?'

'You have used your influence over my wife – or over Daisy Baxter, if you insist – to take photographs of a vile nature. It is my belief that you have corrupted her.' To my surprise, having delivered himself of this dreadful accusation, he burst into tears – copious tears, in fact – such as you might expect from a servant girl. I was taken aback. I myself have not wept since Dr Lloyd admonished me that day in his study when I was fourteen years old, and I think it weak of a man to give in to hysteria in this way. But clearly he did not know what he was saying. How could I have 'corrupted' my darling Daisy simply by taking her picture? She was just the same sweet creature afterwards as she was before. And if he found her less lovely because she had shown herself to me in all her innocence, then the fault was with him.

'Neither Daisy nor I did anything we were ashamed of,' I said. 'You have seen something you do not like – something that does not meet with your own narrow view of morality – and you have jumped to some wild conclusion.'

'I don't think so,' he said, shaking his head and swallowing back his tears. 'Margaret – my wife – has more or less admitted her sin.'

My innards churned about in a dreadful way as I thought how all the Mrs Grundys in the world would rejoice at my downfall if it was thought I had sinned against a child. But why had Daisy turned against me and born false witness? 'What has she said?' I demanded. 'What is this "more or less"?'

'She has hardly *described* it, Mr Jameson,' he said, sarcastically. 'She is a modest woman, after all. But she admitted that she had misled me as to her character before our marriage and that she was "not as she should be".'

'Daisy said that?'

'And I have my own very cogent reasons for thinking that her connection with you was of an unchaste nature.'

'What reasons do you have? *State them at once.*' I was almost choked with a mixture of fear and rage.

'They are – intimate and private,' he said, looking decidedly uncomfortable.

I saw immediately that he was not on such firm ground as he was pretending to be. I suspected that he was seeking clarification of something he did not understand, on the evidence of something Daisy did not exactly say (at least, I hoped she had not cast such calumny on me). It seemed that he had come to his conclusion before even hearing the evidence. 'You cannot come here making terrible accusations against me, and then claim "private and intimate" reasons for not saying why you are making them,' I said. 'At least you can – but it would get you nowhere in a court of law. So don't expect me to take such accusations with any seriousness. And if I hear that you have – in any way, shape or form – spread such accusations abroad, I will invoke the law myself and have you arraigned for slander.'

He looked horrified. 'This is not a matter for the courts, Jameson. Do you think I care nothing for my wife's reputation? If I attack you, I bring her down with you – in the full glare of public opinion. I would not do such a thing to her, whatever she may have done to me. I wish only to arrive at the truth.'

'The truth? *Ah, what is Truth, as jesting Pilate said* – although, notably, he did not stay for an answer. Perhaps he knew that there is no truth in this world. There is only the truth of God.'

This seemed to enrage him. 'Swear to me, then,' he said. 'Swear to me on the *truth of God* that nothing impure occurred between you.' He got up and seized a New Testament from my desk, thrusting it at me as if we were engaged in a particularly urgent game of pass-the-parcel.

'I'm not obliged to do anything of the sort,' I said, declining to take it from him. 'I am not in the dock at the Old Bailey, for all you think you are both judge and jury in this case. It is enough for me to know I am innocent of all charges.' But then it occurred to me that a man as bitter and confused as

Constantine was best appeased, if only to stifle further rumour. 'But for Daisy's sake, I will swear,' I said. And I did, taking the book, and reverently and solemnly invoking Christ to be my witness at the Awful Day of Judgement, that I had never laid unchaste hands on Daisy Baxter; that she was as pure when she left my company as when she had come into it.

When I had finished, Constantine put the Testament back on the desk. He seemed uncertain, then, like Dinah used to when she pounced on her prey, only to discover it had unexpectedly escaped. 'I suppose I must accept what you have said,' he murmured finally.

'Indeed you must, unless you think I would put my eternal soul in jeopardy,' I said. 'Daisy was one of the purest-minded children I have ever met, and unless she has changed with the onset of wifehood' – I could not help saying that – 'I cannot imagine how there can be any charge made against her.'

He sat down abruptly and put his head in his hands. 'I can only think that her father's madness has affected her more than I thought. It seems he has the power to frighten her still.'

'*Still?* I am astonished to hear he ever *did*. In my experience, Daniel Baxter was devoted to his daughter.'

'Forgive me,' he said, glaring up at me. 'But you weren't in the house. You never had to listen to his unfortunate ravings; you never had to restrain the poor man by main force. She's had dreadful dreams about it. She can't clear him from her mind.'

Poor Daisy. I knew she suffered much in that household, trying to meet her father's exacting standards. But I had always thought that Baxter's fierceness had invariably been tempered with love. And he showed that love to all his children, even the imperious Christiana, and the disatisfied Sarah. To tell the truth, I had always envied the ease with which he accepted the due rewards of fatherhood – in particular, of course, Daisy's rosy kisses, and her loving presence on his lap. And I'd seen (not without some jealousy on my own part) how his love for her had latterly blossomed, and how pleased she had been to be the object of his new-found attention. Indeed, I'd begun to feel that she no longer looked forward quite so much to the company of a rather eccentric, stammering don when she could have her handsome, doting father to herself. And when she fell ill, I believe no one could have cared for her as devotedly as Daniel – certainly I could not have done so.

'I still fail to see how my photographs are connected with Daisy's alleged fear of her father,' I said. 'Or perhaps you intend to slip up to heaven and accuse *him* of unnatural acts, too?' It was, of course, an appalling notion. Indeed, the idea was so horrific I didn't wish to think about it. I immediately thrust it back into the hell-pit whence it had come. 'I beg your pardon,' I said. 'I take back that remark; I disown it utterly.'

'I should think so; I thought you were supposed to be his friend. But it seems that friendship means little to you, Jameson.'

'On the contrary,' I said, stung by this calumny, 'I think friendship the highest form of human connection.'

'Then why did we never see you at the vicarage when Daniel needed your help? It seems you are a fair-weather friend at best.'

It was a very palpable hit – but I would not allow him his moment of victory. 'Again, you are wrong. I wished to help very much,' I said. 'Indeed, I came to the vicarage with Mr Warner as soon as Baxter's indisposition was reported. But I was forbidden from visiting the house.'

He looked at me with renewed triumph, as if he had pinned me down at last. 'Ah. So Baxter knew of your unauthorized activities with Daisy? He knew what you were doing and he took action against you to keep you away from her?'

'Nothing of the sort,' I retorted. 'It was *Mrs* Baxter who made the request.'

'Then *Mrs* Baxter knew?'

'Knew that I had taken pictures of Daisy? Yes – that was open knowledge. Knew that I had taken these particular pictures – these pictures that have upset you so much? No, she did not.'

'You see?' He shot up from his chair.

'What do I see?'

'You were secretive about them, because you knew that if they had come to light, people would have been appalled by them.'

'As you are now, Mr Constantine. Yes, I knew that would happen. Which is precisely why I kept the matter secret. You have proved my point.'

Constantine looked annoyed. 'Then *why* did Mrs Baxter disapprove of you? There must have been a reason.'

'If you must know, it was the matter of a haircut.'

'A haircut?' He laughed – as well he might. 'That hardly seems likely.'

'I agree. But when the hair was on Daisy and the scissors in my possession, it seems that rationality fled through the window. One would think I had half killed the child – instead of improving her appearance and taking away a source of great discomfort. But Mrs Baxter decided on that basis that I was untrustworthy. And once Daniel succumbed to his affliction – well, Mrs Baxter was head of the household and made the rules.'

'How dare you speak so slightingly of her? She endured more than a woman ever should. And with unfailing dignity.' He looked ready to strike me down in her defence.

'I don't doubt it,' I said, retaining the equable manner that seemed to infuriate him so. 'But the fact remains that I was shut out of Daisy's life and could do nothing about it. Or rather, I *could* do something – I could make good my estrangement by imagining that she was here with me, in these rooms, and that I was telling her some of the stories that she liked so much. You may possibly have heard of a little book called *Daisy's Daydream*.

It has been something of a success.' I thought I had bested him there, but he came at me with a final thrust.

'I wonder,' he said, 'if the parents who buy that popular story book are aware of this other, more *esoteric* interest of yours?'

I shrugged, although my heart was beating fast. 'I make no secret of my leisure interest. I have photographed the lowest and the highest in the land, the old and the young, the humble shepherd and the celebrated poet. I am only interested in beauty, Mr Constantine. And may I remind you that *to the pure, all things are pure*?'

He seemed to be unable to find a reply to this, and, as we stood in an uneasy truce, Donnelly came in to tell me that the bell had gone for luncheon. 'It's steak and kidney pudding today,' he said, adding coals to the fire. 'Then cherry tart with custard.'

'Excellent,' I said. 'All my favourites.'

'Will the other gentleman be lunching, sir?'

'No,' we both said with one voice, although Constantine added, 'Thank you.'

I let him go down the staircase first. At the bottom, as we said our awkward farewells, I ventured to hope that, as his wife knew nothing of our little contretemps, I might still look forward to a visit from her the next day.

He gave no answer, and, as I watched him stride across the quadrangle and under the arch of the lodge, I did not feel optimistic. How irritating it is that women and girls are so dependent on the whims of their fathers and husbands and cannot do just as they like. If I were in charge of the world (which will never be the case as I have no ambition worth speaking of) I would make it a law that girls and women should have equal rights not just to be educated, but also to go to tea with whomsoever they choose.

*

As I listen to the gentle bubbling of the kettle, I try to imagine exactly what brought Constantine to me in such a furious state. His story is confused at best – but I deduce from his embarrassment over the 'intimate and private' matters, that his distress has as much to do with the marital relations between himself and Daisy as with the pictures themselves. I don't like to think of marital relations when it comes to Daisy, but I am sorry if she is prevented by some scruple or other from doing what is necessary in order to become a mother. She was always drawn to infants, and it did my heart good to see how she cared for Benjy in those long afternoons we spent in the vicarage garden. And, in my selfish way, I have looked forward to seeing her own infants come to the age when an old bachelor can have them to tea, and make them laugh.

I can't account, though, for this so-called sin that her husband talks about. Daisy always had a proper sense of right and wrong, but she was never preoccupied with evil. Of course, the nature of her father's insanity may have changed her. I remember how chastened she seemed when I last spoke to her, how lacking in that vitality that had so endeared her to me. But that would still not account for the 'heinous act' that Constantine says she has confessed to. After all, with whom could that act have possibly been committed? Constantine's thwarted passion has clearly blinded him to the dictates of common sense.

All the same, I have taken his visit as a warning. I occupy a delicate position of respectability with regard to children, such that the slightest frisson of scandal will do for me. So, after luncheon yesterday, with the steak and kidney pudding in my stomach and Constantine's words ringing in my ears, I went into my studio and broke all the photographic plates that might give rise to any ambiguity. Daisy's lovely limbs went under the hammer, as did Annie Warner as the Spirit of Dawn, her sister Louisa as Venus, and the Malcolm girls as the

Three Graces. I asked Donnelly to cart away all the broken glass in the coal scuttle, and I burned the paper copies in my grate. It was dreadful to destroy the beautiful images, and I hesitated over more than a few. But it is best to put them out of harm's way.

It is nearly five o'clock, now. The kettle is still simmering away, the tarts are untouched. The window is already dark, and there are splashes of sleet against the panes. My bones ache and I recognize that I am in the autumn of my life. I miss Dinah. I miss Benson, too. And most of all I miss Daisy. I look back with such joy at the golden afternoons when she and I were all in all to each other. I see so clearly her sweet face, her grey eyes, her mass of unruly hair. In my mind, she is always eleven years old. I hear her now, her delicate voice fluting into my fuzzy brain. 'Mr Jameson?' she says.

'Daisy? Can it be you?' I lift my head. I have been dozing in the half-light, and she has come to me, stepping into my sitting room like a fairy, with the lightest of steps. She is wearing a pretty white fur bonnet and is carrying a white muff. My heart fills with gladness.

'Please, I'm not Daisy,' says the child. 'I'm Amy.'

I sit up. I see now that it's not Daisy at all. In fact, it is not the slightest bit like her. This child has golden hair and cherry-red lips, and she is about eight years old.

'Where have you sprung from?' I say, rubbing my eyes.

'I knocked, but you didn't reply,' she says.

'I was in the Land of Nod. But I have come back now and I am very pleased to see you. But you have surely not come on your own?' I look to see if there is a mama lurking in the shadows.

She shakes her head. 'My Uncle Neville lives downstairs. He brought me to the door, but wouldn't come in as he says he is a – *person ungrata* – with you.'

'Ah, is your uncle by any chance Mr Smith-Jephcott?' How could such a delightful child be related to that boorish person? But stranger things have happened.

'I don't know his surname.'

'Of course you don't. But you seem to know *my* name, don't you?'

She draws a copy of *Daisy's Daydream* from her muff. 'You've got two names,' she says. 'One unreal one for writing and one real one for everything else. Uncle Neville says you will write both in my book if I ask nicely.'

'And are you asking nicely?'

'Not yet. I haven't found the page.'

'Of course not. What was I thinking of?'

She puts down the muff and opens the book at the title page. 'Please will you put your name *there*?' she says, pointing at a space one inch below the title. 'Can you put *my* name too, and say it's for me?'

'By all means,' I say, as I get up to find my pen. 'Do you have any unreal names yourself – or were they all given to you at your baptism wherein you were made a child of God?'

'They are all real,' she says solemnly. 'I have three Christian names and one surname. My Christian names are Amy Frances Elizabeth – and there is an "e" in Frances as otherwise it's a boy's name. And my surname is Edgerton.'

'That's a very fine set of names,' I say. I take the book to my desk and she follows me.

She watches me carefully as I write. 'What neat writing!' she says. 'You can see every letter.'

'What is the point of writing something that cannot be read? But the test is – can you read it aloud?' I say.

'Oh, yes,' she says. 'I read aloud all the time.'

'You could of course read it aquiet, but I might have to get my ear-trumpet and that would be very inconvenient.'

'I've never heard of "aquiet",' she says.

'That's because you haven't "aquiet" enough knowledge. Come now, read it to me.'

And she reads, in slightly halting speech: '*To Miss Amy Frances Elizabeth Edgerton, from her friend and admirer, John Jameson, November 1872.*' She pauses. 'Are you really my friend and admirer?'

'No doubt about it. You won my heart in an instant with your fur hat and muff. But are you mine? That is to say, did you like *Daisy's Daydream?*'

'Oh, it's my favourite book. I read a chapter every night before bed.'

'Then I expect you know it better than I do, as I've only read it the once – for it's nonsense, you know. But which part do you like best?'

'Oh.' She pauses, thinking. 'I can't choose. But I like it when Daisy goes to sea with all the four-legged creatures and they use her hair as a sail, and the Fatted Calf says how much he loves the *sea hair!* And the dormouse wakes up and says –'

'– *Hair, hair!*' I chorus with her. We both laugh.

She is so delightful as she laughs, as her cheeks grow pink with merriment, her soft blue eyes crinkling up like little crescent moons. 'Do you live in Oxford?' I say, hoping against hope that this is the case, and that she has not been sent merely to enchant and then disappear. So many of my little friends are merely pen-friends, which is pleasant enough, but I like it best when I can be in their company.

'Yes,' she says. 'We've just moved here. We live on Cumnor Hill.'

'So you will be able to visit me whenever you like?' I say. 'Whenever you come to tea with your uncle, perhaps? If you are very good, I will tell you some other stories.'

'About Daisy?'

'Yes, about Daisy. She is a most interesting child, and the world quite rightly loves her. And so do I, my dear, more than I can say.' I find my eyes filling with tears. I know for certain now that Daisy has gone from my life. I'll never entertain her in my rooms again, never hand her a sandwich or make her laugh, never see that wondering look in her grey eyes as she asks a question. Never, never, never, never.

'Mr Jameson?' Amy fixes her blue eyes on me. 'Are you crying?'

'Crying? By no means. These are not real tears, you know. They are of the crocodile variety; pure glycerine and treacle, and you must take no notice. But I am thinking that maybe it is time to write about someone else.'

'Someone *else*?' She looks crestfallen.

'How would you like it,' I say, 'if I made up a story about a child called – let us say quite spontaneously and at random – Amy?'

'*Me?*' Amy clasps her hands excitedly. 'Oh, yes please!'

'Very well,' I say. 'And now I have another question to ask you, but it's not at all hard, because there is only one answer and that is, yes.'

She looks at me expectantly. She is as lovely as a dream in her white fur.

'Will you permit me to take your photograph?'

Harley Street,
London.

November 1872

My dear Charcot,
I had a most interesting case brought before me this week: a young woman – a very attractive young woman, with considerable education and a finely wrought sensibility – who is displaying some interesting features of nervous amnesia. She has recurrent nightmares, waking dreams, and a form of hysterical paralysis which prevents her consummating her marriage. I've been looking for a case like this since I returned from Paris and I am very excited to have found Mrs C. (as I shall call her), whom I hope to treat over the coming weeks.

The way she came to my attention was interesting. Her own family doctor, who is not without some experience in these matters, had heard of my work with you, and when the lady's husband wrote asking for assistance, he referred the matter for my attention. As it happens (I think serendipity was at work here) I had an engagement the very next week to speak at a public lecture in the city where this lady resides – my subject being, naturally – *The Supremacy of the Brain*. It was an evening event, followed by a dinner, as these things tend to be, and I had put the following afternoon aside to examine the lady at my leisure. However, the moment my train arrived in the city, Dr L. (as I shall call the family doctor) was on the platform to meet me, saying that the husband had written that very morning to cancel the appointment. I was extremely disappointed, as you can imagine, especially as I had previously understood Mr C. to be quite distraught, and anxious to resolve the matter as quickly as possible. I asked Dr L. if he knew the reason for the change of heart, and he said that he did not, and he was very embarrassed to have advocated so strongly on their behalf and then find them unwilling.

I suggested that perhaps the lady was anxious about a physical examination. 'Is she of a nervous disposition?' I asked. Whereupon he disclosed to me that her father had been subject to religious mania, and had been committed to an asylum where he ended his days. But he said that the young woman herself had always been of a modest and agreeable nature, with no signs of insanity. This intrigued me the more, and I was aggrieved not to be able to meet her. Dr L., however, said that he had spoken to the young man inviting his attendance at my lecture, hoping it might influence a change of heart.

Therefore, after I had given my talk (conveying much I had learned from your eminent self), and was enjoying a little hospitality with some of the university's more prominent scientific men, I was not completely surprised when I was approached by a young clergyman who introduced himself as Mr C., the very husband in question. He was most apologetic, and hoped it would be possible to reinstate our original appointment. He said his wife's circumstances had previously changed (although the nature of the problem remained the same), but he had listened to my lecture and felt I might be of assistance. I accepted with alacrity and arranged to see the couple the very next day.

I now précis the results of my findings:

It would seem that Mr and Mrs C. have been married for some ten weeks. Prior to that, they had enjoyed each other's company over a number of years – since Mrs C. was a child, in fact (she is six years younger than her husband). Once engaged, they had looked forward as any couple might to the nuptial event. They were well-matched in intelligence and social station, and their families (such as they were – Mr C. being an orphan, and Mrs C. having no effective father) were in favour of the betrothal. However, it would seem that the young man, being a clergyman of high morals and little experience, had not made even the most modest of sexual advances during their engagement. I believe, in fact, that the couple had hardly kissed. So, on the wedding night, both parties were largely ignorant of what was required of them. (Of course, my dear Charcot, we know that this is no uncommon occurrence among the respectable middle classes, especially, I may say, in England – but generally nature takes its course, a man gains confidence, and within a year we are celebrating a happy event.)

However, it seems that ignorance alone was not the cause of the unhappiness in this case. Mr C. had read Acton and believed his bride would enjoy little pleasure from the act, but he was appalled to find that she would not engage in it at all. Her body became rigid (we have seen similar cases of paralysis in Paris, of course) and she became hysterical at the prospect of his advance. I questioned Mr C. closely and he is convinced that there was more than maidenly modesty on the part of his bride. Being a man of a sensitive nature, however, he did not press matters, but soothed his wife's distress (which continued for up to an hour) and departed to the dressing-room where, if he consoled himself as best he could, I am not the man to blame him.

I also established that this was not a case of vaginal spasm; Mr C. admitting that he had not even touched his wife's body, let alone attempted penetration. He said that it seemed to be the sight of him in his nightshirt which caused the outbreak of hysteria, and that the young woman went so far as to shelter under the bed in her attempts to evade his advance. I think from that evidence it is safe to say that the problem lies not in the young man's performance, but the young woman's irrational fear.

Now I come to the nub, and it is most interesting. As I have already mentioned, Mrs C.'s father (Mr B.) had suffered a nervous collapse a number of years before, followed by severe religious mania which eventually necessitated his committal to an asylum. He was a clergyman himself, I should say, and a brilliant one, although given perhaps to an excess of passion in both his religious and domestic life. (In fact, Mr C. was a devotee of Mr B.'s particular style of preaching and commitment to the poor of the parish. He had attached himself to him during his first term at the university, and was eager to follow in his footsteps.) The circumstances of the collapse of Mr B. are somewhat shrouded in mystery, but it seems that his natural monomania became distilled into an obsession with water and nakedness, both of which were seen by him as representing the Love of God. At the time, he alienated himself from his entire family, all except for Mrs C., then a child of eleven. It seems that she often spent time with her father during this period, but she has very poor recollection of it now, except that it was by turns pleasurable and frightening.

There is one curious aspect to this case, which I have not yet mentioned, and that is that Mrs C., as a child, was befriended by a gentleman of some repute, who interested himself in her situation and took her about with him when the family were preoccupied with other matters. At one stage, the husband feared that this gentleman (who is so well-known that I will not even refer to him by his initials) had in some way violated his wife. I could hardly credit this, as she was a child, and the enormity of the crime would be beyond belief. Mr C. contends that it was based on an alleged 'confession' that Mrs C. had made to him. However, it transpires that this confession is not to be trusted. The gentleman in question is above reproach and, in any case, when confronted by Mr C., he swore most solemnly on the Bible that no such act had taken place. Interestingly, when I questioned Mrs C. myself, she denied that she ever made such an allegation, and insisted that it was her husband who had misunderstood her meaning. I suspect, therefore, that Mrs C., in spite of her charm, is an unreliable witness – as we have found many of our Hysterics to be – and I have no doubt that her fears with regard to the sexual act will prove to have stemmed from similarly disordered thoughts.

It is clear to me that the source of her condition is her father's unfortunate habit, while mad, of revealing himself in an undressed state (attested to by Mr C. himself). This exposed the young Mrs C. to views of the male body that may have frightened her. It is easy to see that such an experience would have rendered Mr B. a fearful figure in the eyes of a young child, and that the repetition of such a scene on her wedding night, with her husband in a state of undress, might have brought back all these unpleasant recollections.

In discussion with Mr C., I have agreed to treat Mrs C. until her antipathy to the marital act is overcome. I am confident that if Mrs C. (with my help) exerts the power of the Brain in a positive fashion to subdue the weakness of the Body, she will tame all her irrational fears. I have arranged to put her in a hypnotic trance next week so I may imbed in her the healthful thoughts that will lead, I hope, to a diminution of her symptoms and a happy conclusion of this case. She is understandably nervous, fearful of what she might disclose while under hypnosis, and apprehensive that what (she feels) lurks in her deepest mind may come unbidden to the surface. She even thinks it may shock me. I had to explain to her that as a specialist in the manifestations of brain disorders, all kinds of situations are every day put before me: rage and jealousy, fear and hatred, excess of will and weakness of will, extreme agitation and extreme melancholia – and so on ad infinitum. The genteel fears of a lady of the English middle classes, I said, are unlikely to surprise me. But she is persistently anxious. All she wishes, she says, is to be a good wife to her husband, to love him fully and have children. In short, she wishes to be no different from any other woman. However, she made me promise that I would not, under any circumstance, tell her husband anything that she discloses. And although I think it is generally a husband's right to know the details of his wife's condition, I have, in order to gain her compliance, agreed to keep silent.

What is interesting is that Mrs C. retains an adamant belief that she has in some way misbehaved herself with her father. She is most sincere in this and can recount vivid dreams about lions and walruses and crocodiles – all of whom make attempts on her virtue. The choice of animal is interesting and peculiar, but of course it is nonsense. I am only surprised that such a gentle-minded female has the capacity to conceive of such things out of her own head (perhaps, dear Charcot, you will not be surprised, knowing as you do the strange convolutions of the human mind), but I understand she has read widely on all manner of subjects, and her reading, when young, was unsupervised. I venture to suggest that, being an imaginative child, she found herself drawn into the fearful worlds of demons and monsters, hermaphrodites and anthropomorphs, and in her unformed mind has conflated what is real with what is false. I suggest that this should be a warning to all parents to keep their daughters away from questionable reading matter, including, I may say, some of the more extreme kind of so-called 'fairy stories'.

I reassured Mrs C., of course, saying I would make her forget everything wicked she had ever thought about her father. 'Such thoughts, however lucid they appear to you, are not the purveyors of truth,' I told her. 'They are deceptive vehicles, full of art and fancy, and not to be trusted. Without them, you will be a new person and a fit companion to your husband.'

I am confident that I will be successful, and I will keep you apprised of my progress, which I hope eventually to present (in similar anonymous form) to the important medical societies. I fear, of course, that my ideas will be too advanced for those who are still convinced that a little letting of blood will answer all distemper. It would serve me best if I could collect more similar case studies to convince them that this kind of brain-generated paralysis is not uncommon, but I fear that, owing to the delicacy of the subject, I am unlikely to find many other patients willing to put themselves into my hands. Therefore, Mrs C. is very special to me, and I intend to make the best use of her that I can. She might even enjoy, as Patient C., a modicum of celebrity in the annals of medical science.

To that end, I remain,

Your most sincere pupil and friend,

Edward Franklin.

Afterword

I was initially wary about writing another novel set in the nineteenth century, and featuring yet another famous writer. But the idea of exploring the relationship between 'Lewis Carroll' and Alice Liddell was tempting for a number of reasons. Carroll (or rather, the real-life Charles Dodgson) has suffered a generally bad press on account of his fondness for small girls, a predilection of which we are highly suspicious in our post-Freudian age. Having worked in Child Protection myself, and being aware of the distorted thought processes of most abusers, I was interested in how a man such as Dodgson, in spite of behaviour that would now be considered as the most blatant kind of 'grooming', maintained an apparently unstained reputation while he lived. I did not, however, want to focus only on Dodgson. Many writers of the epoch (for example, Ruskin and Dickens) seem to have held idealized (and sometimes highly confused) views on the desirability of 'child-women' and even the apparently well-balanced Rev. Francis Kilvert is not above giving voice to feelings about little girls that we would regard as very questionable today. In fact, nineteenth-century writers for children, particularly male clergymen such as Charles Kingsley, seem to have been given to exorcising their own religious and sexual demons through the apparently innocent stories they devised. Thus, *After Such Kindness* is not just the Alice Liddell and Charles Dodgson tale in disguise; it is an exploration of a number of themes that interest me; and my made-up story of Daisy Baxter has ramifications that never, as far as I know, affected either the real-life Alice or those around her.

Acknowledgements

Apart from the fiction of Lewis Carroll, I have taken information and inspiration from a number of other sources:

The Life and Letters of Lewis Carroll (ed. Stuart Dodgson Collingwood, 1898)

Aspects of Alice: Lewis Carroll's Dream Child as Seen Through the Critics' Looking Glass, 1865–1971 (ed. Robert Phillips, Penguin Books, 1972)

The Beast and the Monk: Life of Charles Kingsley (Susan Chitty, Hodder & Stoughton, 1974)

Charles Kingsley: His Letters and Memories of His Life, Volume 1 (ed. Frances Eliza Kingsley, 1877)

Secret Gardens (Humphrey Carpenter, Houghton Mifflin, 1985)

Kilvert's Diary, 1870–1879 (ed. William Plomer, Penguin Books, 1977)

John Keble: A Study in Limitations (Georgina Battiscombe, Constable, 1963)

THANKS

I would like once more to thank all at Tindal Street Press, especially my editor, Alan Mahar, whose detailed advice, suggestions and words of encouragement helped me knock this book into a much better shape. My thanks are also due to Luke Brown and Emma Hargrave for their additional comments and many pertinent queries, and to Melissa Baker, who has worked in many unseen ways to ease the book into its public life. I'm also grateful to the current members of Tindal Street Fiction Group for their feedback when the manuscript was in its early, unformed stages. And, of course, to my husband, for all the meals he cooked and all the cups of tea he brought me during the entire period when I was writing this book, especially during the late night sessions, of which there were rather too many.

About the Author

Gaynor Arnold was born and brought up in Cardiff and studied English at St Hilda's College, Oxford before becoming a social worker. She worked in childcare for many years, most recently for Birmingham's Adoption and Fostering Service. Her first novel, *Girl in a Blue Dress* (a fictionalized account of the marriage of Charles Dickens), was longlisted for the Man Booker Prize 2008 and the Orange Prize 2009. Her second book, *Lying Together*, a collection of short stories, was published in 2011. She is married, with two grown-up children.